MW01629105

Lakota Texts

STUDIES IN THE ANTHROPOLOGY OF NORTH AMERICAN INDIANS SERIES

Editors

Raymond J. DeMallie
Douglas R. Parks

Lakota Texts

Narratives of Lakota Life and Culture in the Twentieth Century

Translated and analyzed by REGINA PUSTET

Published by the UNIVERSITY OF NEBRASKA PRESS, Lincoln,
in cooperation with the
AMERICAN INDIAN STUDIES RESEARCH INSTITUTE, Indiana University, Bloomington

Library of Congress Cataloging-in-Publication Data
Names: Pustet, Regina, 1963–2013, author. | Indiana University, Bloomington. American Indian Studies Research Institute, issuing body.
Title: Lakota texts: narratives of Lakota life and culture in the twentieth century / translated and analyzed by Regina Pustet.
Description: Lincoln: Published by the University of Nebraska Press; Bloomington: In association with the American Indian Studies Research Institute, Indiana University [2021] | Series: Studies in the anthropology of North American Indians | Includes bibliographical references. | Lakota and English.
Identifiers: LCCN 2020034269
ISBN 9780803237353 (hardback)
ISBN 9781496226426 (pdf)
Subjects: LCSH: Lakota dialect—Texts. | Lakota Indians—Social life and customs—Folklore. | Dakota philosophy.
Classification: LCC PM1024.Z9 L3346 2021 | DDC 897/.5243—dc23
LC record available at https://lccn.loc.gov/2020034269

Designed and set in MeropePonca by L. Auten.

Dedicated to the Lakota people

May their culture endure

CONTENTS

TABLES

PREFACE

The language materials presented in this monograph were compiled in Denver, Colorado, between April 1994 and November 1995. The in-depth analysis of the data and preparation of the final manuscript were completed during shorter field trips spanning the years 1996 to 1998. This research was, for the most part, funded by a grant from the Deutsche Forschungsgemeinschaft (German Research Association). The last finishing touches were added to the manuscript during a stay at the Research Centre for Linguistic Typology at LaTrobe University in Melbourne, Australia, in 2001, which has supported my work with a research grant. Considerable time and effort went into the stylistic improvement of the original tape-recorded texts. Since repetitions, redundancies, inaccuracies, and other infelicities are almost inevitable in spoken language, the texts were reviewed with the help of the narrators again and again, until no more changes were suggested.

The Lakota community in the Denver area is coherent enough to enable speakers to use the language on an everyday basis. But like any Native American language in the United States, Lakota is facing a rapid decline of speakers and the eventual threat of extinction. The young people both within and outside of the reservations usually learn English only. Fortunately, Lakota is a relatively well-documented language. Some classical works include the Boas and Deloria grammar (1941), the grammar and dictionary by Buechel (1939, 1970), and the text collection by Deloria (1932). What is more, Lakota is an extremely popular language. Many non-Indians, in the United States as well as overseas, want to learn Lakota. The fact that there are textbooks, such as *Beginning Lakhota* by the University of Colorado Lakhota Project (1976), greatly facilitates dealing with the language. But despite these favorable circumstances, it must be kept in mind that a language lives only through people who use it in everyday life and who are familiar with the cultural heritage and traditions connected with it. Language and culture are inseparably entwined. Whenever a culture is changing or disappearing, the language or languages associated with it will also be affected. Language loss results in a weakening of a people's sense of ethnic affiliation. Native Americans have undergone a process of acculturation that has extended over centuries, and which is still in progress. Exposure to white culture and an English-speaking environment leaves its imprints in the language. For instance, Lakota is borrowing syntactic patterns from English and is producing a vast amount of neologisms which, for the most part, designate elements of white culture. On the other hand, Native American culture also influences white culture, which is adopting not only the more trivial aspects of material culture such as turquoise jewelry and beadwork but also knowledge about alternative medical practices and elements of Native American spirituality. This scenario of cultural interaction, adaptation, and inevitable decline brings about changes in the structure of Native American languages that call for detailed documentation. Collections of texts in Native American languages usually focus on mythology—on trickster stories, creation tales, fables, etc. These narrative genres have been deliberately neglected in the present monograph, partly because Deloria (1932) already offers a wealth of data in this respect. Instead, an attempt has been made to document contemporary Native American culture, a culture in transition that is struggling for survival. Although many elements of traditional Plains Indian culture are addressed in the present text collection—such as the use of herbs, production of tools, preparation of food, ceremonies, and spirituality—its general focus is on autobiographical material. The native speakers who have participated in the project were asked to consider this monograph a mouthpiece for communicating the things that moved them and the things they wanted people to know about the Native American way of life in the late twentieth century to a broader audience. Consequently, the choice of the topics to be covered was mainly up to the native speakers. However, several Lakota speakers who were encouraged to participate in this project were reluctant to do so. A prevalent attitude toward projects of this kind among Native Americans is that data on language and culture should not be disclosed to non-Indians—a point of view that I am able to sympathize with, given the historical facts. Other native speakers who were willing to share their knowledge and experience with me, and with prospective readers of the book, also advanced very good reasons for doing so. Neva Standing Bear, spiritual leader, healer, and instructor, who contributed the larger part of the language materials included in this book, feels that the Lakota language must be taken care of and preserved by white researchers because it will not be kept alive by the Lakota people. Neva's hope, and my hope as well, is that both Native Americans and non-Indians will take books like this as an inspiration to engage with the Lakota language, as well as with other Native American languages, and that such efforts, in turn, will help to further the mutual understanding and respect between the races.

I have studied Lakota for over twenty years, first on an autodidactic basis, then as part of an academic career in linguistics. The language has never stopped fascinating me. Lakota presents an inexhaustible source for new discoveries about language structure in general, since it differs significantly from English and other Indo-European languages in many respects. Non-linguists may find this hard to imagine, but as a matter of fact, one language cannot, as a rule, be directly translated into another by simply substituting words or grammatical forms. Languages diverge considerably with respect to the complexity of their grammatical and lexical inventories and with respect to the organization of these inventories. Each time a language becomes extinct, we lose a unique, self-contained system of thought that enables us to grasp, analyze, and reflect upon the world around us. Thus, it is astonishing to see that even when all the lexical and grammatical components of a Lakota text have been identified, one is left with text passages that stubbornly resist the attempt to assemble the bits and pieces into a correct English sentence. When questioned about seemingly twisted text passages, native speakers usually insist upon the appropriateness of the formulation, adding a comment such as: "Don't worry, this is the Lakota way of saying things. Lakota is all different from English."

All in all, Lakota is not a hard language to learn. To make an in-depth understanding of the language materials presented in the text section possible, the texts are accompanied by a thorough interlinear gloss, which is supplemented with a short grammar sketch in section 1.1. In addition, an appendix provides an analysis of the neologisms that occur in the text section. This text collection can be used by anyone interested in Lakota language and culture — by linguists, anthropologists, speakers and semi-speakers of Lakota, as well as by laypersons. It could not have been completed without the constant and patient cooperation of the Lakota speakers: Mary Light, Florine Red Ear Horse, and Neva Standing Bear. Neva adopted me as her daughter according to an ancient Plains Indian tradition in 1997. Her help and advice at all stages of analysis have been as invaluable as her unfailing sense of humor, which made hard work seem like no work at all on so many occasions. I would like to express my gratitude to the native speakers who participated in the project. We deeply regret losing Mary Light, who died of the consequences of a stroke on August 21, 1997. The Linguistics Department at the University of Colorado Boulder proved to be an operation base I could count on while conducting my research. I am particularly indebted to David Rood for putting me in contact with native speakers and for offering help, advice, and support through the years.

Denver, Colorado, April 1999

Lakota Texts

1 An Introduction to Lakota Language and Culture

1.1. The Lakotas and the Lakota Language

Lakota is the language of the Western, or Teton, branch of the Sioux Nation. Until approximately 1880, Lakota was spoken in an area that embraces what is now North Dakota and South Dakota, as well as parts of today's Nebraska, Wyoming, and Montana. Currently, the majority of Lakota speakers live in South Dakota, mainly in the Standing Rock, Cheyenne River, Lower Brule, Crow Creek, Pine Ridge, and Rosebud reservations. There are, presumably, no monolingual speakers left.

The language of the ethnic group that is referred to as "Sioux" is composed of three mutually intelligible dialects: Santee-Sisseton, Yankton-Yanktonai, and Teton (Parks and DeMallie 1992). The closest relative of these dialect groups is Assiniboine, which is distinct enough from Sioux to be considered a separate language. Stoney, a language which shares a common historical background with Assiniboine, has, partly through innovation inspired by Cree, changed to the extent that Assiniboine is now "closer to the Sioux dialects than it is to Stoney" (Parks and DeMallie 1992:251). One of the major phonological characteristics that has been cited in the literature over and over to differentiate between the languages and dialects which make up the Sioux-Assiniboine-Stoney group is the varying distribution of the consonants [d], [n], and [l], as shown in the self-designations for the ethnic subgroups. The Santee-Sisseton and the Yankton-Yanktonai refer to themselves as *Dakhóta*; the Teton call themselves *Lakhóta*; and the Assiniboine and Stoney self-designation is *Nakhóta* (Parks and DeMallie 1992). However, *Dakota* functions as a widely accepted cover term for the Sioux language as a whole. This is due to the fact that Dakota was the first Sioux dialect to be documented by whites.

The Sioux language is part of the Siouan language family, which, at one time, extended across the Midwest, the plains area, and part of the southeastern United States. Today, most Siouan languages are extinct. Siouan is genetically linked to the Caddoan and Iroquioan language families. Numerous other genetic affiliations have been proposed over the years, but the majority of scholars working in this field reject most of them as too speculative.

Plains Indian culture has, to some degree, been a corollary of the European invasion of the Americas. Originally, the plains were largely uninhabited because of the relative scarcity of water, the difficulty of making a living by hunting the species that dominated this habitat, i.e., the buffalo, and extreme climatic conditions in winter. Later, the introduction of horses helped to overcome these obstacles. The endemic horse had disappeared during the glacial periods in the Americas; later, horses that the Spanish had brought with them to Mexico during the *conquista* spread north. The plains area turned out to be an ideal habitat for these horses, and they multiplied quickly. The mustangs were domesticated by the Native Americans living in adjacent areas, and the exodus to the plains began. These migrations were also conditioned by white settlement pressure. In the eighteenth century, when Native Americans set out to conquer the plains, there were hardly any whites to be found in the area. Most of them were explorers, mountain men, and traders. However, the eastern tribes had constantly been pushed west by white settlers, and as a consequence, laid claims on the homelands of their western neighbors. Thus, the white invasion emitted shock waves long before the actual arrival of whites in the Midwest and West.

1.2. Lakota Spelling and Sounds

Section 1.2.1 explains Lakota pronunciation and the spelling of Lakota words used in this text collection. Section 1.2.2 explains some of the ways in which the sounds of Lakota prefixes, suffixes, and stems can change when these elements are put together into words, and how the sounds of words can change when they are put into a sentence.

1.2.1. TRANSCRIPTION AND PRONUNCIATION

For fuller guidance on pronunciation, the reader is referred to the relevant sections in Boas and Deloria (1941), Buechel (1939), Buechel (1970),

Rood and Taylor (1996), and textbooks that are supplemented with tape-recorded materials, such as *Beginning Lakhota* by the University of Colorado Lakhota Project (1976), and, if possible, should consult speakers of Lakota. It is impossible to describe sounds that are foreign to English properly without resorting to audiovisual aids. The hints for pronunciation in table 1 are meant to serve as a preliminary guide to help keep the reader from being misled by differences between Lakota orthography and English spelling.

TABLE 1. Hints for pronunciation of the Lakota transcription

Symbol used in the transcription	Hints for pronunciation
a	as in *father* (not like English *a* in ***hat*** or ***make***!)
ą	(nasal *a*: no real English equivalent, but somewhat like *un* in ***hunt***, ***hunk***, or like French *an* in ***langue***)
e	as in *pet* (not like English *e* in *scene*!)
i	as in *machine* (not like English *i* in ***ride***!)
į	(nasal *i*: no real English equivalent, but a little like *in* in ***hint***)
o	as in ***rode***
u	like *oo* in ***food***
ų	(nasal *u*: no English equivalent)
b	as in ***bad***
c	like *ch* in ***rich*** (not like English *c* in *rice* or ***cool***!)
ch	aspirated *c*: like *ch* in ***cheese***
cʔ	(glottalized *c*: no English equivalent)
g	as in ***good***, ***get*** (not like English *g* in ***gem***!)
ǧ	(voiced velar fricative: no English equivalent; somewhat like French *r* in ***rouge***)
h	as in ***help***
ȟ	voiceless velar fricative: like German *ch* in ***Bach***
k	as in ***skin***

kh	aspirated *k*: (1) before *i, į, u,* and sometimes before *e*: like *k* in ***keep***, or *c* in ***cool***; (2) before *a, ą, o, ų,* and sometimes before *e*: like Lakota *k* plus *ȟ*
*k*ʔ	(glottalized *k*: no English equivalent)
l	as in ***lead***
m	as in ***make***
n	as in ***now***
p	as in *s**p**in*
ph	aspirated *p*: (1) before *i, į, u,* and sometimes before *e*: like *p* in ***pin***; (2) before *a, ą, o, ų,* and sometimes before *e*: like Lakota *p* plus *ȟ* (never like English *ph* in ***ph**ysics*!)
*p*ʔ	(glottalized *p*: no English equivalent)
s	as in ***see, so***
š	like *sh* in ***sh**oot*
t	as in *s**t**and*
th	aspirated *t*: (1) before *i, į, u,* and sometimes before *e*: like *t* in ***tall, tin***; (2) before *a, ą, o, ų,* and sometimes before *e*: like Lakota *t* plus *ȟ* (never like English *th* in ***th**eater*!)
*t*ʔ	(glottalized *t*: no English equivalent)
w	as in ***well***
y	as in ***young***
z	as in ***zone***
ž	like *s* in *mea**s**ure*, or the second *g* in *gara**g**e*
ʔ	glottal stop: like the break between the syllables in *uh-oh!*

The acute accent mark over a vowel (e.g., *á, ą́, é, í,* etc.) indicates that the syllable is stressed. (Most often, stress falls on the second syllable of the word, but many words have stress on the first syllable.) Extreme prolongation of vowels—which occurs only in interjections—is marked by a double colon, :: . For more detailed discussion of the pronunciation of the aspirated sounds *ch, kh, ph,* and *th,* see Rood and Taylor (1996:442) and Lakota Language Consortium (2008: 697–98). Glottal stops are written only word internally or word finally, not in word-initial position; word-initial vowels are typically preceded by a glottal stop in careful pronunciation of Lakota.

In table 2, the transcription used in this book is contrasted with those employed in the standard works by Boas and Deloria (1941), by Buechel (1939, 1970), and by the Lakota Language Consortium (LLC) (2008). The rightmost column shows equivalents in the International Phonetic Alphabet (IPA).

TABLE 2. Other transcriptions of Lakota

Transcription in this book	Boas/Deloria	Buechel	LLC	IPA symbol
a	a	a	a	ɑ
ą	ą	aŋ	aŋ	ɑ̃
e	e	e	e	e
i	i	i	i	i
o	o	o	o	o
u	u	u	u	u
į	į	iŋ	iŋ	ĩ
ų	ų	uŋ, oŋ	uŋ	ũ
b	b	b	b	b
c	c	ċ, c	č	tʃ
ch	c‘	c	čh	tʃʰ
c'	c’	c'	č’	tʃ’
g	g	g	g	g
ğ	ġ	ġ	ğ	ɣ
h	h	h	h	h
ȟ	ḣ	ḣ	ȟ	x
k	k	k̇, k	k	k

kh	k‘	k, kᶜ	kh, kȟ	kʰ, kx
kˀ	k’	k'	k’	k’
l	l	l	l	l
m	m	m	m	m
n	n	n	n	n
p	p	ṗ, p	p	p
ph	p‘	p, pᶜ	ph, pȟ	pʰ, px
pˀ	p’	p'	p’	p’
s	s	s	s	s
š	ṡ	ś	š	ʃ
t	t	ṫ, t	t	t
th	t‘	t, tᶜ	th, tȟ	tʰ, tx
tˀ	t’	t'	t’	t’
w	w	w	w	w
y	y	y	y	j
z	z	z	z	z
ž	ż	j	ž	ʒ
ˀ	’	'	’	ʔ

1.2.2. PHONOLOGY AND MORPHOPHONEMICS: SOME IMPORTANT RULES

When two vowels are adjacent to each other within a complex word, they are frequently contracted. Some common contraction rules are:

a + *a* => *a*
a + *i* => *i*
a + *o* => *o*
o + *o* => *o*
i + *i* => *i*

For example, the verb *oyáka* means ‘tell it’; when the nonspecific patient prefix *wa-* ‘something, things’ is added to *oyáka*, the result is *w-**ó**yaka* ‘tell things, tell a story’.

When *i* is followed by *a*, *o*, or *u*, *y* is inserted between the two vowels.

i + *a* => *iya*
i + *o* => *iyo*
i + *u* => *iyu*

thi-y-óhą
house-EI-between
'between the houses'

In the analysis of the texts, such epenthetic elements are glossed as EI (euphonic insertion). In some contexts, *w* is inserted instead of *y*.

Stress in Lakota always falls on the first or the second syllable of a word. When a prefix is added to the beginning of word that is stressed on the second syllable, therefore, the stress moves to an earlier syllable:

kašná
miss
'He/she missed it.'

wa-kášna
1SG.AG-miss
'I missed it.'

An important phonological rule of Lakota, though one with many exceptions, prescribes that the consonants *k*, *kh*, and *k'* be transformed into *c*, *ch*, and *c'*, respectively, when preceded by the vowels *e*, *i*, or *į*. Thus, for example, when the second person patient (object) prefix *ni-* is added to the verb stem *kağí* 'to avoid someone (as a mark of respect or awe)', the result is *ni-**c**áği* 'he/she avoids you (as a mark of respect)'; compare *ma-**k**áği* 'he/she avoids me'.

Lakota has various processes whereby the form of lexical stems or grammatical items is modified when they are combined with specific grammatical items. A particularly important process of this sort is the change of *a* or *ą* at the end of many stems or grammatical elements into a different vowel (*e* or *į*). Not every final *a* or *ą* undergoes these changes, but which ones do, and which do not, is entirely unpredictable; those that do undergo the changes are referred to here as "unstable" *a* or *ą*, and those that do not, as "stable." Unstable *a* or *ą* is an inherent feature of the individual phonetic makeup of lexical stems or grammatical elements. (A complicating factor is that native speakers sometimes disagree on whether the stem-final *a* or *ą* of particular forms is unstable or not; see Rood and Taylor 1996:449.)

What triggers the change of unstable *a* and *ą* is the following grammatical element; certain grammatical elements trigger a change, while others do not. Whether the unstable vowel changes to *e* or to *į* also depends on the following element. One simply has to learn which grammatical elements have which effects. Examples of elements that trigger change of unstable *a* and *ą* to *e* include (among others) *hą́tąhąš* 'if, when', *kštó* 'assertive (female speaker)', *sʔa* 'habitually', *sʔe* 'like, as though, as if', and *-šni* 'not'. Thus, for example, the unstable final *a* of *kaksá* 'chop' and the unstable final *ą* of *pehą́* 'fold' change to *e* before the negator *-šni*:

chą́ *ki* *wa-kákse-šni*
wood DEF 1SG.AG-chop-NEG
'I didn't chop the wood.'

šiná *ki* *pehé-šni*
blanket DEF fold-NEG
'He/she didn't fold the blanket.'

Unstable *a* and *ą* at the end of a declarative sentence change to *e* as well.

chą́ *ki* *wa-kákse*
wood DEF 1SG.AG-chop
'He/she chopped the wood.'

šiná *ki* *wa-péhe*
blanket DEF 1SG.AG-fold
'I folded the blanket.'

Stable *a* and *ą* are unaffected in these contexts; the stable final *a* of *kakšá* 'to coil it, to roll it up' does not change to *e* before *-šni* or at the end of a sentence:

*wa-kákš**a**-šni*
1SG.AG-coil-NEG
'I didn't coil it up.'

wíkhą	*ki*	*wa-kákš**a***
rope	DEF	1SG.AG-coil

'I coiled up the rope.'

A smaller number of grammatical elements, such as *-kta* 'future' (whose own *a* is unstable) and *na* 'and' (and some other elements beginning with *na*, such as *nahą́* 'and, and then' and *na'į́š* 'or, and'), change unstable *a/ą* into *į*, as is seen for the lexical stems *yá* 'go' and *kaksá* 'chop' in the following examples:

yį́	*na . . .*
go	and

'he/she/it went and . . .'

chą́	*ki*	*wa-káksį-kte*
wood	DEF	1SG.AG-chop-FUT

'I will chop the wood.'

However, the unstable *a* of *-kta* 'future', in an exception to the usual pattern, itself changes to *e* rather than *į* before *na* 'and':

ú-kte	*na . . .*
come-FUT	and

'he/she/it will come and . . .'

Not all grammatical elements trigger change of unstable vowels. For example, the question marker *he* does not:

chą́ *ki* *ya-káks**a*** *he*
wood DEF 2SG.AG-chop QS
'Did you chop the wood?'

šiná *ki* *peh**ą́*** *he*
blanket DEF fold QS
'Did he/she fold the blanket?'

Another process affects stem-final vowels (especially *a*) in stems that are longer than one syllable. In certain syntactic environments, such as when verbs are juxtaposed to each other, stem-final vowels are not changed but rather are omitted ("truncation"). This process, in turn, affects the consonant that precedes the omitted vowel: *z, ž,* and *ǧ* become *s, š,* and *ȟ*, respectively, while *p, t, č,* and *k* become *b, l, l* (or sometimes *g*), and *g*, respectively. Some of these changes are shown in the following examples, where the stem-final *a* of *púza* 'dry', *šíča* 'bad', and *wąyą́ka* 'see' disappears through truncation; *z* is then replaced by *s, l,* and *g*, respectively.

*pú**s*** *áye*
dry PRC
'it gets dry'

*ší**l*** *áye*
bad PRC
'it becomes bad'

*wąyą́**g*** *ma-hí*
see 1SG.PAT-come
'she/he came to see me'

Sometimes truncation happens to words other than verbs too; for example, it can happen to nouns in compounds or close phrases, such as *Lakȟóta* 'Lakota' in the following expression:

Lakȟól *wičhóȟʔą*
Lakota tradition
'Lakota traditions'

After a nasal vowel, word-final *p* becomes *m* and word-final *t* usually becomes *n* (rather than becoming *b* and *l*, respectively). For example, *nų́pa* 'two' is often truncated to *nų́m*.

1.3. Outline of Lakota Grammar

This section sketches the basics of Lakota grammar as an aid to interpreting the texts and their glossing, beginning with syntax (§§1.3.1–1.3.4) and then turning to the inflection of nouns, verbs, and other types of words (§§1.3.5–1.3.8). Of course, it is beyond the scope of this short introduction to offer an exhaustive description of the Lakota language; it is not a substitute for a full grammar. Based primarily on Neva Standing Bear's Rosebud dialect of Lakota, it focuses on those aspects of Lakota grammatical structure that are likely to cause the greatest difficulties to speakers of English and considers only grammatical elements that occur in this text collection. To make it more accessible to nonlinguists, unnecessary use of linguistic terminology is avoided. For a deeper understanding of the complexities of the Lakota language, grammars such as those by Boas and Deloria (1941) and Buechel (1939) should be consulted. Compact descriptions of Lakota grammar are provided by Rood and Taylor (1996), by Ingham (2003), and by the Lakota Language Consortium (2008: 689–777).

The grammatical sketch is followed by an alphabetical list of some additional terms that are used in the glossing of Lakota (§1.4).

1.3.1. SENTENCE STRUCTURE

Word order in Lakota is very different from English. In the clause, the verb is normally the last word (except for grammatical elements); it is preceded not only by the subject but also by the object—for example, *wį́yą ki lé* 'this woman' and *phežúta* 'medicine' in the following sentences:

wį́yą	*ki*	*lé*	*phežúta*	*k'ú-pi*	*nahą́*	. . .
woman	DEF	this	medicine*	give-IPS	and then	

'they would give the woman medicine and . . .'

chą́	*wį́yą*	*ki*	*lé*	*waché-we-ci-chiyį*	*na*
then	woman	DEF	this	ST-1SG.AG-BEN-pray	and

'Then I prayed for the woman.'

Adverbs likewise precede rather than follow the verb:

wakhą́-yą	*ma-wá-ni*
sacred-ADV	ST-1SG.AG-walk

'I'm walking in a spiritual way.'

However, clauses in which more than one noun phrase appears are rare in Lakota. Where English would use a pronoun such as *I, you, us, he, she, him, they,* etc., Lakota most often simply uses no noun phrase. Sometimes this results in ambiguity, but much of the information that would be supplied by independent pronouns in English is provided by the person markers in verb inflection in Lakota (see §§1.3.5–1.3.8).

A variety of grammatical elements occur after the verb. (These elements are sometimes referred to as "clitics" or "enclitics" in Lakota studies, although some of them bear stress.) The markers of future tense and of negation are among these elements:

-kta 'future' (FUT) (the *a* of *-kta* is unstable; *-kta* changes a preceding unstable vowel to *į*)
-šni 'not' (NEG) (changes preceding unstable vowel to *e*)

Other such elements mark mood—declarative/assertive, imperative, interrogative, and similar categories. Some of the mood markers vary depending on whether the speaker is male or female.

k'ų, wą, -': assertive (ASS) (statement of a fact; rendered by declarative mood in English; used by both sexes; *k'ų* changes a preceding unstable vowel to *e*) (In the Pine Ridge [i.e., Oglala] dialect, *k'ų* may be realized as *ų*.)

kštó: assertive (ASS) (used only by female speakers; changes a preceding unstable vowel to *e*)

ló: assertive (ASS) (used only by male speakers; changes a preceding unstable vowel to *e*)

ló has the following variants:

yeló when following stable *a*, stable *ą*, *i*, *į*, or an *e* that does not result from transformation of unstable *a/ą*;

weló when following *o*, *u*, or *ų*;

ló when following an *e* that results from the transformation of unstable *a* or *ą* (but sometimes *yeló* appears in this context)

ló also normally combines with a preceding plural marker *-pi* (see §§1.3.5–1.3.8) to form *-pe ló* (though *-pi yeló* occasionally occurs)

hé, *hųwó*, *só*: interrogative (QS) (indicating that the sentence is a question; *hųwó* is used only by male speakers)

ná, *yé*, *yó*: imperative (IMP) (expressing commands or requests; *ná* is used by female speakers only to express a request; *yé* is used by male speakers to express a request and occasionally by female speakers to express a command; *yó* is used by male speakers to express a command)

After *o*, *u*, or *ų*, *yé* and *yó* appear as *wé* and *wó* respectively, and *ná* appears as *waná*. They contract with a preceding plural marker *-pi* to form *pé* and *pó* respectively (written as separate words; *ná* does not contract with *-pi*).

It is not always clear whether postverbal grammatical markers are best considered suffixes or separate words. In the present volume, the future and negative markers are written as suffixes, while the mood markers are written as separate words. (In some other works, the future and negative markers are also treated as separate words.) The above is not a complete list of Lakota postverbal markers; others are not discussed here because they do not occur in the texts. (For details, see Rood and Taylor [1996:475].) The plural suffix *-pi* is discussed in §§1.3.5–1.3.8.

Lakota articles, such as the definite article *ki* 'the' or the indefinite article *wą*, follow the noun they modify.

wičháša *ki*
man DEF
'the man'

wičháša *wą*
man IDF.SG
'a man'

The definite articles change preceding unstable *a/ą* to *e*. (For additional discussion of the articles, see "Definite" and "Indefinite" in the alphabetical list in §1.4.)

Demonstratives such as *lé* 'this' and *hé* 'that' occur together with the definite article; the demonstrative may be either at the beginning or at the end of the noun phrase.

lé *wičháša* *ki*
this man DEF
'this man'

wašícu *wičhó'ų* *ki* *lé*
white man way of life DEF this
'this white man's way of life'

Numerals, adjectives, and other modifiers also follow the noun they modify but precede articles and demonstratives:

waníyetu *nų́pa*
year two
'two years'

šųgmáyetu *thą́ka* *wą*
wolf big IDF.SG
'a big wolf'

Strictly speaking, Lakota equivalents of English adjectives are stative verbs (see §1.3.5.2). Relative clauses are discussed in §1.3.4.

1.3.3. POSTPOSITIONS AND POSTPOSITIONAL PHRASES

Lakota has various postpositions—elements that are functionally equivalent to English prepositions but follow their noun phrase or pronoun object, as the example given below demonstrates: the noun phrase *thípi ki* 'the house' is the object of the postposition *él* 'in'.

thípi	*ki*	*él*
house	DEF	in

'in the house'

Some Lakota postpositions can also be used with reference to time as well as to space:

hį́hąni	*ki*	*él*
morning	DEF	in

'in the morning'

Postpositional phrases (that is, phrases ending in postpositions) precede the verb of the clause, just as subjects and objects do:

na	*he-tą́*	***wašícu***	***makhóche***	***ektá***	*wa-híyu.*
and	that-from	white man	country	to	1SG.AG-come

'and from there I went **to the white man's land**.'

Some of the most common Lakota postpositions are:

aglágla	'along the edge of, beside'
akʰą́n / akʰą́l	'on top of'
chóla	'without'
ektá	'in, at, to, toward'
él	'in, at, to, toward'
etą́(hą)	'from'
étkiya	'to, toward'
glakį́yą	'across'

ih̆éyab	'away from'
ihákab	'behind'
ikhą́yela	'near, close to'
ikhíyela	'near, close to'
ikhówakatą(hą)	'across (from)'
ilázata	'behind'
isákhib	'beside, next to, together with'
isą́pha / isą́m	'beyond'
ithókab	'before, in front of'
iwą́kab	'above, up'
iyókogna	'between'
kichí	'(together) with' (singular object)
mahél	'inside'
ób	'(together) with' (plural object)
ogná	'in, inside, among, along, according to'
óhą	'among'
ohómni	'around'
oh̆láthe	'under'
ókšą	'around'
ópta	'through'
ų́	'because of, for, in order to'
ų́	'with, by means of, using'
yuhá	'with, taking along'

Postpositions are sometimes inflected for the person and number of their object; see §1.3.7. Many Lakota postpositions can also be used as adverbs; for example, *ektá* 'there, at/in/to this place', *él* 'there, at/in/to this place', *etą́(hą)* 'from there', *ikhą́yela* 'nearby', and *ikhíyela* 'nearby'.

Besides the postpositions, there are also location- or direction-marking forms which are directly suffixed to a noun. These suffixes, which convey a locative or directional meaning, include:

-ta	'at, in, on, to, toward'
-(ta)kiya	'to, toward'
-tą(hą)	'from'

However, the locative-directional suffixes are more restricted in usage than the corresponding postpositions listed above. Only a small set of nouns and adverbs can be combined with these suffixes.

pahá-ta
hill-on
'on the hill'

pahá-tąhą
hill-from
'from the hill'

1.3.4. SUBORDINATE CLAUSES

Many subordinate clauses are marked by a subordinator at the end of the clause. Clause-final subordinators include *hą́tąhaš* and *kihą* 'if; when', *héci* 'whether', and *ki* 'if, when' (a special use of the definite article).

ya-hí i	*hą́tąhaš*
2SG.AG-come	if/when

'if/when you come'

For some subordinate clauses referring to time, a postposition is used as the subordinator, like *él* in the example below. In such cases the respective postposition can often be translated by an English conjunction.

akísni	*él*
recover	when

'when he/she/it had recovered'

The Lakota postposition at the end of clauses like this is often best translated by an English conjunction; thus, *él* is rendered as 'when' in this example.

Some complement clauses have final subordinators (glossed as LK for "linker") as well, which can typically be translated as 'that'; common ones are *ki* and *cha*.

ya-ˀú-kta	***cha***	*slol-wá-ya*
2SG.AG-come-FUT	LK	ST-1SG.AG-know

'I know that you are coming'

ho	*cha*	*ištámaza*	*sápa*	*mų́*	***ki***	*i-má-yųǧa-pi*	*cha . . .*
well	so	glasses*	black	wear.1SG.AG	LK	ST-1SG.PAT-ask-1PS	so

'They asked me if I wear dark glasses, so . . .'

Not all complement clauses involve a linker; in many cases, a complement clause can simply be juxtaposed to the higher-order verb.

ho	*cha*	*tuktógna kˀéyaš*	*mi-thá-ˀoˀiye*	*oyáte*	*ki*
well	so	whichever way	1SG.POR-ALP-word	people	DEF
na-má-ȟˀų	*wa-chį́.*				
ST-1SG.PAT-hear	1SG.AG-want				

'I want people to hear my words, whichever way.'

Whether a linker is needed or not depends on what higher-order verb is used. Some higher verbs require a linker, while with others it is optional. Complement clauses precede the higher-order verb. If a linker is employed, it appears between complement clause and higher-order verb (in the following example, *slolyá* 'to know' functions as the higher-order verb).

Another marker of subordinate clauses is *héci*, glossed as SUB (subordinator); it too is placed at the end of the subordinate clause. In many cases, *héci* can be translated as 'whether'; in other contexts, an English translation is not available. At least in the texts in this monograph, *héci* marks complement clauses that usually contain an interrogative element such as *táku* 'what' and *tókhel* 'how'.

hé *táku-ȟca* ***héci*** *slolyé-šni*
that what-INT SUB know-NEG
'he/she doesn't know what that is', 'he/she doesn't know what that is all about'

For further discussion of *héci*, see Lakota Language Consortium (2008: 758).

As the examples above show, subordinate clauses, including complement clauses, normally precede the main-clause verb, as ordinary subjects and objects do. Occasionally, however, conjunctions such as *na* 'and', *yųkhą́* 'and then', and *nahą́ke* 'and then' function as linkers that connect complement clauses and higher-order verbs. In this case, the complement clause follows the higher verb (in the following example, *oyáka* 'to tell' functions as the higher verb), and the linker appears between the higher verb and the complement clause.

oyáka-pi *na* *Denver* *él* *hihų́ni*
tell-PL LK Denver in arrive
'they say that he has arrived in Denver'

Relative clauses follow the noun they modify. Between the noun and the relative clause, one of the two indefinite articles is inserted: *wą* after a singular head noun, and *eyá* after a plural head noun. The status of the whole complex noun phrase (including the relative clause) as definite or indefinite is indicated by an article that follows the relative clause. If the complex noun phrase is definite, the definite articles *ki*, *kihą*, *k'ų*, and *k'ųhą* are used:

šiná *wą* *sų́* *ki*
rug IDF.SG weave DEF
'the rug he/she/it is weaving'

šiná *eyá* *sų́* *ki*
rug IDF.PL weave DEF
'the rugs he/she/it is weaving'

cha wicháša wą hįgná-wa-ye ki slol-wá-ye-šni.
so man LK ST-1SG.AG-marry DEF ST-1SG.AG-know-NEG
'I didn't know the man I married.'

If the complex noun phrase is indefinite, indefiniteness is marked after the relative clause not by the ordinary indefinite articles *wą* and *eyá* (see §1.3.2 and "Definite" and "Indefinite" in §1.4) but rather by *cha* 'qualifier':

šiná wą sų́ cha
rug LK weave QL
'a rug he/she/it is weaving'

šiná eyá sų́ cha
rug LK weave QL
'rugs he/she/it is weaving'

1.3.5. INFLECTION OF VERBS

Lakota verbs include prefixes and suffixes that mark the person and number of grammatical roles corresponding to English subjects and objects and in many cases roles such as beneficiary, recipient, or possessor.

1.3.5.1. Basic inflection of transitive verbs. The basic inflection employed for transitive verbs—i.e., verbs with both a subject and an object—is given in paradigm 1 below. Most elements of this paradigm also occur in the inflection of intransitive verbs (see paradigms 2 and 3). In most cases in the transitive paradigm, verbs mark both their subject and their object by prefixes or suffixes. Subjects are marked by the agent (AG) set of prefixes (first person singular *wa-* 'I', second person *ya-* 'you'), and objects by the patient (PAT) prefixes (first person singular *ma-*, second person *ni-* 'you'). However, the combination of first person singular subject and second person object ('I [verb] you') is marked by a special prefix *chi-* (glossed 1SG.AG.2SG.PAT- or 1SG.AG.2PL.PAT-), and a single prefix *ų-* (or *ųk-* before a vowel) is used for first person dual inclusive or plural as either subject or object ('we', 'us'; see below for the dual inclusive). Third person subjects and third person singular objects are not marked by an overt prefix; this absence of a prefix is rendered by *Ø-* in the paradigms given below but is not graphically represented in the texts. Plurality of either the subject or the object is marked by the suffix *-pi*, except for third person plural object (which is marked just by the special prefix *wicha-*); the prefix *ų(k)-* not accompanied by *-pi* is first person dual inclusive subject, meaning that just two people are acting—specifically, 'you and I'. (In the patient role, *ų(k)-* plus *-pi* can be interpreted as either dual 'you and me' or as plural.) The symbol X in the paradigms indicates the position of the lexical stem in complex word forms that include both a prefix and a suffix.

In the texts, the second person prefixes *ya-*, *ni-*, and *chi-* are glossed either as singular (SG) or plural (PL), and the prefix *ų-* is glossed as either dual inclusive (DU) or plural, depending on how they are interpreted in the context. Thus, for instance, *ų-* is rendered by "1PL.AG-" in the following form:

ų-yúta-pi
1PL.AG-eat-PL
'we eat (it)'

PARADIGM 1: transitive

	1SG.AG	2SG.AG	3SG.AG	1DU.AG	1PL.AG	2PL.AG	3PL.AG
1SG.PAT	*	*ma-ya-*	*ma-*	*	*	*ma-ya-X-pi*	*ma-X-pi*
2SG.PAT	*chi-*	*	*ni-*	*ų-ni-*	*ų-ni-X-pi*	*	*ni-X-pi*
3SG.PAT	*wa-*	*ya-*	*Ø-*	*ų(k)-*	*ų(k)-X-pi*	*ya-X-pi*	*ø-X-pi*
1DU/PL.PAT	*	*ų-ya-X-pi*	*ų(k)-X-pi*	*	*	*ų-ya-X-pi*	*ų(k)-X-pi*
2PL.PAT	*chi-X-pi*	*	*ni-X-pi*	*ų-ni-X-pi*	*ų-ni-X-pi*	*	*ni-X-pi*
3PL.PAT	*wicha-wa-*	*wicha-ya-*	*wicha-*	*wicha-ˀų(k)-*	*wicha-ˀcų-X-pi*	*wicha-ya-X-pi*	*wicha-X-pi*

1.3.5.2. Basic inflection of intransitive verbs. The subject of intransitive predicates is coded by two distinct sets of person markers in Lakota. (This phenomenon is usually referred to as split intransitivity.) The two sets of intransitive person markers, which are reproduced below, more or less coincide with the two paradigms most commonly employed for coding transitive agents and patients, respectively: active intransitive verbs inflect with the agent prefixes (paradigm 2), and stative intransitive verbs inflect with the patient prefixes (paradigm 3).

PARADIGM 2: active intransitive

	SG	DU	PL
1	*wa-*	*ų(k)-*	*ų(k)-X-pi*
2	*ya-*	*	*ya-X-pi*
3	*Ø-*	*	*ø-X-pi*

PARADIGM 3: stative intransitive

	SG	DU	PL
1	*ma-*	*ų(k)-*	*ų(k)-X-pi*
2	*ni-*	*	*ni-X-pi*
3	*Ø-*	*	*ø-X-pi*

Unsurprisingly, the special transitive prefix *chi-* 'first person singular agent acts upon second person patient' (i.e., 'I [verb] you') does not appear in the intransitive paradigms. Also note that all intransitive verbs, both active and stative, normally mark third person plural subject by the suffix *-pi*; the prefix *wicha-* marks third person plural patient of transitive verbs. (When *wicha-* is used for the subject of an intransitive verb, it implies not simple plurality but rather a group of people acting collectively; in this use, it is glossed as COLL, for "collective," e.g., *wich-ómani* 'a group of people travel', from *ománi* 'travel'.) Another difference from transitive verb inflection is that stative intransitive verbs can mark their subject as first person dual inclusive ('you and I') by the prefix *ų(k)-* without the plural suffix *-pi*; the patient of a transitive verb is never marked by *ų(k)-* without *-pi*.

As a rule, any given intransitive verb takes agent or patient person affixes exclusively. Stems which imply a high degree of agency on the part of the subject, like *psíca* 'to jump', select the active (agent) set of person markers:

wa-psíce
1SG.AG-jump
'I jumped.'

Stems which imply a low degree of agency, or a high degree of stativity, like *kakíža* 'to suffer', are combined with the stative (patient) set:

ma-kákiže
1SG.PAT-suffer
'I suffer.'

Words that correspond to English adjectives, such as *wašté* 'good', are treated as stative verbs in Lakota:

ni-wášte
2SG.PAT-good
'You are good.'

Agency is not always a reliable indicator of the set of person markers used with a given verb. There are verbs that do not imply agentivity semantically that nonetheless are inflected by means of the agent paradigm and therefore count as active verbs, like *nawízi* 'to be jealous' (e.g., *na-**wá**-wizi* 'I am jealous'; see the next section for the position of *wa-* inside the verb stem). There are also verbs whose subject is clearly an agent semantically that nonetheless take the patient paradigm of affixes and thus count as stative verbs, like *šką́šką́* 'to move'.

1.3.5.3. Infixation of person prefixes. For many Lakota verb stems, the person prefixes do not precede the whole verb, but rather are inserted ("infixed") within it. Examples of this type of stem are *naȟʼų́* 'to hear' and *slolyá* 'to know'.

na-má-ya-ȟʼų

ST-1SG.PAT-2SG.AG-hear

'you hear me'

slol-ʼų́-yą-pi

ST-1PL.AG-know-PL

'we know (it, him, her)'

Verb stems that end in a final element *ya* (*yą* after a nasal vowel) or *khiya*, such as *slolyá* 'know' in the examples above, regularly follow this pattern, inserting the personal prefixes immediately before the final element. Very often the *ya, yą,* or *khiya* can be identified as a causative suffix (see "Causative" in the alphabetical list of terms). It is convenient to refer to stems ending in *ya, yą,* or *khiya* as causative even when—as with *slolyá*—the final element does not have a clear causative meaning.

A common pattern for verb stems of more than one syllable whose first syllable begins with a vowel is for the first person plural (or dual) prefix to precede the vowel (taking the form *ųk-*, as it normally does before vowels in other circumstances as well), but for the other person prefixes to be infixed after the vowel. Examples of this type of stem are *okíhi* 'to be able, can' and *olé* 'look for, seek':

ųk-ókihi-pi

1PL.AG-can-PL

'we can, we are able'

o-wá-kihi

ST-1SG.AG-can

'I can, I am able'

o-má-le

ST-1SG.PAT-seek

'he/she/it looked for me'

ų̨k-ó-ni-le-pi
1PL.PAT-ST-2SG.PAT-seek-PL
'we looked for you'

When personal prefixes are infixed into the stem, the part of the stem that precedes the personal prefixes is given the gloss ST- (part of the stem), and the stem's full gloss appears with the part of the stem that follows the personal prefixes. This can be seen in the examples above, and in many places in the texts.

1.3.5.4. Y-stems and other special forms of agent inflection. There are lexical stems whose inflectional paradigms diverge from the ones reproduced above, especially as regards the form of the agent prefixes. For instance, most verbs that insert person prefixes before a syllable that starts with *y* ("y-stems") employ a special inflectional paradigm. The overwhelming majority of these y-stems are transitive. The consonant *y* is retained in the third person agent forms, but it is replaced by *bl* to code first person agent, and by *l* to code second person agent.

hé *yuštą́*
that finish
'he/she/it finished it'

hé *bluštą́*
that 1SG.AG.finish
'I finished it'

hé *luštą́*
that 2SG.AG.finish
'you finished it'

(Note that causative stems, such as *slolyá* 'know' in the preceding section, have the ordinary forms of the agent prefixes, not the y-stem forms; thus 'I know [it, him, her]' is *slol-wá-ye* [ST-1SG.AG-know].)

Lexical stems whose inflectional paradigms are highly irregular are also encountered in Lakota, although irregular inflection, in general, is rather marginal in this language.

1.3.5.5. Reflexive and reciprocal inflection. Reflexive verbs (verbs whose object in English would be a form ending in *-self* or *-selves,* such as *myself, yourself, ourselves, themselves,* etc.) and reciprocal verbs (verbs whose object in English would be *each other*) take special inflections in Lakota. The most straightforward type of reflexive inflection involves an element *icʔi-* with special forms of the personal prefixes, as shown in paradigm 4.

PARADIGM 4: reflexive inflection (basic form)

	SG	DU	PL
1	*micʔi-*	*ųkicʔi-*	*ųkicʔi-X-pi*
2	*nicʔi-*	*	*nicʔi-X-pi*
3	*icʔi-*	*	*icʔi-X-pi*

micʔi-kte
1SG.RFL-kill
'I killed myself'

iyé	*cha*	*hécha*	*i-ʔícʔi-ʔų*
he	QL	such	ST-3RFL-do to

'He had done that to himself . . .'

For certain kinds of verbs, reflexives are formed not with the element *icʔi-* but by replacing the first consonant of the stem by *igl-*. These include y-stems (see §1.3.5.4) and stems with the instrumental prefix *ka-* (see "Instrumental" in §1.4). Thus some reflexive forms of *yužáža* 'to wash (something/someone)' are as follows:

miglúžaža
1SG.RFL.wash
'I washed myself'

niglúžaža-pi

2PL.RFL.wash-PL

'you washed yourselves'

iglúžaža

3SG.RFL.wash

'he washed himself, she washed herself'

And a reflexive form of *kašká* 'to bind' is:

nigláška

2SG.RFL.bind

'you bound yourself'

Verbs with the instrumental prefix *pa-* form the reflexive by *ik-* before the *p*.

patítą 'to push'

mik-pátitą

1SG.RFL-push

'I pushed myself'

Reciprocal inflection is basically marked by an element *kichi-* with agent prefixes, as in paradigm 5. Since reciprocals imply two or more individuals acting on each other, the singular agent prefixes are not used. The second person agent prefix *ya-* contracts with *kichi-* to form *yéchi-*.

PARADIGM 5: reciprocal inflection

	DU	PL
1	*ų-kichi-*	*ų-kichi-X-pi*
2	*	*yéchi-X-pi*
3	*	*kichi-X-pi*

gnáyą 'to deceive' (unstable *a*)

ų-kíchi-gnaye
1PL.AG-REC-deceive
'you and I deceived each other'

yéchi-gnayą-pi
2PL.AG.REC-deceive-PL
'you deceived each other'

kichí-gnayą-pi
REC-deceive-PL
'they deceived each other'

1.3.5.6. Dative, benefactive, and possessive inflection of verbs. Further person-marking paradigms of the Lakota verb establish reference to beneficiaries, recipients, and possessors. Three such categories can be recognized: benefactive (BEN), which indicates that the action is done for the benefit of someone else, or in someone's stead; dative (DAT), which indicates that the action is done in such a way as to affect another person or that it involves transfer of something to another person; and reflexive-possessive (RPOSS), which indicates that the action is done to something that belongs to the subject (agent). The following examples of benefactive, dative, and reflexive possessive forms of the same basic verb show the contrasts in meaning:

Basic verb: *pazó* 'to show, to exhibit, to display (something)'

šų́kawakh	*ki*	*pazó-pi*
horse	DEF	show-PL

'They showed (exhibited) the horse.'

Benefactive: *kíci-pazo* 'to show (something) on (someone's) behalf'

chįkší-tku	*táku*	*káǧe*	*ki*	*kíci-pazo*
son-3POR	what	make	DEF	BEN-show

'He exhibited his son's work.'

mí-ci-pazo
1SG.PAT-BEN-show
'He showed/displayed it for me (on my behalf).'

Dative: *ki-pázo* 'to show (something) to (someone)'

táku *ma-kí-pazo*
something 1SG.PAT-DAT-show
'She showed something to me.'

Reflexive possessive: *k-pazó* 'to show one's own, to display one's own'

cheží *k-pazó*
tongue RPOSS-show
'He showed his tongue.'

wówaštelake *wa-k-pázo*
love 1SG.AG-RPOSS-show
'I have shown my love.'

The basic form of the benefactive marker is *kíci-*, with agent and patient personal prefixes added before it; the patient prefixes indicate the beneficiary. However, after any personal prefix other than *ų(k)-*, *kíci-* loses its *k* and contracts with the personal prefix. Thus, for example, when the beneficiary is first person singular ('me'), the patient prefix *ma-* contracts with *kíci-* to form *mí-ci-*, as seen in the second beneficiary example above; the benefactive form with second person singular agent is *yé-ci-*, from *ya-* 'second person singular agent' plus *kíci-*. (Despite the contraction, it is convenient to divide the prefixes as indicated.)

The basic form of the dative marker is *ki-*; patient personal prefixes indicate the affected person or the recipient. For most verbs, dative *ki-* does not contract with the personal prefixes. The recipient is marked by a patient prefix; thus, for example, in the prefix combination *ma-ki-* (1SG.PAT-DAT-), the patient prefix indicates the recipient, 'me'.

The form of the reflexive-possessive is complicated. For some verbs, it is marked by a prefix *ki-* like the dative, except that the reflexive possessive often loses its *k* and contracts with personal prefixes (so that the first person singular agent form of many reflexive possessive verbs is *wé-*, from *wa-* plus *ki-*). But for many kinds of verbs, it has a different form. Before *pa*, the reflexive-possessive marker is *k-*, as in *k-pazó* 'to show one's own' above. (As it happens, there are no examples of reflexive-possessive *k-* in the texts.) With y-stems and stems beginning with *ka*, the reflexive-possessive form replaces the *y* or *k* of the stem with *gl*:

wakšíca *ki* *yužáža*
plate DEF wash
'he/she is washing the plate'

wakšíca *ki* *glužáža*
plate DEF RPOSS.wash
'he/she is washing his/her/its (own) plate'

Benefactive, dative, and reflexive-possessive inflection is one of the most complex and least explored areas of Lakota grammar; such forms involve many idiosyncrasies and irregularities, most of which cannot be discussed here. One complication that can be noted is that while the benefactive and dative inflections are clearly distinct in form, the difference in meaning between them is not always as straightforward as in the above examples; many dative forms can be given benefactive-like translations ('do something for someone').

As noted above, the reflexive-possessive inflection means that the object (patient) of the verb belongs to the agent. Benefactive verbs, on the other hand, often imply that the object belongs to the beneficiary:

wakšíca *ki* *mí-ci-pakhį̣te*
plate DEF 1SG.PAT-BEN-wipe
'he/she wipes the plate (that belongs to me) for me', 'he/she wipes my plate'

Dative inflection tends not to carry this implication:

wakšíca *ki* *ma-kí-pakhı̨te*
plate DEF 1SG.PAT-DAT-wipe
'he/she wipes the plate (that does not belong to me) for me'

For some verbs, however, dative inflection does imply that the object belongs to the affected person but with the added implication that the action is to the detriment of the affected person:

wóyute *ma-kí-yu-sota-pi*
food 1SG.PAT-DAT-INSTR-use up-PL
'They used up all my food.'

1.3.6. INFLECTION OF NOUNS

While Lakota very often marks possessive relationships on the verb of the clause (see §1.3.5.6), possessive relationships can also be expressed by means of possessor affixes attached to the possessed noun.

PARADIGM 6: possessor

	SG	DU	PL
1	*mi- / ma-*	*ų̨kí-*	*ų̨kí-*X*-pi*
2	*ni-*	*	*ni-*X*-pi*
3	*Ø- / -cu / -ku / -tku*	*	*-pi / -cu-pi / -ku-pi / -tku-pi*

mi-nápe
1SG.POR-hand
'my hand'

Plural possessors are coded by means of the affix *-pi* (see §§1.3.5.1–1.3.5.2), which combines with the person markers. The first person singular form *ma-* occurs only with certain lexical items designating body parts. Third person possessors are, in most cases, marked by the affix Ø-. The alternative third person singular forms *-cu / -ku / -tku*, and the corresponding plural forms, are found only in combination with terms of relationship.

lekší-tku-pi
uncle-3POR-PL
'their uncle'

The element *tha-* is prefixed to nouns to indicate that a possessive relationship holds between the extralinguistic referents of a given noun and some other entity. The semantic role of this entity is that of possessor. A possessive relationship specified by *tha-* can be interpreted as terminable and non-inherent in many cases. Thus, *tha-* is always used when alienably possessed items, such as material objects, are involved. *tha-* also occurs very frequently with possessed abstract nouns. *tha-* is encountered less frequently in combination with nouns designating body parts or terms of relationship; these concepts are conceived of as implying inherent, non-terminable (inalienable) possession. Pronominal possessor affixes precede *tha-*.

mi-thá-ˀogle
1SG.POR-ALP-shirt
'my shirt'

Possessors expressed by full noun phrases precede the possessed noun phrase.

John *tha-ˀógle*
John ALP-shirt
'John's shirt'

John *napé* *ki*
John hand DEF
'John's hand'

Sometimes possessor affixes are added to a special form *tháwa* to form possessive pronouns that follow the possessed noun, e.g., *mitháwa* 'my, mine', *nitháwa* 'your, yours', *tháwa* 'his, her(s), its':

wanáǧi *nitháwa*
spirit your
'your spirits'

While most English nouns inflect for number (e.g., singular *dog* vs. plural *dogs,* and so on), Lakota nouns do not normally do so. Rather, their singular or plural status can be deduced from other words. Indefinite articles (singular *wą,* plural *eyá*) or demonstratives (e.g., singular *lé* 'this' and *hé* 'that', plural *lená* 'these' and *hená* 'those') mark the number of the noun they modify:

wanáǧi *eyá*
spirit IDF.PL
'some spirits'

wanáǧi *ki* *lená*
spirit DEF these
'these spirits'

The inflection of the verb of the clause usually indicates the person and number of its subject and object (see §§1.3.5.1–1.3.5.2); in the following sentences, *šų́ka* 'dog' and *šų́kawakhą́* 'horse' are understood as plural ('dogs', 'horses') because of the plural suffix *-pi* and the plural patient prefix *wicha-* on the verbs of these sentences.

šų́ka *ki* *hó-pi*
dog DEF howl-PL
'The dogs were howling.'

ehą́ni *šų́kawakhą́* *wichá-ʔų-yuha-pi*
long ago horse 3PL.PAT-1PL.AG-have-PL
'long ago we had horses'

1.3.7. INFLECTION OF POSTPOSITIONS

The objects of postpositions are sometimes coded by a special additional set of person markers.

PARADIGM 7: objects of postpositions

	SG	DU	PL
1	*mi-*	*ų̨kí-*	*ų̨kí-*
2	*ni-*	*	*ni-*
3	*Ø-*	*	*wichí-*

mi-sákhib
1SG-beside
'beside me'

The affixes included in paradigm 7 are directly attached to postpositions. However, pronominal objects of postpositions very often are not coded on the postposition itself, but rather on the predicate of the clause the postposition is contained in. For this purpose, the stative (patient) paradigm of person affixes (see paradigms 1 and 3) is used.

sakhíb	*ma-yą́ke*
beside	1SG.PAT-sit

'he/she/it is sitting beside me'

In some cases, the object of the postposition may be marked both on the postposition and on the verb of the clause:

wichí-y-ohomni	*i-wícha-yaye*
3PL-EI-around	ST-3PL.PAT-go

'he/she/it is walking around them'

In this example, third person plural is coded on the postposition *ohómni* 'around' by means of the prefix *wichí-* and on the verb by means of the prefix *wicha-* (for the latter, see §1.3.5.1).

1.3.8. INDEPENDENT PRONOUNS

Lakota has a set of independent personal pronouns. However, these elements are normally used only to convey the pragmatic notions of emphasis or contrast, since the inflection of verbs and nouns usually indicates the person and number of subjects, objects, possessors, and sometimes other participants.

PARADIGM 8: independent personal pronouns

	SG	DU	PL
1	*miyé*	*ųkíye*	*ųkíyepi*
2	*niyé*	*	*niyépi*
3	*iyé*	*	*iyépi*

miyé *wa-ˀú*
I 1SG.AG-come
'I am coming', 'I am the one who is coming', 'I am coming (rather than someone else)'

1.4. Alphabetical List of Grammatical Terms

This section explains grammatical terms that are used to gloss Lakota grammatical elements (prefixes, suffixes, or grammatical words such as articles and auxiliary verbs).

Additive (ADD): *aké*. This word is equivalent to English *-teen* in numerals. It is placed before single-digit numerals to form the numerals between eleven and nineteen.

aké *wąží*
ADD one
'eleven'

aké *záptą*
ADD five
'fifteen'

Adjective (A). Used to disambiguate English words in glosses; see §1.6.

Adverb (AV). Used to disambiguate English words in glosses; see §1.6.

Adverbializer (ADV): *-ya, -yahą, -yą, -yela.* These suffixes derive adverbs from adjectives (like English *-ly*) and from verbs.

Agent (AG). See §§1.3.5.1–1.3.5.2.

Alienably possessed (ALP): *tha-*. See §1.3.6.

Assertive (ASS): *kštó, k'ų, ló, wą, -'*. See §1.3.1.

Benefactive (BEN). See §1.3.5.6.

Causative (CAU): *-khiya, -ya* (both with unstable *a*; see §1.2.2) 'to cause; to make'. These suffixes are added to verbs to form new verbs whose subject is the causer or instigator of the action coded by the base verb, while the subject of the base verb is the object of the causative verb. (Another affix with a similar function is the instrumental prefix *yu-* (see "Instrumental" below.)

aphé-ya
wait-CAU
'to make (someone) wait'

aphé-khiya
wait-CAU
'to make (someone) wait'

Person-marking prefixes are placed before the causative suffix:

aphé-wa-ye
wait-1SG.AG-CAU
'I made him/her wait.'

ų́thų-wicha-ya-pi
be injured-3PL.PAT-CAU-PL
'They hurt them.'

Causative *-ya* tends to become *-yą* (with nasal vowel) after a nasal vowel or after the sequence of a nasal consonant plus a vowel (e.g., after the first person dual/plural prefix *ų-* or after the second person patient prefix *ni-*). To *ų́thų-wicha-ya-pi* 'they hurt them', with no nasalization of the vowel of the causative suffix, compare:

ų́thų-yą-pi
be injured-CAU-PL
'They hurt him/her.'

ų́thų-ni-yą-pi
be injured-2SG.PAT-CAU-PL
'They hurt you.'

Celeritive (CEL): *éyaya, iyáya, iyéya* 'abruptly; at once; immediately; in a hurry; quickly; suddenly'. The verbs *éyaya* 'to take along', *iyáya* 'to go', and *iyéya* 'to send; to make go' may function as auxiliaries denoting immediate, sudden, or quick action. These elements follow the syntactic constituent they modify, which in most cases is a verb, and trigger truncation of the preceding lexical item. All three of these verbs end in unstable *a*. (For truncation and unstable *a*, see §1.2.2.)

nážį	*iyáya*
stand	CEL

'he gets up quickly'

Collective (COLL): *a-, wichó-* 'they (all)'. These affixes indicate that several individuals that are conceived of as constituting a group are involved in a given event. *a-* and *wichó-* may occur along with the plural marker *-pi* (for which, see §§1.3.5.1–1.3.5.2).

a-híyu(-pi)
COLL-come(-PL)
'they all come'

wichó-ˀų(-pi)
COLL-exist(-PL)
'they all exist'

Continuative (CNT): *a'ú / nážį / ų́ / yąká* 'to keep on; to continue'. The verbs *a'ú* 'to come to', *nážį* 'to stand', *ų́* 'to exist', and *yąká* 'to sit' may function as auxiliaries denoting continuative aspect. These elements follow the syntactic constituent they modify, which, in most cases, is a verb, and trigger truncation of the preceding lexical item. *yąká* ends in unstable *a*. (For truncation and unstable *a*, see §1.2.2.)

lową́	*yąké*
sing	CNT

'he/she keeps on singing'

Copula (COP): *hécha* 'to be'. When functioning as predicates, nouns are usually combined with the copula *hécha*.

John	*Lakhóta*	*hécha*
John	Lakota	COP

'John is a Lakota'

hécha is not an exact equivalent of the English copula 'to be', mainly because the latter can indicate not only group membership ("is a . . .") but also identification ("is the . . ."). *hécha* exclusively expresses group membership with nominal predicates; this element is not admissible in identificational contexts. In identificational contexts, the copular element *é* must be used (discussed below as identity predicator).

hécha can always be omitted in the third person singular.

John	*Lakhóta*
John	Lakota

'John is a Lakota'

In some contexts, *hécha* is most appropriately glossed as 'such'.

Lakota equivalents of English adjectives are usually stative verbs (see §1.3.5.2), and thus can be predicates without needing the copula.

mi-chą́te	*ki*	*wašté*
1SG.POR-heart	DEF	good

'My heart is good.'

Counterfactual (CNF): *tkhá* 'almost; would'. *tkhá* follows the verb that it modifies.

yá *tkhá*
go CNF
'he/she/it almost went', 'he/she/it would have gone'

Dative (DAT): *ki-*. See §1.3.5.6.

Definite (DEF): *ki, kihą* 'the'; *k'ų, k'ųhą* 'the aforesaid'. The basic function of definite articles is signaling that a given noun phrase has previously been mentioned in discourse. In this respect, *ki* and *kihą* on the one hand, and *k'ų* and *k'ųhą* on the other, convey slightly different meanings. The most frequently occurring definite articles are *ki* and *kihą*, which can usually be rendered by English 'the'. *k'ų* and *k'ųhą* are used with noun phrases that refer to participants in an event having not been mentioned in discourse for quite a while, and thus can be rendered by 'the aforesaid'. Lakota articles follow the noun they modify (see §1.3.2); they change preceding unstable *a* and *ą* to *e* (see §1.2.2).

Desiderative (DES): *ešá* 'may it happen that'. The particle *ešá* is always combined with *-šni* 'negative' (see §1.3.1), which is suffixed to the predicate. In this construction, *-šni* has no negative meaning and is left untranslated (though in grammatical glosses it is still glossed as NEG).

ešá *hokšíla* *i-ní-chağe-šni*
DES boy ST-2SG.PAT-grow-NEG
'may you grow up to be a boy'

Diminutive (DIM): *-la*. This element, which is homonymous with the limitative marker *-la* (cf. "Limitative"), can be attached to various parts of speech; it expresses diminution or sympathy.

wicháša-la
man-DIM
'little man', 'cute little man'

-la changes preceding unstable *a* and *ą* to *e* (see §1.2.2).

Dual inclusive (DU): *ų(k)-* 'you and I'. Lakota first person inflectional forms distinguish three number categories: singular, plural, and dual. First person dual indicates a group of two people, the speaker and the addressee ('I and you'). (Strictly speaking, then, the Lakota category is first person dual inclusive.) For subjects of transitive and intransitive verbs, this category is coded by the prefix *ų-* (*ųk-* before a vowel) without the plural suffix *-pi*.

ųk-íyųǧį-kte
1DU.AG-ask-FUT
'We (you and I) will ask him.'

ųk-íȟat'e
1DU.AG-laugh
'We (you and I) laugh.'

When the plural suffix *-pi* is present, *ų(k)-* simply denotes first person plural subject ('we'). Objects (patients) of transitive verbs do not distinguish between first person plural and first person (inclusive) dual; *ų(k)-* combined with *-pi* is used for both (and can be translated 'us'). See §§1.3.5.1–1.3.5.2.

Emphatic (EMPH): *-š*. This element expresses emphasis. Although it can be suffixed to various parts of speech, it is particularly frequent with adverbs.

Euphonic insertion (EI). In specific phonological environments, certain prefixes require the insertion of an additional sound element, usually *w* or *y*, in order to facilitate pronounciation (see §1.2.2). With a few verbs, certain prefixes require the insertion of *k* after the prefix. For instance, when the verb *icú* 'to take' is combined with the reflexive-possessive prefix *ki-* (see §1.3.5.6), the resulting form is *i-kí-k-cu* 'to take one's own'; the expected form **i-kí-cu* is ungrammatical.

False assumption (FASS): *tókhįš* 'I thought that . . . (but that was wrong)'. An example of this form is seen below:

tókhį̣š	*wachí-kte-šni*	*s'e*	*léchecha*	*yų̣khą̣*	*wachí*
FASS	dance-FUT-NEG	like	like this	and then	dance

'I thought he was not going to dance, but he did'

Female speaker (F): Certain sentence-final particles are used only by female speakers; F is used in the glosses of such particles. See §1.3.1.

Future (FUT): *-kta*. The future suffix *-kta* is the only tense marker that exists in Lakota. When the context makes it clear that future tense is indicated, *-kta* is frequently omitted. Sometimes *-kta* conveys an intentional meaning ('to want to', 'to intend to'). *-kta* ends in unstable *a*, and changes preceding unstable *a* or *ą* to *į* (see §1.2.2).

Habitual (HAB): *s'a*, *-šna* 'always; commonly; whenever'. *-šna* is primarily suffixed to adverbs expressing time or location and to conjunctions such as *na* 'and', while *s'a* is usually placed after verbs. *s'a* changes preceding unstable *a* or *ą* to *e* (see §1.2.2).

Identity predicator (IP): *é* 'it is'. To identify a particular individual or group, Lakota uses the special element *é*, rather than its ordinary copula *hécha* (for the latter, see "Copula" in this list).

John	*é*
John	IP

'it is John'

The identity predicator *é* is frequently used as a topic marker—that is, to mark a person or thing that the speaker's attention is focused on. In this case, *é* is usually followed by *cha* 'qualifier' (see "Qualifier" in this list).

Imperative (IMP): *ná, pé, pó, wé, wó, yé, yó*. These markers are placed at the end of the sentence; see §1.3.1.

Impersonal (IPS): *-pi*. Lakota has no close equivalent to the English passive, but it has an impersonal construction that serves partially similar functions. The plural suffix *-pi* (see §1.3.5.1–1.3.5.2) can be used when the indvidual identity of the agent is not of concern. This use of *-pi* is analogous to that of English *they* in *they told him,* when this sentence is understood as meaning something similar to the passive sentence *he was told* (simply leaving unspecified the identity of the person or persons who did the telling). Thus, the impersonal *-pi* construction can be translated by an English passive. In some cases, it is hard to decide whether *-pi* should be glossed as 'plural' or as 'impersonal'. In the texts, the gloss 'impersonal' is used whenever the extralinguistic referents of *-pi* cannot be clearly identified.

Inclusive. See "Dual inclusive" in this list.

Indefinite (IDF): *wą* 'a', *eyá* 'some'. These are the singular and plural forms of the indefinite article, respectively (see §1.3.2 and §1.3.6). Sometimes the form *wąží* (which is basically the numeral 'one') is also used for indefinite singular referents. *wąží* is, presumably, the historical source of *wą*.

Ingressive (IGR): *ahí, aʔú, éyaya, iyáya* 'to start'. The verbs *ahí* 'to come to', *aʔú* 'to come to', *éyaya* 'to take along', and *iyáya* 'to go' may function as auxiliaries expressing ingressive aspect. These elements follow the word they modify, which is in most cases a verb, and trigger truncation of the preceding word. *éyaya* and *iyáya* end in unstable *a*. (For truncation and unstable *a*, see §1.2.2.)

chéya *iyáya*
cry IGR
'he/she/it starts crying'

Instrumental (INS): *ka-* 'by striking; by a sudden impact', *na-* 'with the foot; with the leg', *na-* 'by an inner force; by itself', *pa-* 'by pushing; by drawing; by rubbing; by pressing', *wa-* 'by a sawing motion; with a knife', *wo-* 'by shooting; by punching; by pounding; from a distance', *ya-* 'by biting; by talking; with the mouth', *yu-* 'by pulling; with the hands; with no particular instrument'. The basic function of the instrumental prefixes is to add a causer or instigator for the verb root that they are attached to and to specify how this causer or instigator brings about the state of affairs expressed by the root. The instrumental prefix most frequently encountered is *yu-*; this element usually does not imply a particular mode of action and therefore can often be rendered as 'to cause, to make'.

yu-bláya
INS-flat
'to make flat, to flatten'

Verbs containing *ya-* and *yu-* are y-stems, which employ a special inflectional paradigm (see §1.3.5.4). Combinations of an instrumental prefix with a root often form an inseparable unit, either because the root in question cannot be used independently anymore or because the combination of prefix and root has taken on a meaning that diverges from that of the sum of its components. In such cases the instrumental prefix is not separated from the root in the morphological analysis.

Intensifier (INT): *áta, átaya, -lahčaka, -lahči, líla, -ȟca, -ȟci, -ȟcį* 'altogether, entirely, really, very'. This collection of suffixes and grammatical words is subsumed under a single category 'intensifier' because they can all be translated by the English adverbs listed above. Some of them are evidently related, but it is not yet clear just how the relationships should be characterized in detail. It is safe to assume, however, that *áta* is a shortened version of *átaya*. Rood and Taylor (1996: 474) report that *-lahčaka,* as well as some variant forms of this element which do not occur in the present text collection, may express emotions such as "mild yearning, mild discomfort, amusement," etc.

The adverbial intensifiers *áta, átaya,* and *líla* precede the words that they modify; *-lahčaka, -lahči, -ȟca, -ȟci,* and *-ȟcį* are suffixed to the word that they modify and change preceding unstable *a* or *ą* to *e*. *-lahčaka* and *-ȟca* themselves end in unstable *a*. (For stable and unstable *a* and *ą*, see §1.2.2.)

Interjection (IJ): *é, háųw, hé, hóȟ, hųhųhé, í, má, ma éya, wą́*. This list of interjections includes only those that occur in the texts in this volume; the total set of interjections in Lakota is much larger. *é* and *í*, which are usually pronounced with considerable vowel lengthening, do not seem to convey a particular meaning. *hóȟ* indicates disagreement. *háų̨w* and *hų̨hų̨hé* express sadness or regret and can be translated by 'alas'. *hé* is used to attract attention and is thus functionally equivalent to English 'hey'. *má, má éya,* and *wą́* are hesitation particles that can be rendered by 'well' or 'oh'. *í, má,* and *má éya* are used by women only, while *háų̨w, hé, hóȟ, hų̨hų̨hé,* and *wą́* are used by men only. *é* is used by both sexes.

Intransitive verb (VI). Used to disambiguate English words in glosses; see §1.6.

Limitative (LIM): *-la* 'only'. This element is usually suffixed to numerals. It is homonymous with, and functionally related to, *-la* 'diminutive' (see "Diminutive" in this list).

záptą-la
five-LIM
'only five'

Linker (LK): certain uses of *ki, k'ų, cha, na*. Grammatical markers placed at the end of certain subordinate clauses; see §1.3.4.

Locational (L): *a-* 'at; on; over; to', *é-* 'toward; to', *i-* 'at; from; with; in; by means of', *o-* 'at; into; to; on; in'. The locational prefixes are usually attached to verbs. They fulfill a variety of functions. As a rule, they specify the spatial setting of the state of affairs expressed by the verb.

a-glé
L-put
'to put on'

These prefixes often form inseparable units with the verb stem that they are combined with, in which the connection of the meaning of combination to the meaning of the locational prefix or the verb stem can no longer be easily detected. In such cases the locational prefix is not separated from the verb stem in the morphological analysis.

Male speaker (M). Certain sentence-final particles are used only by male speakers; M is used in the glosses of such particles. See §1.3.1.

Negative (NEG): *-šni* 'not'. This element can be added to various types of lexical items (see §1.3.1); it changes preceding unstable *a* or *ą* to *e* (see §1.2.2). Various negative pronouns, such as *tuwéni* 'nobody' and *tákuni* 'nothing', require that *-šni* be present on the predicate of the clause (not on the pronoun, unless the pronoun is itself the predicate):

tákuni	*slolyé-šni*
nothing	know-NEG

'he/she/it knows nothing'

Nonspecific patient (NSP.PAT): *wa-* 'something; things'. This prefix is frequently used as a way of leaving the patient of a transitive verb indefinite, unspecified, or implied; it can often be translated as 'something' or 'things'.

wopté
dig
'He/she digs it up.'

wa-wópte
NSP.PAT-dig
'He/she digs things up.'

Noun (N). Used to disambiguate English words in glosses; see §1.6.

Obligative (OBL): *hécha* 'must, should'. *hécha* follows the predicate that it modifies and is frequently preceded by a linker (see §1.3.4).

Ordinal number (ORD): *icí-*. Prefixing *icí-* transforms a cardinal number into an ordinal number.

icí-yamni
ORD-three
'third'

Partitive (PART): *etą́* 'some (of)'. This element is homonymous with and functionally related to the postposition *etą́(hą)* 'from'. It follows the syntactic constituent it modifies.

mní *etą́*
water PART
'some (of the) water'

Part of stem (ST). When personal prefixes are infixed into the stem (see §1.3.5.3), the part of the stem that precedes the personal prefixes is given the gloss ST- (part of the stem), and the stem's full gloss appears with the part of the stem that follows the personal prefixes. For example, the first person singular form of *nah̆ʔų́* 'to hear' appears as follows:

na-wá-h̆ʔų
ST-1SG.AG-hear
'I hear'

Patient (PAT). See §§1.3.5.1–1.3.5.2.

Plural (PL). *-pi*. See §§1.3.5–1.3.8. PL also appears as part of the gloss of the plural indefinite article *eyá* (see "Indefinite"), of the plural object prefix *wicha-*, and sometimes as part of the gloss of other pronominal prefixes (see §§1.3.5.1–1.3.5.2).

Possessor (POR). See §1.3.6.

Processual (PRC): *áya* 'to become (increasingly)'. This auxiliary, which follows the verb it modifies, denotes gradual intensification of a given state of affairs. *áya* triggers truncation of the preceding lexical item and ends in unstable *a*. (For truncation and unstable *a*, see §1.2.2.)

šóka *áye*
thick PRC
'it becomes thick', 'it becomes thicker and thicker'

Progressive (PRG): *-hą* 'to keep on, to continue; for a while; again and again; always'. This element can also be translated by continuous tense ('to be . . . ing'). It ends in unstable *ą* (see §1.2.2).

yúta-he
eat-PRG
'He/she/it is eating it.'

ų-yúta-hą-pi
1PL.AG-eat-PRG-PL
'We are eating it.'

Qualifier (QL): *cha*. This grammatical element fulfills a variety of syntactic functions (for instance, see the discussion of relative clauses in §1.3.4). Sometimes it can also be translated by 'such', or it functions as a conjunction that can be rendered by 'so'. In the latter case it is glossed as 'so' instead of 'qualifier'. In many cases a translational equivalent for *cha* is not available at all.

Question (QS): *hé, hųwó, só*. These sentence-final particles indicate that the sentence is a question. The elements *hé* and *só* are used by male and female speakers; *hųwó* is used by male speakers only. See §1.3.1. (There are additional question markers in Lakota, but they are not listed here because they do not occur in the texts in this volume.)

Quotative (QT): *kéye, škhé* (also variant form *škhá*) 'it is said'. These sentence-final particles indicate that the statement made is based on hearsay, rather than on the speaker's own experience. They are usually not translated in the English versions of the texts.

Reciprocal (REC) *íchi-, kichí-* 'each other'. See §1.3.5.5.

Reduplication (RED). In Lakota, the process of reduplication consists in repeating a syllable. A reduplicated syllable may undergo certain phonologically conditioned changes and is therefore not necessarily identical with the basic syllable in phonetic shape. Reduplication conveys the notions of intensification and repetition.

slí-slipe
RED-lick
'He licked it repeatedly.'
(cf. unreduplicated *slípe* 'he licked it')

In the case of inanimate entities, reduplication can also express pluralization:

táku	*cik-cík'ala*
things	RED-small

'small things'
(cf. unreduplicated *cík'ala* '[be] small')

wówapi	*ki*	*lená*	*wašté-šte*
book	DEF	these	good-RED

'These books are good.'
(cf. unreduplicated *wašté* '[be] good')

Reflexive (RFL). See §1.3.5.5.

Reflexive-possessive (RPOSS). See §1.3.5.6.

Singular (SG). In Lakota, the category of singular is not marked by a separate prefix or suffix within inflectional paradigms. Some articles, demonstratives, and pronominal prefixes include it as part of their meaning, however; see §§1.3.5.1–1.3.5.2 and §1.3.6.

Subordinator (SUB): *héci*. See §1.3.4.

Syntactic particle (SYP): *ki(hą) / k'ų(hą)*. These elements are homonymous with the definite articles *ki(hą)* and *k'ų(hą)* (see "Definite"). Syntactic particles subordinate the preceding clause. In most cases, they can be rendered by 'after', 'when', and 'while'. In other cases, an English translation is not available.

hí	*ki*
come	SYP

'when he/she/it came'

Transitive verb (VT). Used to disambiguate English words in glosses; see §1.6.

1.5. Lakota Speakers

The transcripts of the original tape-recorded texts were repeatedly revised with the help of the native speakers of Lakota who participated in the project, mainly to eliminate redundancies, repetitions, inaccuracies, and other stylistic infelicities which are almost inevitable in spoken language. The original version has been retained whenever it did not contain any such infelicities. Fillers and hesitation particles indicating interruptions in speech production, such as *į̨s*, *į̨ska*, and *eya*, have been removed. Although spoken language is inevitably not as polished as written language, the English translation given is kept as close to the Lakota original as possible, sometimes at the cost of stylistic elegance.

Below, some detailed information about the native speakers who participated in the project is given.

Mary Light (Wį́yą Ehákе 'Last Woman') was born on December 10, 1918, in Oglala, Pine Ridge Indian Reservation, South Dakota. She died on August 21, 1997, in Boulder, Colorado. Mary acquired Lakota as her first language. She spoke the Oglala dialect of Lakota. Mary started to learn English at school at the age of eight. She attended school until the age of seventeen. She lived (in chronological order) in Oglala, South Dakota; Manderson, South Dakota; Chadron, Nebraska; Hot Springs, South Dakota; Longmont, Colorado; Greely, Colorado; Fort Collins, Colorado; Denver, Colorado; and Boulder, Colorado. She was married to a Lakota man from Pine Ridge Indian Reservation, South Dakota, and a Lakota man from Rosebud Indian Reservation, South Dakota. She spoke both Lakota and English with her former husbands. In the more recent past, she used the Lakota language to communicate with Lakota friends who reside in the Denver–Boulder area. None of her thirteen children speaks or understands Lakota.

Florine Lucille Red Ear Horse (Thašína Ská Wį 'White Shawl Woman') was born on March 4, 1925, in Oglala, Pine Ridge Indian Reservation, South Dakota. Florine acquired Lakota as her first language. She represents the Oglala dialect of Lakota. Florine started to learn English at school at the age of six. She attended school until the age of seventeen. She has lived in Oglala, South Dakota; Pine Ridge, South Dakota; Custer, South Dakota; Legion Lake, South Dakota; Denver, Colorado; and Morris, Minnesota. Florine has worked at a hotel, as a nurse's aid, at a moccasin factory, at the Denver Indian Center, and as a restaurant manager. She was married to a Lakota man, with whom she spoke Lakota only. All of her six children understand Lakota, but only one daughter also speaks the language. Today, Florine uses Lakota on an everyday basis when she talks to her children and grandchildren, although her grandchildren's knowledge of Lakota is limited, and when communicating with Lakota friends who reside in the Denver–Boulder area.

Neva Elizabeth Standing Bear Light-in-the-Lodge (Zįtká Zí Wį 'Yellow Bird Woman') was born on August 3, 1924, in Rosebud, Rosebud Sioux Reservation, South Dakota. Neva is a Lakota woman who grew up in a bilingual Lakota- and English-speaking environment. She represents the Brulé dialect of Lakota. She attended school from age ten to fourteen. Neva has lived in Parmalee, South Dakota; Kyle, South Dakota; Alliance, Nebraska; and Denver, Colorado. She worked at a public school in South Dakota and as a civil servant at an air base in Nebraska, ran a trading post in Golden, Colorado, and has been part of the University of Colorado Lakhota Project in Boulder, Colorado. She was married to a Lakota from Pine Ridge and to several white Americans. One of her ten children speaks Lakota. Today, Neva uses Lakota on an everyday basis when talking to her daughter and Lakota friends who reside in the Denver–Boulder area.

Neva is the niece of Luther Standing Bear, author of several books on Sioux culture and history (*Land of the Spotted Eagle, My Indian Boyhood*, etc.). She is living a very active life as a spiritual leader, healer, and instructor. Her awards include the Colorado Woman of Color Award, awarded on March 22, 1990; the Certificate of Appreciation in Recognition of Accomplishments and Contributions to the Indian Community and the Winyan Wašaka Program, awarded on August 2, 1991, and again on June 20, 1992; the Social Responsibility

Award in Honor of Dr. Martin Luther King Jr., awarded on January 17, 1992; the Native American Women's Business Organization Mile High City Woman of the West Award, awarded on February 2, 1995; and the Native American Women's Association Award, awarded on May 13, 1995.

1.6. The Presentation of the Lakota Texts

The Lakota texts in this book are presented in an interlinear format that includes grammatical analysis. Complex Lakota words are divided into their smaller meaningful units, which are separated from each other by means of hyphens. The meaningful elements are glossed in the second line. Most lexical stems are glossed by ordinary English words in lowercase, while grammatical elements are glossed by abbreviations in small capitals. For instance, the complex word *yápi* 'they go' is composed of a lexical stem (*yá* 'to go') and a grammatical unit (the suffix *-pi* 'plural').

yá-pi
go-PL

When it is necessary to gloss a single meaningful element by more than one word or abbreviation, the words or abbreviations in the gloss are connected by periods. For example, the sentence-final grammatical marker *yó* is an imperative form that is used by men only (women use different imperative markers); *yó* is glossed by the abbreviation IMP, which stands for 'imperative', plus the abbreviation M, for 'male speaker', connected by a period:

yó
IMP.M

An exception is that no period is used after the abbreviations 1, 2, and 3, which stand for 'first person', 'second person', and 'third person' respectively. Thus, for example, the first person singular agent prefix *wa-* is glossed as 1SG.AG. (See §§1.3.5.1–1.3.5.2 for discussion of such grammatical categories as person and agent.)

Some Lakota words and phrases have idiomatic meanings that are hard to deduce from their lexical and grammatical components. These words and phrases are treated as units for purposes of glossing in the text; in such cases the gloss is marked with an asterisk (*) as an indication that the word or phrase can be found in the appendix, "Analysis of Neologisms and Idioms," an alphabetical list where such idiomatic expressions are analyzed into their lexical and grammatical components. Thus, for example, *hoyékhiya* is glossed as 'call to*' in the texts, but in the appendix it is explained as:

hó-ye-khiya
voice-go-CAU

(where CAU stands for 'causative'). Similarly, the phrase *wahˇté-šni inít'e ló* in the texts is treated as a unit and glossed 'doggone you*'; in the appendix it is explained thus:

wahˇté-šni	*i-ní-t'e*	*ló*
worthless	L-2SG.PAT-die	ASS.M

(See the list of abbreviations for explanations of the glosses of the grammatical elements.)

In English, many lexical items are ambiguous as to part of speech. For instance, *back* may function as an adverb, as a noun, as an adjective, and as a verb (e.g., *to back up*). Further, many English verb stems are ambiguous with respect to their transitivity status; for instance, *to dry* may function both as an intransitive and as a transitive verb (*the shirt is drying* vs. *I am drying the shirt*). In some cases where such ambiguities could interfere with the correct interpretation of the Lakota form, an abbreviation for part of speech (A for 'adjective', AV for 'adverb', N for 'noun', VI for 'intransitive verb', VT for 'transitive verb') is added to the English gloss of a Lakota stem or word. Thus, for example, the noun stem *wówachįye* is glossed as 'help.N', while the transitive verb stem *ókiya* is glossed as 'help.VT'.

Besides the interlinear grammatical analysis, the Lakota texts are accompanied by free translations into English. Sentences in the English translations do not necessarily correspond one-to-one to sentences in Lakota. For instance, in Lakota, many long sequences of clauses connected by *na* 'and' are treated as single sentences; in the free translations, these are often divided into several sentences.

A peculiarity of Lakota narrative style is that sentence-final predicates tend to be repeated at the beginning of the following sentence. This may seem inelegant to native speakers of English; however, no attempt has been made to change that characteristic trait in the texts presented in this volume.

Personal Histories 2

2.1. A Short Autobiography

NEVA STANDING BEAR

Tape recorded September 31, 1994

lé	*ą̨pétu*	*ki*	*tókhel*	*i-má-chağa*	*héci*	*hé*
this	day	DEF	how	ST-1SG.PAT-grow	SUB	that

o-wá-glakį-kte.	*ehą́ni*	*ma-cík'ala*	*k'ų*	*héhą*
ST-1SG.AG-POSS.tell-FASS	long ago	1SG.PAT-little	SYP	then

South Dakota	*él*	*i-má-chağe.*	*hé*	*Sichą́ğu*	*oyą́ke*	*él*
South Dakota	in	ST-1SG.PAT-grow	that	Rosebud*	reservation	in

i-má-chağį	*na*	*he-tą́*	*wa-híyu*	*na*	*Oglála*
ST-1SG.PAT-grow	and	that-from	1SG.AG-come	and	Oglala

makhóche	*ektá*	*hįgná-wa-thų*	*na*	*he-tą́*	*wašícu*
country	in	ST-1SG.AG-marry*	and	that-from	white man

makhóche	*ektá*	*wa-híyu.*	*ho*	*héhą*	*ehą́ni*	*wa-má-khąyeža*
country	to	1SG.AG-come	well	then	long ago	ST-1SG.PAT-child

cha	*héhą*	*iná-wa-ye*	*ki*	*máni-šni.*	*waníyetu*
QL	then	mother-1SG.AG-have as	DEF	walk-NEG	year

wikcémna	*máni-šni*	*na*	*ą̨pétu*	*wą*	*él*	*máni-kta*	*yųkhą́*
ten	walk-NEG	and	day	IDF.SG	in	walk-FASS	then

ichų́hą hįgná-wa-thų na léchiya Oglála makhóche ektá
meantime ST-1SG.AG-marry* and here Oglala country to

wa-híyu-ˀ. ho héhą Lakhóta étkiya
1SG.AG-come-ASS well then Lakota toward

hįgnáthų-ma-khiya-pi cha wichá-ma-kˀu-pi. cha
marry*-1SG.PAT-CAU-IPS QL 3PL.PAT-1SG.PAT-give-IPS so

wicháša wą hįgná-wa-ye ki slol-wá-ye-šni.
man LK ST-1SG.AG-marry* DEF ST-1SG.AG-know-NEG

slol-wá-ye-šni éyaš hįgná-wa-yį na waníyetu
ST-1SG.AG-know-NEG but ST-1SG.AG-marry* and year

yámni séca héchi wa-ˀų́. na he-tą́ wašícu
three maybe there 1SG.AG-live and that-from white man

makhóche ektá wa-híyu, Chasmú Okáȟmi ektá
land to 1SG.AG-come Alliance* to

wa-híyu, na héchiya wa-ˀų́. na hél wówaši
1SG.AG-come and there 1SG.AG-live and there work.N

echámų na hokší icháȟ-wa-khiyį na he-tą́
do.1SG.AG and child grow-1SG.AG-CAU and that-from

iyópteya Ȟé Ská étkiya wa-híyu na hehą́tą
further on Rocky Mountains* toward 1SG.AG-come and since then

Ȟé Ská Oyą́ke léchiya othų́wahe wą thą́ka cha héchiya wa-ˀų́.
Denver* here city LK big QL there 1SG.AG-live

waná	*waníyetu*	*wikcémna*	*tóp*	*są́m*	*aké*	*šaglóǧą*	*henákecha*
now	year	ten	four	more	ADD	eight	so many

léchiya	*wa-ʔų́.*	*ho*	*éyaš*	*wašícu*	*ų́pi*	*ki*	*othéȟikį*
here	1SG.AG-live	well	but	white man	existence	DEF	hard

na	*Lakhóta*	*wichóʔų*	*ki*	*są́m*	*gnúni*	*ųk-áya-pi*
and	Indian	way of life	DEF	more	lose	1PL.PAT-PRC-PL

chąkhé	*oʔíyokišice.*	*ho*	*lehą́n*	*ųkʔ-ų́-pi*	*ki*	*nąké*
then	sad	well	now	1PL.AG-exist-PL	SYP	now

ų-Lákhota-pi-kteȟci	*éyaš*	*ųk-ókihi-pi-šni.*	*takómni*
1PL.PAT-Indian-PL-crave	but	1PL.AG-can-PL-NEG	at all costs

wašʔág-yahą	*wašícu*	*wichóʔų*	*ogná*	*ųkʔ-ų-pi*	*cha.*
strong-ADV	white man	way of life	inside	1PL.AG-exist-PL	QL

othéȟi-ya	*núni*	*sʔe*	*ųkʔų́-pi*	*lé*	*ąpétu*	*ki.*
terrible-ADV	lost	like.AV	1PL.AG-exist-PL	this	day	DEF

ho	*yųkhą́*	*etą́*	*Lakhól-wichóȟʔą*	*naʔį́š*	*táku*	*ki*	*lená*
well	then	from	Indian-traditions	or	what	DEF	these

héktakiya	*yu-kíni-pi*	*na*	*echél*	*thokátakiya*	*yuhá*
backwards	INS-revive.VI-PL	and	so	in the future	have

máni-pi-kte	*na*	*echél*	*Lakhól-wichóʔų*	*ki*	*lená*	*héchų sʔe*
walk-PL-FASS	and	so	Indian-way of life	DEF	these	that way*

Lakhóta	*oyáte*	*ki*	*ų́-pi*	*hą́tąhąš*	*tąyą́*	*ų́-pi-kte.*
Indian	people	DEF	be-PL	if	well	exist-PL-FASS

kta *kéyá-pi* *na* *hená* *héchų-pi* *éyaš* *mnišíca* *wą* *líla*
FASS say that-PL and those do that-PL but liquor* IDF.SG INT

khicáyą-pi *na* *ų́* *núni-pi.* *ho* *chąkhé* *lehą́n* *o'ínikağe*
abuse-PL and therefore lost-PL well then now sweatlodge

él *a-wícha-ya-pi* *na* *mní* *wichá-k'u-pi* *na'į́š*
to ST-3PL.PAT-take to-PL and water 3PL.PAT-give-PL or

chąnų́m-wichá-khiya-pi *lená* *waníce.* *héhą́ni* *yukhé* *yųkhą́*
smoke-3PL.PAT-CAU-PL these lack at that time exist then

lehą́n *hená* *waníce.* *cha* *hená* *akhé* *héktakiya* *kú-'.* *ho*
now those lack so those again backwards come-ASS well

cha *lená* *wochékhiye* *ų́* *oyáte* *kihą* *ób-šna*
so these prayer using people DEF with-HAB

iní-'ų-kağa-pi *na*
ST-1PL.AG-perform sweatlodge ceremony-PL and

waché-wicha-'ų-kici-chiya-pi, *hógna* *ka-'ówothą* *iyáya-pi*
ST-3PL-1PL.AG-BEN-pray-PL that way* INS-straight IGR-PL

hą́tąhąš, *hógna* *ecéla* *lená* *Lakhóta* *kihą* *tąyą́* *ų́-pi-kte.*
if that way* only these Indian DEF well exist-PL-FASS

ho *na* *hé* *ų́,* *wašícu* *ų́pi* *ki* *hé* *ų́,*
well and that because of white man existence DEF that because of

kakíža-pi. *ho* *cha* *lehą́n* *wichó'ų* *kihą* *hų́ȟ* *wó'ųspe*
suffer-PL well so now generation DEF some knowledge

wąkátuya	*yuhá-pi*	*kˀéyaš*	*Lakhóta*	*hų́ȟ*	*wa-yáwa-pi-šni,*
high	have-PL	but	Indian	some	NSP.PAT-read-PL-NEG

hená	*ó-wicha-kiya-pi-šni*	*cha*	*lehą́n*	*othų́wahe*	*ektá*
those	ST-3PL.PAT-help.VT-IPS-NEG	so	now	city	in

thi-níca-pi	*na*	*lochí̜-pi*	*na*	*wóchi̜*	*ománi-pi*	*naˀí̜š*
house-lack-PL	and	hungry*-PL	and	beg	walk about-PL	or

tuktéktel	*thi-ˀáglagla*	*iští̜ma-pi*	*kˀų.*	*na*	*osní*	*hą́tąhąš*
here and there	house-along	sleep-PL	ASS	and	cold	when

chąkú	*naˀí̜š*	*wakpála*	*ektá*	*aglágla*	*hená*	*héchiya*	*iští̜ma-pi*	*na*
road	or	river	at	along	those	there	sleep-PL	and

hená	*héchiya*	*thí-pi.*	*naˀí̜š*	*héchi*	*cheyákthųpi*	*oȟláthe*
those	there	live-PL	or	there	bridge	underneath

chethí-pi	*na*	*hená*	*o-khál-ˀicˀi-ya*	*yąká-pi.*	*ho*	*lená*
build a fire-PL	and	those	L-warm-3RFL-CAU	sit-PL	well	these

é	*cha*	*Lakhóta*	*kihą*	*i-wícha-ˀųk-icu-pi*	*na*	*echél*
IP	QL	Indian	DEF	ST-3PL.PAT-1PL.AG-take-PL	and	so

owóthąla	*asní-wicha-ˀų-yą-pi*	*hą́tąhąš*	*akhé*	*hená*
straight	recover-3PL.PAT-1PL.AG-CAU-PL	if	again	those

wówaši	*echų́-pi*	*naˀí̜š*	*ó-ˀicˀ-iye*	*wa-chí̜-pi-kte*
work.N	do-PL	and	ST-3RFL-help.VT	NSP.PAT-want-PL-FASS

na	*thi-yúha-pi-kte*	*naˀí̜š*	*thiwáhe*	*yąká-pi-kte.*	*éyaš*	*lená*
and	home-have-PL-FASS	and	family	sit-PL-FASS	but	these

waná wanícį na tha-chį́cha-pi ki hená iyúha wašícu
now lack and ALP-child-PL DEF those all white man

icháȟ-wicha-ya-pi. chąkhé othéȟike. nakų́ lehą́n
grow-3PL.PAT-CAU-PL then hard also now

phežúta wichášа na waphíya wichášа lená waníca-pi na
herbalist* and healer* these lack-PL and

wakhą́ wichášа lená henála áya-pi chąkhé tuwá
spiritual man* these gone PRC-PL then someone

wachį́-ˀų-yą́-pi-kta wą waníce. wówachįye
ST-1PL.AG-depend on-PL-FASS IDF.SG lack help.N

wichá-ˀų-ki-la-pi ki lená hų́ȟ itéšniyą
3PL-1PL.AG-BEN-ask for-PL DEF these some truthfully

hécha-pi-šni. itéšniyą wochékhiye él nážį-pi-šni tkhá lená
COP-PL-NEG truthfully prayer in stand-PL-NEG but these

wa-ˀínapišką́ye hécha-pi. ho chąkhé tuktél
NSP.PAT-play around COP-PL well then where

ų-híyaya-pi-kta thąį́-šni. ho cha ųkíyechįka
1PL.AG-go on-PL-FASS evident-NEG well so by ourselves

ųk-íyaya-pi na wochékhiye ųk-éya-pi na oyáte ki
1PL.AG-go and prayer 1PL.AG-say-PL and people DEF

lená ób na-ˀų́-žį-pi. hógna ecéla, kawítaya
these with ST-1PL.AG-stand-PL that way* only together

ų-khínažį-pi ki, ų-wáš'aka-pi-kte. na táku
1PL.AG-stand up-PL if 1PL.PAT-strong-PL-FASS and things

abléza-pi-kte na héchel ų́ši-kichi-la-pi-kte. na'į́š
notice-PL-FASS and so ST-REC-pity.VT-PL-FASS and

abléza-pi hą́tąhą wašícu wichó'ų ki lé ogná tąyą́
notice-PL if white man way of life DEF this inside well

ų́-pi-kte. héchel táku ehą́ni
exist-PL-FASS so what long ago

thųkášila-wicha-'ų-yą-pi na'į́š
grandfather-3PL.PAT-1PL.AG-have as-PL and

ųcí-wicha-'ų-yą-pi táku
grandmother-3PL.PAT-1PL.AG-have as-PL what

ųk-ó-ki-yaka-pi héci hená lehą́n hená é cha
1PL-ST-BEN-tell-PL SUB those now those IP QL

ų-kíksuya-pi na ų́ lechála icháğe ki
1PL.AG-remember-PL and this way recently grow DEF

w-ó-wicha-'ų-ki-yaka-pi. ho cha lehą́n wakhą́yeža
NSP.PAT-ST-3PL.PAT-1PL.AG-BEN-tell-PL well so now child

ki líla óta ipáyeȟ iyáya-pi na mázawakhą́ khicáyą-pi na
DEF INT many wrong go-PL and gun* abuse-PL and

lechála-š Lakhóta hokšíla wą Lakhóta hokšíla wą
recently-EMPH Indian boy IDF.SG Indian boy IDF.SG

ka-tʔá iyéye chąkhé átaya wóchątešice hécha. ho lé
INS-die CEL then INT sadness OBL well this

ithánųgya chąté šíca-pi na lená héchel wichóʔų-šni
on both sides sad*-PL and these so way of life-NEG

chąkhé tohą́n okíhilaka hų́-ku-pi ki kakíža-pi na
then as much as can be* mother-3POR-PL DEF suffer-PL and

at-kúku-pi ki nakų́. ho éyašchį takómni wašícu
father-3POR-PL DEF also well but at all costs white man

wichóʔų na lená héchel ųspé-pi cha theȟíke. ho
way of life and these so know-PL so terrible well

thokátakiya waníyetu eháke tóna kaphíyehą
in the future year yet so many for a longer time

zaní-ya wa-ʔų́ hą́tąhąš lená oyáte ki ób
healthy-ADV 1SG.AG-exist if these people DEF with

thokátakiya ma-wá-ni-kte. miyé héchel
in the future ST-1SG.AG-walk-FASS I so

mi-thá-wachį. ho chąkhé lená ehą́ni
1SG.POR-ALP-thought well then these long ago

até-wa-ye ki lená w-í-wahokų-ma-khiya-pi
father-1SG.AG-have as DEF these NSP.PAT-LST-1SG.PAT-preach-PL

na lekší-wicha-wa-ye ki hená na
and uncle-3PL.PAT-1SG.AG-have as DEF those and

thųwį-wicha-wa-ye ki hená waná henála-pi-kte, tkhá
aunt-3PL.PAT-1SG.AG-have as DEF those now gone-PL-FASS but

waná wąží-la bluhá. thųwį-wa-ye ki
now one-LIM have.1SG.AG 1SG.AG-aunt-1SG.AG-have as DEF

wąží-la. ho chąkhé iyé kayéš kakíža chąkhé wochékiye hé
one-LIM well then she even suffer then spirituality that

š'ag-yáhą líla gluhá na-wá-žį. hógna oyáte ki
strong-ADV INT POSS.have ST-1SG.AG-stand that way* people DEF

akísni-pi na tąyą́ iyáya-pi na waš'áka-pi-kta ų́
recover-PL and well go-PL and strong-PL-FASS because of

lená héchamų. héchel iyé thitákuye-pi hená
these do that.1SG.AG so they relative-3PL.POR those

ó-wicha-kiya-pi-kta cha hé ų́ léchetu. léchų s'e
ST-3PL.PAT-help.VT-PL-FASS QL that because of so this way*

wa-'échamų. ho lehą́n oyáte kihą miyé étkiya
NSP.PAT-do.1SG.AG well now people DEF 1SG toward

wówachįye ma-kí-la-pi na'į́š wochékhiye na wó'asniye
help.N 1SG-BEN-ask for-PL or prayer and recovery

ki lená ma-kí-la-pi chąkhé othéȟika tkhá
DEF these 1SG-BEN-ask for-PL then difficult but

phežúta wicháša wąží-la ų́ cha hé ecéla wachį-wa-ye.
medicine man* one-LIM exist QL that only ST-1SG.AG-depend on

chą́-šna ektá masˀá-mi-ci-pha-pi chą́-šna tókhel
then-HAB there ST-1SG-BEN-give a phone call*-IPS then-HAB how

wa-ˀéchųkˀų-kte lená ųk-ó-ki-yaka-pi hą́tąhąš.
NSP.PAT-do.1PL.AG-FASS these 1PL-ST-BEN-tell-PL so that

hé ogná ecéla oyáte kihą wochékhiye ų́
that way* only people DEF prayer using

asní-wicha-ˀų-yą-pi naˀį́š ó-wicha-ˀų-kiya-pi.
recover-3PL.PAT-1PL.AG-CAU-PL and ST-3PL.PAT-1PL.AG-help.VT-PL

na hená oyáte kihą Sichą́ǧu naˀį́š Oglála oyáte ecéla-pi-šni,
and those people DEF Rosebud* or Oglala people only-PL-NEG

lená áta oyáte makhá sitómniya ų́-pi ki, lená áta
these all people earth everywhere be-PL DEF these all

ó-wicha-ˀų-kiya-pi-kta ų́ hená
ST-3PL.PAT-1PL.AG-help.VT-PL-FASS in order to those

héchųkˀųpi. naˀį́š ská oyáte naˀį́š há-sápa oyáte
do that.1PL.AG-PL and white people and skin-black people

naˀį́š há-zí oyáte ki lená iyúha
and skin-yellow people DEF these all

ó-wicha-ˀų-kiya-pi-kta cha ų́ léchel
ST-3PL.PAT-1PL.AG-help.VT-PL-FASS so that way so

ų-hí-nažį-pi na hógna ųkícˀi-chųza-pi chąkhé
1PL.AG-come-stand-PL and that way* 1PL.RFL-promise-PL then

othéȟike. tókheškhe waníyetu óta ų-yą́-pi na tohą́n
hard this is why year many 1PL.AG-go-PL and when

waná ųk-ókihi-pi-šni hą́tąhą́š tuwá lená áyį-kte
now 1PL.AG-can-PL-NEG when someone these carry on-FASS

ki lená waníca-pi. cha othéȟike. ho éyaš lé ąpétu kihą
DEF these lack-PL so terrible well but this day DEF

lená wówachįye na wóʼokhiye wichá-ʼų-ki-la-pi. ho
these assistance and help.N 3PL-1PL.AG-BEN-ask for-PL well

eché-ȟcį-š wį́yą wą wichókhuže šíca yuhá na akísni
SO-INT-EMPH woman IDF.SG disease bad have and recover

chį́ na ní chį́ na wašícu wakhą́ ki wí yámni-la
want and live want and white doctor* DEF month three-LIM

kʼú-pi ho éyaš waná wí šakówį ní, waná
give-PL well but now month seven live now

wąbláke-šni tkhá hohú echécha kéyá-pi. ho hé waná
see.1SG.AG-NEG but bone be that way say that-IPS well that now

le-tą́ hį́hąni akhó-tąhą khignį́-kta cha ho
this-from tomorrow beyond-from go home-FASS so well

icínųpani hé wą-ʼų́-yąka-pi-kte-šni škhá iníhąšni
never again that ST-1PL.PAT-see-PL-FASS-NEG but nevertheless

ų-kíksuya-pi-kte. ho héhą lená tha-thítakuye na
1PL.PAT-remember-PL-FASS well then these ALP-relative and

chįchá	*lená*	*wókakiže*	*él*	*ikhóyaka-pi*	*lená*	*abléza-pi-šni*	*cha*
child	these	suffering	to	connected-PL	these	realize-PL-NEG	so

ho	*tkhá*	*hená*	*įȟąhą*	*kéchį-pi*	*éyaš*	*lená*	*tohą́n*	*ų́yą*
well	but	those	temporary	think that-PL	but	these	when	leave

ųk-íyaya-pi	*chą́-šna*	*othéȟike.*	*thą́kake*	*ki*	*ų́yą*
1PL.PAT-go-PL	then-HAB	hard	elders	DEF	leave

ųk-íyaya-pi	*hą́tąhąš*	*héhą*	*othéȟike.*	*tuktél*	*ų-híyaya-pi-kta*
1PL.PAT-go-PL	when	then	terrible	where	1PL.AG-go-PL-FASS

ų-híyaya-pi-kta	*waníce.*	*ho*	*wašícu*	*wichóˀų*	*ki*	*lé*
1PL.AG-go-PL-FASS	lack	well	white man	way of life	DEF	this

tohą́n okíhilaka	*othéȟike.*	*cha*	*blihé-ˀųkicˀi-ya-pi-kte*	*na*
as much as can be*	hard	so	energetic-1PL.RFL-CAU-PL	and

ó-ˀų-kichi-ya-pi-kta	*wą*	*hécha.*	*ho*	*lé*	*ąpétu*
ST-1PL.AG-REC-help.VT-PL-FASS	IDF.SG	OBL	well	this	day

kihą	*lé*	*waná̌ǧoyapi*	*ki*	*lé*	*táku*	*lená*	*oyáka-pi*	*naˀį́š*
DEF	this	tape recording*	DEF	this	things	these	tell-IPS	or

ųgnáš	*wówapi*	*káǧa-pi.*	*hé*	*hená*	*ųkí-chįcha-pi*	*na*
maybe	book	make-IPS	that	those	1PL.POR-child-PL	and

ųkí-thakožakpaku-pi	*ki*	*hená*	*yawá-pi*	*hą́tąhąš*	*ųgná*
1PL.POR-grandchild-PL	DEF	those	read-PL	if	maybe

he-tą́	*táku*	*slolyá-pi-kta*	*ų́*	*lená*
that-from	something	know-PL-FASS	because of	these

héchamų.	*ho*	*cha*	*tuktógna k'éyaš*	*mi-thá-ʔoʔiye*
do that.1SG.AG	well	so	whichever way	1SG.POR-ALP-word

oyáte	*ki*	*na-má-ȟʔų*	*wa-chį́*	*na*	*ų́*	*lená*
people	DEF	ST-1SG.PAT-hear	1SG.AG-want	and	therefore	these

léchel	*wa-káǧe.*	*thokátakiya*	*wakȟą́yeža*	*ki*	*lená*	*wašícu*
so	1SG.AG-make	future	child	DEF	these	white man

étkiya	*wa-ʔų́spe-pi*	*na*	*Lakȟól-ʔiyá*	*nakų́*	*wa-ʔų́spe-pi*
toward	NSP.PAT-know-PL	and	Indian-speak	also	NSP.PAT-know-PL

hą́tąhąš,	*iyé*	*táku*	*ehą́ni*	*ųspé-ʔų-khiya-pi*	*ho*	*hená*
if	they	what	long ago	know-1PL.PAT-CAU-IPS	well	those

į́š	*eyá*	*lehą́n*	*wayúphika-pi*	*hą́tąhąš*	*héchel*	*núni-šni-ye*
they	also	now	skillful*-PL	if	so	lost-NEG-ADV

ksab-yáhą	*thokáta-kiya*	*máni-pi-kte.*	*lehą́n*	*iyótą-š*
wise-ADV	future-toward	go-PL-FASS	now	most-EMPH

wičháša itháchą	*khó*	*waníce*	*cha*	*tuwéni*	*oʔíye*	*naȟʔų́-pi-kta*
leader	also	lack	so	nobody	word	hear-PL-FASS

waníce.	*cha*	*othéȟike.*	*ho*	*lehą́yela*	*wa-ʔéphį-kte*
lack	so	terrible	well	this is all	NSP.PAT-say.1SG.AG-FASS

nahą́	*táku*	*thókecha*	*wąží*	*oblákį-kte.*
and then	something	different	IDF.SG	tell.1SG.AG-FASS

Today I will tell about how I grew up. A long time ago, when I was little, I grew up in South Dakota. I grew up on the Rosebud Reservation, and then I left and got married in the Oglala country [Pine Ridge Reservation]. From there I went to the white man's land. Back then, long ago, when I was a child, my mother could not walk. She couldn't walk for ten years. One day she would walk again [after being in the hospital], but meantime I was married and had moved over there to the Oglala country. They made me marry the Lakota way, as I was given to them [to my husband's family]. I didn't know the man I married. I didn't know him, but I married him and lived over there [with him] for about three years. And from there I went on to the white man's country, I went to Alliance, Nebraska, and stayed there. And I worked there and raised my child. From there I went on toward the Rocky Mountains and I have lived here in Denver ever since, in a big city. Now I've been living here for over forty-eight years. But the white man's way of life is tough, and we are losing our Indian way of life more and more, which is sad. Living today, we now crave to be Indians but we cannot. We exist in the white man's world, trying to be strong, come what may. We live like being terribly lost [culturally] these days. If from now on people brought the Indian traditions or whatever back to life, and if they went on with these things in the future, and if the Indian people lived that way, according to the Indian way of life, they would be doing alright. People say it will be like this, and act like that, but they abuse liquor a lot, and therefore they are lost. Today there is no one who takes them to the sweatlodge, gives them water [to pour on the stones in the sweatlodge] or makes them smoke [the sacred pipe]. Those things existed back then, but they are gone today. They are coming back again. If we regularly had sweats with the people [who have trouble], using prayers, and if we prayed for them, and if they straightened out that way, that way only the Indians would have a good life. Because of the white man's way of life they are suffering. Some of today's generation have a high education, but there are other Indians who cannot read, they do not get any assistance. So they are homeless in the city, and they are hungry and roam about begging, or they sleep anywhere among the buildings. And when it is cold they sleep by the roadside or by the creek [Cherry Creek in Denver], and they live there. Or they build a fire there under the bridge and sit there warming themselves. If we took care of these Indians and put them on the right track they would work again, and they would have the willpower to help themselves, and they would have homes and a family to stay with. But these things do not exist right now, and their children are all being raised by white people. This is sad. Now there are no herb doctors and healers, either, and the spiritual men are becoming extinct, so there is no one for us to depend on. Some of those we ask for help are not really that kind [i.e., true spiritual leaders]. They do not really live up to their prayers, but rather, they are the kind who merely play around. It is not clear where we should go. So we [the spiritual leaders] go on by ourselves and say prayers, and stand by the [Indian] people. Only that way, if we stand together, we will be strong. And people will be insightful, and therefore will care for each other. And being insightful, they will be doing alright in the white man's world. Today we remember what our grandfathers and grandmothers told us a long time ago, and so we tell it to today's generation. Today many, many of the children go wrong and abuse guns. Recently an Indian boy killed another Indian boy, and this is a reason for great sorrow. There is sadness on both sides [in both families]; that was not the people's way of life [violence was not tolerated among tribal members in the old days]. Their mothers [of the two boys] are suffering as much as can be, and their fathers [are suffering] too. But this is definitely a white man's world; this is the behavior they know, and this is terrible. If I'll be in good health for many more years to come, I will accompany these people into the future. This is my thought. Long ago my fathers [the Lakota used the same word for 'father' and the 'father's brother(s)'] preached to me about these things. My uncles and aunts will be gone soon. Now I have only one [older relative] left. Only one aunt. She is suffering herself. I stand up for spirituality with a lot of conviction. I do that because that way people will recover and be alright on their journey, and be strong. That way they [in turn] will help their relatives, that's the way it works. I do things this way. Now people ask me for help, or they ask me for prayers and healing. It's difficult, but there is only one medicine man that I still depend on [to assist me]. I regularly call him, or people call on my behalf, so he tells us what to do. Only that way, by using prayers, we heal the people and help them. We do that in order to help the people, not just Rosebud Sioux or Oglala Sioux, but all the people on earth. White people, black people, and yellow people, we will help them all. We have come this far that way; this is what we commit ourselves to, and it is difficult. This is the reason why we have been going on for many years, and when we'll be unable to go on any longer, there will be no one left to carry on. It is terrible. But today we [can] ask them [the spiritual leaders] for assistance and help. Likewise, a certain woman had a bad disease [cancer], and she wanted to recover and live. The white doctors gave her only three months, but she has lived for seven months now; I haven't seen her now, but people say that she is nothing but bones. Now she will go home the day after tomorrow [her family told me so], so we will never see her again, but we will still remember her. Her relatives and children had not even realized how much they were caught in suffering; rather, they thought that it was a temporary condition [because the doctors sent her home]. But when people leave us it is always terrible. When the elders leave us, it is terrible. We don't have a place to go to anymore [for emotional support]. The white man's way of life is as tough as can be. So we should make ourselves strong and help each other. Today people tape record things, or maybe they make books. If our children and grandchildren read them, maybe they'll get some knowledge from that; that's why I do that [language recording]. I want people to hear my words, whichever way. This is why I do this. If the children of the future learn the white man's ways and the Indian ways, too, if they also receive education now in what we were taught long ago, they will walk into the future without being lost, with wisdom. Now there is no leader, either, so there is nobody whose words they could listen to. It is terrible. This is as much as I will say about it. I will talk about something else now.

2.2. My Roots

MARY LIGHT

Tape recorded September 15, 1994

ehą́ni	*ma-théca*	*na*	*wi-má-chįcala*	*wahéhątu*	*cha*
long ago	1SG.PAT-young	and	ST-1SG.PAT-girl	about that time	QL

le-tą́	*oblákį-kte*	*nahą́*	*lehą́l*	*waná*
this-from	1SG.AG.tell-FASS	and then	now	now

wi-má-nuȟcala.	*cha*	*hehą́l*	*o-wá-glakį-kte.*
ST-1SG.PAT-old woman	so	then	ST-1SG.AG-POSS.tell-FASS

wi-má-chįcala	*wą*	*héhą*	*Oglála*	*na*	*Grass Creek*	*ektá*	*iyúha*
ST-1SG.PAT-girl	IDF.SG	then	Oglala	and	Grass Creek	in	all

ų-thí-pi.	*nahą́*	*hél*	*owáyawa*	*nahą́*
1PL.AG-live-PL	and then	there	school*	and then

Number 5 Day School	*eyá-pi*	*cha*	*tókhi*	*waníyetu*	*ma-šágloǧą*
Number 5 Day School	say-IPS	QL	about	year	1SG.PAT-eight

na'į́š	*ma-nápcįyąka*	*wahéhą*	*Wabláwa.*	*na*	*hél*
or	1SG.PAT-nine	about that time	go to school*.1SG.AG	and	there

ųk-íchaǧa-pi.	*Makhá Są́*	*oyáte*	*ki*	*hél*	*ų-thí-pi.*
1PL.PAT-grow-PL	White Clay	community	DEF	there	1PL.AG-live-PL

cha	*he-tą́*	*hél*	*wabláwa*	*nahą́*	*ho*
so	that-from	there	go to school*.1SG.AG	and then	well

até-wa-ye ki t'á cha iná-wa-ye ki
father-1SG.AG-have as DEF die so mother-1SG.AG-have as DEF

é na thibló-wa-ye ki é cha héchegla hél
IP and older brother-1SG.AG-have as DEF IP QL that is all there

ų-thí-pi cha. ho hél tókhi ųk-íchağa-pi ki hél
1PL.AG-live-PL QL well there where 1PL.PAT-grow-PL DEF there

o-wá-'ų-yawa-pi nahą́ ho he-tą́ tókhi
L-ST-1PL.AG-go to school*-PL and then well that-from about

ma-nineteen na'į́š twenty wahéhą hé
1SG.PAT-nineteen or twenty about that time that

Pine Ridge Boarding School é cha akhé hél wabláwa.
Pine Ridge Boarding School IP QL again there go to school*.1SG.AG

na hél iná-wa-kiyį na ho he-tą́ héchena Oglála él
and there ST-1SG.AG-quit and well that-from afterwards Oglala in

ų-thí-pi na he-tą́ wicháša wą áta-wa-yį na
1PL.AG-live-PL and that-from man IDF.SG ST-1SG.AG-meet and

hé kichí wa-'ų́ na he-tą́ miyé family mitháwa ki
that with 1SG.AG-exist and that-from I family my DEF

start na ho lehą́l wakhą́yeža óta wichá-bluha na
start and well now child many 3PL.PAT-have.1SG.AG and

iyúha icháğa-pi. cha áta tókhiškhiya California na į́š eyá
all grow-PL so INT in all directions California and also

hųȟ	*Pine Ridge*	*héchikchiya*	*hená*	*nahą́ȟci*	*ní*	*ų́-pi*	*cha*
some	Pine Ridge	here and there	those	still	live	CNT-PL	QL

miyé	*ho*	*hé*	*thiwáhe*	*thą́ka*	*bluhá*	*cha*	*ho*	*lehą́l*	*waná*
I	well	that	family	big	have.1SG.AG	QL	well	now	now

léchiya	*akhé*	*wakhą́yeža*	*icháǧa-pi.*	*ho*	*hená*	*iyúha*	*hįgnáthų-pi*
here	again	child	grow-PL	well	those	all	marry*-PL

na	*thawícuthų-pi*	*cha*	*iyéchįkala*	*thí*	*glé-pi*	*chą́na*	*lehą́l*
and	marry*-PL	QL	on their own	house	put up-PL	then	now

miyé	*m-išnála*	*thiwáhe*	*wą*	*él*	*mąké*	*nahą́*
I	1SG.PAT-alone	household	IDF.SG	in	sit.1SG.AG	and then

iyúha	*icháǧa-pi.*
all	grow-PL

I'm going to talk about the time long ago when I was young, a little girl.

Now I'm an old woman. I will tell my story. When I was a girl we all lived in Oglala and Grass Creek [on Pine Ridge Reservation]. And there was a school. It was called Number 5 Day School (today it is Lone Man Day School), and I went to school there from when I was about eight or nine years old. And there we grew up. We lived in the White Clay community.

I went to school there from that time. Then my father died, so I lived there alone with my mother and my older brother. Where we grew up we also went to school, and when I was about nineteen or twenty I went to a boarding school, Pine Ridge Boarding School. After I had finished there we lived in Oglala, and I met a man. I lived with him and started my own family. Now I have many children, and they have all grown up. They spread in all directions, to California, and some [other relatives] are still living over there in Pine Ridge. I have a big family, and now another generation of children has grown up. They all have husbands and wives, and their own homes. Now I am alone in the house; they are all grown.

2.3. Growing Up on the Reservation

MARY LIGHT

Tape recorded September 15, 1994

lé	*táku*	*ki*	*léchel*	*o-wá-glakį-kte.*	*ehą́ni*
this	something	DEF	so	ST-1SG.AG-POSS.tell-FASS	long ago

Oglála	*él*	*ų-thí-pi*	*nahą́*	*šų́kawakhą́*
Oglala	in	1PL.AG-live-PL	and then	horse*

wichá-ʼų-yuha-pi	*na*	*ptebléška*	*nakų́.*	*wi-má-chįcala*	*kʼų*
3PL.PAT-1PL.AG-have-PL	and	cattle*	also	ST-1SG.PAT-girl	SYP

héhą	*hená*	*mní*	*wichá-wa-kʼu*	*sųkʼákąmąkį*	*na-šna*
then	those	water	3PL.PAT-1SG.AG-give	ride*.1SG.AG	and-HAB

kaȟáb	*iyéya*	*a-wícha-mnį*	*na-šna*
in all directions	send	ST-3PL.PAT-take to.1SG.AG	and-HAB

mni-yátką-pi	*na*	*héchel*	*akhé*	*héktakiya-šna*	*pasture*	*ektá*	*thimá*
water-drink-PL	and	so	again	back.AV-HAB	pasture	to	home

khiglé-wicha-wa-ye.	*na*	*héchel*	*akhé*	*ptąyétu*	*ikhíyela*
go home-3PL.PAT-1SG.AG-CAU	and	so	again	fall	near

chą́na	*akhé*	*hél*	*pheží*	*nąkséya-pi*	*iyéhątu*
then	again	there	grass	cut with a machine-IPS	when it is time

chą́na-šna	*thibló-wa-ye*	*ki*	*hé*	*kichí*
then-HAB	older brother-1SG.AG-have as	DEF	that	with

ó-wa-kiye na-šna pheží
ST-1SG.AG-help.VT and-HAB grass

ną̨ksé-ʔų-yą-pi nahą́ ų-yúhįta-pi
ST-1PL.AG-cut with a machine-PL and then 1PL.AG-rake hay-PL

ų-yúhįta-pi na pheží pahá óta é-ʔų-gle-pi na hé
1PL.AG-rake hay-PL and grass hill many ST-1PL-put-PL and that

ptebléška ki hená waníyetu ópta yúta-pi sʔa héchel-šna
cattle* DEF those winter through eat-PL HAB SO-HAB

héchųkʔų-pi sʔa chą́na ųkí-tha-makha-pi-la ektá-šna
do that.1PL.AG-PL HAB then 1PL.POR-ALP-earth-PL-DIM in-HAB

é-ʔų-thi-pi nahą́ tókhi wí wąží naʔį́š wahéhą-šna
L-1PL-live-PL and then about month one or about that time-HAB

héchiya manį́l ų-thí-pi na pheží
there in the wilderness 1PL.AG-camp.VI-PL and grass

ną̨ksé-ʔų-yą-pi na é-ʔų-gle-pi na
ST-1PL.AG-cut with a machine-PL and L-1PL.AG-put up-PL and

é-ʔų-gle-pi chą́ akhé héktakiya-šna ų-thí-pi
L-1PL.AG-put up-PL then again back.AV-HAB 1PL.AG-camp.VI-PL

ektá ų-glá-pi nahą́ ho hehą́l akhé wagmíza naʔį́š
to 1PL.AG-go home-PL and then well then again corn and

táku cik-cíkʔala icháȟ-ʔų-yą-pi-la ki hená nakų́ akhé
things RED-small grow-1PL.AG-CAU-PL-DIM DEF those also again

ų-yúksa-pi na hená iyúha-šna pusʾ-ų́-yą-pi.
1PL.AG-husk.VT-PL and those all-HAB dry.A-1PL.AG-CAU-PL

pusʾ-ų́-yą-pi. waštų́kala ų-káğa-pi naʾį́š
dry.A-1PL.AG-CAU-PL hominy 1PL.AG-make-PL or

héchekche-šna héchųkʾų-pi na hená iyúha waníyetu
like this-HAB do that.1PL.AG-PL and those all winter

ópta ų-yúta-pi-kta cha hé é-ʾų-ki-gle-pi. ho
through 1PL.AG-eat-PL-FASS QL that L-1PL.AG-PSS-put-PL well

héchel waníyetu theȟíke éyaš héchel ųyą́ka-pi waníyetu
so winter terrible but so sit.1PL.AG-PL winter

ópta. na akhé wétu chą́na-šna įšé waná ma-thą́ka
through and again springtime then-HAB just now 1SG.PAT-big

cha wa-wó-wa-kiyį na wichį́cala ma-cíkʾala kʾų
so NSP.PAT-ST-1SG.AG-help.VT and girl 1SG.PAT-small SYP

héhą tákunikel echámų-šni. cha hená hehą́yela hé
then nothing at all do.1SG.AG-NEG so those that is all that

wéksuye.
remember.1SG.AG

So I will tell a story now. Long ago we lived in Oglala, and we had horses, and cattle, too. At the time when I was a little girl I took them [the horses] to the water, riding on them. I let them go in all directions. Then they drank, and I drove them back home to their pasture again. And when fall was close again, the grass would be cut again. I helped my brother with this, and we mowed the grass and raked it. We put up many haystacks. The cattle ate that throughout the winter, that's why we always did that. So we lived on our little piece of land, and for one month or so [per year] we went to camp in the wilderness. We cut grass and piled it up, and then we returned to where we lived. And then we also harvested the corn and the other small things we had grown and dried them all. We made hominy and similar things, and we stored all these things in order to eat them throughout the winter. The winter was terrible, but this way we made it through the winter. And when it was springtime again I'd always have grown bigger, so I helped with the work to be done. When I was a little girl I didn't do anything at all [to help]. So that's all I remember.

2.4. Wounded Knee

MARY LIGHT

Tape recorded September 15, 1994

ho *Pine Ridge* *oyáte* *ki* *hél* *ehą́ni* *owíchakte* *wą*
well Pine Ridge people DEF there long ago massacre IDF.SG

Wounded Knee *eyá-pi* *cha* *hé* *tohą́yą* *slol-wá-ye* *ki*
Wounded Knee say-IPS QL that as far as ST-1SG.AG-know DEF

hé *obláki̹-kte.* *hé* *iná-wa-ye* *kihą* *hél* *ópha.*
that tell.1SG.AG-FASS that mother-1SG.AG-have as DEF there join

na *táku* *thitákuye* *nakų́* *hél* *ų́-pi* *ki* *hų́ȟ* *wichá-kte-pi*
and what relatives also there be at-PL DEF some 3PL.PAT-kill-IPS

nahą́ *hų́ȟ* *iyáyekiya-pi* *na* *lehą́l* *iná-wa-ye*
and then some run away-PL and now mother-1SG.AG-have as

kihą *hų́ȟ* *thitákuye* *cha* *hená* *naphá-pi.* *iná-wa-ye*
DEF some relatives QL those flee-PL mother-1SG.AG-have as

ki *é* *nahą́* *sųká-ku* *wą* *é* *cha* *hehą́l*
DEF IP and then younger brother-3POR IDF.SG IP QL then

tókhiya *ní* *ų́-pi.* *héchegla* *slol-wá-ye* *cha*
somewhere live CNT-PL that is all ST-1SG.AG-know QL

o-chí-ci-yaki̹-kte.
ST-1SG.AG.2SG-BEN-tell-FASS

I will tell what I know about the massacre that happened on Pine Ridge Reservation long ago [1890], which is called Wounded Knee. My mother was in there. And all her relatives were in there too. Some were killed, and some got away. Some of my mother's relatives escaped. My mother and one of her younger brothers managed to stay alive [by hiding] somewhere. That is all I know and that I wanted to tell you.

2.5. A Miracle

NEVA STANDING BEAR

Tape recorded September 16, 1994

ehą́ni	*waníyetu*	*tókhi*	*1979*	*wahéhąn*	*ų̨gnáhelakha*	*ištáǧųǧa*
a while ago	year	then	1979	around	suddenly	blind

a-má-hi.	*yųkhą́*	*ištá-ma-ǧųǧa*	*ki*	*hé*	*théhą-šni*
ST-1SG.PAT-become	then	ST-1SG.PAT-blind	DEF	that	long-NEG

tkhá	*líla*	*othéȟike.*	*tákuni*	*wąbláke-šni*	*yųkhą́*	*átaya*	*othéȟike.*
but	INT	terrible	nothing	see.1SG.AG-NEG	then	INT	terrible

chąkhé	*ąpétu wakhą́*	*hį́hąni*	*cha*	*wachékhiye*	*mnį́-kta*
then	Sunday*	morning	so	pray	go.1SG.AG-FASS

wa-šką́-he	*yųkhą́*	*othą́kaye*	*ektá*	*thimá*	*iblámnį*	*na*
1SG.AG-move-PRG	then	bathroom	to	inside	1SG.go	and

wa-nų́we.	*wa-nų́wį*	*na*	*wa-glínaphį*	*na*
1SG.AG-swim	1SG.AG-swim	and	1SG.AG-POSS.come out	and

hawéčʔų	*na*	*héktakiya*	*thimá*	*ibláble*	*yųkhą́*	*hél*
1SG.get dressed	and	backwards	inside	1SG.go	then	there

vacuum cleaner	*wą*	*hą́*	*cha*	*hú*	*ki*	*él*	*na-ʔíyapehe*
vacuum cleaner	IDF.SG	stand	so	leg	DEF	in	INS-wrap around

iyé-wa-yį	*na*	*ma-kátʔe.*	*yųkhą́*	*hé*	*ihą́ke*	*ki,*	*lé*
ST-1SG.AG-CEL	and	1SG.PAT-fall	then	that	end.N	DEF	this

wakhą́gli wíkhą ikhóyake ki hé é cha hú él cha-má-phį
power* rope plug DEF that IP QL leg in ST-1SG.PAT-stab

na makhíya ma-phá cha hú etą́ wa-glúžų,
and to the ground 1SG.PAT-fall QL leg from 1SG.AG-POSS.pull up

na iyáskab wé-thų na héchena thi-y-ų́ma-takiya,
and bandage.VT 1SG.AG-apply and thus house-EI-other-to

olólʾiȟʾą étkiya thimá iblábla yųkhą́ tókheškhe ųgnáhelakha
kitchen toward inside 1SG.go then somehow suddenly

na-wa-šlute-šni kʾéyaš ma-yų́kahe cha
ST-1SG.AG-slip-NEG but 1SG.PAT-fall down so

ma-ká-cązekį na "tókheškhe šik-šíca o-má-ya-khuwa
1SG.PAT-INS-angry and somehow RED-bad L-1SG.PAT-2AG-treat

éyaš takómni wachékhiye mnį́-kte kʾų" ephé. "tókhel
but at all costs pray go-FASS ASS say.1SG.AG somehow

aná-ma-ya-ptį-kte éyaš iníhąšni wachékhiye
ST-1SG.PAT-2AG-stop-FASS but nevertheless pray

mnį-kte kʾų" ephé, tuwé cha hé
1SG.go-FASS ASS say.1SG.AG who QL that

w-ó-wa-ki-yake-lakha. héchena iyéchįkyąka ogná
NSP.PAT-ST-1SG.AG-BEN-talk-kind of thus car* inside

íblutakį na iblábla. cha hé tókheškhe
1SG.AG.sit down and go.1SG.AG so that somehow

wa-káȟape-ka *héchi,* *m-išnála* *iblábla* *cha.* *cha*
1SG.AG-drive-kind of there 1SG.PAT-alone 1SG.go QL so

mnį́ *na* *owáchekiye* *thą́ka* *wą* *ektá* *wachékhiye*
1SG.go and church big IDF.SG to pray

ų-yą́-pi *cha* *hé* *Ská Ų́* *owáchekiye* *cha* *hél*
1PL.AG-go-PL QL that Episcopal* church QL there

ų-thí-pi *ki* *he-tą́* *makhíyuthapi* *aké* *šaglóǧą* *echétu*
1PL.AG-live-PL DEF that-from mile* ADD eight so

cha *hé* *hiyágleya* *tókheškhe* *wa-káȟape* *ki*
QL that to that point how 1SG.AG-drive LK

wéksuye-šni. *áta-š* *ho* *éyaš* *héchi* *wa-ˀí*
remember.1SG.AG-NEG INT-EMPH well but there 1SG.AG-go to

na *waná* *owáchekiye* *ki* *él* *thimá* *iblábIe* *kˀų* *héhą*
and now church DEF to inside 1SG.go LK then

wéksuye. *íblutakį* *na* *átaya* *chéya*
remember.1SG.AG 1SG.AG.sit down and INT cry

waché-wa-khiyį *na* *mi-glúštą.* *chąškékha-ma-gle*
ST-1SG.AG-pray and 1SG.AG.PSS-POSS.finish ST-1SG.PAT-kneel down

na-wá-žį *na* *waché-wa-khiya* *yųkhą́* *léchel*
ST-1SG.AG-stand and ST-1SG.AG-pray then so

mi-glúštą *na* *owákąyąke* *ki* *él* *íblutakį*
1SG.AG.PSS-POSS.finish and bench* DEF in 1SG.AG.sit down

na wachékiya wicháša kihą w-ó-wahokųkhiya-hą cha. ektá
and priest* DEF NSP.PAT-L-preach-PRG QL there

anáǧoptą mąkį́ nahą́ke ablúta yųkhą́ léchegla-ke
listen sit.1SG.AG and then look at.1SG.AG then close-kind of

s'e nážį na w-óglake s'e léchecha. anáǧoptą
like.AV stand and NSP.PAT-POSS.tell like.AV like this listen

mąká-hį na waná wachékhiya-pi iglúštą-pi cha áta
sit.1SG.AG-PRG and now pray-IPS POSS.finish-PL so all

a-glínąpha cha wa-glínąphį na thąkál ókšą-kšą
COLL-come out so 1SG.AG-come out and outside around-RED

é-tųwą na-wá-žį-hą yųkhą́ lé chąkú él lé inážį-pi
L-look ST-1SG.AG-stand-PRG then this road in this stop-IPS

chą́na-šna na'íle eyá yukhé hená é cha na-'íle-le cha
then-HAB traffic light* LK exist those IP QL INS-light-RED LK

wąyą́g na-wá-žį-hį na ephé "ųgnáhelakha
see ST-1SG.AG-stand-PRG and say.1SG.AG suddenly

wąbláka" cha wą́cag héchel i-má-nihą na
see.1SG.AG so immediately so ST-1SG.PAT-excited and

w-íyuškį-ma-hįgnį na nahą́ke wóphila
NSP.PAT-be happy-1SG.PAT-suddenly and and then thanks

ephį́ na aglágla lé wówapi ki hená wąbláke
say.1SG.AG and along this writing DEF those see.1SG.AG

yųkhą́	*léchel*	*ášlayela*	*wąbláka*	*chąkhé*	*átaya*	*Thųkášila*
then	so	plainly	see.1SG.AG	then	INT	God*

wóphila	*e-wá-kiyį*	*na*	*átaya*	*líla*	*w-íbluškį.*
thanks	L-1SG.AG-say to	and	INT	INT	NSP.PAT-happy.1SG.AG

na	*héchena*	*wa-glíyacu*	*na*	*į̨šé*	*ehą́ni*
and	thus	1SG.AG-go back home	and	just	a while ago

ithókamna	*ištámaza*	*kithų́*	*wa-ˀų́*	*tkhá.*	*na*	*líla*	*ištá*
before	glasses*	wear	1SG.AG-CNT	used to	and	INT	eye

i-má-kakiže	*yųkhą́*	*héhą*	*wa-hínažį.*	*cha*	*héhą*
L-1SG.PAT-suffer	then	then	1SG.AG-get that far	so	then

thi-yáta	*wa-glí*	*nahą́ke*	*o-wá-glakį.*
house-to	1SG.AG-arrive at home	and then	ST-1SG.AG-POSS.tell

tókha-šni-yą	*wąblákį*	*na*	*líla*	*į̨šé*	*wóˀiyuškį*
not alright-NEG-ADV	see.1SG.AG	and	INT	just	joy

o-má-žula.	*ho*	*cha*	*héchena*	*a-má-kisni*	*na*
ST-1SG.PAT-full	well	so	continuously	ST-1SG.PAT-recover	and

he-tą́	*lehíyagleya*	*ištámaza*	*chóla*	*wa-ˀų́*	*na*	*éyaš*	*hé*
that-from	to this day	glasses*	without	1SG.AG-exist	and	but	that

tuktéhą	*lé*	*wé*	*wąkál*	*iyáya-pi*	*ki*
sometimes	this	blood	upwards	go-1PS	DEF

he-má-checha	*cha*	*ištá*	*ki*	*lazáta*	*wéyotha*	*wą*
ST-1SG.PAT-affected with	QL	eye	DEF	behind	blood clot	IDF.SG

í-ma-yutaka cha ištá ma-sáni-la. éyaš iníhąšni
ST-1SG.PAT-sit so eye 1SG.PAT-one sided-LIM but nevertheless

héchiya-tąhą khó eyášna ų́ tąyą́ wąbláke. yųkhą́ lehą́n
there-from also sometimes with well see.1SG.AG then now

ȟtálʼehą ištá wašícu wakhą́ wą wąyą́g wa-ʼí yųkhą́
yesterday eye white doctor* IDF.SG see 1SG.AG-go to then

átaya-š ištá to-má-kheca-šni echíyatąhą átaya-š
INT-EMPH eye ST-1SG.PAT-not alright-NEG on that side INT-EMPH

ištámaza mų́ o-wá-kihi-šni ki tókha-šni
glasses* wear.1SG.AG ST-1SG.AG-can-NEG LK not alright-NEG

kéyé cha wa-bláwa hą́tąhąš lé ištámaza ikcéka
say that so NSP.PAT-read.1SG.AG when this glasses* common

hé é cha ų-má-ši cha. líla iblúšk̨į cha éyaš hé
that IP QL use-1SG.PAT-ask QL INT happy.1SG.AG so but that

lé há-sápa wį́yą ki wówaši echų́ cha hé é cha
this skin-black woman DEF work.N do QL that IP QL

wicá-ma-la-šni hé ištámaza chóla waníyetu wikcémna
ST-1SG.PAT-believe-NEG that glasses* without year ten

wa-ʼų́ cha. yųkhą́ i-má-yuthe éyaš tókha-šni-yą
1SG.AG-exist QL then ST-1SG.PAT-try but not alright-NEG-ADV

wa-bláwa táku ma-kí-pazo na bláwa na
NSP.PAT-read.1SG.AG what 1SG-BEN-show.VT and read.1SG.AG and

a-wá-bleze *cha.* *líla* *iyúšʔįyą* *na* *ištá* *saní*
ST-1SG.AG-recognize QL INT surprised and eye one sided

ma-šíce *echíyatąhą* *ų́* *wa-yáwa-ma-ši* *éyaschį*
1SG.PAT-bad on that side with NSP.PAT-read-1SG.PAT-ask but

wąbláke-šni. *cha* *hé* *ska-yéla* *nážį* *cha* *wąbláke* *cha*
see.1SG.AG-NEG so that white-ADV stand LK see.1SG.AG so

o-wá-ki-yakį *na* *táku* *wą* *ská* *ma-kʔú*
ST-1SG.AG-BEN-tell and something IDF.SG white 1SG.PAT-give

cha *i-wá-cu* *nahą́ke* *o-wá-ki-yake* *yųkhą́* *hé* *é*
QL ST-1SG.AG-take and then ST-1SG.AG-BEN-tell then that IP

cha *iyúšʔįyą* *nahą́* *cha* *"tókheškhe* *echíyatąhą* *hąhépi*
QL surprised and then QL how on that side night

wąláka *hé?* *oʔíyokpaze* *ektá* *wąláke.* *cha* *hená* *wóʔinihą*
see.2SG.AG QS darkness in see.2SG.AG so those astonishment

hécha *kʔų"* *eyá* *o-má-ki-yake.* *ho* *cha* *ištámaza* *sápa*
OBL ASS say ST-1SG-BEN-tell well so glasses* black

mų́ *ki* *i-má-yųğa-pi* *cha* *"hiyá,* *ehą́ni*
wear.1SG.AG LK ST-1SG.PAT-ask-IPS so no long ago

mų́ *tkhá* *éyaš* *tóhąni* *hehą́yą* *mų́-šni."* *cha*
wear.1SG.AG used to but never no more wear.1SG.AG-NEG so

phežúta *ištá* *o-mí-ci-yušʔe-pi* *na* *ištá* *wą-mí-ci-yąka-pi*
medicine* eye L-1SG-PSS-drop-IPS and eye ST-1SG-PSS-see-IPS

éyaš áta-š ištá ki to-má-kheca-šni. cha waná
but INT-EMPH eye DEF ST-1SG.PAT-not alright-NEG so now

oglíną̨phe él ištámaza sápa ų-má-khiya-pi cha áta
exit at glasses* black wear-1SG.PAT-CAU-IPS so INT

yuthą́-thą wa-kú na wa-glíną̨phe. cha
touch-RED-PL 1SG.AG-come and 1SG.AG-go outside so

a-ˀí-ma-ȟatˀa-hą-pi éyaščhį ištámaza chóla léhąn
L-ST-1SG.PAT-laugh-PRG-IPS but glasses* without now

wa-ˀų́. hená wakhą́-yą tókheca cha ų́
1SG.AG-exist those mysterious-ADV happen so because of

wakhą́-yą ma-wá-ni ištá ma-sáni-la éyaš.
sacred-ADV ST-1SG.AG-walk eye 1SG.PAT-one sided-LIM although

hená é cha įšé o-wá-glake.
those IP QL just ST-1SG.AG-POSS.tell

A while ago, around 1979, I suddenly went blind. My blindness didn't last long but it was horrible. I didn't see anything, and that was terrible. One morning, one Sunday morning, when I was getting ready for church, I went into the bathroom and took a shower. I took a shower and came out [of the shower]. I got dressed and went back inside [the bathroom]. Then a vacuum cleaner was standing there. My leg got entangled in it [the power cord], and I fell. The end, the plug of the power cord, stabbed into my leg and I fell on the floor. I pulled it out of my leg, and put on a bandage. I went into another room, the kitchen, and all of a sudden, somehow, I didn't slip, but I collapsed. That made me angry. "Somehow you [the dark spirit] treat me badly but I'll go to church no matter what. Somehow you are trying to stop me but I'll go to pray nevertheless," I said, whoever I was talking to. So I got into the car and went on my way. Somehow I drove there, [blind as I was], all by myself. I went there; I don't remember how I managed to drive to a certain big church, an Episcopal church that we go to to pray, which is about eighteen miles from where we live. I don't remember how I drove there. But I got there and went into the church, that I remember. I sat down, and I cried as I was praying. Then I stopped [praying]. I knelt down and prayed. After finishing my prayer, I sat down on the bench, and the priest made a sermon. I sat listening, looking at him. It seemed like he was standing close and talking [even though he was some distance away]. I sat listening, and after people had finished their prayers, they all went outside. So I went outside; I was standing outside, looking around. As I was standing there, I saw the [traffic] lights that were there changeing whenever they [the cars] stopped in the street. I said: "Suddenly I see." At that point I suddenly got excited and happy, and then I expressed my gratitude. I saw the signs [traffic signs, ads] all along [the road]. I saw them clearly; I thanked God and was very, very happy. I went back home. Before that, I used to wear glasses all the time. I was suffering very much from my eyes, and now I had made such progress. Then I went back home and told my story. I have no trouble seeing, and I am full of happiness. I recovered more and more, and to this day I live without glasses. But sometimes I'm suffering of high blood pressure. Behind my eye there is a blood clot; I am blind on one eye. But despite that, sometimes I see well with it, too [the bad eye]. Right now, yesterday, I went to see a white eye doctor. He said it's alright that I cannot wear glasses on the one eye which is okay. He told me to wear these common glasses [reading glasses] when I'm reading. I was very happy, but the black woman working there didn't believe that I have lived for ten years without glasses by now. She tested me, but I had no trouble reading what she showed me; I read it and recognized it. She was very surprised, and she asked me to read with my one bad eye [with the good eye covered]. [At first] I didn't see anything. [Then] I saw that she was standing there dressed in white [the room was completely dark], and I told her so. She gave me something white [i.e., she held it in her hands and let me grab it]. I took it and told her [that I could see it]. She was surprised because of that, and said: "How come you see in the night on one side [the blind one]? You see in the dark. This is astonishing." They asked me if I wear dark glasses, so [I said]: "No, I used to wear them in the past, but I don't wear them anymore." They dropped medicine into my eye, and looked into my eye, but there is nothing wrong with my eyes. Since they had made me wear dark glasses at the exit [I couldn't see well because of the eye exam], I was moving along feeling about, and finally got outside. They had laughed at me [because they didn't believe me], but now I'm living without glasses. Because of this miracle I'm walking in a spiritual way, although I'm blind on one eye. I'm just telling it as it is.

Note: Before this incident in 1979, Neva had diabetes and lost much of her eyesight because of it. This story describes the day she lost her eyesight completely. Neva believes that she was able to drive to the church because a "spiritual eye" guided her. This "spiritual eye" also enables her to see in the dark and to baffle optometrists that way.

2.6. A Sweatlodge Ceremony

NEVA STANDING BEAR

Tape recorded September 19, 1994

yukhą́	*wóphila*	*iníkağa-pi.*	*ho*	*cha*	*hé*
then	thanks	perform sweatlodge ceremony-IPS	well	so	that

thakóža	*wą*	*hąblécheya*	*cha*	*hé*	*waná*	*iglušta-kta*
grandchild	IDF.SG	seek a vision*	so	that	now	POSS.finish-FASS

cha	*wóphila*	*káğį*	*na*	*hé*	*ąpétu*	*ki*
so	thanks	make	and	that	day	DEF

iní-ˀų-kağa-pi.	*lé*	*thakóža*
ST-1PL.AG-perform sweatlodge ceremony-PL	this	grandchild

Wallace Black Elk	*é*	*nahą́*	*thakóža*	*Lydia Black Elk*	*na*
Wallace Black Elk	IP	and then	grandchild	Lydia Black Elk	and

isą́m	*thakóža*	*Bernard Ice*	*lená*	*ób*	*oˀínikağe*	*wą*
beyond	grandchild	Bernard Ice	these	with	sweatlodge	IDF.SG

ų-yúha-pi.	*ų-yúha-pi*	*yųkhą́*	*hél*	*thimá*	*wochékhiye*
1PL.AG-have-PL	1PL.AG-have-PL	then	there	inside	prayer

ų-káğa-pi.	*líla*	*wich-óta-pi*	*thimá,*	*óhiye*	*nų́m*	*átaya*
1PL.AG-make-PL	INT	people-many-PL	inside	row	two	INT

thimá	*yąká-pi.*	*ho*	*cha*	*hé*	*thimá*	*hená*	*iyúha*
inside	sit-PL	well	so	that	inside	those	all

wachékhiya-pi cha él ma-glíhųni. ho cha
pray-PL so to 1SG.PAT-POSS.arrive well so

w-ó-wa-glake. w-ó-wa-glakį na
NSP.PAT-ST-1SG.AG-POSS.tell NSP.PAT-ST-1SG.AG-POSS.tell and

tókhel táku ų́ i-má-kakiža héci hená é cha
how things because of L-1SG.PAT-suffer SUB those IP QL

i-w-ó-wa-glake. na oyáte ki thą́tahą-pi
L-NSP.PAT-ST-1SG.AG-POSS.tell and people DEF for the sake of-PL

ų́ ma-kákiža cha hé é nahą́ hokšíla wą
for 1SG.PAT-suffer QL that IP and then boy IDF.SG

ka-hį́ȟpe-ma-ya cha waníyetu wąží ų́
INS-fall-1SG.PAT-CAU QL year one because of

i-má-kakiža cha hená ų́ hél
L-1SG.PAT-suffer so those because of there

iníkağa-pi ki hél
perform sweatlodge ceremony-IPS DEF there

yųkhą́ wanáği eyá hí-pi, hená wicháša
then spirit IDF.PL come-PL those man

e-wícha-kiya-pi, wicháša eyá chažé-wicha-yata-pi. yųkhą́
ST-3PL.PAT-say to-IPS man say ST-3PL.PAT-call-IPS then

hí-pi na m-ígną-pi. m-ígną-pi na phaȟté
come-PL and 1SG.PAT-console-PL 1SG.PAT-console-PL and forehead

wíyaka wą ų́ é-ma-kaȟtaka cha. hé ų́ phaȟté
feather IDF.SG with ST-1SG.PAT-touch QL that with forehead

él é-ma-kaȟtake, hé é, nahą́ wagmúha wą ų́
in ST-1SG.PAT-touch that IP and then squash IDF.SG with

ka-ȟlá-ȟla phaȟté él é-ma-kaȟtake. ho yųkhą́
INS-rattle-RED forehead in ST-1SG.PAT-touch well then

mi-thákoža ki lé o-má-ki-yakį nahą́
1SG.POR-grandchild DEF this ST-1SG-BEN-tell and then

wachékhiya-pi ki ichų́hą hená thó éyaš w-óyakį-kta cha
pray-IPS DEF during those but first NSP.PAT-tell-FASS so

thó éyaš é-ki-gnąg-wicha-ši. ho yųkhą́ hená wanáǧi kihą
but first L-PSS-put-3PL.PAT-ask well then those ghost DEF

hé wicháša ki hená ų́ši-ma-la-pi nahą́
that man DEF those ST-1SG.PAT-pity.VT-PL and then

m-íkcąta-pi kéyé. táku ų́ wochékhiye
1SG.PAT-console-PL say that what because of prayer

wa-káǧį naʾį́š táku ų́ lená wa-ʾéchamų éyaš
1SG.AG-make and what because of these NSP.PAT-do.1SG.AG but

éyaš takómni ma-kákiža cha hená
but at all costs 1SG.PAT-suffer LK those

i-w-óglag-ma-ši-pi. héchel
L-NSP.PAT-ST-POSS.tell-1SG.PAT-ask-PL so

ó-ma-kiya-pi-kta *kéyá-pi* *wicá-wa-kha*
ST-1SG.PAT-help.VT-PL-FASS say that-PL ST-1SG.PAT-honest

ehą́tąhąš. *ho* *cha* *hená* *i-w-ó-wa-glakį* *na*
if well so those L-NSP.PAT-ST-1SG.AG-POSS.tell LK

hokšíla *wą* *waníyetu* *šaglóǧą* *cha* *Ųcíyapi Thamákha* *etą́* *hí.*
boy LK year eight QL England* from come

ho *yųkhą́* *hé* *oníya* *šíca* *cha* *hé* *ų́* *hų́-ku*
well then that breathe bad so that because of mother-3POR

ki *ektá* *a-má-hi.* *hé* *thi-yáta* *South Dakota* *ektá*
DEF to ST-1SG.PAT-take to that home-to South Dakota to

aglá-pi-kte *éyaš* *lél* *ahí-pi* *na* *wą-má-yąkį-kta*
take home-PL-FASS but here take to-PL and ST-1SG.PAT-see-FASS

škhá *cha* *ahí-pi.* *yųkhą́* *hokšíla* *ki* *hé* *waché-we-ci-chiyį*
QT so take to-PL then boy DEF that ST-1SG.AG-BEN-pray

na *lé* *oníya* *šíce* *ki* *lé* *akísni-kta* *képhį* *na*
and this breathe bad DEF this recover-FASS say that.1SG.AG and

phežúta *wą* *azíl-wa-ye.* *ho* *yųkhą́*
medicine* IDF.SG ST-1SG.AG-burn incense well then

tókha-šni-yą *niyá* *kéyį* *nahą́ke* *o-má-ki-yakį* *na*
not alright-NEG-ADV breathe say that and then ST-1SG-BEN-tell LK

hu-má-šte *ki* *hé* *asní-ma-yį-kta* *kéyé*
ST-1SG.PAT-lame DEF that recover-1SG.PAT-CAU-FASS say that

naˀį́š	*ma-khúže*	*ki*	*hé*	*a-má-kisni-kta*	*cha*
and	1SG.PAT-sick	DEF	that	ST-1SG.PAT-recover-FASS	QL

ų́	*hé*	*chąkpé*	*ki*	*él*	*oȟláthe*	*é-ma-pathą-kta*
in order to	that	knee	DEF	at	under	ST-1SG.PAT-touch-FASS

kéyį	*na*	*waché-mi-ci-chiye.*	*yųkhą́*	*átaya*	*napé*	*kihą*
say that	and	ST-1SG-BEN-pray	then	INT	hand	DEF

tohą́n okíhilaka	*kháte.*	*naˀį́š*	*sí*	*ki*	*áta*	*khó*	*makhá-ta*
as much as can be*	hot	and	foot	DEF	INT	also	earth-to

yųkhą́	*ka-ˀóȟlaya*	*i-má-yaye*	*sˀe*	*léchecha.*	*líla*
then	INS-loose	ST-1SG.PAT-go	like.AV	like this	INT

ma-tą́yą.	*ho*	*cha*	*hená*	*é*	*cha*	*i-w-ó-wa-glakį*
1SG.PAT-well	well	so	those	IP	QL	L-NSP.PAT-1SG.AG-POSS.tell

na	*hená*	*khoškálaka,*	*hokšíla*	*ki*	*lé*	*ų́*
and	those	young man	boy	DEF	this	for

waché-we-ci-chiyį-kta	*képhé.*	*na*	*hená*	*wóphila*
ST-1SG.AG-BEN-pray-FASS	say that.1SG.AG	and	these	thanks

ephá	*képhé.*	*ho*	*na*	*oyáte*	*kihą*	*líla*	*ų́*
say.1SG.AG	say that.1SG.AG	well	and	people	DEF	INT	for

i-w-í-ma-kakiže.	*cha*	*hé*	*o-wá-glake.*	*tohą́n*
L-NSP.PAT-L-1SG.PAT-suffer	so	that	ST-1SG.AG-POSS.tell	when

mi-chų́kši	*ki*	*hé*	*wówaši*	*echų́*	*ábla*	*chą́-šna*
1SG.POR-daughter	DEF	that	work.N	do	take to.1SG.AG	then-HAB

Lakhóta ki áta othų́wahe aglágla wa-yátką nážį-pi naˀį́š
Indian DEF INT town along NSP.PAT-drink stand-PL and

ištį́ma-pi tuktéktel él é-ˀicˀi-k-tųwą-pi-šni cha hená
sleep-PL where in L-3RFL-EI-look-PL-NEG so those

i-chą́te ma-šíca képhį na tókhel echámų
L-ST 1SG.PAT-sad* say that.1SG.AG and how do.1SG.AG

hą́tąhąš na héktakiya tąyą́ wachį-ksapa-pi na mnišíca ki hé
if and back.AV well mind-sober-PL and liquor* DEF that

ayúštą-pi na Thųkášila étkiya wąkáta-kiya é-tųwą-pi nahą́
quit-PL and God* toward up-toward L-look-PL and then

lená tąyá máni-pi-kta képhį na héchel chąkú wą
these well walk-PL-FASS say that.1SG.AG and so road LK

lúta cha ogná chąnúpa ki hé yuhá máni-pi-kta
red QL along pipe DEF that have walk-PL-FASS

i-w-ó-wa-glake. yųkhą́ hená tąyą́
L-NSP.PAT-ST-1SG.AG-POSS.tell then those well

wa-ˀépha škhé. na wochékhiye wa-káǧį na
NSP.PAT-say.1SG.AG QT and prayer 1SG.AG-make and

ehą́ni waphíya wicháša wą hékta waníyetu wikcémna
long ago medicine man* IDF.SG back.AV year ten

kiníca kˀų héhą ųspé-ma-khiye lená táku kįhą
almost SYP then know-1SG.PAT-CAU these things DEF

ų́ Lakhóta ki ní-pi nahą́ ų́
by means of Indian DEF live-PL and then because of

zaní-pi-kta ki hená o-má-ki-yakį na
healthy-PL-FASS LK those ST-1SG-BEN-tell and

ma-híyohi-pi. wanáǧi eyá ób ma-híyohi-pi.
1SG.PAT-come after-IPS spirit IDF.PL with 1SG.PAT-come after-IPS

ho cha hená kiksúya na-wá-žį yųkhą́ héktakiya
well so those remember ST-1SG.AG-stand LK back.AV

waníyetu nų́pa yųkhą́ héhą wichį́cala wą hąblécheya yį́-kta
year two then then girl LK seek a vision* go-FASS

cha thi-yáta a-wá-khi yukhą́ hą'íyachįkešni wicháša
QL home-to ST-1SG.AG-take home then late at night man

ki lé waná makhá mahél ȟpáye k'éyaš héchiya-tąhą lową́ na
DEF this now earth inside lie but there-from sing and

olówą wą ma-k'ú. cha hé a-wá-hiyaye. hé
song IDF.SG 1SG.PAT-give so that ST-1SG.AG-sing that

a-wá-hiyayį na mi-glúštą yųkhą́ lé wanáǧi
ST-1SG.AG-sing and 1SG.AG.PSS-POSS.finish then this spirit

ki lená o-má-ki-yaka-pi na táku ephá héci hená
DEF these ST-1SG-BEN-tell-PL and what say.1SG.AG SUB those

wówicakhe na hená ų́ši-ya Thųkášila hóye-wa-khiya
truth and those humble.A-ADV God* ST-1SG.AG-call to*

cha na-mí-ci-ȟʼų-pi nahą́ le-tą́ thokátakiya
so ST-1SG-PSS-hear-PL and then this-from in the future

o-w-íyuškį-yą zaní-ya ma-wá-ni-kta
L-NSP.PAT-happy-ADV healthy-ADV ST-1SG.AG-walk-FASS

kéyá-pi. ho yukhą́ iyéchel a-má-ye cha
say that-PL well then so ST-1SG.PAT-PRC so

tohą́n okíhilaka i-chą́te ma-wášte. ho na tákuni
as much as can be* L-ST 1SG.PAT-happy* well and nothing

ítokha-šni-ma-ši-pi héchel tókša iyé lená
worry-NEG-1SG.PAT-ask-PL so soon they these

khicháyą-pi na tókša iyéchįka lená oyáte kihą mnišíca
take care of-PL and soon by itself these people DEF liquor*

ki hé ayúštą-pi-kte na Wakhą́thąka étkiya kiksúya-pi-kte
DEF that quit-PL-FASS and Great Spirit* toward remember-FASS

na chąnų́pa ki lé yuhá chąkú wą lúta cha ogná
and pipe DEF this have road LK red QL along

máni-pi-kta kéyį na hená Lakhóta ki išnála-pi-kte-šni
walk-PL-FASS say that and those Indian DEF alone-PL-FASS-NEG

tkhá há-sápa oyáte na wicháša lúta na wicháša zí
but skin-black people and man red and man yellow

oyáte ki na ská oyáte ki chąkú wą wašté cha ogná
people DEF and white people DEF road LK good QL along

máni-wicha-wa-khiya wa-chį́ k'ų, hé ogná
walk-3PL.PAT-1SG.AG-CAU 1SG.AG-want ASS that along

máni-pi-kta ták-eya-pi o-má-ki-yaka-pi. ho cha
walk-PL-FASS something-say-PL ST-1SG-BEN-tell-PL well so

tákuni i-chą́te šíce-šni-ma-ši-pi. ho cha he-tą́ líla
nothing L-ST sad*-NEG-1SG.PAT-ask-PL well so that-from INT

wóphila eyá wa-glínąphe. ho tókha-šni-yą
thanks say 1SG.AG-go outside well not alright-NEG-ADV

wa-glínąphį na sagyé chóla ma-wá-ni na lé
1SG.AG-go outside and cane without ST-1SG.AG-walk and this

ąpétu kihą líla ma-tą́yą cha mi-tháchą kihą zaní cha
day DEF INT 1SG.PAT-well so 1SG.POR-body DEF healthy so

waná wašícu wakhą́ wą ektá wa-'í yųkhą́ thą-máhel
now white doctor* IDF.SG to 1SG.AG-go to then body-inside

wichókhuže tákuni i-má-khoyake-šni na wé mitháwa
sickness nothing ST-1SG.PAT-adhere to-NEG and blood my

ki wašté na mi-chą́te ki wašté nahą́ ažų́tka ki
DEF good and 1SG.POR-heart DEF good and then kidney DEF

ma-wášte nahą́ thezí nahą́ phí nahą́ chağú ki
1SG.PAT-good and then stomach and liver and lungs DEF

lená iyúha to-má-kha-šni kéyé ho cha líla
these all ST-1SG.PAT-not alright-NEG say that well so INT

i-chą́te ma-wášte. ho tkhá lé chąhą́pi khúžapi ki lé é

L-ST 1SG.PAT-happy* well but this diabetes* DEF this IP

cha nahą́ wé ki wąkál i-má-yaye watóhąšna éyaš

QL and then blood DEF up ST-1SG.PAT-go sometimes but

hená tókša ehákela hená khicháyį-kte. ho cha héchegla éyaš

those soon finally those fix-FASS well so so far but

líla chąté i-má-wašte. ho cha hená ų́

INT ST L-1SG.PAT-happy* well so those because of

thokáta wóphila wąží wa-káǧį-kte na'į́š

in the future thanks IDF.SG 1SG.AG-make-FASS and

léna-kte-šni tkhá thokátakiya. cha lená táku kihą

right now-FASS-NEG but in the future so these things DEF

ó-ma-wakhąkhą-šni tkhá lená líla wóphila thą́ka ephé.

ST-1SG.PAT-lie-NEG but these INT thanks big say.1SG.AG

[Recently] an appreciation sweatlodge ceremony was held. One of my grandchildren was on a vision quest, and now he wanted to finish it and express his appreciation [for the vision he had received]; so we had a sweatlodge ceremony that day. At this sweatlodge ceremony my grandson Wallace Black Elk, my granddaughter Lydia Black Elk, and my great-grandson Bernard Ice were present. We held it [the ceremony] and made prayers inside it [the sweatlodge]. There were many people; people were sitting in there in two rows. They were all praying in there. Then it was my turn [to pray]. So I spoke. I spoke and talked about the things that were torturing me. [I said that] I was suffering for the people's sake. That [I talked about], and [I also said that] a boy had run me down, and that I had been suffering for one year from this injury, and that I was inside this sweatlodge for this reason. Then a few spirits came, the kind that is called *wicháša* [man]; their name is *wicháša*. They came and consoled me. They consoled me and touched me on the forehead with an eagle feather. With that they touched my forehead, that's what it was, and then they touched me on the forehead with a gourd rattle. Then my grandson [Wallace Black Elk, a medium] interpreted [the spirits] for me. Then he told me that while people were praying, he was going to speak, so he asked them to put it [the praying] off for a while. He said that those spirits, those *wicháša*, pitied me and were trying to comfort me. They were asking me to explain why I was making prayers, and why I was doing these things [healing, instructing, preaching etc.], but still suffering that much. They said they would help me if I was serious about it. I talked about these things, and about a certain eight-year-old boy who had come from England. His mother had brought him to me because he had asthma. They were going to bring him home to South Dakota [to meet with medicine men or women] but then it was said that they would bring him [here] in order to see me. I prayed for the boy, and I said he would recover from the asthma, and burned some medicine. After that he said that he could breathe very well, and he told me that he would heal my stiff leg [from the accident with the other boy]. He said that in order to heal my injury he would touch me below the knee, and he prayed for me. His hand was extremely warm. And my foot, too, [was hot], it was like it went down my leg to the ground. I was feeling very good. I talked about these things [to the people in the sweatlodge], I expressed my gratitude. And [I said that] I was suffering very much for the people's sake. This is what I said. Whenever I take my daughter to work, the Indians all over town are standing there drinking, and they don't care where they sleep. I said I was sad because of that. And I said that if only I knew what to do so they sobered up again, quit drinking liquor, and looked up to God. Then, I said, they would be on the right track. I told them that that way they would travel on the red road with the pipe in their hands. They said that I had spoken well. And I made prayers.

Long ago, almost ten years ago, a medicine man had instructed me by telling me that by means of these things [spirituality] the Indians would survive, and that they would be in good health because of them. And I was chosen [to be a spiritual instructor]. I was chosen through some spirits. I stood fast, remembering that two years ago a girl was going on a vision quest, so I took her home [to South Dakota]. In the middle of the night this man who is now under the earth sang [from his grave], and he gave me a song. So I sang it. I sang it, and when I was through with it, these spirits instructed me. What I'm saying is the truth. When I sing to God in a humble way my calling is heard. They [the spirits] said that I'd be walking happy and healthy in the future. Since I'm getting to be like this I'm as happy as can be. They told me not to worry about anything because soon they would take care of these things, and soon people would quit drinking liquor all by themselves. They would remember the Great Spirit, and they would travel on a red road with the pipe in their hands. And the Indians would not be alone. I'd like to make the black people and the red people and the yellow people and the white people travel on a good road. They said they would travel on it; that's what they told me. They asked me not to be sad about anything. After that I went outside, expressing my deep gratitude. I went outside without trouble and walked without a cane. Today I feel very well and healthy, and I went to a white doctor. There is no trace of sickness in my body. He said that my blood is good, my heart is good, my kidneys are good, my stomach, my liver, and my lungs are all okay, so I'm very happy. It's only diabetes [that I have], and sometimes I have high blood pressure, but soon he [the doctor] will fix that for good. So far I'm very happy. For this reason I will have an appreciation ceremony, not now, but soon. I don't lie about these things. My story is true. Therefore I say many, many thanks.

Note: "Red road" and "black road" are metaphors for good and evil, respectively. The red road has numerous exits that lead to the black road. The pipe metaphor symbolizes peace.

2.7. A Visit to South Dakota

NEVA STANDING BEAR

Tape recorded October 14, 1994

hékta	*bloké-hą*	*wiwą́yąg wachípi*	*ų-khí-pi.*	*yųkhą́*
back.AV	summer-PRG	sundance*	1PL.AG-go home-PL	then

waphíya wichášą	*wą*	*eyášna*	*léchiya-šna*	*hóchoka*
medicine man*	IDF.SG	sometimes	here-HAB	ceremony

wé-ci-cağa-he	*yųkhą́*	*héchel*	*thí*	*ektá*	*olé*
1SG.AG-BEN-make-PRG	then	so	house	at	search

ųk-í-pi	*yųkhą́*	*Oglála-ȟce*	*héchiya*	*wąkáta*	*tuktél*
1PL.AG-go to-PL	then	Oglala-INT	there	upwards	where

wiwą́yąg wachípi	*waȟpé okhíye*	*wą*	*káğa*	*cha*	*manį́n*	*ų́*
sundance*	arbor*	IDF.SG	make	so	outdoors	be

škhé	*cha*	*ektá*	*olé*	*ųk-í-pi.*	*yųkhą́*	*aphé*
QT	QL	there	search	1PL.AG-go to-PL	then	wait

ų-yą́ka-hą-pi	*yųkhą́*	*glí*	*nahą́ke*	*hé*	*"wą́*
1PL.AG-sit-PRG-PL	then	come home	and then	that	IJ.M

líla	*tąyą́*	*ya-hí-pe*	*ló"*	*eyé.*	*"théhąn*	*léchiya*	*wa-ˀų́,*
INT	well	2AG-come-PL	ASS.M	say	long	here	1SG.AG-be

įthó	*éyaš*	*wówaši*	*echámų*	*cha*	*hé*	*ų́*	*léchiya*
first	but	work.N	do.1SG.AG	so	that	because of	here

wa-ʔų́-he”	*eyá*	*o-má-ki-yake.*	*w-ó-ʔų-ki-yaka-hą-pi.*
1SG.AG-be-PRG	say	ST-1SG-BEN-tell	NSP.PAT-ST-1PL-BEN-tell-PRG-PL

nahą́ke	*“líla*	*tąyą́*	*wą-chí-yąka-pi*	*kʔų,*	*tóhąni*
and then	INT	well	ST-1SG.AG.2PAT-see-PL	ASS	never

wą-chí-yąke-šni	*yųkhą́*	*lé*	*othókaheya*
ST-1SG.AG.2SG.PAT-see-NEG	then	this	for the first time

wą-chí-yąke	*kʔų”*	*eyį́*	*na*	*“táku*	*tókha”*	*kéyį*
ST-1SG.AG.2SG.PAT-see	ASS	say	and	something	happen	say that

na	*o-má-ki-yake.*	*“hená*	*léchiya*	*hų́ȟ*	*waphíya-pi*
and	ST-1SG-BEN-tell	those	here	some	doctor*-PL

ké-ʔicʔi-ya-pi	*na*	*wakhą́ wicháša-pi*	*kéyá-pi*	*na*
ST-3RFL-say that-PL	and	spiritual man*-PL	say that-PL	and

kʔéyaš	*hená*	*iyéchetu-šni*	*škhá*	*héyá-pi*	*kéye”*
but	those	so-NEG	but	say that-PL	QT

o-má-ki-yake.	*hená*	*w-óglag*	*yąká-hį*	*na*	*hé*	*“wą́*
ST-1SG-BEN-tell	those	NSP.PAT-POSS.tell	CNT-PRG	and	that	IJ.M

lél	*watóhąšna*	*šųgmáyetu*	*thą́ka*	*wą*	*eyášna*	*híyutakį*
here	sometimes	wolf	big	IDF.SG	sometimes	sit down

na-šna	*ahí-tųwą*	*yąká-he*	*kʔų”*	*eyé.*	*“akhé*	*tókhaȟʔą*	*na-šna*
and-HAB	come-look	sit-PRG	ASS	say	again	disappear	and-HAB

akhé	*tuktél*	*ipáyeȟ*	*híyutakį*	*na-šna*	*yąká-he”*	*eyá*	*cha.*
again	somewhere	other place	sit down	and-HAB	sit-PRG	say	QL

"tókhi hé lél itówapi naškąškąyapi wą kąğa-pi ki hél
maybe that here movie* LK make-IPS DEF there

Kevin Costner ecíya-pi wą hél škáta cha hé tókhi olé
Kevin Costner call-IPS LK there play QL that maybe search

hí-hą nachéce" ephá cha tohą́n okíhilaka iȟát'į
come-PRG maybe say.1SG.AG so as much as can be* laugh

na "hóȟ" eyį nahą́ke "lé itéšniya w-ó-wa-glaka
and IJ.M say and then this seriously NSP.PAT-ST-1SG.AG-POSS.tell

škhá" eyį na iȟát'e. "na'į́š ųgná héchų s'e cha. ųgnáš hé
but say and laugh or maybe that way* QL maybe that

olé ahí-he séce k'ų́" eyá cha. "takómni héchų kštó,
search arrive-PRG maybe ASS say QL at all costs do that ASS.F

ų́yą khi-glá cha" ephé yųkhą́ iȟát'a-hį
lose sight of come-go home QL say.1SG.AG then laugh-PRG

nahą́ kéyé "wą́ éna yąká pó,
and then say that IJ.M right there sit IMP.PL.M

wa-'ų́-yuta-pi-kte" cha éna ųyą́ka-hą-pi
NSP.PAT-1PL.AG-eat-PL-FASS so right there sit.1PL.AG-PRG-PL

yųkhą́ hé "iní-'ų-kağa-pi-kta cha
then that ST-1PL.AG-perform sweatlodge ceremony-PL-FASS so

niyé khó iní-'ų-kağa-pi-kte ló"
you too ST-1PL-perform sweatlodge ceremony-PL-FASS ASS.M

eyá cha. "ohá, éyaš tákuni gluhá wa-hí-šni k'ų"
say QL okay but nothing POSS.have 1SG.AG-come-NEG ASS

ephé. "chuwígnaka na'į́š itípakįte tákuni gluhá
say.1SG.AG dress or towel* nothing POSS.have

wa-hí-šni k'ų" ephé yųkhą́ wichįcala wą kichí
1SG.AG-come-NEG ASS say.1SG.AG then girl LK with

wa-'í ki hé é cha "etą́ bluhá cha tókša
1SG.AG-go to DEF that IP QL PART have.1SG.AG so right away

o-chí-c'u-kte k'ų" eyé. cha tohą́n cha áta
L-1SG.AG.2SG.PAT-give-FASS ASS say so then so INT

manį́n o'íyaye šíca wą ektá ųk-í-pi yųkhą́
wilderness path bad IDF.SG to 1PL.AG-go to-PL then

iní'okağe wą héchi manį́n hé, pahá akąń. cha
sweatlodge IDF.SG there outdoors stand hill on top so

ųk-í-pi yųkhą́ wį́yą wą tókhi pahá akąń
1PL.AG-go to-PL then woman LK somewhere hill on top

hąblécheya cha aglí-pi cha hé é cha
seek a vision* QL bring home-IPS so that IP QL

waché-kici-chiye-ma-ši na hé ų́
ST-BEN-pray-1SG.PAT-ask and that because of

iníkağa-pi-kta kéyá cha ektá
perform sweatlodge ceremony-PL-FASS say that so there

ųk-í-pi	*na*	*kichí*
1PL.AG-go to-PL	and	with

iní-ˀų-kaǧa-pi	*tókhįš*	*iyé*	*cha*
ST-1PL.AG-perform sweatlodge ceremony-PL	FASS	he	QL

wachékhiyį-kte	*séce*	*yųkhą́*	*wachékhiye-ma-khiye*	*cha*
pray-FASS	maybe	then	pray-1SG.PAT-CAU	so

waché-wa-khiye.	*chą́*	*wį́yą*	*ki*	*lé*	*waché-we-ci-chiyį*	*na*
ST-1SG.AG-pray	then	woman	DEF	this	ST-1SG.AG-BEN-pray	and

ų-pákįta-pi	*na*	*ų-glínąpha-pi*	*na*	*héchiya*	*hukhúta*
1PL.AG-wipe-PL	and	1PL.AG-go outside-PL	and	there	downwards

thí	*ektá*	*ų-khí-pi*	*na*	*wa-ˀų́-yuta-pi.*
house	to	1PL.AG-arrive at-PL	and	NSP.PAT-1PL.AG-eat-PL

wa-ˀų́-yuta-pi	*na*	*héchena*	*ų-glíyacu-pi.*	*thi-yáta*
NSP.PAT-1PL-eat-PL	and	immediately	1PL.AG-start home-PL	home-to

Rosebud	*Owákpamni*	*héchi*	*ų-khí-pi*	*na*	*hé*
Rosebud	agency*	there	1PL.AG-go home-PL	and	that

wiwą́yąg wachípi-kte	*ki*	*šką́-hą-pi*	*ki*	*héchi*	*ų-khíhųni-pi*
sundance*-FASS	DEF	move-PRG-IPS	DEF	there	1PL.AG-arrive-PL

ȟtayétu	*ehą́n*	*éyaš*	*líla*	*ma-tą́yą-šni*	*éyaš*	*akhé*
evening	then	but	INT	1SG.PAT-well-NEG	but	again

ų-khí-pi	*kˀų*
1PL.AG-come home-PL	SYP

iníkaȟ-ˀų-ši-pi	*chąkhé*
perform sweatlodge ceremony-1PL.PAT-ask-IPS	then

iní-ˀų-kağa-pi.	*wį́yą*	*ki*
ST-1PL.AG-perform sweatlodge ceremony-PL	woman	DEF

iní-wicha-ˀųki-ci-cağa-pi.	*cha*
ST-3PL-1PL.AG-BEN-perform sweatlodge ceremony-PL	so

héchekche-kel	*táku*	*wóˀiȟaka*	*na*	*į́š*	*eyá*	*itéšniya*	*táku*
like that-kind of	things	fun	and	it	also	seriously	things

eyášna	*i-w-ó-ˀų-glaka-pi.*	*ho,*	*henákecha.*
sometimes	L-NSP.PAT-ST-1PL.AG-POSS.tell-PL	well	enough

Last summer we went to a sundance. We went looking for a medicine man whom I sometimes help with ceremonies. We went looking for him at his house. We were told that he was somewhere up in the real Oglala [the town of Oglala on Pine Ridge Reservation] putting up the sundance arbor; people said that he was out there, so we went looking for him there. We sat waiting for a while, and he came home. He said to me: "It is very nice that you came. I've been here for a long time, since I had some work to do. That's why I am here." He kept talking to us. Then he said: "It is very nice to see you. I have never met you, I'm seeing you for the first time." And he said: "Something is going on." And he told me: "Rumor has it that some people here call themselves medicine men and say that they are spiritual men. Even though they are not, they say so," he said to me. He kept on talking about these things, and then he said: "From time to time a big wolf comes and sits down here. He always sits watching. Then he disappears again, sits down somewhere else, and stays there." I replied: "Maybe he is coming to look for the guy named Kevin Costner who played in the movie they made here." He laughed as much as he could, and said: “Hey! I’m talking seriously [but you are fooling around]!” And he laughed. “Or maybe it is like that. Maybe he is coming to look for him,” he said. “I’m sure he that this is what he is doing. He [Kevin Costner] left him behind,” I said. He kept on laughing and said: “Stay here, we will eat.” So we stayed there. “We will have a sweat. You guys will have a sweat with us,” he said. “Okay, but I don’t have anything with me,” I said. “I don’t have a dress or towel with me.” Then the girl I had come with said: “I have some, I’ll lend it to you right away.” Then we went on a bad wilderness trail. A sweatlodge had been put up there in the wilderness, on top of a hill. We went there. Meantime they had brought a woman who had been on a vision quest on the hill back [to the lodge]. He [the medicine man] asked me to pray for her, and he said that the sweatlodge ceremony was to be held because of her. We went there and had a sweat with them. I thought that he was going to pray himself. But he asked me to pray, so I prayed. Then I prayed for the woman, we purified her [with incense], and then we left. We went back down to the house and ate. We ate, and right after that we got on our way home. We went back home to Rosebud Agency. In the evening we arrived at the place where the preparations for the sundance were being made. I was feeling very bad, but after we had come back we were invited for a sweat, so we had another sweat. We made a sweat for the women. This was fun. We also talked about some serious matters. That’s it.

2.8. A Scary Ride

NEVA STANDING BEAR

Tape recorded October 14, 1994

ehą́ni	*iyéchįkyąke*	*wanı́ca*	*cha*	*héhą*	*hé*	*tókhi*	*1922*	*naˀį́š*	*23*
long ago	car*	lack	so	then	that	around	1922	or	23

nachéce	*cha*	*héhą*	*até*	*é*	*cha*	*iyéchįkyąke-la*	*wą,*
maybe	so	then	father	IP	QL	car*-DIM	IDF.SG

model T Ford	*wą,*	*yuhá*	*kéye,*	*iyéchįkyąke*	*cha.*	*yųkhą́*
model T Ford	IDF.SG	have	QT	car*	QL	then

awókheye	*ki*	*yuȟpá-pi*	*cha*	*eyášna*	*ogná*	*yąkį́*	*na*	*įšé*	*lı́la*
cover.N	DEF	loosen-IPS	so	sometimes	inside	sit	and	just	INT

lúzahe-šni,	*hená*	*iyéchįkyąke*	*ki.*	*éyaš*	*ogná*	*yąkį́*	*na*
fast-NEG	those	car*	DEF	but	inside	sit	and

hąˀíyachįkešniyą	*glá*	*kéye.*	*Ųžį́žįtka*	*Owákpamni*
in the middle of the night	go home	QT	Rosebud*	Agency*

étkiya	*ochą́ku*	*wą*	*ehą́ni*	*ȟpáye.*	*lehą́n*	*į́š*	*hąké*
toward	wagon trail	IDF.SG	long ago	lie	now	it	part

yuksá-pi,	*chąkú*	*ki,*	*na*	*chąkú*	*wą*	*lechála*	*hél*	*é-ˀųpa-pi.*
cut-IPS	road	DEF	and	road	IDF.SG	recently	there	L-put-IPS

cha	*hé*	*ogná*	*aˀíyakapteya*	*glá-pi*	*chą́-šna*	*iyéchįkyąke*	*ki*
so	that	along	uphill	go home-IPS	then-HAB	car*	DEF

tokhécela įyąka kéye, aˀíyakapteya. yųkhą́ até oyákį na
barely run QT uphill then father tell LK

táku wą sápa cha iyéchįkyąke ki isákhib įyąka kéye.
something IDF.SG black QL car* DEF beside run QT

cha ektá é-tųwą yųkhą́ lazá-tąhą íyutaka kéye nahą́ke lé
so to L-look then behind-from sit down QT and then this

hékta-tąhą oyą́ke hé ektá o-ˀíȟpe-icˀi-ya kéye. cha líla tké
behind-from seat that into L-ST-3RFL-throw QT QL INT heavy

kéye cha. áta tokhécela aˀíyakapteya gnį́ na waná
QT QL INT barely uphill go home and now

khiyáhį na hakíkta éyaš tuwénišni yųkhą́ akhé isákhib
reach the top and look back but nobody then again beside

híyutaka kéye cha. ektá é-tųwe éyaš tuwénišni kéye cha.
sit down QT QL there L-look but nobody QT QL

thokátakiya é-tųwą chą́-šna isákhib yąká kéye. cha átaya
in the future L-look then-HAB beside sit QT SO INT

gnį́ na Sápa Ų́ othí étkiya glá kéye,
go home and Catholic* mission toward go home QT

St. Francis-takiya. lową́ yąká kéye. áta lową́ yąkį́ na
St. Francis-toward sing CNT QT INT sing CNT and

ȟná-hįgnį na hakíkta kéye. yųkhą́ tuwénišni
snort like a bear-suddenly and look back QT then nobody

kéye.	*áta*	*iyéchįkyąke*	*kap'óžela-hįgla*	*kéye*	*cha.*	*átaya*
QT	INT	car*	light weighted-suddenly	QT	QL	INT

pąȟyá	*khi-gnį́*	*na*	*thi-yáta*	*khihų́ni*	*kéye*	*yųkhą́*
fast	come-go home	and	home-at	arrive at home	QT	then

ogláka	*kéye*	*yųkhą́*	*thųką́-ku*	*ki*	*é*	*cha*	*héyá*	*kéye*
POSS.tell	QT	then	father in law-3POR	DEF	IP	QL	say that	QT

"wą́	*hél*	*eyášna*	*wicháša*	*wą*	*tuwá*	*išnála*	*glá*
IJ.M	there	sometimes	man	IDF.SG	someone	alone	go home

chą́-šna	*khuwá*	*škhé*	*yelő"*	*eyá*	*kéye.*	*"n-išnála*	*ománi-šni*
then-HAB	chase	QT	ASS.M	say	QT	2SG.PAT-alone	travel-NEG

yő"	*eyá*	*kéye.*	*yųkhą́*	*įšé*	*íyohakab,*	*waníyetu*	*tónakecha*
IMP.SG.M	say	QT	then	just	after	year	so many

íyohakab,	*hé ogná*	*thųwį́*	*wą*	*oglákį*	*na*	*iyéchįkyąke*
after	that way*	aunt	IDF.SG	POSS.tell	and	car*

ogná	*glá-pi*	*yųkhą́*	*héchų s'e*	*įšé*	*akhé*	*wich-ísakhib*
inside	go home-PL	then	that way*	just	again	3PL.PAT-beside

įyąka	*kéye*	*chąkhé*	*naphá-pi*	*nahą́ke*	*chąkú*	*ka'ípayeȟ*
run	QT	then	flee-PL	and then	road	the wrong way

iyáya-pi	*yųkhą́*	*lé*	*a'íyakapteya*	*chąkpágmiyąpi*	*wą*
go-PL	then	this	uphill	wagon*	IDF.SG

hiyáhą	*cha*	*kahįȟpeya.*	*kahįȟpeya-pi*	*na*
appear on top of a hill	so	run over	run over-PL	and

chąpágmiyąpi ihúpa kihą lé kaȟápe ki í opázą na
wagon* handle DEF this driver DEF mouth push in and

átaya chehúpa o-pážužu kéye. nahą́ šų́kawakhą́ ki lé
entirely jaw L-dislocate QT and then horse* DEF this

ožą́žąglepi ki choką́ naȟtákį na ité ogná naȟtáka cha
window* DEF middle kick and face inside kick so

áta ité ki iną́phą. cha okhúže thípi ektá é-wicha-ˀųpa-pi
entirely face DEF smash so hospital* to L-3PL.PAT-put-IPS

yųkhą́ o-wícha-ki-yaka-pi na ehą́ni hél wanáǧi eyá wiwíla
then ST-3PL-BEN-tell-IPS LK long ago there spirit LK spring

wicháša e-wícha-kiya-pi cha héchacha hená eyášna
man ST-3PL.PAT-call-IPS QL that kind those always

wichá-khuwa-pi kéyá oyáka-pi. ho cha hé
IPS-chase-PL say that tell-IPS well so that

até-wa-ye ki hé wanáǧi wą kichí yąkį naˀį́š
father-1SG.AG-have as DEF that spirit IDF.SG with sit or

hená wiwíla e-wícha-kiya-pi kéye cha. cha hé
those spring ST-3PL.PAT-call-IPS QT QL so that

otóhąn gnį́ na pahá-ta khinážį yųkhą́ gliyópsicį
a short distance go home and hill-on stop then jump off

na tókhiya iyáye kéye.
and somewhere go QT

Long ago there were no cars. Around 1922 or perhaps 1923 my father had a Model T Ford, that kind of car. Sometimes he would ride in it with the cover taken off. They were not very fast, those cars. But he rode in it, and he drove home in the middle of the night. Long ago there was a wagon trail leading toward Rosebud Agency. Today part of it is cut off, part of the trail, and recently a highway was built there. Whenever people went uphill on it [the trail], the cars just barely made it going up the hill. My father reported that one time something black was running along with him beside the car. He looked at it. It sat down from behind. It threw itself in the back seat from behind. It was very heavy. He was barely moving uphill, but when he had reached the hilltop and looked back, there was nobody sitting with him anymore. He looked around but there was nobody. When he looked again, it was there again. He rode fast, toward the Catholic mission, toward St. Francis. He was singing [to overcome his fear]. He was singing loudly, and uttered bear-like sounds [an old Lakota strategy to make oneself feel courageous]. He looked back. There was nobody. Suddenly the car became extremely light [before that it had felt like someone was pulling it back]. He was driving fast, and when he arrived at home he told his story. His father-in-law said: "Rumor has it that sometimes a man chases people riding alone. Don't go all by yourself!" After that, many years after that, an aunt [of mine] told a story like that, that she and some others were driving home in a car, and it [that being] ran with them again just the same way. They tried to escape, but they took the wrong road. On top of the hill a wagon appeared, and they collided with it. They collided, and the wagon's hitch pierced the driver's mouth, entirely dislocating his jaw. The horse [of the wagon] kicked in the middle of the windshield and kicked her [my aunt] in the face; it smashed her face completely. They were brought to the hospital, and people told them that long ago spirits called "spring men" sometimes chased people. So my father rode with a spirit or one of those beings called spring men. When he had made part of his way home, and stopped on the hill, it jumped off and disappeared.

2.9. Going to School on the Reservation

MARY LIGHT

Tape recorded October 25, 1994

lehą́l	*akhé*	*tak̨ų́l*	*Lakhótiya*	*oblákį-kta*	*cha*	*hé*	*ų́*
now	again	something	in Lakota	tell.1SG.AG-FASS	so	that	so that

Lé	*wį́yą*	*kihą*	*echél*	*yuʾíyeska-kte*	*thokáta.*	*lehą́l*	*įšé*
this	woman	DEF	so	interpret-FASS	in the future	now	just

wakhą́yeža	*mitháwa*	*ki*	*hų́ȟ*	*Sápa Ų́*	*owáyawa*	*cha*	*él*
child	my	DEF	some	Catholic*	school*	QL	to

wayáwa-pi.	*Holy Rosary*	*hél*	*wayáwa-pi*	*na*	*iyúha*
go to school*-PL	Holy Rosary	there	go to school*-PL	and	all

wóʾųspe	*gluštą́-pi.*	*na*	*hé*	*įšé*	*oblákį-kte*	*na*
education	POSS.finish-PL	and	that	just	1SG.AG.tell-FASS	and

thokála-ȟci	*wayáwa-pi*	*ho*	*héhą*	*Manderson*	*ektá*
at first-INT	go to school*-PL	well	then	Manderson	in

ų-thí-pi	*cha*	*lé*	*wichįcala*	*ki*	*šųkʾákąyąkį*	*na-šna*
1PL.AG-live-PL	so	this	girl	DEF	ride*-PL	and-HAB

he-tą́	*wayáwa.*	*wayáwa*	*na-šna*	*ȟtayétu*	*chą́na-šna*
that-from	go to school*	go to school*	and-HAB	evening	then-HAB

khí	*na*	*akhé*	*hįhąni*	*chą́*	*kiktá*	*na*	*líla*	*osní*	*na*
go home	and	again	morning	then	get up	and	INT	cold	and

wa-šmé chą́na-šna hél hokšíla wąží eyášna hékta-kta-kiya
snow-deep then-HAB there boy IDF.SG always back.AV-RED-to

glá cha hé owáyawa ektá éȟpeye. waná ąpétu áta
go home so that school* at drop off now day entire

wayáwa na ȟtayétu chą́ hiyó-ˀi na-šna akhé
go to school* and evening then come for-come and-HAB again

akhí. hékta-kiya ų-thí-pi ektá akhí. na tohą́l
bring home back.AV-to 1PL.AG-live-PL to bring home and then

hé owáyawa ki hél iglúštą ho he-tą́ cha
that school* DEF there POSS.finish well that-from so

Holy Rosary ektá akhé wayáwa. hų́ȟ hél wayáwa-pi,
Holy Rosary at again go to school* some there go to school*-PL

wakhą́yeža mitháwa ki. tókhi záptą-pi sˀe léchecha hél
child my DEF about five-PL like.AV like this there

wayáwa-pi na iyúha wayáwa-pi iglúštą-pi. éyaš
go to school*-PL and all go to school*-PL POSS.finish-PL but

hél Sápa Ų́ owáyawa ki hé líla táku óta ogláki̜-kta.
there Catholic* school* DEF that INT things many POSS.tell-FASS

tayą́-šni-šni o-wícha-khuwa-pi éyaš iníhąšni hél
well-NEG-RED L-3PL.PAT-treat-IPS but nevertheless there

waníyetu tóna iyúha ų́-pi na iglúštą-pi. áta
year so many all be at-PL and POSS.finish-PL INT

wóta-pi	*naˀį́š*	*táku*	*echų́-pi*	*ki*	*iyúha*	*líla*	*wówasukiye*
NSP.PAT.eat-PL	or	what	do-PL	DEF	all	INT	rule

óta	*cha*	*iglúžaža-pi*	*naˀį́š*	*wa-glúžaža-pi*	*ki*	*iyúha*
many	so	POSS.wash-PL	or	NSP.PAT-POSS.wash-PL	DEF	all

thogyé	*echų́-pi.*	*ho*	*iyúha*	*thog-thógye*	*na*	*ipáyeȟ*
differently	do-PL	well	all	RED-differently	and	wrong

icháȟ-wicha-ˀų-yą-pi	*nahą́*	*wayáwa-pi*	*ki*	*hél*
grow-3PL.PAT-1PL.AG-CAU-PL	and then	go to school*-IPS	DEF	there

i-thókecha	*cha.*	*éyaš*	*iníhąšni*	*hél*	*waníyetu*	*tóna*	*iyúha*
L-different	QL	but	nevertheless	there	winter	so many	all

ų́-pi	*na*	*iglúštą-pi.*	*hé*	*nakų́*	*táku*	*eyá*	*hél*	*tókha*
be at-PL	and	POSS.finish-PL	that	also	things	some	there	happen

ki	*lé*	*ogláke*	*kihą*	*hé*	*obláke-šni.*	*įšé*	*hená*	*líla*	*hél*
DEF	this	POSS.tell	DEF	that	tell.1SG.AG-NEG	just	those	INT	there

wówasukiye	*óta.*	*takų́l*	*echų́-pi-šni*	*ehą́tąhąš*	*cha*	*áta*	*hú*
rule	many	something	do-PL-NEG	if	QL	INT	leg

ki	*él*	*a-wícha-pha-pi*	*kéye.*	*belt*	*naˀį́š*	*táku*	*ų́.*	*cha*	*táku*
DEF	on	ST-3PL.PAT-hit-PL	QT	belt	or	what	with	so	things

ki	*hél*	*líla*	*wówasukiye*	*suk-súta*	*ų́.*	*cha*	*éyaš*	*he-tą́*
DEF	there	INT	rule	RED-hard	exist	so	but	that-from

líla	*wóˀųspe*	*óta*	*ųspé-pi.*	*cha*	*wa-glúžaža-pi*	*naˀį́š*
INT	knowledge	much	know-PL	QL	NSP.PAT-POSS.wash-IPS	and

nųwą́-pi	*ki,*	*hená*	*nakų́*	*líla*	*wówasukiye*	*óta.*	*mní*	*cónala*
bathe-IPS	DEF	those	also	INT	rule	many	water	a little bit

ų́-pi.	*owíchakaške*	*él*	*ų́-pi*	*iyéchel-ya*	*hená*
use-PL	prison*	in	be at-PL	like that-ADV	those

wichá-khuwa-pi.	*hená*	*iyúha*	*lehą́l*	*tąyą́*	*iglóˀaya-pi*
3PL.PAT-treat-IPS	those	all	now	well	self supporting-PL

nahą́	*waná*	*iyé*	*chįchá-pi*	*ki*	*hená*	*hél*
and then	now	they	child-PL	DEF	those	there

wichá-gloˀaya-pi	*chį́-pi-šni.*	*cha*	*lehą́l*
3PL.PAT-take one's own to-PL	want-PL-NEG	so	now

thokhą́-khą-l-ya	*wóˀųspe*	*yuhá-pi.*
elsewhere-RED-ST-ADV	education	have-PL

hená	*ipáyeȟ*	*wayáwa-ki-chiya-pi*	*nahą́*	*léchiya*	*lehą́l*
those	elsewhere	go to school*-PSS-CAU-PL	and then	here	now

iyúha	*tąyą́*	*ų́-pi.*	*ho*	*héhą*	*įšé*	*hél*	*owáyawa*	*Holy Rosary*	*él*
all	well	be-PL	well	then	just	there	school*	Holy Rosary	in

tókhel	*ų́-pi*	*cha*	*ogláka-pi.*	*cha*	*hé*	*ų́*	*obláke.*
how	be-PL	QL	POSS.tell-PL	QL	that	because of	1SG.AG.tell-FASS

cha	*hehą́yą*	*bluštą́*	*sˀe*	*léchecha.*
so	that is all	finish.1SG.AG	like.AV	like this

Now I will tell a story in Lakota again, so this woman [refers to the author] can translate it later on. Some of my children went to a Catholic school. They went to school in Holy Rosary [on Pine Ridge Reservation], and they all finished their education there. This is the topic of my story. When they first went to school we lived in Manderson [on Pine Ridge Reservation]. This girl [Mary's daughter Helen] got on a horse and went to school. She went to school, and in the evening she always went back home. And when she got up in the morning, and it was very cold, and the snow was deep, she always rode back and forth with a certain boy on a horse; he dropped her off at the school. She was in school all day, and in the evening he would pick her up again and bring her home. He brought her back home to where we lived. And after finishing that school she went to school again at Holy Rosary. Some of them went to school there, some of my kids. About five of them went to school there, and they all finished this school. They would tell many stories about that Catholic school. They were not treated right, but they stayed there nevertheless for so many years, and they finished. There were many rules for eating and whatever they did, for example for washing oneself or washing one's belongings. It was all done differently. It was all different, and the way we raised them was wrong. At school everything was different. But they [my kids] stayed there nevertheless. They stayed there for many years, and they finished. Some of the things that happened there, as she [Helen] reported, I don't mention here. There were many, many rules. If they [the kids] didn't do certain things they would spank them on the legs. With belts or whatever. For everything there were extremely strict rules. But from that they have a very good education. The areas in which they were treated extremely badly were doing laundry and taking a bath; there very many rules to that, too. They used little water. They were treated almost as if they were in prison. Now they are all taking good care of themselves. They would not want to put their own children in that school. They get their education elsewhere. They [my children] put them [their children] into different schools, and they are all doing well there. They [my kids] had talked about what it's like to be in the Holy Rosary school. This is why I have talked about it. I think I stop here. That's it.

2.10. Crow Fair

MARY LIGHT

Tape recorded October 25, 1994

lehą́l Psáloka oyáte kihą tókheškhe wa-ʔéchų-pi hená tókhel
now Crow people DEF how NSP.PAT-do-PL those as

slol-wá-ye ki obláki̜-kte. waníyetu nų́pa ho
ST-1SG.AG-know DEF tell.1SG.AG-FASS year two well

wahéhą-šna héchiya ųk-í-pi. wótakuye héchiya
then-HAB there 1PL.AG-go to-PL relatives there

wichá-bluha. cha héchiya-šna wa-ʔí na-šna
3PL.PAT-have.1SG.AG so there-HAB 1SG.AG-go to and-HAB

mi-tákuye hená ób-šna tókheškhe thí-pi naʔį́š tókheškhe
1SG.POR-relatives those with-HAB that way live-PL and that way

tónachą hél wachí-pi. hená áta oʔíyokiphi-ya iyúha ptáyela
many days there dance-PL those INT happy-ADV all together

wichó-thi nahą́ thiʔóblecha ki hená cónala na lé
COLL-camp.VI and then regular tent* DEF those few and there

thi-phéstola ki hé é líla óta. éyaš líla oʔíyokiphi sʔa.
house-pointed DEF that IP INT many but INT happy HAB

ho na hél tókhi nų́pa naʔį́š yámni chą echél-šna wachí-pi.
well and there maybe two or three days so-HAB dance-IPS

Lakhóta oyáte ki na Psálokaoyáte ki holá iyúha

Lakota people DEF and Crow people DEF those all

thog-thógye iglúza-pi. hé ecéla wachí-pi ki ákhilechecha

RED-differently dress up-PL that only dance-IPS DEF alike

éyaš táku echų́-pi ki héchel líla o'íyokiphi kéye. ihį́hąni

but things do-IPS DEF so INT fun QT in the morning

chą́na six o'clock héhą́ni-šna áta wichá-yuȟica-pi

then six o'clock then-HAB INT 3PL.PAT-wake up.VT-IPS

na-šna éyapaha wą áta óhįniya-šna táku echų́-pi-kte ki

and-HAB herald IDF.SG INT always-HAB things do-IPS-FASS DEF

holá ya-'óthąį. ho héhą-šna waná ikpázopi hé yuhá-pi.

those INS-evident well then-HAB now parade there have-PL

líla šų́kawakhą́ óta-pi cha holá šųk'ákąyąka-pi na holá

INT horse* many-PL so those ride*-IPS and those

iglúthą-pi na šųk'ákąyąka-pi ki holá wókhoyake iyúha

POSS.dress up-PL and ride*-PL DEF those costume all

kic'ų́-pi na-šna ikpázopi yuhá-pi ki hé líla hą́ska cha líla

wear-PL and-HAB parade have-PL DEF there INT long so INT

o'íyokiphi-ya wówąyąke. ho na hé iglúštą-pi chą́na-šna

happy-ADV sight well and there POSS.finish-IPS then-HAB

ho hehą́l chokáta waȟpé wakhéya thą́ka wą hą́ cha

well then in the middle leaf tent big IDF.SG stand so

hél iyúha-šna khiwítaya-pi na-šna ho hehą́l hél
there all-HAB get together-IPS and-HAB well then there

ąpétu ki áta-šna wachí-pi. waná akhé ȟtayétu chą́
day DEF entire-HAB dance-IPS now again evening then

owáphe nų́m ecé iyúha glá-pi nahą́ ȟtayétu
hour* two always all go home-IPS and then evening

wóta-pi na ho hé iglúštą-pi chą́ héktakiya
NSP.PAT.eat-IPS and well that POSS.finish-IPS then back.AV

waȟpé wakhéya héchiya he-tą́ akhé wachí-pi na-šna éyaš
leaf tent there that-from again dance-PL and-HAB but

wachí-pi ki hená líla wich-óta-pi na líg-lila oʔíyokiphi
dance-IPS DEF those INT COLL-many-PL and RED-INT fun

yuhá-pi. ho líla wówąyąke thą́ka. cha hehą́yą slol-wá-ye
have-PL well INT sight big so that is all ST-1SG.AG-know

cha. héchi wichó-thi na léchi wichó-thi ki í-thokecha
QL there COLL-camp.VI and here COLL-camp.VI DEF L-different

éyaš héchiya ki hé líla wówąyąke wašté. cha hehą́yela
but there DEF that INT sight good so that is all

obláki̜-kte.
1SG.AG.tell-FASS

Next, I will tell all I know about the things the Crow people do. Every other year we go there, since I have relatives there. Whenever I go there my relatives camp with them [the Crow], in their own special way, and they dance there for many days. They all camp together in tipis, having a lot of fun. There are few common tents, and many, many tipis. This is always a very joyful event. People dance there for maybe two or three days. The Lakota and the Crow dress up quite differently. Only the dancing style is similar, but whatever people do, there is a whole lot of fun. In the morning, at six o'clock, they wake everybody up and a herald always announces and explains what will be going on. They always have a parade. There are many, many horses. People ride them and dress them up, and all the riders wear costumes. The parade they have is very long and a very beautiful sight to see. When this is over people all get together in the middle of the fairgrounds where there is a big shade, and there they dance all day. Then, in the evening, they all go home [to their tents] for two hours and have dinner. After that they go back to the shade and dance again. There are many, many dancers, and they have lots of fun. It is a great sight to see. This is all I know. The way they camp there and the way they camp here are different, but over there it is a beautiful sight to see. This is all I wanted to tell.

2.11. Extrasensory Perception

NEVA STANDING BEAR

Tape recorded October 31, 1994

ehą́ni	*tókhi*	*waníyetu*	*aké*	*záptą*	*wahéhąn*	*héktakiya*	*héhą*
long ago	about	year	ADD	five	by that time	back.AV	then

líla	*ma-kákiže.*	*tohą́n*	*išt-ógmus*	*íblutake*	*hą́tąhą*	*wich-íte*
INT	1SG.PAT-suffer	when	eye-close	sit.1SG.AG	when	human-face

wąblákį	*naˀį́š*	*táku*	*ipáyeȟ,*	*thókecha*	*wąbláka*	*chą́-šna*
see.1SG.AG	or	things	wrong	different	see.1SG.AG	then-HAB

ųgnáš	*tokhíyothą*	*ománi*	*blé*	*hą́tąhąš*	*ho*	*na*	*hé*	*étkiya*
maybe	anywhere	travel	go.1SG.AG	when	well	and	that	toward

blá	*wa-chį́-šni*	*khéš*	*ipáyeȟ-ya-šna*	*blá*
go.1SG.AG	1SG.AG-want-NEG	but	wrong place-ADV-HAB	go.1SG.AG

chą́	*lé*	*táku*	*wąbláke*	*kˀų*	*hená*	*eyášna*	*wašícu*	*wą*
then	this	things	see.1SG.AG	DEF	those	always	white man	IDF.SG

kichí	*wa-ˀų́.*	*yųkhą́*	*he*	*natá*	*wi-má-tko*	*kéyį*
with	1SG.AG-be	then	that	head	ST-1-SG.PAT.crazy	say that

na	*héchel*	*wašícu wakhą́*	*wą*	*wąyą́g-ma-ši.*	*cha*	*ektá*
and	so	white doctor*	IDF.SG	see-1SG.PAT-ask	so	there

wa-ˀí	*na*	*o-wá-ki-yake.*	*cha*
1SG.AG-go to	and	ST-1SG.AG-BEN-tell	so

kichí	*w-ó-ma-glakį*	*na*	*“hé*	*táku*	*ki*	*lená*
with	NSP.PAT-ST-1SG.PAT-POSS.tell	and	that	things	DEF	these

wąláke	*ki*	*lená*	*niyé*	*ni-Lákhota*	*cha*	*lená*	*táku*	*ki*
see.2SG.AG	DEF	these	you	2SG.PAT-Lakota	so	these	things	DEF

lená	*ithókamna*	*slol-yá-ye*	*k’éyaš*	*nų́*
these	before	ST-2SG.AG-know	but	use.2SG.AG

ya-chį́-šni	*na’į́š*	*a-yá-bleze-šni*	*cha*	*hé*
2SG.AG-want-NEG	and	ST-2SG.AG-notice-NEG	so	that

ų́	*w-í-ni-cakiže*	*k’ų”*	*eyá*	*cha.*
because of	NSP.PAT-L-2SG.PAT-suffer	ASS	say	QL

“slol-yá-yį	*na*	*hená*	*a-yá-bleze*	*hą́tąhąš*	*ųgná*
ST-2SG.AG-know	and	those	ST-2SG.AG-notice	when	maybe

ni-cákižį-kte-šni	*k’ų”*	*eyé*	*cha*	*héphé*	*“hená*
2SG.PAT-suffer-FASS-NEG	ASS	say	QL	say that.1SG.AG	those

héchel	*wąbláka-he*	*éyaš*	*lená*	*é*	*cha*	*héchel*	*bluhá*
so	see.1SG.AG-PRG	but	these	IP	QL	so	have.1SG.AG

hécįhą	*wó’ilag-wa-ye*	*wa-chį́-šni*	*k’ų”*	*ephé.*	*“tuwéni*
if	ST-1SG.AG-use	1SG.AG-want-NEG	ASS	say.1SG.AG	nobody

w-í-ma-yųğe-šni	*tkhá*	*tha-’ó’ų*	*ki*	*wąblákį*	*na*
NSP.PAT-ST-1SG.PAT-ask-NEG	but	ALP-life	DEF	see.1SG.AG	and

echą́ni	*ni-t’į́-kte*	*k’ų”*	*ephá*	*o-wá-kihi-šni*
soon	2SG.PAT-die-FASS	ASS	say.1SG.AG	ST-1SG.AG-can-NEG

kˀų”	*ephé.*	*cha*	*“ho*	*héchel*	*mų́*	*wa-chį́-šni*
ASS	say.1SG.AG	QL	well	so	use.1SG.AG	1SG.AG-want-NEG

kˀų”	*ephé.*	*“cha*	*tókša*	*thokáta*	*tohą́n*
ASS	say.1SG.AG	so	after a while	in the future	when

iyé-mi-ci-hątu	*hą́tąhąš*	*ųgná*	*wóˀilag-wa-yį-kte*	*kˀų”*
ST-1SG-BEN-it is time	when	maybe	ST-1SG.AG-use-FASS	ASS

eyá	*o-wá-ki-yake.*	*yųkhą́*	*hé*	*“ni-Lákhota*	*na*	*Lakhóta*
say	ST-1SG.AG-BEN-tell	then	that	2SG.PAT-Indian	and	Indian

ki	*hená*	*iyúha*	*hé*	ESP	*yuhá-pi*	*cha*
DEF	those	all	that	extrasensory perception	have-PL	so

héchacha	*luhá-pe*	*lő”*	*eyá*	*cha.*	*“cha*	*hená*	*ų́*	*tohą́n*
like that	have.2AG-PL	ASS.M	say	QL	so	those	with	when

waphíya-pi	*naˀį́š*	*ųgnáš*	*takún*	*echų́-pi-kte*	*hą́tąhą*	*hená*
doctor.VT*-PL	or	maybe	something	do-IPS-FASS	when	those

ehą́ta	*slolyá-pi*	*kˀų”*	*eyé.*	*“cha*	*níš*	*eyá*	*hé*	*luhá-š*
already	know-PL	ASS	say	so	you	too	that	2SG.AG.have-EMPH

cha	*hé*	*é*	*cha*	*wóˀilag-ya-yį-kta*	*škhá*	*echánų-šni*	*cha*	*hé*
so	that	IP	QL	ST-2SG.AG-use-FASS	but	2SG.AG.do-NEG	so	that

ų́	*ni-cákiže*	*lő”*	*eyé.*	*eyá*	*cha*	*“éyaš*
because of	2SG.PAT-suffer	ASS.M	say	say	so	but

wóˀilag-wa-ye	*wa-chį́-šni*	*kˀų”*	*ephé*	*cha.*	*“ho*	*cha*
ST-1SG.AG-use	1SG.AG-want-NEG	ASS	say.1SG.AG	QL	well	so

tókša	*ųspé-chi-chiyį*	*na*	*takún*	*héchel*
after a while	know-1SG.AG.2SG.PAT-CAU	and	something	so

i-yá-hąble	*éyaš*	*icínųpani*	*wąlákį-kte-šni"*	*eyá*
ST-2SG.AG-dream.VT	but	never again	see.2SG.AG-FASS-NEG	say

cha	*"ohą́,*	*ho*	*cha*	*icínųpani*	*wąbláke-šni."*	*yųkhą́*	*lehą́n*
so	okay	well	so	never again	see.1SG.AG-NEG	then	now

wichóʼų	*ki*	*lél*	*ichų́hą*	*táku*	*óta*	*iblúkcą*	*chą*
existence	DEF	here	during	things	many	think about.1SG.AG	then

slol-wá-yį	*na*	*o-wá-kaȟniǧe.*	*na*	*ųgnáš*	*tuwá*
ST-1SG.AG-know	and	ST-1SG.AG-understand	and	maybe	someone

takún	*iyúkcą*	*ešáš*	*tókhiya*	*ų́*	*na-šna*
something	think about	although	somewhere	be	and-HAB

ųgnáhelakha	*wicháša*	*ki*	*hé*	*naʼį́š*	*wį́yą*	*ki*	*hé*
suddenly	man	DEF	that	or	woman	DEF	that

a-w-íblukcą	*hą́tąhąš*	*hená*	*táku*	*iyúkcą-pi*
L-NSP.PAT-think about.1SG.AG	when	those	what	think about-PL

ki	*slol-wá-ye.*	*cha*	*otúyachį*	*hená*	*slol-wá-ye-šni*
DEF	ST-1SG.AG-know	so	for no reason	those	ST-1SG.AG-know-NEG

įšé	*na*	*tókhi*	*wakhą́*	*héchiya-tąhą*	*hená*	*héchetu.*	*ho*	*cha*
just	and	maybe	sacred	there-from	those	so	well	so

wa-má-khą-šni	*éyaš*	*įšé*	*hená*	*wóʼilake.*	*na*	*hená*
ST-1SG.PAT-sacred-NEG	but	maybe	those	tool	and	those

oyáte ki wa-ˀó-wa-kiyį-kta cha hé ų́
people DEF NSP.PAT-ST-1SG.AG-help.VT-FASS QL that because of

lená héchecha. cha tákuni šíca héchel
these like that so nothing bad so

w-íblukcą-šni. takómni hená wašté. cha
NSP.PAT-think about.1SG.AG-NEG at all costs those good so

lehą́n enágnakiya wóˀilag-wa-ye éyaš tákuni tóhųweni
now here and there ST-1SG.AG-use but nothing never

šil-ˀá-w-iblukcą o-wá-kihi-šni. cha
bad-L-NSP.PAT-think about.1SG.AG ST-1SG.AG-can-NEG so

héchel įšé o-wá-glake. tohą́n hená wóˀilag-wa-ye
so just ST-1SG.AG-POSS.tell then those ST-1SG.AG-use

hą́tąhąš įšé cha héchel mąkį́ na tuwá tak-tókhų-kte
when just QL so sit.1SG.AG and someone whatever-do-FASS

ki ithókamna o-wé-ci-yaka-hą o-wá-kihi éyaš héchel
DEF before ST-1SG.AG-BEN-tell-PRG ST-1SG.AG-can but so

wóˀilag-wa-ye wa-chį́-šni cha. lená wochékhiye ogná hé
ST-1SG.AG-use 1SG.AG-want-NEG QL these prayer inside that

wóˀilag-wa-ye. cha hé ogná iyó-ma-kiphi. kštó. lé é cha
ST-1SG.AG-use so that way* ST-1SG.PAT-happy ASS.F this IP QL

henákecha.
enough

A while ago, about fifteen years ago, I was suffering very much. Whenever I was sitting with my eyes closed I saw faces, or I saw wrong, different things [things that were different from what I was trying to envision]. When I was going somewhere, and didn't even want to go, I ended up at the wrong places; there I always encountered and witnessed the things I had seen before. Back then I was living with a white man. He said that I had gone insane and told me to see a white doctor. So I went there and talked to him [the doctor]. He counseled me and said: "These things, the things you see, you know beforehand because you are an Indian. You know these things, but because you don't want to use them and notice them you are suffering. If you know that and if you deal with it, maybe you will not suffer any more," he said. I replied: "I see those things this way, but even if I have this ability I don't want to use it. Even if nobody asks me about it I see people's lives, and I cannot say 'soon you will die.' I don't want to use this ability. Maybe sometime in the future when it's time for me I will use it," I told him. He said: "You are an Indian, and all Indians have ESP [extrasensory perception]. This is what you folks have. When they [the Indians] cure people with it, or are planning to do something, they know about these things [people's diseases or actions] beforehand. You also have that [ability], and you are supposed to use it, but you don't do that, and for this reason you suffer from it." I said: "But I don't want to use it." He said: "I will instruct you and whatever visions you had, you will never see that again." I said: "Okay, I will never see this again." Now when I think about any of the many things to do with people's lives, I know and understand. And maybe if someone thinks about something, no matter where he or she is, and I think of that man or woman, all of a sudden I know what they are thinking. I don't just know these things for no reason; maybe these things have a spiritual origin. I am no saint, but maybe this [talent] is a tool. And it is the way it is because I'm supposed to help people. I don't have any bad thoughts. They have to be good by all means [in order to avoid foretelling bad things]. Now I use my ability here and there but I am unable to think badly of anybody. I'm just reporting this. When I use it [my ESP] I could be just be sitting there telling beforehand what someone will do, but I don't want to use it that way. I always use it in my prayers. That way I feel comfortable. That's the way it is. That's all.

2.12. The Invisible Passenger

NEVA STANDING BEAR

Tape recorded November 4, 1994

ká	*Winner,*	*South Dakota*	*echíyatąhą*	*khoškálaka*	*nų́m*
over there	Winner	South Dakota	from there	young man	two

él	*inážį-pi*	*na*	*wa-yátką-hą-pi*	*nahą́ke*	*mní wakhą́*
at	stop-PL	and	NSP.PAT-drink-PRG-PL	and then	liquor*

owíyophe	*wą*	*hél*	*hą́*	*cha*	*hél*	*khinážį-pi*	*nahą́ke*
store*	IDF.SG	there	stand	so	there	stop-PL	and then

mnipíǧa	*ophéthų-pi*	*kéye.*	*chąkhé*	*oyáte*	*eyá*	*Oak Creek*	*etą́*
beer*	buy-PL	QT	then	people	IDF.PL	Oak Creek	from

cha	*a-wą́yąg*	*wichá-khuwa-pi*	*kéye.*	*a-wą́yąg*
QL	L-see	3PL.PAT-chase-PL	QT	L-see

a-wícha-ku-pi	*kéye.*	*lená*	*itómni-pi*	*cha*	*"ųgná*	*mayá*
COLL-3PL.PAT-come-PL	QT	these	drunk-PL	so	maybe	cliff

mahél	*iyáya-pi-kte*	*lő"*	*eyá-pi*	*kéye.*	*wicháša*	*nų́b-la-la-pi*
inside	go-PL-FASS	ASS.M	say-PL	QT	man	two-LIM-RED-PL

cha.	*cha*	*a-wą́yąg*	*a-wícha-ku-pi*	*kéye.*	*cha*	*iyéchįkyąke*
QL	so	L-see	COLL-3PL.PAT-come-PL	QT	QL	car*

nų́m	*wich-íhakab*	*glá-pi*	*kéye.*	*cha*	*hél*	*iyéchįkyąke*	*ki*
two	3PL.PAT-after	go home-PL	QT	QL	there	car*	DEF

wąží él lekší-wa-ye ki yąká kéye. na itómni-pi ki
one in uncle-1SG.AG-have as DEF sit QT and drunk-PL DEF

líla nųphį́ wíyutha w-óglag yąká-pi na glá-pi na
INT both motion NSP.PAT-POSS.tell CNT-PL and go home-PL and

pahá aką́n khinážį-pi kéye. chąkhé ikhíyela khihų́ni-pi na
hill on top stop-PL QT then near arrive-PL and

į́š eyá tohą́yą akhínažį-pi chąkhé ųmá glicú nahą́
they at that point stop-PL then one of them get out and then

ohómni iyáyį na ųmáchiyatąhą íyutaka kéye cha
go around go and on the other side sit down QT so

ųmá thogthóg kaȟápa-pi kéye chąkhé ųmá kaȟápe-šni ki
taking turns* drive-PL QT then one of them drive-NEG DEF

echíyatąhą hé ohómni iyáyį na lé kaȟápe ki héchiya
from there that go around go and this drive DEF there

íyutake. cha éyaš nų́b-la-la yąká-pi éyaš líla w-óglag
sit down so but two-LIM-RED sit-PL but INT NSP.PAT-POSS.tell

yąká-pi na lé iyóžąžą chóla glá-pi kéye. iyéchįkyąke
CNT-PL and this light without go home-PL QT car*

ki iyóžąžą waníca cha. cha hé ų́ wich-íhakab
DEF light lack QL so that because of 3PL.PAT-after

glá-pi kéye yųkhą́ líla w-ó-glag yąká-pi kéye nųphį́
go home-PL QT then INT NSP.PAT-POSS.tell CNT-PL QT both

cha yųkhą́ glá-pi na khiyóȟpaya-pi yųkhą́ waná

so then go home-PL and go down-PL then now

iȟpéya-wicha-khiya glá-pi. yųkhą́ lé itómni-pi ki

leave behind-3PL.PAT-CAU go home-PL then this drunk-PL DEF

lená é cha hé pahá akąń khinážį-pi ki héhą hél

these IP QL that hill on top stop-PL SYP then there

Lakhóta wį́yą wą ektá yuhá glá-pi na hé yuhá

Lakota woman IDF.SG there have go home-PL and that have

khinážį-pi kéye cha. hé mnipíǧa yatką́-pi na lé wį́yą ki

stop-PL QT QL that beer* drink-PL and this woman DEF

hé k'ú-pi kéye, cha hų́ȟ icú na yatką́ kéye. héchena

that give-PL QT so some take and drink QT continuously

chąlí o-kí-paǧi-pi cha icú na ų́pa kéye,

tobacco ST-BEN-load the pipe-PL so take and smoke tobacco QT

wį́yą ki lé. chąkhé líla kichí w-óglag yąká-pi

woman DEF this then INT with NSP.PAT-POSS.tell CNT-PL

éyaš iyóžąžą cha héčheš tókha-šni-yą glá-pi kéye.

but light QL so not alright-NEG-ADV go home-PL QT

glá-pi nahą́ke lé Úta Wakpá kihą isą́m khiglá-pi na

go home-PL and then this Oak Creek* DEF beyond go home-PL and

ká manį́ta-kiya chąkú ikcéka wą cha ogná

over there wilderness-on road common IDF.SG QL along

glá-pi kéye. na hehą́n hél thípi wą hą́ cha él
go home-PL QT and then there house IDF.SG stand so there

khinážį-pi kéye. yųkhą́ léyaš hé thípi-šni, chą́ thą́ka cha hél
stop-PL QT then but that house-NEG tree big QL there

hą́ kéye. yųkhą́ héhą wį́yą ki lé é cha "lehą́yela lél
stand QT then then woman DEF this IP QL this far here

wa-glíyacu-kte k'ų" eyá kéye chąkhé iyóžąžą khinážį-pi na
1SG.AG-get out-FASS ASS say QT then light stop-PL and

wį́yą ki hiyú-'ic'i-yį na héchena iyáya cha tókhetkiya
woman DEF come-3RFL-CAU and thus go so which way

iyáye ki olé-pi éyaš tukténi iyáye-šni tókhaȟ'ą kéye cha.
go DEF look for-PL but nowhere go-NEG disappear QT QL

iž́ąžą waníca chąkhé áta yuthą́-thą-pi na lé líla itómni-pi
light lack then INT feel about-RED-PL and this INT drunk-PL

k'ų hená é cha kibléza-pi kéye cha chąkhé héktakiya
SYP those IP QL sober up-PL QT so then backwards

kawį́ǧa-pi na Úta Wakpá ophą́ya khinážį-pi chąkhé
turn around.VI-PL and Oak Creek* along stop-PL then

lekší-wa-ye ki é cha héyá kéye "tóškhe iyéchįkyąke
uncle-1SG.AG-have as DEF IP QL say that QT why car*

ki iyóžąžą chóla ya-kú-pi hé?" eyá kéye "iyóžąžą
DEF light without 2AG-come-PL QS say QT light

chóla ya-kú-pi hé?" eyá kéye yųkhą́ "hiyá, iyóžąžą
without 2AG-come-PL QS say QT then no light

ų-kú-pi éyaš įšé hé wichįcala wą kichí
1PL.AG-come-PL but just that girl IDF.SG with

ų-kú-pi cha" eyá-pi kéye, išnála kú-pi škhá
1PL.AG-come-PL QL say-PL QT alone come-PL but

héyá-pi. "lé mnipíğa na chąlí ų-kʾú-pi cha-š
say that-PL this beer* and tobacco 1PL.AG-give-PL SO-EMPH

chąnų́m yąkį na khó wa-yátką yąké kʾų" eyá cha
smoke tobacco CNT and also NSP.PAT-drink CNT ASS say so

i-wą́yąka-pi yųkhą́ lé chąlí oğú nahą́ mnipíğa žąžą́
L-see-PL then this tobacco scraps and then beer* bottle

ki hená iyúha chą́ʾowįža ektá yąká kéye na tuwénišni.
DEF those all floor* on sit QT and nobody

tuwénišni škhá héchel išnála kú-pi. wanáği cha hé kichí
nobody but so alone come-PL spirit QL that with

kú-pi kéye. a-wícha-khi na
come-PL QT ST-3PL.PAT-bring home and

ų́yą-wicha-khiya glá kéye cha. thąsák tʾá-pi
leave behind-3PL.PAT-CAU go home QT QL struck with fear-PL

na kibléza-pi kéye na héchegla.
and sober up-PL QT and that is all

Over there in Winner, South Dakota, one time, two young men stopped at a bar and drank. Then there was a liquor store [as they went on]. They stopped there and bought some beer. Some people from Oak Creek were watching them. They didn't let them out of their sight and followed them. They [the two young men] were drunk. They [the people from Oak Creek] said: "Maybe they will go down the ditch." There were but two men. So they kept watching them. They followed them in two cars. My uncle was in one of those cars. The drunks were both talking and motioning all the time. They went on and stopped on a hill. They [the pursuers] approached them, and they also stopped at that point. One [of the drunks] got out, went around the car, and sat down on the other side. They took turns driving. The one who didn't drive from then on went around it [the car], and the driver sat down there [in the driver's seat]. There were only two people. But they were talking all the time, and they were driving without lights. The car didn't have lights. For this reason they [the people from Oak Creek] were following them. They were still talking very much, both of them, as they went on. They went down [the hill]. Now they left them [their pursuers] behind. When the drunks stopped on a hill they had a Lakota woman with them, and they stopped there with her. [This is the story the two young men related later on.] They were drinking beer and gave it to the woman. She took some and drank. They offered her cigarettes. She took them and smoked, this woman. They kept on talking to her. There was light [i.e., the car had lights], so they had no trouble going on. They went on, and when they had passed Oak Creek, they took an ordinary wilderness road [a wagon trail]. And then there was a house. They stopped there. But this was not a house, there was [only] a big tree [as it turned out later]. By then the woman said: "I'm getting off here." They stopped with the lights on. The woman jumped out and took off. They looked for her in the direction she had taken. But she had vanished without a trace. They had no light, so they were feeling about, and even though they were very drunk they sobered up. Then they turned back and stopped on the banks of Oak Creek [meeting their pursuers]. My uncle said: "How come you are driving with a car that has no lights? Have you been driving without lights?"

They said: "No, we did have lights, and we picked up a girl." Actually, they had been alone, but that's what they said. "We gave her beer and cigarettes. She smoked and drank, too, for a while." They [the people from Oak Creek] looked inside, and there were cigarette stubs and beer bottles lying on the floor, and there was nobody else around. There was nobody, they had been riding alone. They had been driving with a spirit. She directed them to where she lived and went on without them. They were scared to death and sobered up. That is all.

2.13. A Gambling Trip

NEVA STANDING BEAR

Tape recorded November 16, 1994

ehání	*até-wa-ye*	*kihą*	*khoškálaka*	*k'ų*	*héhą*	*líla*
long ago	father-1SG.AG-have as	DEF	young man	SYP	then	INT

ȟleté	*kéye.*	*chąkhé*	*tuktétu k'éyaš*	*khąsúkhute-pi*	*cha*	*ektá*
wild	QT	then	wherever	gamble*-IPS	QL	to

iyáza	*ománi*	*na*	*khąsúkhute*	*ohíya*	*ománi*	*na-šna*
one after the other	travel	and	gamble*	win	travel	and-HAB

táku	*maschą́'ųpha*	*na'į́š*	*wíkhą*	*na'į́š*	*chą́wak'į*	*na'íš*
things	bridle*	or	rope	or	saddle*	or

ak'į́	*na'į́š*	*ųgnáš*	*lé*	*mas'ínaȟtake*	*hécha*	*na'į́š*	*eyá*
saddle blanket	or	maybe	this	spurs*	such	or	also

takúšnišni	*ohíya-šna*	*ománi*	*kéye.*	*na*	*mázaska*	*khó.*	*ho*
all kinds of things	win-HAB	travel	QT	and	money*	also	well

chąkhé	*waná*	*khąsúkhute-pi*	*škhá*	*chąkhé*	*étkiya*	*yá-hį*	*na*
then	now	gamble*-IPS	QT	then	toward	go-PRG	and

í	*kéye*	*éyaš*	*lé*	*héhą́ni*	*lé*	*akícitaki,*	*lená*	*wawóyuspa*
arrive	QT	but	this	already	this	policeDEF	these	policeman*

ki,	*lená*	*tókhi*	*a-ná-wicha-slata-pi*	*éyaš*	*slolyé-šni*
DEF	these	somewhere	L-ST-3PL.PAT-sneak up-PL	but	know-NEG

cha	*ektá*	*í*	*na*	*waná*	*thimá*	*íyutaka*	*kéye,*	*lé*	*akícita*
so	there	go to	and	now	inside	sit down	QT	this	soldier

thiyóblecha	*hécha*	*cha.*	*thimá*	*khąsúkhute-pi*	*na*	*lé*
tent*	COP	QL	inside	gamble*-PL	and	this

phetížąžą ǧeǧéya	*yuhá-pi*	*hécha*	*cha,*	*thi-máhel-ya*
lantern*	have-PL	such	QL	house-inside-ADV

iyóšni-šniš-ya-kel	*ilé-ya*	*hą́*	*cha*	*thimá*	*iyáyį*	*na*
dim-RED-ADV-kind of	burn.VI-ADV	stand	so	inside	go	and

waná	*íyutaka*	*kéye.*	*cha*	*éyaš*	*tuwéni*	*ayúta-šni*	*waphóštą*
now	sit down	QT	so	but	nobody	look at-NEG	hat

a-ˀíyoȟpa	*i-kí-k-cu*	*cha*	*tuwéni*	*ayúta-šni*	*kéye*	*cha.*	*hechél*
L-down	ST-PSS-EI-take	so	nobody	look at-NEG	QT	QL	so

íyutakį	*nahą́ke*	*waná*	*khąsúkhute*	*na*	*ohíya*	*áya*	*kéye.*
sit down	and then	now	gamble*	and	win	PRC	QT

wahéhąn	*tuwá*	*thimá*	*hiyú*	*cha*	*ektá*	*é-tųwe-šni*
about that time	somebody	inside	come	so	to	L-look-NEG

phamágle	*yąkį́*	*nahą́ke*	*iníhąšni*	*khąsúkhute*	*yųkhą́*	*sí*
bow the head	sit	and then	nevertheless	gamble*	then	foot

ektá	*wąyą́ka*	*yųkhą́*	*lé*	*ehą́ni*	*hą́pa*	*eyá*	*iškáhu*	*hą́ska-ska*	*cha*
to	look	then	this	old time	shoe	LK	ankle	long-RED	QL

siphá	*ki*	*gmigmá-gma*	*cha*	*lé*	*wawóyuspa*	*ki*	*lená*	*ohą́-pi*
toe	DEF	round-RED	QL	this	policeman*	DEF	these	wear-PL

kéye cha. akícita ki lená hą́pa ki wichá-k'u-pi cha
IP QL police DEF these shoe DEF 3PL.PAT-give-IPS QL

hécha cha ohą́-pi na ųzóğe eyá tho-thó cha hé ų́-pi
such QL wear-PL and pants LK blue-RED QL that wear-PL

kéye. héchų s'e wąyą́ka chąkhé átaya nážį iyáyį na
QT that way* see then INT stand CEL and

ųgnáhelakha lé wawóyuspa ki é cha ité ki ogná aphį́
suddenly this policeman* DEF IP QL face DEF inside hit

na ka'ų́ka kéye chą́ "wawóyuspa cha hí-pe ló"
and knock down QT then policeman* QL come-PL ASS.M

eyį́ na héchena átaya lé phetížąžąye ki hé é cha
say and thus entirely this lamp* DEF this IP QL

ka-sní iȟpéya cha áta hená iyúha mázaska k'ų hená ayúštą-pi
INS-cold throw so INT these all money* DEF these let go-PL

na ka'ábekiya naphá-pi kéye. ata naphá-pi cha waphóštą
and in all directions flee-PL QT INT flee-PL so hat

glušlókį na lé mázaska k'ų hená iyúha okšú nahą́ke
POSS.pull off and this money* DEF those all load and then

khiną́phį na iyáyekiya kéye cha įšé íyohakab lé wawóyuspa
go outside and run away QT so just after this policeman*

ki lé kiktá íyutakį na o-wícha-le éyaš tuwénišni
DEF this get up sit up and ST-3PL.PAT-look for but nobody

kéye. chąkhé tuwénišni chąkhé héchena šųk'áką'iyé'ic'iyį na
QT then nobody then thus mount* and

khiglá kéye. yųkhą́ até-wa-ye ki é cha
go home QT then father-1SG.AG-have as DEF IP QL

šųk'ákąyąkį na itkób yá chąkhé "lé tókhiya lá hé?"
ride* and toward go then this where go.2SG.AG QS

eyá chąkhé "lé étkiya ománi blé k'ų" eyá kéye yųkhą́
say then this toward travel go.1SG.AG ASS say QT then

"wą́ léchiya khąsúkhute-pi škhá cha ektá wa-'í éyaš
IJ.M here gamble*-PL QT so there 1SG.AG-go to but

áta tókhaȟ'ą-pi k'ų" eyá kéye cha "wą́ átaya-š
entirely disappear-PL ASS say QT SO IJ.M INT-EMPH

slol-wá-ye-šni k'ų" eyá kéye, "ehą́ni-š mázaska ki
ST-1SG.AG-know-NEG ASS say QT before-EMPH money* DEF

hená iyúha icú-pi na naphá-pi éyaš ųmá tuwéni hé
those all take-IPS and flee-IPS but other nobody that

khąsúkhute ki wąžíni mázaska wąží-la kayéš yuhá-pi-šni" kéye.
gamble* DEF none money* one-LIM even have-PL-NEG QT

"iyúha wichá-khi. cha áta lé Silas wawóyuspa wą
all 3PL.PAT-rob so INT this Silas policeman* IDF.SG

áta-š šų́šųla naȟtáka-pi s'e aphį na ka-t'á
entirely-EMPH mule kick-PL like.AV hit and INS-unconscious

cha ka'ábekiya naphá-pi k'ų" eyá kéye. ho henákecha.
so in all directions flee-PL ASS say QT well that is all

Long ago, when my father [Silas Standing Bear] was a young man, he was pretty crazy. He went to all the places where people were gambling, one after the other. He traveled around gambling, and he always won. It was things like bridles, ropes, saddles, saddle blankets, spurs, or all kinds of other things that he won when he was traveling around. And money, too. One time rumor had it that there was gambling going on. So he got on his way and arrived there. But the [Indian] police [on the reservation], the cops, had already sneaked up on them [the gamblers]. But he didn't know that, so he went there. He sat down inside. It was an army tent. Inside people were gambling. They had a lantern inside which gave a dim light. He went inside and sat down. But nobody recognized him. He had pulled his hat down [over his face], so nobody recognized him. So he sat down and gambled and won all the time. Then somebody came in. He [my father] didn't look at him, he sat with his head bowed and kept on gambling all the same. Then he [my father] looked at his [the newcomer's] feet. They [his shoes] were old-time high-topped boots with round toes, the kind the policemen wore. The policemen were given such shoes to wear, and they wore blue pants. That was what he saw, so he got up quickly and all of a sudden hit the policeman in the face, knocking him down. He hollered: "The cops are here," and he put out the light, knocking it over. All of them [the gamblers] left their money behind and fled in all directions. When they were gone he pulled off his hat and stuffed in all the money. Then he went outside and ran away. Right after that the policeman sat up again, looking for them, but there was nobody. Since there was nobody, he got on his horse and went back. My father was sitting on his horse and moved in his direction. "Where are you going?" he [the policeman] asked. He [my father] replied: "I am just going this way." He added: "People said that there is gambling going on here, so I came here, but they have all disappeared." He continued: "Well, I have absolutely no idea. Someone has already taken all the money and gotten away. Not one of the other gamblers has even a single dollar. He has taken it all from them. Silas hit a policeman like a bunch of kicking mules and knocked him out, so they fled in all directions." That's it.

2.14. The Eagle Spirit

NEVA STANDING BEAR

Tape recorded November 16, 1994

Wallace Black Elk	*hé*	*thakóža*	*ki*	*hé*	*táku*	*wakhą́*	*wanáǧi*
Wallace Black Elk	that	grandchild	DEF	that	things	sacred	spirit

tháwa-pi	*ki*	*iyé-wicha-kici-ska*	*ki*	*thoká*
his-PL	DEF	ST-3PL-BEN-interpret	DEF	for the first time

héchų-kta	*cha*	*héhą*	*wąblí*	*wą*	*wąyą́ke*	*cha*	*hé*	*é*	*cha*
do that-FASS	so	then	eagle	IDF.SG	see	so	that	IP	QL

ogláke.	*chąkú*	*ogná*	*glá*	*yųkhą́*	*léchel*	*mniȟúha*	*sápa*	*cha*
POSS.tell	road	along	go home	then	so	cloth	black	QL

kaȟwóka-he	*sʔe*	*léchecha.*	*líla*	*iníhą*	*cha*	*éna*	*inážį*
flutter-PRG	like.AV	like this	INT	worry	so	right there	stop

na	*héktakiya*	*ųzíhekta*	*gnį́*	*na*	*apsíl*	*ektá*	*kaʔísakhibya*
and	backwards	back up	go back	and	jump	there	beside

khinážį	*na*	*glicú*	*na*	*chų́kaške*	*ki*	*iyáyį*	*nahą́ke*	*étkiya*
stop	and	get out	and	fence*	DEF	go	and then	toward

yá-hą	*kéye.*	*lé*	*wąblí*	*cha*	*tuwá*	*ó*	*cha*	*lé*	*ȟupáhu*	*ki*
go-PRG	QT	this	eagle	QL	someone	shoot	so	this	wing	DEF

kawéǧa	*cha*	*kįyą́*	*iyáyį-kteȟcį*	*éyaš*	*okíhi-šni.*	*yųkhą́*	*hé*
break.VT	so	fly	go-want very much	but	can-NEG	then	that

wąblí	*ki*	*hé*	*é*	*cha*	*héyá*	*kéye.*	*wąblí*	*gléška*	*cha*	*išnála*
eagle	DEF	that	IP	QL	say that	QT	eagle	spotted	QL	alone

chąkhé	*w-ó-ki-yakį*	*na*	*héyá*	*kéye*	*"lé*
then	NSP.PAT-ST-BEN-tell	and	say that	QT	this

wa-ní-kte-šni	*yeló"*	*eyá*	*kéye.*	*"ho*	*éyaš*	*echą́ni*
1SG.AG-live-FASS-NEG	ASS.M	say	QT	well	but	soon

iblámnį-kta	*cha*	*le-tą́*	*wíyaka*	*wąží*
go.1SG.AG-FASS	so	this-from	feather	IDF.SG

i-má-ya-cu	*na*	*ųmá*	*ki*	*lená*	*ya-ȟá-kte*
ST-1SG.PAT-2SG.AG-take	and	other	DEF	these	2SG.AG-bury-FASS

ló"	*eyá*	*kéye*	*na*	*"wíyaka*	*ki*	*lé*	*tóhąni*	*tuwéni*	*k'ú-šni*
ASS.M	say	QT	and	feather	DEF	this	never	nobody	give-NEG

yó"	*eyá*	*kéye,*	*"lé*	*ecéla*	*ų́*
IMP.SG.M	say	QT	this	only	using

w-íyo-ya-kihi-kte	*ló"*	*eyá*	*kéye.*	*eyá*	*cha*
NSP.PAT-ST-2SG.AG-accomplish-FASS	ASS.M	say	QT	say	so

hé	*wíyaka*	*ki*	*hé*	*icú*	*nahą́*	*manį́ta-kiya*	*áya-hį*	*na*
that	feather	DEF	that	take	and then	wilderness-to	take to-PRG	and

manį́n	*éȟpeya*	*kéye.*	*cha*	*tókhi*	*hé*
in the wilderness	leave behind	QT	so	where	that

manį́n	*wąblí*	*ki*	*hé*	*é*	*t'á*	*nachéce*	*cha.*	*he-tą́*
in the wilderness	eagle	DEF	that	IP	die	perhaps	QL	that-from

wíyaka ki hé óhį̨ni waphóštą él opázą ų́ cha hé
feather DEF that always hat on push into wear so that

wíyaka ki hé zį̨tkála ki he-tą́ icú kéye. ho cha
feather DEF that bird DEF that-from take QT well so

he-tą́ tohą́n ománi na'į́š ųgná héchel
that-from when travel or maybe so

iníkağa-pi na thimá wachékhiya-pi
perform sweatlodge ceremony-IPS and inside pray-IPS

chą́-šna hé zį̨tkála ki hená ókiya-pi cha ektá-šna hí-pi.
then-HAB that bird DEF those help.VT-PL so to-HAB come-PL

cha héchel ób lé wanáği w-óglaka cha táku ki
so so with this spirit NSP.PAT-POSS.tell so things DEF

hená slolyá cha hé ų́ wąblí ki lená wó'ilag-wicha-ye.
those know so that in order to eagle DEF these ST-3PL.PAT-use

ho míš eyá hená wąblí cha, míš anų́khasą eyá-pi cha
well I too those eagle QL I bald eagle* say-IPS QL

héchacha hená wó'ilag-wicha-wa-yį-kta škhé. hená tókhel
like that those ST-3PL.PAT-1SG.AG-use-FASS QT those how

wachį-wicha-wa-yį-kte ehą́tąhąš
ST-3PL.PAT-1SG.AG-depend on-FASS when

ó-ma-kiya-pi-kta kéyá-pi. ho cha hená héchel
ST-1SG.PAT-help.VT-PL-FASS say that-PL well so those so

wakhą́-yą zįtkála ki lená ų́-pi cha. tuwéni otúyachį
sacred-ADV bird DEF these exist-PL QL nobody for nothing

wichá-kte-šni. tuwéni otúyachį wóˀilag-wicha-ye-šni.
3PL.PAT-kill-NEG nobody for nothing ST-3PL.PAT-use-NEG

cha héchegla.
so that is all

My grandson Wallace Black Elk told me that he first started to interpret sacred messages from his spirits when he had an encounter with an eagle. He was on his way home. Then it seemed like a piece of black cloth was moving in the wind. He was alarmed, so he stopped right there and backed up. He stopped right there beside it, got out, jumped over the fence, and went near it. It was an eagle that someone had shot, breaking its wing. It was trying hard to fly away but couldn't. Then this eagle started talking. It was a spotted eagle that was all by itself. It talked to him. It said: "I won't survive that. I will pass away soon. Take a feather from me and bury the rest. And never give this feather to anyone. This is all you will need to be powerful." That way it spoke, so he pulled out the feather, took it [the bird] to the wilderness, and left it there. Somewhere there in the wilderness the eagle probably died. From then on he [my grandson] always wore the feather on his hat, the feather he had taken from the bird. From then on, whenever he was traveling around, or maybe when people were having a sweat, and were praying inside [the sweatlodge], those birds always came to him to assist him. Through them he talks to the spirits. He uses the eagles to obtain knowledge. I was told [by the spirits] that I would also use eagles, the ones called bald eagles [back then I didn't know that I would also do spiritual work some day]. I was told that they [the eagles] would help me whenever I'd need them. These birds live in a sacred way [because they exist on a spiritual plane as well]. Nobody kills them without a reason. Nobody uses them without a reason. That's all.

2.15. A Girl Turns into a Werewolf

NEVA STANDING BEAR

Tape recorded November 11, 1994

ehą́ni wi-má-chįcala kʼų héhą wikhóškalaka wą kichí
long ago ST-1SG.PAT-girl SYP then young woman IDF.SG with

wabláwa. cha ehą́ni thoká wa-ʼų́-yawa-pi
go to school*.1SG.AG so long ago first ST-1PL.AG-go to school*-PL

cha héhą hų́ȟ waníyetu óta-pi éyaš lé nakéš othókaheya
so then some year many-PL but this just now first time

wayáwa-pi cha. lé kindergarden ki lé é cha. cha
go to school*-PL QL this kindergarden DEF this IP QL so

wikhóškala ki lé tókhi wikcémna nų́m isą́m iyáye kʼéyaš
young woman DEF this about ten two beyond go but

nakéš héchiya o-wáyawa. cha héhą įšé miyé waníyetu
just now there L-go to school* so then just I year

ma-wíkcemna. yųkhą́ wikhóškalaka ki lé hél wayáwa
1SG.PAT-ten then young woman DEF this there go to school*

na hąkéya wayáwa-šni yųkhą́ oyáka-pi na khúža
and finally go to school*-NEG then tell-IPS LK sick

kéyá-pi cha. wiyóhiyąpata-kiya é-ya-ya-pi kéyá-pi,
say that-IPS QL east*-to L-go-CAU-PL say that-IPS

héchiya okhúže thípi wą ektá. asní-yą-pi-kta cha
there hospital* IDF.SG to recover-CAU-IPS-FASS so

é-ya-ya-pi kéye. ho yųkhą́ líla théhą glí-šni
L-go-CAU-IPS QT well then INT for a long time come home-NEG

éyaš oyáka-pi na wašícu wakhą́ ki hená glicú-ya-pi
but tell-IPS LK white doctor* DEF these start going home-CAU-PL

glicú-ya-pi okíhi-pi-šni kéyá-pi. líla khúža cha.
start going home-CAU-PL can-PL-NEG say that-IPS INT sick QL

yųkhą́ hų́-ku na at-kúku ki eyášna ektá wąyą́g
then mother-3POR and father-3POR DEF sometimes there see

í-pi yųkhą́ otóhą oyáka-pi na wikhóškalaka ki hé tohą́n
go-PL then for a while tell-IPS LK young woman DEF that when

thąkáyąkį-kta chą́na-šna nihįciya kéye cha wašícu wakhą́
have the menses*-FASS then-HAB afraid QT so white doctor*

ki eyášna o-wícha-ki-yakį na tohą́n héchecha-kta chą́-šna
DEF always ST-3PL-BEN-tell LK when afflicted with-FASS then-HAB

khúžį na tak-tókhų-kte ki slol-kí-ye-šni. líla waš'áka áya
sick and what-do-FASS LK ST-PSS-know-NEG INT strong PRC

kéye cha tohą́n héchecha-kte hą́tąhąš ikhą́yą é-gnaka-pi
QT so when afflicted with-FASS when restrain L-place-IPS

chį́ kéye chąkhé eyášna áta thiyópa ki hená khó
want QT then always entirely door DEF these also

a-'ónathaka-pi chą́-šna átaya tókhi gnáškįyą nachéce.
L-lock up-IPS then-HAB entirely maybe insane maybe

gnaškį́yį na-šna átaya owákąyąke na'į́š wágleyutapi hená
insane and-HAB entirely chair* or table* those

ékayeš khó áta ka-wéȟ-weǧa. chąkhé hąkéya máza
even also entirely ST-RED-break up then finally iron

ikhą́yą gnáka-pi kéye. héchena hąkéya líla áya cha
restrain place-IPS QT thus finally INT progress.VI LK

abléza-pi yųkhą́ lé há ki hįšmá áya kéyá-pi. lé
notice-IPS then this skin DEF furry* PRC say that-IPS this

ithų́kala hį́ ki hécha s'e áya chąkhé a-wą́yąg khuwá-pi
mouse fur DEF such like.AV PRC then L-see chase-IPS

yųkhą́ hąkéya iyá okíhi-šni. cha líla wókhokiphe-ka kéyá-pi.
then finally speak can-NEG so INT fear.N-kind of say that-PL

tohą́n wí wąží ihų́ni chą́-šna lé thąkáyąkį-kte
when month one arrive then-HAB this have the menses*-FASS

wahéhą-šna héchecha. ho cha wahéhą-šna
about that time-HAB afflicted with well so about that time-HAB

gnáka-pi éyaš hąkéya líla áya kéye na óhįniyakašká
place-IPS but finally INT progress.VI QT and always tie

héchecha cha. ho cha lé wašícu wakhą́ ki lé
afflicted with QL well so this white doctor* DEF this

thųkášilayapi ektá hená iyáya-pi nahą́ wó'okiye lá-pi
government* to those go-IPS and then help.N ask for-PL

nahą́ ųgná hų́-ku na at-kúku kihą iyówįyą-pi
and then maybe mother-3POR and father-3POR DEF agree-PL

hą́tąhąš wį́yą ki lé phežúta k'ú-pi nahą́
if woman DEF this medicine* give-IPS and then

ištį́me-khiya-pi-kta kéyá-pi. ištį́me ki héchena t'į́-kta cha
sleep-CAU-IPS-FASS say that-PL sleep SYP that way die-FASS LK

kéyá-pi. hų́-ku na at-kúku ki o-wícha-ki-yaka-pi
say that-PL mother-3POR and father-3POR DEF ST-3PL-BEN-tell-IPS

cha takómni tókhel okíhi-pi-šni cha wąglág í-pi khéš
so at all costs somehow can-PL-NEG so POSS.see go-PL but

hąkéya iyé-wicha-ki-ye-šni. cha hąkéya átaya hįšmá
finally ST-3PL.PAT-PSS-recognize-NEG so finally entirely furry*

áya. cha ayúštą-pi. ayúštą-pi na chažé o'ígwa-pi kéye cha
PRC so finish-IPS finish-IPS and sign*-IPS QT so

wikhóškalaka hé ištį́me-khiya-pi na héchena t'á škhé. kéyá
young woman that sleep-CAU-IPS and that way die QT say that

oyáka-pi. cha hé tókhi wikhóškalaka kihą ehą́ni táku
tell-IPS so that maybe young woman DEF ancient something

wicháša eyá chąkú ogná enágna omani-pi na henä́
man IDF.PL road along here and there travel-PL and those

šųgmáyetu-pi škhé cha hécha nachéce, ųgnáhelakha
wolf-PL QT QL such perhaps suddenly

hécha-hįgla kéyá oyáka-pi. ho henákecha.
such-suddenly say that tell-IPS well enough

Long ago, when I was a girl, I went to school with a certain young woman. Long ago, when we [Indians] started to go to school, some [kids] were pretty old. They were just now beginning to go to school. It was the beginners' class. This young woman was about twenty years old, or maybe past that, but she had just started to go to school. I was ten years old. This young woman went to school there, and one day she didn't show up any more. People reported that she was ill. It was said that she had been moved to the east, into a hospital. She was sent there for treatment. But people also reported that she didn't come home for a long time, and that the white doctors could not let her go home. She was very sick. Her parents sometimes went there to see her. For a while people reported that the young woman was scared when she got her period. The white doctors always told them [the parents] that when she was going to get it she was very sick and didn't know what she was doing. She became very strong, so when she was going to get it she wanted to be tied up. They always locked up the doors, too, since chances were that she went berserk. Whenever she went insane she even broke chairs or tables into pieces. Finally, they put chains on her. In the end they noticed that the disease was progressing rapidly. Her skin became furry. It became like mouse fur. They watched over her, and finally she couldn't speak any more. It was very scary, they said. Whenever one month had passed and she was about to have her period she was like that. During that time, she was confined, but in the end it became even worse, and she was always like that. The white doctors went to see the authorities and asked for help. They [the government officials] said that if her parents agreed they would give the woman medicine and put her to sleep. She'd die when she'd be sleeping. They talked to her parents. They could not do that by any means. They went to see her, but finally she did not recognize them anymore. In the end, she became furry all over. So they put an end to it. They put an end to it and signed the papers. They put the young woman to sleep; that way she died. This is what people reported. People say that the young woman might have been something like those ancient beings who travel on the road here and there, like those werewolves. People say that she suddenly became like that. That's enough.

Note: Werewolves were not part of the old-time Lakota folklore.

2.16. Spiritual Healing

NEVA STANDING BEAR

Tape recorded November 16, 1994

lél	*héktakiya*	*tókhi*	*okó*	*tópa*	*séce*	*isą́mya*	*hehą́n*	*wį́yą*
here	backwards	about	week	four	maybe	further	then	woman

wą	*kichí*	*iní-ˀų-kağa-pi*	*éyaš*	*lé*
IDF.SG	with	ST-1PL.AG-perform sweatlodge ceremony-PL	but	this

ská	*wį́yą*	*hécha*	*cha*	*kichí*
white	woman	COP	QL	with

iní-ˀų-kağa-pi	*yųkhą́*	*héhą*	*lé*
ST-1PL.AG-perform sweatlodge ceremony-PL	then	then	this

gliną́phį	*na*	*hé*	*“átaya*	*wanáği*	*nitháwa*	*ki*	*hená*	*ahą́nažį*
go outside	and	that	INT	spirit	your	DEF	those	bother

ma-khúwa-pi	*cha*	*átaya*	*iȟéyab*	*iblábla*	*o-wá-kihi-šni*
1SG.PAT-chase-PL	so	INT	away	go.1SG.AG	ST-1SG.AG-can-NEG

šką-šką́-šni	*mąké*	*kˀų”*	*eyá*	*cha.*	*“o::*	*į́šé*	*hená*
move-RED-NEG	sit.1SG.AG	ASS	say	QL	oh	just	those

ų́thų-ni-yą-pi-kte-šni	*kštó”*	*ephé,*	*“ųgná*
injured-2SG.PAT-CAU-PL-FASS-NEG	ASS.F	say.1SG.AG	maybe

to-ní-kheca	*héci*	*hé*	*ų́*	*héchų-pi*	*kˀų.”*	*ho*
ST-2SG.PAT-not alright	SUB	that	because of	do that-PL	ASS	well

yųkhą́ he-tą́ tókhi okó wą́žíca yųkhą́ hįgná-ku ki
then that-from about week one then husband-3POR DEF

oyákį na hé "mi-thá-wicu ki lé wašícu wakhą́ wą
tell LK that 1SG.POR-ALP-wife DEF this white doctor* IDF.SG

eyášna wąyą́kį nahą́ke o-kí-yakį na wašícu wakhą́ wą́ží
sometimes see and then ST-BEN-tell LK white doctor* IDF.SG

ektá naʔį́š okhúže thípi wą́ží ektá yį́ na wąyą́g-ʔicʔi-chiye-ši,
to or hospital* IDF.SG to go and see-3RFL-CAU-ask

thezí mahél táku wą ų́ cha." ho yųkhą́ hąkéya
stomach inside something IDF.SG be QL well then finally

líla khúža áya chąkhé okhúže thípi ektá aʔí-pi yųkhą́ thezí
INT sick PRC then hospital* to take to-IPS then stomach

ektá waglúla wą ų́ kéyá-pi. chąkhé kaʔísakhibya líla
in tapeworm IDF.SG be say that-IPS then besides INT

óta ihé-wicha-ya kéye, nakų́. yųkhą́ héchetu waná líla
many ST-3PL.PAT-discharge QT also then so now INT

khúža kéye. glí na ihą́bla yųkhą́ héyá kéye,
sick QT come home and dream then say that QT

wichá-ho wą líla hó hukhúchiyela cha héyá kéye
human-voice IDF.SG INT voice low QL say that QT

"ų-ní-kte-pi-kte lő" eyá kéye chąkhé
1PL.AG-2SG.PAT-kill-PL-FASS ASS.M say QT then

thąsák tˀe-yá-pi *cha* *léchiya* *ma-kí-yuȟla-pi*
scared to death*-CAU-IPS so here 1SG-BEN-give a phone call*-PL

cha *o-wá-ki-yakį* *na* *"hé* *táku* *cha* *thezí* *mahél* *ní*
QL ST-1SG.AG-BEN-tell LK that thing QL stomach inside live

ų́ *héci* *hé* *é* *cha* *waná* *tˀį́-kta* *cha* *hé* *ų́*
CNT SUB that IP QL now die-FASS so that because of

ni-kų́za-he *kštó"* *ephé* *cha.* *"šˀag-yáhą* *wachékhiyį*
2SG.PAT-curse-PRG ASS.F say.1SG.AG QL strong-ADV pray

yé *na* *ni-tˀį́-kta* *kéchį-šni* *yé"* *ephé.*
IMP.SG.F and 2SG.PAT-die-FASS think that-NEG IMP.SG.F say.1SG.AG

éšˀéš *a-ní-cisni-kta* *kéyá* *yé,* *tókša*
just ST-2SG.PAT-recover-FASS say that IMP.SG.F soon

echél i-ní-yayį-kte *kštó"* *ephé.* *na* *hįgná-ku* *ki*
ST-2SG.PAT-get well-FASS ASS.F say.1SG.AG and husband-3POR DEF

wa-khį́ *na* *"thi-y-ó-w-azilyį* *nahą́* *ikcéya*
1SG.AG-say to LK house-EI-L-NSP.PAT-burn incense and then ordinary

lé *mní* *ki* *lécha* *cha* *icú* *nahą́* *yatkį́-kte* *hą́tąhą*
this water DEF such QL take and then drink-FASS when

azíl-ya-thų *nahą́* *a-wáchekhiyį* *na* *kˀú* *wé,*
ST-2SG.AG-burn incense and then L-pray and give IMP.SG.F

tókša *echél iyáyį-kte* *kštó"* *ephé* *yųkhą́* *héchų-kta* *kéyé.*
soon get well-FASS ASS.F say.1SG.AG then do that-FASS say that

mní a-wáchekhiyį na azílyį nahą́ke k'ú yųkhą́ léchel
water L-pray and burn incense and then give then so

líla áta thezí ki yazą́ na átaya pehą́-hą kéye chąkhé
INT INT stomach DEF hurt and INT curled up-RED QT then

héktakiya okhúže thípi ektá a'í-pi yųkhą́ įthó él
backwards hospital* to take to-IPS then just there

aphé-khiya-pi cha hécheya líla khúže éyaš aphé ȟpáya-hą
wait-CAU-IPS so really INT sick but wait lie-PRG

yųkhą́ thąkáye-kínicha chąkhé lé oyų́ke él-šna o'íheye
then ease oneself*-anxious then this bed in-HAB bed pan

wą wichá-k'u-pi cha hé é cha ų́-kta cha k'ú-pi yųkhą́
LK IPS-give-IPS QL that IP QL use-FASS QL give-IPS then

lé waglúla wą hé é cha áta ihéya kéye na
this tapeworm IDF.SG that IP QL entirely discharge QT and

cik-cík'ala khó átaya ihé-wicha-ya kéye.
RED-small also entirely ST-3PL.PAT-discharge QT

ihé-wicha-yį nahą́ke al-'áta lé thezí yazą́
ST-3PL.PAT-discharge and then RED-INT this stomach hurt

na-thíp-thipe k'ų hé akísni kéye. chąkhé wašícu wakhą́ ki
ST-RED-cramp SYP that recover QT then white doctor* DEF

thimá hiyú nahą́ke "ehą́ni
inside come and then for a long time

aphí-ˀų-ni-yą-pi-šni, tókheškhe echánų-welakha
ST-1PL.AG-2SG.PAT-treat*-PL-NEG how do.2SG.AG-indeed

waglúla ki ihé-ya-ye kˀų" eyá kéye. chąkhé "hą́,
tapeworm DEF ST-2SG.AG-pass.VT ASS say QT then yes

įchį́ líla théhą a-wá-phe cha hé ų́
because INT for a long time ST-1SG.AG-wait so that because of

hąkéya thezí ma-yázą" cha hé "éyaš lé phežúta
finally stomach 1SG.PAT-hurt so that but this medicine*

chóla ihé-ya-ya o-yá-kihi-šni škhá
without ST-2SG.AG-discharge ST-2SG.AG-can-NEG but

héchanų kˀų́" eyá kéye. cha glicú-ya-pi cha
do that.2SG.AG ASS say QT so come home-CAU-IPS so

thi-yáta glí na lé táku phąphą́la hená é cha
home-to go home and this things soft those IP QL

yul-wá-ši. héchel lé thezí mahél táku ų́ ki átaya
eat-1SG.AG-ask so this stomach inside things be DEF entirely

ihé-ki-ya cha. hé ų́ tákuni thezí mahél ų́
ST-PSS-pass.VT QL that because of nothing stomach inside be

okíhi-šni kéye. ho cha héchų-wa-ši yųkhą́ áta
can-NEG QT well so do that-1SG.AG-ask then INT

ųgnáhelakha akhé masˀá-ma-ki-pha-pi. tókhi
suddenly again ST-1SG-BEN-give a phone call*-PL about

hékta okó kˀų héhą masˀá-ma-ki-pha-pi nahą́ke
back.AV week SYP then ST-1SG-BEN-give a phone call*-PL and then

akhé eché-ȟci w-ákhipha cha átaya makhú khó yazą́ cha
again SO-INT NSP.PAT-encounter so INT chest also hurt so

hįgná-ku ki wa-khį́ na “héktakiya okhúže thípi ektá
husband-3POR DEF 1SG.AG-say to and backwards hospital* to

áya yé, ųgná į́yą wąží thezí mahél ų́ séce
take to IMP.SG.F maybe stone IDF.SG stomach inside be maybe

kštó” ephé yųkhą́ léchel aʾí-pi cha héche-ȟci aphé
ASS.F say.1SG.AG then so take to-IPS so SO-INT wait

ȟpáye yųkhą́ iyéchįka į́yą ki hé ihéya kéye. į́yą ki
lie then by herself stone DEF that discharge QT stone DEF

hé ihéya cha kaʾéchel iyáyį na lehą́n waná akísni.
that discharge so get well by herself and now now recover

akísni éyaš eháke thezí ki nahą́ȟci mahél phąphą́la cha.
recover but still stomach DEF still inside tender QL

otóhąyą hokšícala tha-wóyute ecéla yúta-hį-kta
for a while baby ALP-food only eat-PRG-FASS

képhé. tókša kaʾéchel iyáye kihą hehą́n okáblaya
say that.1SG.AG soon get well by herself when then unhampered

zaní-ya ų́-kta képhá o-wá-ki-yaka cha.
healthy-ADV exist-FASS say that.1SG.AG ST-1SG.AG-BEN-tell QL

cha lé a-w-íyuškį-laȟcake. héchegla.
so this L-NSP.PAT-happy-INT that is all

About four weeks ago, maybe more, we had a sweat with a woman. She was one of the white women that have sweats with us. After a while she went outside [the sweatlodge] and said: "Your spirits [which are always around in the sweatlodge] are haunting me. Since I cannot leave, I sit here motionlessly." [Leaving the sweatlodge before the ceremony is over activates bad spirits.] I said: "Oh, they won't harm you. Maybe they do that because there is something wrong with you." Then, about one week later, her husband told us this story: "Every now and then my wife goes to see a white doctor. He examined her and told her to go to some other white doctor or into a hospital for a check-up because there is something in her stomach." She had finally become very sick. When she was brought to the hospital she was told that there was a tapeworm in her stomach. In addition to [the big one] she passed a whole lot of them [small ones]. At that time she was very sick. When she got back home she had a dream. She said that there was a human voice, a very low voice, which said: "We will kill you." She was scared to death, so they [she and her husband] called me over here. I told her: "Whatever the thing living in your stomach may be, it is going to die now [because of the medical treatment]. Therefore, it is cursing you. Pray hard and don't think you're going to die. Just say that you will recover; soon you'll be alright." And I told her husband: "Burn incense in the house. Take ordinary water, and when she wants to drink it, smudge it, pray over it, and then give it to her. Soon she'll be alright." He said that he would do that. He prayed over the water, smudged it, and gave it to her. Then her stomach started hurting very much. She was all curled up [in pain] when she was brought back to the hospital. But they just had her wait there. Even though she was really very sick, she was lying there waiting. She wanted to use the bathroom. She was supposed to use one of those bed pans that people are usually given in bed. She passed all of the tapeworm. She also passed all the small ones. She passed them, and after having a series of very painful stomach cramps, she recovered. Then the white doctor came in and said: "We didn't treat you for quite a while, it is quite incredible that you managed to pass the tapeworm." She replied: "Yes, because I've waited for so long my stomach finally revolted." He said: "But you shouldn't have been able to pass it without medicine; but that's what you did." They let her go home, so she went home. I told her to eat soft things. That way she passed all the things that were in her stomach. Therefore [because soft food does not remain in the stomach] nothing could be in her stomach. I told her to do that. All of a sudden they called me again, last week or so. They called me, and the same thing was happening to her again. Now her chest also hurt. So I said to her husband: "Take her back to the hospital. Maybe there is a stone in her stomach." So they took her there. Just like before, she was lying there waiting. Then she passed the stone all by herself. She passed the stone and got well all by herself. Now she has recovered. She has recovered, but [the lining inside] her stomach is still tender [because the tapeworm takes part of the skin with it when it is being discharged]. I said that she should eat baby food only for a while. I told her that soon, after she would have recovered all by herself, she would live without trouble and be healthy. She was very happy about that. That's all.

2.17. The Hole in the Eardrum

NEVA STANDING BEAR

Tape recorded November 30, 1994

wí nų́pa kʼų héhą thakóža-la wą líla khúže. isą́m
month two SYP then grandchild-DIM IDF.SG INT sick beyond

thakóža hécha cha. tohą́n okíhilaka khúža cha okhúže thípi
grandchild COP QL as much as can be* sick so hospital*

ektá aʼí-pi kéye yųkhą́ lél nų́ǧe opháya yazą́ na áta
to take to-1PS QT then here ear canal hurt and INT

tʼeblézešni chąkhé wašícu wakhą́ ki hé eyá kéye "lé nų́ǧe
frantic then white doctor* DEF that say QT this ear

mahél oȟlóka wą" eyá kéye cha, "éyaš aphí-ʼų-yą-pi
inside hole ASS say QT QL but ST-1PL.AG-treat*-PL

ųk-ókihi-pi-šni kʼų, ųgná aphí-ʼų-yą-pi kihą naȟʼų́
1PL.AG-can-PL-NEG ASS maybe ST-1PL.AG-treat*-PL if hear

okíhi-kte-šni ho he-tą́" eyá kéye chąkhé thakóža ki
can-FASS-NEG well that-from say QT then grandchild DEF

nihį́ciyį na lé isą́m thakóža-la ki ahí-pi. ahí-pi
afraid and this beyond grandchild-DIM DEF bring-PL bring-PL

na aphíye-ma-ši-pi cha miyé tákuni wakhą́ wa-ȟʼą́
and treat*-1SG.PAT-ask-PL so I nothing miraculous 1SG.AG-act

o-wá-kihi-šni *į̇šé* *Thųkášila* *hená* *echų́.* *yųkhą́* *cha* *lél*
ST-1SG.AG-can-NEG just God* those do then so here

ahí-pi *cha* *chąlí* *o-wá-pağ̌i* *na* *lé* *waché-wa-khiyį*
bring-PL so tobacco ST-1SG.AG-fill a pipe and this ST-1SG.AG-pray

nahą́ *chąnų́pa* *cha* *iblátą* *nahą́ke* *thakóža*
and then pipe so light up.1SG.AG and then grandchild

isą́m *thakóža* *ki* *i-wá-cu* *na* *nų́ğe* *ektá* *átaya*
beyond grandchild DEF ST-1SG.AG-take and ear to INT

šóta *o-bláblu* *na* *"ho* *tókša* *thakóža*
smoke L-blow.1SG.AG and well soon grandchild

a-ní-cisni-kte *kštó.* *lená* *léchų-pi* *chą́-šna* *hená*
ST-2SG.AG-recover-FASS ASS.F these do this-IPS then-HAB those

ų́ *akísni-pi"* *cha* *ephé.* *ho* *cha* *waná*
because of recover-IPS QL say.1SG.AG well so now

lechála-kel *tohą́n* *hų́-ku* *ki* *o-má-ki-yakį* *na*
recently-kind of when mother-3POR DEF ST-1SG-BEN-tell LK

mi-thákoža *ki* *isą́m* *thakóžakpaku* *ki* *áta* *héktakiya*
1SG.POR-grandchild DEF beyond grandchild DEF INT backwards

wašícu wakhą́ *ektá* *a'í* *yųkhą́* *lé* *nų́ğe* *ohlóka* *kéyá-pi* *k'ų*
white doctor* to take to then this ear hole say that-IPS DEF

hé *na-'ókhiyuthį* *na* *átaya* *tókheca-šni* *cha* *tókheškhe*
that INS-heal and INT not alright-NEG so how

héchamų	*héci*	*i-má-yųğa-pi*	*k'ų*	*cha*	*"įchį*
do that.1SG.AG	SUB	ST-1SG.PAT-ask-IPS	SYP	QL	because

waché-ya-khiya-pi	*ų́*	*hená*	*héchecha*	*k'ų"*	*ephé.*	*cha*
ST-2AG-pray-PL	because of	those	such	ASS	say.1SG.AG	so

é-'e	*lehą́n*	*tókheca-šni-yą*	*o-'įyąka-he.*	*cha*	*ehą́ni*
IP-RED	now	not alright-NEG-ADV	L-run-PRG	so	long ago

ókowąžila	*khátį*	*nahą́*	*khuš-yáhą*	*ų́*	*yųkhą́*	*líla*	*lehą́n*
all the time	have a fever	and then	sick-ADV	CNT	then	INT	now

áta	*tókheca-la-šni*	*cha*	*khó-š*	*waná*	*iyį́*	*na*
INT	not alright-DIM-NEG	so	also-EMPH	now	speak	and

o-'įyąka-he.	*ho.*
L-run-PRG	well

Two months ago one of my grandchildren was very sick. She is one of my great-grandchildren. She felt horribly sick, so she was brought to the hospital. She had an ear infection, and she was crazy from pain. The white doctor said: "She has a hole in her eardrum. But we cannot doctor her. If we treat her, maybe she won't be able to hear any more afterwards." My granddaughter [the girl's mother] was scared. They brought my great-granddaughter [to me]. They brought her and asked me to doctor her. I myself cannot do miracles, God does that. When they had brought her I filled a pipe with tobacco and prayed. I lit the pipe. Then I picked up my great-granddaughter. I blew the smoke into her ear and said: "Grandchild, soon you will be alright. Whenever people do that, they get well from it." Only recently her mother told me that she had taken my great-grandchild back to the white doctor. The hole in the eardrum they [the medical staff] had talked about had healed, and she [the girl] is doing just fine. When I was asked how I had accomplished that I said: "When you pray it will happen that way." Now she [the girl] is running around, doing fine. In the past, she had had fever all the time, and had always been sickly. Now she is doing just fine. She also talks [she was too young for that before], and she is running around. That's the way it is.

2.18. Denver International Airport

NEVA STANDING BEAR

Tape recorded November 30, 1994

tókhi	*lé*	*waníyetu*	*tópa*	*sece*	*cha*	*héhą́ni*	*lé*
about	this	year	four	maybe	QL	at that time	this

kįyékhiyapi oʾínažį	*hécha*	*cha*	*hé*	*líla*	*thą́ka*	*káǧa-pi*	*cha*
airport*	such	QL	that	INT	big	make-IPS	so

héchiya	*lé*	*Lakhóta*	*ki*	*ehą́ni*	*hená*	*tuktéktel*
there	this	Indian	DEF	long ago	those	in this area

wichá-ȟa-pi	*škhé*	*cha*	*hená*	*wichá-kʾa-pi*	*na*	*héhą́ni*
3PL.PAT-bury-PL	QT	so	those	3PL.PAT-dig-IPS	and	at that time

yu-ȟéyab	*i-wícha-cu-pi*	*hą́tąhąš*	*ecéla*	*hé*	*thi-káǧa-pi*
INS-away	ST-3PL.PAT-take-IPS	if	only	that	house-make-IPS

okíhi-pi	*kéyá-pi*	*naʾį́š*	*lé*	*oʾį́yąke*	*cha.*	*ho*	*cha*	*yųkhą́*
can-IPS	say that-IPS	and	this	runway	QL	well	so	then

héchiya	*wąží*	*iyéya-pi*	*cha*	*kʾá-pi*	*na*	*yu-ȟéyab*	*icú-pi*
there	one	find-IPS	so	dig-IPS	and	INS-away	take-IPS

kéyá-pi.	*cha*	*tuktéktel*	*hiyéye*	*séce*	*éyaš*	*tókhi*
say that-IPS	so	here and there	lie about	maybe	but	maybe

a-náȟma-pi	*naʾį́š*	*tóktu nachéce.*	*ho*	*cha*	*hé*	*é*	*cha*	*waná*
L-hide-IPS	and	who knows*	well	so	that	IP	QL	now

yuštą́-pi na yuǧą́-pi-kta cha ektá wachékhiye-ma-ši-pi

finish-IPS and open.VT-IPS-FASS so there pray-1SG.PAT-ask-IPS

cha ektá wa-ʔí-šni hą́ni iblámnį na ká lé

so there 1SG.AG-go to-NEG before go.1SG.AG and over there this

wašícu eyá lé táku hohú kʔá-pi naʔį́š táku ehą́ni

white man IDF.PL this things bone dig-PL or things long ago

makhá mahél hiyéye ki iyé olé-pi na hé icú-pi na

earth inside lie about DEF they look for-PL and that take-PL and

hená ų́ táku slolyá-pi cha hená héchų-pi. yųkhą́ ektá

those using things know-PL QL those do that-PL then there

wichá-wa-ʔi na i-wícha-mųǧe. "lé

3PL.PAT-1SG.AG-go to and ST-3PL.PAT-ask.1SG.AG this

kįyékhiyapi oʔínažį wą káǧa-pi ki lél tákuni wichá-thą

airport* LK make-PL DEF here nothing human-body

yąké-šni hé?" ephé-ʔ. "wichá-thą yąké hą́tąhąš hená

sit-NEG QS say.1SG.AG-ASS human-body sit if those

thokéya yu-ȟéyab i-wícha-cu-pi na hé yuǧą́-pi ki

first INS-away ST-3PL.PAT-take-PL and that open.VT-PL DEF

wašté kʔų" ephé. yųkhą́ "hiyá, tákunišni kʔų, átaya hená

good ASS say.1SG.AG then no nothing ASS entirely those

ųk-óle-pi éyaš tákunišni kʔų. cha túwa hé hohú

1PL.AG-look for-PL but nothing ASS so someone that bone

eyá IDF.PL *icú* take *na* and *chą-ká'ichąyą* tree-leaning against *é-gle* L-put *cha* so *hená* those *é* IP *cha* QL *lé* this

chų́kaške fence post* *ki* DEF *aglágla* along *é-gle* L-put *k'éyaš* but *hená* those *wicháša* man *hohú-šni* bone-NEG

kéyá-pi say that-IPS *k'ų,* ASS *hená* those *wamákhašką* animal* *kéyá-pi."* say that-IPS *na* and *hél* there *tuktél* where

táku things *wichóthi* camp.N *k'á-pi* dig-PL *cha* QL *hé* that *átaya-š* entirely-EMPH *makhá* earth *ki* DEF *sápa* black

cha LK *iyéya-pi* find-PL *kéye.* QT *ho* well *yųkhą́* then *"hená* those *į́š* it *ehą́ni* long ago *wašícu* white man

o'éthi village *k'ų"* ASS *kéyá-pi,* say that-PL *"cha* so *tókha-šni* matter.VI-NEG *k'ų"* ASS *eyá-pi* say-PL *cha.* QL

"ohą́," okay *ephé,* say.1SG.AG *"lé* this *é* IP *cha* QL *hé* that *yu-wákhą-ma-ši-pi* INS-sacred-1SG.PAT-ask-IPS

éyaš but *Lakhóta* Indian *kihą* DEF *lená* these *tóhąni* never *mázaska* money* *slolyá-pi-šni* know-PL-NEG *na* and *lé* this

o'ínažį parking area *ki* DEF *lé* this *líla* INT *mázaska* money* *óta* much *na* and *líla* INT *wicháša* man *žicá* rich

hená those *ų́* using *ománi-pi-kta* travel-PL-FASS *cha* so *hé* that *blu-wákhą* INS.1SG.AG-sacred *hą́tąhąš* if

takún-ȟci something-INT *Lakhóta* Indian *ki* DEF *héktakiya* back.AV *wichá-kicu-pi* 3PL.PAT-give back-IPS

ki	*wašté*	*kˀų”*	*ephé.*	*héchų-pi-šni*	*hą́tąhąš*	*takómni*
DEF	good	ASS	say.1SG.AG	do that-IPS-NEG	if	at all costs

hená	*khušéya*	*ų́-pi-kta*	*cha*	*tóhąni*	*echél*	*káǧa-pi*
those	in the way	be-PL-FASS	so	never	right	make-PL

okíhi-pi-kte-šni.	*tóhąni*	*yuštą́-pi-kte-šni”*	*eyá*
can-PL-FASS-NEG	never	finish-PL-FASS-NEG	say

o-wícha-wa-ki-yake.	*cha*	*“hél*	*tákuni*	*ų́-šni*	*škhá*
ST-3PL-1SG.AG-BEN-tell	so	there	nothing	be-NEG	but

héyá-hą-pi	*kˀų”*	*eyá,*	*“hená*	*takómni*	*tókša*
say that-PRG-PL	ASS	say	those	anyway	later

slol-ˀų́-yą-pi-kte	*kˀų”*	*ephé,*	*“héchel*	*hél*	*wanáǧi*
ST-1PL.AG-know-PL-FASS	ASS	say.1SG.AG	so	there	spirit

ų́-pi	*hą́tąhąš”*	*eyá*	*o-wícha-wa-ki-yake.*	*cha*	*waché-wa-khiye*
be-PL	if	say	ST-3PL-1SG.AG-BEN-tell	so	ST-1SG.AG-pray

éyaš	*“į̆šé*	*hená*	*lé*	*yuǧą́-pi*	*hą́tąhąš*	*hél*	*oyáte*	*kihą*	*tąyą́*
but	just	those	this	open.VT-IPS	if	there	people	DEF	well

hí-pi	*na*	*tąyą́*	*khiglá-pi-kta*	*cha*	*ų́*	*waché-wa-khiyį-kte*
come-PL	and	well	go home-PL-FASS	QL	for	ST-1SG.AG-pray-FASS

kˀų”	*ephé.*	*“tóhąni*	*thípi*	*ki*	*na*	*hé*	*kįyékhiyapi*	*oˀįyąke*
ASS	say.1SG.AG	never	house	DEF	and	that	airplane*	runway

hógna	*hená*	*a-wáche-wa-khiya*	*o-wá-kihi-šni*	*kˀų”*
that way*	those	L-ST-1SG.AG-pray	ST-1SG.AG-can-NEG	ASS

ephé, "įšé henáoyáte ki hél hí-pi na etą́
say.1SG.AG just those people DEF there come-PL and from there

kįyą́ yá-pi-kta héci héchel waché-wa-khiyį-kte k'ų" eyá
fly go-PL-FASS SUB so ST-1SG.AG-pray-FASS ASS say

o-wícha-wa-ki-yake. ho cha héchi wachékhiye wa-'í
ST-3PL-1SG.AG-BEN-tell well so there pray 1SG.AG-go to

cha héhą héchų s'e waché-wa-khiyį na tohą́n hé yuğą́-pi
so then that way* ST-1SG.AG-pray and when that open.VT-PL

hą́tąhąš henáoyáte ki ų́ tákuni tókha-šni kįyą́-pi-kta
when those people DEF for nothing happen-NEG fly-PL-FASS

wochékhiye ephé. ho yųkhą́ lehą́n yuštą́-pi éyaš
prayer say.1SG.AG well then now finish-IPS but

táku ipáyeȟ-ya įyąkį na henáwaná áta hél
something wrong-ADV run and those now INT there

įyą okástakapi cha henáátaya na-šlé-šlecį na wanáği ki
concrete* QL those INT ST-RED-cracked and spirit DEF

šicá-yela šką́-pi kéyá-pi kéye cha héchiya lé Šahíyela
bad-ADV act-PL say that-IPS QT so there this Cheyenne

oyáte nahą́ Phaláni na'įš héchekche héchiya hóchoka
people and then Pawnee or this and that there ceremony

yuhá-pi kéyá-pi hé oyáka-pi. cha henálé cha ektá
have-PL say that-IPS that tell-IPS so those this QL there

mnį́ na slol-wá-yį-kta képhé lená táku
go.1SG.AG and ST-1SG.AG-know-FASS say that.1SG.AG these what

ų́ cha héchų-pi héci na wašícu ki
because of QL do that-PL SUB and white man DEF

hená ówakhąkhą-pi hą́tąhąš takómni tóhąni echél iyáyį-kte-šni
those lie-PL if anyway never right go-FASS-NEG

na hé átaya žužúwahį-kta cha hé é cha ų́ lehą́n lé
and that entirely fall apart-FASS so that IP QL be now this

iwánaȟʔų ektá hená oyáka-pi cha ą́paó héhą́ni
radio* in those tell-IPS so in the morning at that time

chįkší-wa-ye ki ma-yúȟicį na o-má-ki-yake.
son-1SG.AG-have as DEF 1SG.PAT-wake up.VT and ST-1SG-BEN-tell

cha "tókša ektá mnį́-kte kʔų" ephį́ "na tókha
so soon there go.1SG.AG-FASS ASS say.1SG.AG and happen

héci tókša ób w-ó-wa-glakį-kte kʔų" ephé
SUB soon with NSP.PAT-ST-1SG.AG-POSS.tell-FASS ASS say.1SG.AG

cha "hená į́šé iyé átaye-la Lakhóta ki
QL those just they entirely-LIM Indian DEF

é-wicha-kiktųža-pi na iyé átaye-la žicá wa-chį́-pi
ST-3PL.PAT-forget-PL and they entirely-LIM rich NSP.PAT-want-PL

cha hé ų́ tóhųweni iyéchecha-kte-šni kʔų" ephé.
so that because of never right-FASS-NEG ASS say.1SG.AG

tókhel	*wa-ˀéchų-pi*	*éyaš*	*takómni*	*echécha-kte-šni.*	*takómni*
how	NSP.PAT-do-IPS	but	at any rate	right-FASS-NEG	at any rate

tóhąni	*į́yąkį-kte-šni*	*cha*	*eyá*	*o-wá-ki-yaka*	*hé*	*hį́hąni.*
never	run-FASS-NEG	QL	say	ST-1SG.AG-BEN-tell	that	morning

héchetu.
true

About four years ago an airport was being built, a very big one. Rumor had it that in the old times, the Indians had buried their dead in this area. It was said that only after they [the remains] had been dug up and removed people would be allowed to construct buildings and a runway. It was said that one body had been found there, that it had been dug up and removed. The bodies may have been lying here and there, but this was probably kept a secret, who knows. When they had finished it [the airport] and were about to open it they asked me to give an invocation. I didn't go before I had been there [to investigate]. Some white men over there had dug up all the bones, or at least everything that was in the earth from long ago. They had collected and secured everything. They did that in order to gain knowledge from these things. I walked up to them and asked some questions. I said: "There are no traces of human bodies under the airport that is being built, are there? If there are human bodies, it would be a good idea to first remove them and then open it [the airport]." One [of them] replied: "No, there is nothing, we have investigated everything but there is nothing. Someone has taken some bones and put them up against a tree. He has lined them up against this fence post, but it is being claimed that they are not human bones. They are animal bones." Where something like the remainders of a village had been dug up they had found that the earth was all black. They said: "Long ago this was a white settlement, so it does not matter." "Okay," I replied. "I have been asked to do a blessing ceremony, but the Indians never knew about money. This airport costs a lot of money, and very rich people will travel by means of it. If

I bless it it would be a good idea if the Indians received something in return [such as better job opportunities]. If this does not happen they [the spirits] will definitely resist, so people will never be able to carry this project through. They will never finish it." That I told them. He [a staff member] said: "No, there is nothing, but people keep on saying that [there is something]." "Then we will certainly find out about it later," I replied. "When there will be spirits," I told them. So I made a prayer, but I said: "At the opening I will just pray that people will arrive safely and leave safely. I could never pray over the buildings and the runway. I will only pray for people to arrive and depart." This is what I told them. So I went there to do the invocation. I prayed like I had said I would. At the opening I prayed that people should fly without any accidents. Now it [the airport] is finished, but something went wrong. It is being reported that all the concrete is cracked, and that the spirits are revolting. People said that the Cheyenne or Pawnee or some other tribe were having a ceremony right there [at the airport, to find out what was going on]. They were going to have a meeting, so I went there. I said that I would find out for what reason these things were happening, and that if the white people had lied it [the airport] would never ever work right and would fall apart. These things [about problems with the airport] are now being reported on the radio. One morning, at dawn, my son woke me up and told me [about the news on the radio]. I said: "Soon I'll go there. Soon I'll talk to them [the white people] about what is happening. They have just entirely forgotten about the Indians and only want to be rich. Therefore it [the airport] will never be alright. Whatever they do, it will never ever be alright. It will never work." This is what I told him [my son] that morning. It's true.

2.19. Scalps

NEVA STANDING BEAR

Tape recorded November 30, 1994

cha	*héhą*	*lé*	*owáchekiye*	*ki*	*lé*	*Mní*	*Wichóni*	*Owáchekiye*
so	then	this	church	DEF	this	water	life	church

eyá-pi	*cha*	*ų-yúha-pi.*	*yųkhą́*	*hél*	*wikhóškalaka*	*wą*
say to-IPS	QL	1PL.AG-have-PL	then	there	young woman	IDF.SG

Lakhóta	*thókecha*	*cha*	*eyášna*	*hél*	*wachékhiye*	*hí*	*yųkhą́*
Indian	different	QL	sometimes	there	pray	come	then

hékta	*tókhi*	*waníyetu*	*yámni*	*na'į́š*	*tópa*	*séce*	*ká*
back.AV	about	year	three	or	four	maybe	over there

ȟé	*ektá*	*othų́wahe*	*wą*	*Kremmling, Colorado*	*eyá-pi*	*cha*
mountain	to	town	LK	Kremmling Colorado	say to-IPS	QL

héchiya	*í*	*kéye*	*yųkhą́*	*tha-wíchaša*	*wą*	*kichí*	*í*	*nahą́ke*	*lé*
there	go	QT	then	ALP-man	IDF.SG	with	go	and then	this

oȟpáye thípi	*cha*	*él*	*í-pi*	*nahą́ke*	*hél*	*ȟpáya-pi-kta*	*cha*
motel*	QL	to	go-PL	and then	there	lie-PL-FUT	QL

he-tą́	*iyáya-pi-kta*	*cha*	*hél*	*í-pi*	*yųkhą́*	*tókheškhe*	*átaya*
that-from	go-PL-FUT	so	there	go-PL	then	somehow	INT

chuwí	*ki*	*sni-sní*	*iyáya*	*kéye*	*chąkhé*	*ókšą-kšą*	*é-tųwį*
back.N	DEF	cold-RED	IGR	QT	then	around-RED	L-look

nahą́ke	*“tókheškhe*	*to-má-kheca*	*kʾų”*	*kéchį*	*kéye.*
and then	somehow	ST-1SG.PAT-not alright	ASS	think that	QT

nahą́ke	*lé*	*thi-tháhepiya*	*wąkál*	*é-tųwą*	*echél*	*lé*
and then	this	house-on the side	upwards	L-look	so	this

wichá-phaha	*hécha*	*nų́m*	*nahą́*	*wahį́kpe*	*na*	*itázipa*
human-scalp*	such	two	and then	arrow	and	bow

héchekche	*otká*	*kéye*	*cha.*	*chąkhé*	*eyá*	*kéye*	*“hená*
all kinds of things	hang.VI	QT	QL	then	say	QT	those

tókhiya-tą	*luhá*	*hé?”*	*eyá*	*kéye*	*yųkhą́*	*wašícu*	*ki*
where-from	have.2SG.AG	QS	say	QT	then	white man	DEF

hé	*eyá*	*kéye*	*“lená*	*até-wa-ye*	*ki*	*ehą́ni*	*léchiya*
that	say	QT	these	father-1SG.AG-have as	DEF	long ago	here

wiyóhiyąpata	*owíchakte*	*cha*	*hél*	*hená*	*phahá*	*ki*	*icú*	*kʾų”*	*eyá*
east*	massacre	QL	there	those	scalp*	DEF	take	ASS	say

kéye.	*cha*	*wichį́cala*	*ki*	*héyá*	*kéye*	*“tákuwe*	*hená*	*luhá*
QT	so	girl	DEF	say that	QT	why	those	have.2SG.AG

hé?”	*eyá*	*kéye,*	*“hená*	*wichá-tʾa*	*hécha-pi*	*škhá*
QS	say	QT	those	person-dead	COP-PL	but

wichá-luha	*kʾų”*	*eyá*	*kéye*	*yųkhą́*	*“hiyá,*	*hená*
3PL.PAT-have.2SG.AG	ASS	say	QT	then	no	those

até-wa-ye	*kihą*	*hená*	*wówitą*	*ų́*	*yuhá*	*kʾų”*
father-1SG.AG-have as	DEF	those	pride	because of	have	ASS

eyá kéye. “hená ohíya cha ų́ iglátą cha yuhá k’ų”
say QT those win so because of brag so have ASS

eyá kéye. chąkhé “hená héchanų-kte-šni škhá
say QT then those do that.2SG.AG-FUT-NEG but

héchanų-pi k’ų” eyá kéye. “éyaš lél wa-ȟpáyį-kte-šni k’ų,
do that.2AG-PL ASS say QT but here 1SG.AG-lie-FUT-NEG ASS

hená Lakhóta phahá cha wichá-luha-pi cha” eyá kéye.
those Indian scalp* QL 3PL.PAT-have.2SG.AG-PL QL say QT

eyį́ na khiną́phį nahą́ke iyéchįkyąke ektá mahél išnála
say and go outside and then car* in inside alone

iyáyį-kta cha íyutakį na iyáyį-kta yųkhą́ táku wą
go-FUT so sit down and go-FUT then something IDF.SG

iyéchįkyąke ki lé ųmáchiyatą hiyú na íyutaka kéye
car* DEF this from the other side come and sit down QT

chąkhé héchena iyáyį-kte éyaš hé eyá kéye “phahá ki hená
then still go-FUT but that say QT scalp* DEF those

aglá yő” eyá kéye. “tákuni tókha-kte-šni cha icú
take home IMP.SG.M say QT nothing happen-FUT-NEG so take

na aglá yő” eyá kéye, “na akhí-ȟa yő”
and take home IMP.SG.M say QT and take home-bury IMP.SG.M

eyá chąkhé chéya iyáyį na héyá kéye “tákuwe cha
say then cry IGR and say that QT why QL

a-má-ya-luštą-pi-šni *hé,* *líla* *hená* *ų́*
ST-1SG.PAT-2AG-stop.2AG-PL-NEG QS INT those because of

kakíš-ma-ya-ya-pi *k'ų"* *héyá* *kéye.* *yųkhą́* *"hená* *icú*
suffer-1SG.PAT-2AG-CAU-PL ASS say that QT then that take

na *aglá* *yó"* *eyá* *kéye.* *"hená* *Lakhóta-pi"* *eyá* *kéye.*
and take home IMP.SG.M say QT those Indian-PL say QT

cha *éyaš* *héchena* *waná* *iyáya* *kéye.* *iyáyį* *nahą́ke* *othų́wahe*
so but still now go QT go and then town

étkiya *iyáyį-kta* *yųkhą́* *tókheškhe* *ųgnáhelakha* *átaya*
toward go-FUT then somehow suddenly INT

iyéchįkyąke *ki* *ka'íthokabya* *átaya* *iléȟ-leȟ-ya* *hą́* *chąkhé*
car* DEF in front of INT shine-RED-ADV stand then

phathág *inážį* *nahą́ke* *hiyú-'ic'i-ya* *yųkhą́* *lé* *hél*
stop abruptly stop and then come-3RFL-CAU then this there

blé *wą* *mnináthakapi* *cha* *ektá* *mahél* *iyáya* *tkhá* *kéye* *cha* *éyaš*
lake LK reservoir* so to inside go well QT so but

lé *wanáği* *ki* *lé* *anápta* *cha* *éna* *inážį* *kéye.* *cha*
this spirit DEF this hinder so right there stop QT so

héktakiya *iyéchįkyąke* *ki* *ektá* *íyutakį* *na* *pa'ų́zi* *ektákiya* *yį́*
backwards car* DEF in sit down and back up*

nahą́ke *héyá* *kéye* *"táku* *cha* *héchamų-kta* *héci*
and then say that QT what QL do that.1SG.AG-FUT SUB

o-má-ki-yaka pé, echél echámų-kte" eyá kéye. cha
ST-1SG-BEN-tell IMP.PL.F so do.1SG.AG-FUT say QT so

héktakiya gle-ší-pi cha ektá khí na wašícu ki
backwards go home-ask-PL so there come and white man DEF

o-kí-yakį na héyá kéye "lená phahá ki
ST-BEN-tell and say that QT these scalp* DEF

aglé-ma-ši-pi cha héktakiya a-wá-gnį
take home-1SG.PAT-ask-IPS so backwards ST-1SG.AG-take home

na wa-ȟá-kte k'ų" eyá kéye. chąkhé wicálašni éyaš
and 1SG.AG-bury-FUT ASS say QT then refuse but

héyá kéye "hé niyé cha ni-cákižį-kte k'ų héchel
say that QT that you QL 2SG.PAT-suffer-FUT ASS so

luhá-he hątąhąš" eyá kéye. "na lená wanáǧi kihą
have.2SG.AG-PRG if say QT and these spirit DEF

tákuni tókha-kte-šni eyá-pi k'ų" eyá kéye. chąkhé héchena
nothing happen-FUT-NEG say-PL ASS say QT then thus

tha-wíchaša ki héyá kéye "hą́, k'ú wó, tókša niyé
ALP-man DEF say that QT yes give IMP.SG.M soon you

é wóka'ižu ni-c'ú-pi-kte" eyá kéye. "ho cha
IP credit 2SG.PAT-give-IPS-FUT say QT well so

ni-y-áte lená héchų-kte-šni škhá lená héchų weló"
2POR-EI-father these do that-FUT-NEG but these do that-IPS ASS.M

eyá kéye. hená į́š eyá oyáte-pi cha wichá-kte-pi-kte-šni
say QT those also people-PL so 3PL.PAT-kill-PL-FUT-NEG

škhá ítą-yą wa-ʔéchų weló" eyá kéye. eyá chąkhé "ohą́,
but proud-ADV NSP.PAT-do ASS.M say QT say then okay

cha lená aglá pó" eyį́ na yuȟpį́ na
so these take home IMP.PL.M say and take down and

wichá-kʔu cha átaya hąʔíyachį́šni yuhá
3PL.PAT-give so INT in the middle of the night have

kú-pi éyaš átaya líla hą-khókipha-pi kéye. cha héchena
come home-PL but INT INT night-fear.VI-PL QT so thus

akú-pi na léchiya thí ektá aglí-pi nahą́ke lé
bring-PL and here house to bring home-PL and then this

wágleyutapi él é-gnaka éyaš líla hąhé-pi átaya lé wanáǧi ki
table* on L-place but INT night entire this spirit DEF

o-phícʔiya-pi kéye, thimá, cha kiktá nahą́ke héyá kéye
L-stir-PL QT inside so wake up and then say that QT

"lená tókheškhe echámų-kta hé?" eyá kéye chąkhé "wą́,
these how do.1SG.AG-FUT QS say QT then IJ.M

Neva ki-yúȟla na iyų́ǧa yó" eyá kéye cha
Neva BEN-give a phone call* and ask IMP.SG.M say QT so

hį́hąni él ma-kí-yuȟla-pi na i-má-yųǧa-pi
morning in 1SG-BEN-give a phone call*-PL and ST-1SG.PAT-ask-PL

cha ephé “ąpétu wakhą́ kihą owáchekiye ektá
so say.1SG.AG Sunday* DEF church to

a-yá-ˀu kihą tókša a-wáche-ˀų-khiya-pi na tohą́n
ST-2SG.AG-take to if first L-ST-1PL.AG-pray-PL and when

iyéhątu kihą héktakiya lé owíchakte héchiya
it is time when backwards this massacre there

a-wícha-ˀų-gla-pi-kte nahą́ ektá
ST-3PL.PAT-1PL.AG-take home-PL-FUT and then there

wichá-ˀų-ȟa-pi-kte kˀų” ephé, “héchel nağí ki
3PL.PAT-1PL.AG-bury-PL-FUT ASS say.1SG.AG so soul DEF

okáblaya iyáya-pi-kte kˀų” eyá o-wá-ki-yake. “cha lehą́n
unhampered go-PL-FUT ASS say ST-1SG.AG-BEN-tell so now

ilánį na mniȟúha wąží lúta cha i-yá-cu na
go.2SG.AG and cloth IDF.SG red QL ST-2SG.AG-take and

phežíȟota é-ya-gnakį na a-ˀó-ya-pemni na
sagebrush* L-2SG.AG-place and L-ST-2SG.AG-wrap and

thi-y-ó-w-azil-ya-ye ki héchel
house-EI-L-NSP.PAT-ST-2SG.AG-burn incense if so

tókheca-kte-šni kštó.” ho cha héchų kéye na o-má-ki-yake.
happen-FUT-NEG ASS.F well so do that QT and ST-1SG-BEN-tell

ho cha hé waná ąpétu wakhą́ él ektá lé phahá ki lená
well so that now Sunday* on there this scalp* DEF these

ahí	*na*	*owáchekiye*	*él*	*a-glé*	*na*	*wachékiyapi*	*ki*	*él*
come and bring	and	church	in	L-put	and	altar*	DEF	on

ahí-gnaka	*cha*	*átaya*	*wąblákį*	*na*	*tókheškhe*	*líla*
come and bring-put	so	INT	see.1SG.AG	and	somehow	INT

chąté šíca	*a-má-hi*	*cha*	*chéya*	*iblámnį*	*na*
sad*	ST-1SG.PAT-IGR	so	cry	IGR.1SG.AG	and

wa-chéya-he.	*cha*	*a-má-kisni*	*él*	*waché-wa-khiye.*
1SG.AG-cry-PRG	so	ST-1SG.PAT-recover	when	ST-1SG.AG-pray

waché-wa-khiyį	*na*	*phi-yá*	*opémni.*	*ho*	*cha*	*héphé*
ST-1SG.AG-pray	and	good-ADV	wrap	well	so	say that.1SG.AG

“lé	*thokáta*	*ąpétu wakhą́*	*kihą*
this	future	Sunday*	DEF

iní-ˀų-kağa-pi	*na*	*héchiya*	*hóchoka*
ST-1PL.AG-perform sweatlodge ceremony-PL	and	there	altar

wąží	*é-ˀų-gle-pi-kte*	*nahą́*	*he-tą́*	*lená*
IDF.SG	L-1PL.AG-put-PL-FUT	and then	that-from	these

azíl-ˀų-thų-pi-kte	*na*	*ektá*	*wichá-ȟa*
ST-1PL.AG-burn incense-PL-FUT	and	there	3PL.PAT-bury

ųk-áya-pi-kte	*kˀų”*	*ephé.*	*“ho*	*cha*
1PL.AG-take to-PL-FUT	ASS	say.1SG.AG	well	so

ni-glú-wįyeya-kte,	*niyé*	*hená*
2SG.AG.PSS-POSS.INS-ready-FUT	you	those

a-wícha-ya-gli *cha"* *hépʰé.* *"cha* *wóyute*
ST-3PL.PAT-2SG.AG-take home QL say that-1SG.AG so food

na *táku* *wíȟpe-ya-yį-kta* *héci* *hená*
and what ST-2SG.AG-practice give away*-FUT SUB those

ni-glú-wįyeya *ki* *ho* *hehą́n* *ektá* *ųk-áya-pi*
2SG.AG.PSS-POSS.INS-ready SYP well then there 1PL.AG-take to-PL

na *wichá-ʔų-ȟa-pi-kte* *kštó"* *epʰé* *chąkhé* *"ohą́"*
and 3PL.PAT-1PL.AG-bury-PL-FUT ASS.F say.1SG.AG then okay

eyé. *waná* *ąpétu wakhą́* *cha* *wachékhiye* *iglúštą-pi* *cha*
say now Sunday* so pray POSS.finish-IPS so

iyópteya *pahá* *ektá* *iníkaȟ* *ųk-í-pi*
straight on hill to perform sweatlodge ceremony 1PL.AG-go to-PL

nahą́ *thimá* *a-wícha-ʔi* *cha* *oʔínithikağe* *phežíȟota*
and then inside ST-3PL.PAT-take to so sweatlodge sagebrush*

owį́š-wicha-wa-khiye. *na* *ektá*
spread.VT-3PL.PAT-1SG.AG-CAU and there

é-gnag-wicha-wa-khiyį *na* *ektá* *isákhib* *yąké-wa-ši.*
L-put-3PL.PAT-1SG.AG-CAU and there beside sit-1SG.AG-ask

héchetu *"lená* *niyé* *a-wícha-ya-gli* *cha* *hená*
so these you ST-3PL.PAT-2SG.AG-take home so those

wichá-gluha *nąkį́* *na* *echél* *tohą́n* *wichá-ȟa-pi*
3PL.PAT-POSS.have sit.2SG.AG and so when 3PL.PAT-bury-IPS

ki hehą́n ni-glúštą-kte kštó" ephé cha.

SYP then 2SG.AG.PSS-POSS.finish-FUT ASS.F say.1SG.AG QL

"niyé hé wó'okiye ni-cáhi-pi cha tákuni

you that goodwill 2SG.PAT-bring-PL so nothing

a-yá-khipha-kte-šni. cha waná hé

ST-2SG.AG-encounter-FUT-NEG so now that

iní-'ų-kağa-pi na waná echél hená

ST-1PL.AG-perform sweatlodge ceremony-PL and now so those

é-'ų-gle-pi na thimá ųk-íyutaka-pi. áta į́yą ki

L-1PL.AG-put-PL and inside 1PL.AG-sit down-PL INT stone DEF

tohą́n okíhilaka kháta cha tuwéni thimá yąká okíhi-šni cha.

as much as can be* hot so nobody inside sit can-NEG QL

iníhąšni m-išnála thimá mąké. cha hená į́yą kihą

nevertheless 1SG.PAT-alone inside sit.1SG.AG so those stone DEF

wačhé-wa-khiyį na iwáštegla kháta-pi-wa-ši. héchel "táku

ST-1SG.AG-pray and moderately hot-PL-1SG.AG-ask so what

echų́k'ų-pi-kte ki ų-glúštą-pi na hená héktakiya

do.1PL.AG-PL-FUT DEF 1PL.AG-POSS.finish-PL and those backwards

hé owíchakte héchiya

that massacre there

wichá-'ų-glogla-pi-kta" képhé

3PL.PAT-1PL.AG-carry home one's own-PL-FUT say that.1SG.AG

o-wá-ki-yake. héchiya yųkhą́ į́yą ki iwáštegla kháta
ST-1SG.AG-BEN-tell there then stone DEF moderately hot

cha héktakiyata thimá glicú-pi cha ób
so backwards inside start going back-PL so with

waché-wa-khiye nahą́ke lé phahá ki lená yuhá
ST-1SG.AG-pray and then this scalp* DEF these have

waché-wa-khiyį yųkhą́ lé wikhóškalaka ki lé é cha átaya
ST-1SG.AG-pray then this young woman DEF this IP that INT

chéya iyáyį nahą́ke "Neva, mi-sákhib
cry IGR and then Neva 1SG.PAT-beside

ma-yá-nąkį-kta kéhá yųkhą́ kákhiya
1SG.PAT-2SG.AG-sit.2SG.AG-FUT say that.2SG.AG then there

mi-chį́cha ki yąké ki ektá héchiya nąké." chįchá ki
1SG.POR-child DEF sit DEF at there sit.2SG.AG child DEF

hé él ų́-šni škhá héyá. eyá cha "tókša
that at be-NEG but say that say so soon

a-ní-cisni-kte kštó. wachékhiya é" ephé.
ST-2SG.PAT-recover-FUT ASS.F pray IMP.SG.F say.1SG.AG

tókha-šni kštó, tuwéni ksúye-ni-yį-kte-šni kštó"
not allright-NEG ASS.F nobody ST-2SG.PAT-hurt-FUT-NEG ASS.F

ephé. ho cha waná ųk-ígluštą-pi él ká
say.1SG well so now 1PL.AG-POSS.finish-PL when over there

Chasmú Wakpá héchi Lakhóta óta wichá-kte-pi cha héchiya
Sand Creek* there Indian many 3PL.PAT-kill-IPS so there

héktakiya hená a-wícha-ˀų-ki-pi na ȟtáyetu ehą́n
backwards those ST-3PL.PAT-1PL.AG-take to-PL and evening then

ųk-íhųni-pi na áta waná ká owíchakte ki
1PL.AG-arrive-PL and INT now over there massacre DEF

isą́m-ya héchiya oˀínažį wą hą́ cha ektá
more-ADV there parking area IDF.SG stand so there

ų-khínažį-pi yųkhą́ átaya thaté thą́ka hí na áta chą́ ki
1PL.AG-stop-PL then INT wind big come and INT tree DEF

hená kawéǧį-kte sˀe léchecha áta ka-wį́š-wįžį na
those break.VI-FUT like.AV like this INT ST-RED-bend.VT and

tókhel okíhi-ka thaté ki wašˀáke cha. thiyóblecha wą
how can-kind of wind DEF strong QL tent* LK

pawóslal iyéya-pi ki hé áta kaˀų́kį-kte sˀe léchecha
upright send-PL DEF that INT knock down-FUT like.AV like this

éyaš iníhąšni thimá mąkį́ na wól mąká-he.
but nevertheless inside sit.1SG.AG and eat.NSP.PAT sit.1SG.AG-PRG

cha wį́kchekche thą́kal wanáǧi ki ománi-pi éyaš
so unconcerned outside spirit DEF walk about-PL but

mąké. cha iyé lená khokípha-pi na átaya lé
sit.1SG.AG so they these scared-PL and INT this

chethí-pi na héchel ókšą yąká-pi na echél a-ˀą́pa-pi.
build a fire-PL and so around sit-PL and so L-dawn.VI-PL

cha waná héphé "ma-yúȟica pé
so now say that.SG.AG 1SG.PAT-wake up.VT-PL IMP.PL.F

lé ą́paó wicháȟpi ki lé hiną́phe-šni hą́ni,
this morning star* DEF this come out-NEG before

ma-yúȟica pé, lená ųk-ígluštą-pi-kte
1SG.PAT-wake up.VT IMP.PL.F these 1PL.AG-POSS.finish-PL-FUT

kštó" ephé. ephé yųkhą́ waná ą́paó wicháȟpi ki
ASS.F say.1SG.AG say.1SG.AG then now morning star* DEF

hé hiną́phį-kta kaˀíthokabya áta ablákela na áta á-ˀinila-hą
that come out-FUT before INT calm and INT L-silent-PRG

cha ma-yúȟica-pi. cha wékta na héchena
so 1SG.PAT-wake up.VT-PL so get up.1SG.AG and thus

héktakiya lé owíchakte ki hé étkiya máni ų-yą́-pi
backwards this massacre DEF that toward walk 1PL.AG-go-PL

na ektá ųk-íhųni-pi na makhá k'a-wícha-wa-khiyį
and there 1PL.AG-arrive-PL and earth dig-3PL.PAT-1SG.AG-CAU

na áta phežíȟota owį́š-wicha-wa-khiye. héchamų
and INT sagebrush* spread.VT-3PL.PAT-1SG.AG-CAU do that.1SG.AG

na lé phahá ki lená é cha nųphį́ mahél
and this scalp* DEF these IP QL both inside

iyé-wicha-ˀų-yą-pi na waché-wa-khiye. na hé
ST-3PL.PAT-1PL.AG-send-PL and ST-1SG.AG-pray and that

wachékhiya wicháša ki hé wiwą́yąg wachí cha wa-khį́
pastor* DEF that do the sundance* QL 1SG.AG-say to

na ephé "wiwą́yąg wa-yá-chi kštó. chąnų́pa ki
and say.1SG.AG ST-2SG.AG-do the sundance* ASS.F pipe DEF

lé icú na yuhá wachékhiya yé, lená héchel wólakhota
this take and have pray IMP.SG.F these so peace

ų-káǧa-pi ki wóˀokiye ų-yúha-pi-kte kštó." cha éyaš
1PL.AG-make-PL if good luck 1PL.AG-have-PL-FUT ASS.F so but

hé iyótą-ȟci tókhiyani yá okíhi-šni. áta wanáǧi ki hóthąˀį-pi
that most-INT nowhere go can-NEG INT spirit DEF shout-PL

cha na-wícha-ȟˀų. ho cha waná hé chąnų́pa ki icú na
LK ST-3PL.PAT-hear well so now that pipe DEF take and

wachékhiye cha wahéhąye-š ą́paó wicháȟpi ki waná
pray so about that time-EMPH morning star* DEF now

hiną́pha yųkhą́ áta lé wachékhiya nážį ki iwą́kab-ya
come out then INT this pray stand SYP above-ADV

é-wa-tųwą yųkhą́ zįtkála nų́m kįyą́-pi. átaya
L-1SG.AG-look then bird two fly-PL INT

phé-ˀichi-ˀa-gle-ya nážį-pi na átaya maȟpíya ektá wąkáta
head-REC-L-put-ADV stand-PL and INT sky to upwards

kįyą́-pi cha. phamágle i-ná-wa-žį na wawaché-wa-khiyį
fly-PL QL bow the head L-ST-1SG.AG-stand and ST-1SG.AG-pray

na ephé "Thųkášila, waná hená
and say.1SG.AG God* now that

wichá-ˀų-glogli-pi cha tąyą́ į́š asníkiya-pi-kte na
3PL.PAT-1PL.AG-take home-PL so well they take a rest-PL-FUT and

tąyą́ tákuni tókha-šni-yą okáblaya tha-ˀóyate ki
well nothing happen-NEG-ADV without trouble ALP-people DEF

ób ų́-pi-kta" képhá waché-wa-khiya yųkhą́ lé
with exist-PL-FUT say that.1SG.AG ST-1SG.AG-pray then this

zįtkála ki henáos kįyą́-pi k'ų lé wachékhiya wicháša ki lé
bird DEF both fly-PL SYP this pastor* DEF this

kákhel iglúštą yųkhą́ zįtkála ki kaˀíthanųgya kįyą́ iyáya-pi.
so POSS.finish then bird DEF on both sides fly go-PL

kįyą́ iyáya-pi yųkhą́ hé ųmá wicháša na ųmá hokšíla
fly go-PL then that one of them man and other boy

cha hé phahá wichá-yuza-pi cha hená é cha
QL that scalp* 3PL.PAT-grasp-PL so those IP QL

wichá-ˀų-ȟa-pi. cha áta líla ąpétu wašté ų-yúha-pi
3PL.PAT-1PL.AG-bury-PL so INT INT day good 1PL.AG-have-PL

na héchiya-tąhą yu-phí-ya ų-kú-pi na léchiya
and there-from INS-good-ADV 1PL.AG-come home-PL and here

ų-glí-pi.	*ho*	*cha*	*hé*	*wówapi*	*wą*	*káğa-pi*	*cha*	*hél*
1PL.AG-go home-PL	well	so	that	book	LK	make-IPS	QL	there

eháke	*hékta*	*yubláyapi*	*tóna*	*ki*	*él*	*owá-pi*	*cha*	*hél*
end.N	in the back	page*	so many	DEF	there	write-IPS	so	there

oyáka-pi.	*wówapi*	*ki*	*hé*	*Songs of Sorrow*	*eyá-pi*	*k'ų.*	*cha*
tell-IPS	book	DEF	that	Songs of Sorrow	say-IPS	ASS	so

tuwá	*chet'ų́-ma-gla*	*hą́tąhąš*	*hé*	*yawá-kte.*	*héchetu.*
someone	ST-1SG.PAT-doubt	if	that	read-FUT	so

We [Native Americans] have this church which is called Living Waters Church. A young woman from another tribe sometimes visits here to pray. About three years ago, maybe four, she went to a town in the mountains called Kremmling, Colorado. She went there with her boyfriend. They checked into a motel to spend the night. They planned to continue the trip after that. While they were checking in she somehow started feeling cold chills running down her back. She looked around and thought: "Somehow something is wrong with me." Then she looked up the wall, and right there two scalps, a bow and arrow, and all kinds of other things, were hanging. She said [to the owner of the motel]: "Where have you got these from?" The white man said: "My father took those scalps a long time ago at a massacre in the east." The girl replied: "Why do you keep them? They belong to dead people, but you keep them nevertheless." He said: "No, my father kept them for pride. He kept them so he could brag about having won [over an enemy]." "You should not do that, but you [guys] do it anyway," she said. "But I will not stay at this place, where you keep Indian scalps," she said. She said that and left [without her boyfriend, she was too upset]. She was going to leave all alone in the car. She got in and was about to leave. Then something got in from the other side of the car and remained there. She was ready to go, but it [the being] said: "Take those scalps home. Nothing will happen [to you], so get them and take them home and bury them." She started crying and said: "Why don't you leave me alone, you make me suffer a lot because of that." It [the being] said: "Get them and take them home, they belong to Indians." But nevertheless, she got on her way now. She drove on, trying to reach a town. Then, all of a sudden, lights appeared in front of the car. She stopped abruptly and jumped out. Ahead of her there was a lake, a reservoir. She would have gone right into it, but this spirit kept it from happening, so that she had stopped on the spot. She got back into the car and backed up. She said: "Tell me what I should do, I will do it." They [the spirits of the scalps] told her to go back, so she went back and said to the white man: "I have been told to take these scalps home. I will take them back home and bury them." He refused [to hand them over to her], but she said: "You are the one who will suffer if you keep them. And these spirits said that everything will be alright." Her boyfriend added: "Yes, give them to her, then it will be you who gets the credit. Your father should not have done this, but he did it anyway. They [the Indians] are human beings, too, so people shouldn't have killed them. But he was proud to do it." He [the white man] said: "Okay, take them home." He took them off [the wall] and handed them over to them. They arrived at home with them in the middle of the night. They were scared all night. They took them, and they brought them into the house. She put them on the table. But the spirits stirred all night in the house. She got up, and asked [some people]: "What should I do with them?" Someone said: "Well, call Neva and ask her." In the morning she called me and asked me. I said: "If you bring them to the church on Sunday we will first pray over them, and when the time is right we will take them back home to the massacre site. We will bury them there. That way their souls will wander about freely." That's what I told them. "If you go now, take a piece of red cloth, put sagebrush on top, wrap them [the scalps] with it, and burn incense in the house [to make the spirits feel comfortable]; nothing will happen." She did that, and told me [that she had done it]. Next Sunday she brought the scalps and put them up in the church; she put them on the altar. I saw them, and somehow I got very sad. I started crying. I cried for quite a while. When I was alright again I prayed. I prayed, and she rewrapped them [the scalps] carefully [they had been unwrapped on the altar]. I said: "Next Sunday we will have a sweat. We will put up an altar there, burn incense on it, and take them [the scalps] back to bury them." I added: "You [the girl and her boyfriend] will get yourselves ready, you will be the ones who take them home. When you will have prepared some food and some things to give away [in a give-away ceremony] we will take them over there and bury them." "Okay," she said. On Sunday, when the sermon was over, we went straight on to the hills to have a sweat. She had them [the scalps] with her. In the sweatlodge I had them spread sagebrush. I had them put them [the scalps] there, and asked her to sit next to them. I said: "It was you who brought them home, so you will be sitting with them, and as soon as they are buried you will have completed your duty. They will bring you good luck, nothing will happen to you." Then we had a sweat. We set them [the scalps] up and sat down inside. The stones were extremely hot. Nobody could sit inside. Still, I sat in there alone. I prayed and asked those rocks to cool down to a moderate temperature. I said to them: "We will finish what we planned to do and take them back to the massacre site." After that the stones had a moderate temperature. So they [the others] came back in. I prayed with them, and I prayed with these scalps. Then the young woman started crying: "Neva, you said that you would sit beside me. [But] you are sitting over there where my son is sitting." [This was a hallucination. Her son had died long ago.] She said that even though her son was not here. I said: "Soon you will be alright again. Pray." I added: "It is alright, no one will hurt you." When we were through with that we took them [the scalps] over to Sand Creek, where many Indians had been killed. We arrived there in the evening. A little ways away from the massacre site there was a parking space. We stopped there. Then a high wind rose and bent the trees to a point at which they almost broke. The wind was very strong. It seemed like it would knock over the tent that they [the people who were with us] had put up, but I sat inside nevertheless and ate. Even though the spirits were roaming about outside I sat there unconcerned. They [the others] were scared. They built a fire and sat around it until daybreak. Then I said: "Wake me up before the morning star appears, wake me up. We will finish this." When they woke me up before the morning star appeared everything was calm and quiet. I got up, and we walked back to the massacre site. When we arrived there I had them dig up the earth and spread sagebrush. I did that, we put the two scalps in there, and I prayed. And I turned to the pastor [of Living Waters Church], who is a sundancer, and said: "You are a sundancer. Take the pipe and pray with it, if we make peace this way we will have good luck [because we did the spirits a favor]." But he was frozen on the spot. He heard the spirits [of the ones who were killed at the Sand Creek massacre in 1864] shout. At last, he took the pipe and prayed. About that time the morning star appeared. While he was standing there praying I looked up, and there were two birds flying. They stood still in the air, bringing their heads together, and flew up to the sky. I was standing with my head bowed and prayed, and I said: "Grandfather [Great Spirit], now we have brought them back. They rest in peace. They will live with their people in peace, undisturbed." This I said in my prayer. While both birds were flying above the pastor finished [his prayer]. Then the birds flew away in separate directions. They flew away. One of the two people that had been scalped, and that we had buried, was a man, and the other was a boy [I just knew that; their spirits had turned into birds now]. We spent a wonderful day. After that, we had a safe trip home, and finally got back. In the last chapter of a book which has been written, this story is included; it covers many pages. The book is called Songs of Sorrow [cf. references, Mendoza 1993]. In there this story is told. And if someone doubts me he should read it. That's the way it is.

2.20. Old-Time Medicine

FLORINE RED EAR HORSE

Tape recorded September 1, 1995

lé táku wąží i-w-ó-wa-glakį-kte ki hé 1918
that thing IDF.SG L-NSP.PAT-ST-1SG.AG-POSS.tell-FUT DEF that 1918

mniwą́cha khowáka-tą okhícize na héchiya-tąhą
ocean* across-from war and there-from

w-azílya-pi yųkhą́ léchiya hihų́ni na oyáte óta
NSP.PAT-set on fire-IPS then here arrive and people many

héchel sóta-pi. yųkhą́ hų́ȟ thiwáhe átaya kiníl héchel
so gone-PL then some family INT most of them so

sóta-pi. yųkhą́ héhą thųkášila ki ní ų́ cha héchel
gone-PL then then grandfather DEF live CNT so so

ųcí thųkášila kichí chįchá óta-pi. chįchá wikcémna
grandmother grandfather with child many-PL child ten

na hé ųcí-wa-ye ki chįchá nų́pa cha aké
and that grandmother-1SG.AG-have as DEF child two QL ADD

nųpa-pi. átaya-kel aké nų́m wichá-yuha-pi. yųkhą́ waná lé
two-PL all-kind of ADD two 3PL.PAT-have-PL then now this

léchetu héhą átaya maȟpíya ki zí škhé nahą́ wichókhuže
so then INT sky DEF yellow QT and then disease

wichókhuže nahą́ ąpétu iyóhila owáchekiye ki lená
disease and then day each church DEF these

wa-ká-ȟla-pi na hená wichá-ȟa-pi nahą́ iyótą-š
NSP.PAT-INS-ring-IPS and these IPS-bury-IPS and then most-EMPH

wį́yą eyá iglúš?aka-pi k?ų hená wichókhuže ki lé icú-pi
woman LK pregnant-PL DEF those disease DEF this take-PL

hą́tąhąš héhą ihą́ke-pi héchel óta héhą t?á-pi. héchel oyáka-pi.
when then end.VI-PL so many then die-PL so tell-IPS

yųkhą́ thųkášila-wa-ye ki lé phežúta ki lená
then grandfather-1SG.AG-have as DEF this medicine* DEF these

slolyá cha iyáyį na phežúta tóna héchel yužų́ na
know so go and medicine* so many so pull out and

aglí na hená héchel hutkhą́ ki hená héchel hų́ȟ
take home and those so root DEF those so some

waksá-ksį na hená áta chéǧa thą́ka wą ų́ mní o-káštą
cut-RED and those all kettle big IDF.SG using water L-pour

lená áta piȟ-yį́ na héchel ícat?a piȟ-yį́ na sni-yá
these INT boil.VI-CAU and so hard boil.VI-CAU and cold-CAU

é-gle na lená átaya ȟpáya-pi kéye, khúža-pi cha ȟpáya-pi kéye,
L-put and these INT lie-PL QT sick-PL QL lie-PL QT

hená iyóhila wíyatke i-y-óžu-gžu-la héchel wichá-k?u, lená
those each cup* L-EI-ST-RED-full so 3PL.PAT-give these

iyúha héchel echá-wicha-kichų yųkhą́ iyúha ni-wícha-khiya
all so ST-3PL.PAT-do to then all live-3PL.PAT-CAU

kéye. ho na ųmá thiwáhe-pi ki lena tókhi héchų-pi-šni
QT well and other family-PL DEF these maybe do that-PL-NEG

cha hų́ȟ t'á-pi. Lakhóta oyáte óta héchel sóta-pi. hé
so some die-PL Lakota people many so gone-PL that

wichó'oyake kihą ųcí-wa-ye ki lená
story DEF grandmother-1SG.AG-have as DEF these

o-má-ki-yake na iná-wa-ye ki lé o-má-ki-yake.
ST-1SG-BEN-tell and mother-1SG.AG-have as DEF this ST-1SG-BEN-tell

yųkhą́ hená waná él ų́-pi-šni éyaš o'íye-pi k'ų hená héchel.
then these now there be-PL-NEG but word-PL DEF that so

nahą́ȟci ní nážį-pi ki iyéchecha hená ąpétu wąžígži hé
still live CNT-PL DEF like that those day some that

eyášna wéksuye. na Lakhóta oyáte ki ų́šika-pi éyaš
sometimes remember.1SG.AG and Lakota people DEF poor-PL but

táku héchel eyá wašté-šte slol-'ų́-yą-pi k'ų lená
things so LK good-RED ST-1PL.AG-know-PL DEF these

ų́ táku ųk-ókihi-pi. átaya-ȟci tóna wicákhe-ya
by means of things 1PL.AG-can-PL INT-INT so many true-ADV

wicála-pi, hená Lakhóta wichóȟ'ą ki sutá-ya gluhá
believe-PL those Lakota tradition DEF strong-ADV POSS.have

nážį-pi. hená líla wašté-pi na hená wóphila hécha.
stand-PL those INT good-PL and those appreciation OBL

My story is about this: in 1918 there was a war overseas, and some of what people were burning there came over here. Many people died for that reason. In some families most people died that way. My grandfather was still alive back then; my grandmother had many children with my grandfather. There were ten children, and my grandmother had two more children [from her first marriage], so there were twelve. All in all they had twelve. When this was happening, the sky was all yellow, and there was a disease [caused by that]. Every day the church bells rang, and there were funerals. Most of the pregnant women who caught the disease passed away; so many people died then. This is what was being reported. My grandfather knew about medicine. He went and gathered some medicine plants and took them home. He cut some of the roots into pieces and boiled them all in a big pot into which he had poured water. He boiled them really hard, put them aside to cool, and gave a cupful to each of those who were lying in bed, lying in bed sick. That way he proceeded with all of them. He saved them all. The other families probably did not do that, so some people died. Many Lakotas died that way. That story was told to me by my grandmother, and my mother told it to me, too. They are not around any more, but their words are. I remember them on some days as if they were still alive. The Lakotas are poor, but by means of the good things we know we are able to accomplish something. There are many, many people who truly believe in and hold on firmly to the Lakota tradition. These are very good people, and the fact that they exist is a reason for gratitude.

2.21. The Flying Saucer

FLORINE RED EAR HORSE

Tape recorded September 1, 1995

táku wąží ąpétu wą él wąbláka cha mi-ˀíšta ų́
something one day IDF.SG in see.1SG.AG QL 1SG.POR-eye with

wąblákį na hé é cha o-wá-glakį-kte. yųkhą́ hehą́l
see.1SG.AG and that IP QL ST-1SG.AG-POSS.tell-FUT then then

wicháša wą kichí wa-ˀų́ ki hé ní ų́. cha eyášna
man LK with 1SG.AG-be DEF that live CNT so always

hų́-ku thí ektá hų́-ku ki thí hé na
mother-3POR house to mother-3POR DEF house that and

ų-thí-pi ki íchi-khąyela cha eyášna héchiya máni
1PL.POR-house-PL DEF REC-nearby so always there walk

ųk-í-pi na akhé-šna máni ų-glí-pi. yųkhą́
1PL.AG-go to-PL and again-HAB walk 1PL.AG-come home-PL then

héchiya ųk-í-pi nahą́ w-ó-ˀų-kˀu-pi cha
there 1PL.AG-go to-PL and then NSP.PAT-L-1PL.PAT-give-PL QL

hél wa-ˀų́-yuta-pi na ób w-óglag
there NSP.PAT-1PL.AG-eat-PL and with NSP.PAT-POSS.tell

ų-yą́ka-hą-pi na waná tókhi hą-chóką-yą khąyéla
1PL.AG-sit-PRG-PL and now around night-middle-ADV near

héchiya-tą máni ų-kú-pi. éyaš waníyetu hą́tu éyaš
there-from walk 1PL.AG-come home-PL but winter then but

hą-ˀósni-šni na wá yąké-ˀ. héchiya-tąhą hél thí kihą
night-cold-NEG and snow sit-ASS there-from there house DEF

ilázatąhą aˀíyoȟpeya cha hél ogná iyé thokáheya
behind down the hill QL there along he first

gliyóȟpayį na choką́gnągya ósmaka sˀe léchecha lé
come down from and in the middle dip.N like.AV like this this

hél kú wahehą́l míš waná wa-glíyoȟpaye
there come home by that time I now 1SG.AG-come down from

ki waléhąl ųgnáhelakha áta iyóyąpa wą héchel
SYP by that time suddenly INT light IDF.SG so

a-ˀó-ˀų-žąžą-pi. yųkhą́ ožą́žą ki hé átaya miméla. máni
L-ST-1PL.PAT-light-PL then light DEF that entirely round walk

kú ki héchena a-ˀóžąžą kú na míš eyá héchel
come home SYP still L-light come home and I too so

wa-kú na hé ikhówakatą él thípi wą
1SG.AG-come come and that from across here house LK

ų-kíci-cağa-pi cha hél ehą́ni ų-yą́ka-pi tkhá ho
1PL-BEN-make-IPS QL there long ago 1PL.AG-sit-PL used to well

hél ų-glí-pi na hél chethí na tókhįš
there 1PL.AG-come home-PL and there build a fire and FASS

i-w-ó-ˀų-glaka-pi-kte	*sˀe*	*léchecha*	*yųkhą́*
L-NSP.PAT-ST-1PL.AG-POSS.tell-PL-FUT	like.AV	like this	then

"slol-yá-ya	*hé*	*tókheca*	*ki"*	*ephá*	*yųkhą́*	*"hą́,"*	*eyį́*	*na*
ST-2SG.AG-know	QS	happen	DEF	say.1SG.AG	then	yes	say	and

héhą	*áta-š*	*i-w-óglaka*	*chį́-šni.*	*ho*	*hé*
then	INT-EMPH	L-NSP.PAT-POSS.tell	want-NEG	well	that

táku	*wąží*	*lehą́l-šna*	*watóhą-šna*	*wéksuye*	*ki*
something	IDF.SG	now-HAB	sometimes-HAB	remember.1SG.AG	DEF

hé	*tákuwe*	*cha*	*hé*	*wąkáta*	*é-wa-tųwe-šni.*	*ho*
that	why	QL	that	upwards	L-1SG.AG-look-NEG	well

echą́mi	*sˀa*	*táku*	*cha*	*a-ˀíyo-ˀų-yąpa-pi*	*héci*	*mahpíya*
think.1SG.AG	HAB	what	QL	L-ST-1PL.PAT-shine-PL	SUB	sky

echíya-tąhą.	*ho*	*hé*	*eyášna*	*iblúkcą*	*sˀa.*	*ho*	*iyé*
there-from	well	that	always	think about.1SG.AG	HAB	well	he

áta-š	*i-w-óglaka*	*chį́-šni.*
INT-EMPH	L-NSP.PAT-POSS.tell	want-NEG

I will talk about something I saw one day, something that I saw with my own eyes. Back then the man I was living with was still alive. We always walked to his mother's house—his mother's house and our house were close together—and after that we walked back again. We went there, they fed us, so we ate there, and sat there talking to them. One time, around midnight, we were on our way home from there. It was winter then, but the night was not cold, and there was snow on the ground. He [my husband] first walked down the slope behind the house [his mother's house]. In the center [of the slope] there was some kind of a dip. While he was approaching it, I was on my way down. Suddenly there was a light on us. That light was all round. While he kept on walking, the light was still on him as he was walking. I kept on walking, too. From over there we arrived here, at the house that had been built for us [on the reservation], where we used to live long ago, and he built a fire. I thought we would talk about the incident. I said: "Do you know what happened there?" He said: "Yes." Then he didn't want to discuss it any more. The one thing that I'm sometimes pondering about now is why I didn't look up. I am always thinking whether the thing that was shining on us was maybe from the sky. I'm constantly thinking about this. But he didn't want to talk about it at all.

2.22. The Fire Ball

FLORINE RED EAR HORSE

Tape recorded September 1, 1995

hąhépi	*wą*	*él*	*héchel*	*ehą́ni*	*oyáte*	*ki*	*thąkáya-pi*	*ki*
night	IDF.SG	in	so	long ago	people	DEF	ease oneself*-PL	SYP

hé	*makhíkceya*	*thąkáya-pi,*	*tókhel*	*héchų-pi*	*ki*
that	on the ground	ease oneself*-PL	why	do that-PL	LK

slol-wá-ye-šni	*éyaš*	*oˀíheye thípi*	*hé*	*glé-pi*	*na*	*khohą́*
ST-1SG.AG-know-NEG	but	outhouse*	that	put-IPS	and	yet

héchų-pi.	*yųkhą́*	*iná-wa-ye*	*ki*	*thąkáya*	*chį́*	*na*
do that-PL	then	mother-1SG.AG-have as	DEF	ease oneself*	want	and

ye-ˀá-ma-phe.	*yųkhą́*	*waná*	*íyutaka*	*cha*	*wąbláke*	*ki*
go-ST-1SG.PAT-wait on	then	now	sit down	LK	see.1SG.AG	SYP

waléhąl	*ižą́žą*	*wą*	*gas lamp*	*eyá-pi*	*cha*	*lehą́l*	*wašícu*	*ki*
by that time	light	LK	gas lamp	say-PL	QL	now	white man	DEF

yuhá-pi	*yųkhą́*	*hécha*	*wąží*	*ilé-ya-pi*	*hą́tąhąš*	*áta*	*ȟmų-yéla*
have-PL	then	such	IDF.SG	light-CAU-IPS	when	INT	hiss-ADV

hé	*yųkhą́*	*hé*	*é-ˀe-ȟci*	*táku*	*wą*	*ȟmų-yéla*	*ú.*	*cha*
stand	then	that	IP-RED-INT	what	IDF.SG	hiss-ADV	come	so

él	*é-wa-tųwą*	*yųkhą́*	*m-íthokab*	*léchel*	*thápa*	*cha*	*thó*
there	L-1SG.AG-look	then	1SG.PAT-before	so	ball	QL	blue

s'e léchecha cha iž̨ą́ž̨ą héchel ȟmų-yéla makhá etą́
like.AV like this QL light so hiss-ADV earth from

iwátohą hiyáyį na héchena iyáye. yųkhą́ ehą́ni į́š
a little distance go by and thus go then long ago they

thųkášila-wicha-wa-ye-la na
grandfather-3PL.PAT-1SG.AG-have as-DIM and

até-wicha-wa-ye hehą́yą wichóȟ'ą ki lé táku
father-3PL.PAT-1SG.AG-have as all there is incident DEF this things

ki hé lé oyáka-pi ki hé tukté'el makhóche wą él
DEF that this tell-PL DEF that wherever land IDF.SG in

wígli yąké hą́tąhą hé táku kihą wąyą́ka-pi škhé. ho cha táku
oil sit if that things DEF see-IPS QT well QL what

ki slol-wá-ye-šni éyaš tokháš héchetu séce
LK ST-1SG.AG-know-NEG but maybe right maybe

lepcé-ȟce. eyášna hená lehą́l waná waníyetu ma-'óta
think so.1SG-INT always those now now year 1SG.PAT-many

nahą́ tákuni o-wá-kihi-šni éyaš tukté-kte-l-šna
and then nothing ST-1SG.AG-can-NEG but sometimes-RED-ST-HAB

mąká chą́ wichóȟ'ą ki lená héktakiya hená kiksúya
sit.1SG.AG then event DEF these back.AV those remember

mąké-' na hená táku ų́ lé echą́mi s'a. yųkhą́
sit.1SG.AG-ASS and those what be this think.1SG.AG HAB then

waná	*waléhąl*	*wa-hí-nažį*	*kihą*	*a-wá-bleza*
now	by that time	1SG.AG-come-stand	SYP	ST-1SG.AG-realize

héchetu,	*lé*	*wichóˀoyake*	*ki*	*echíyatąhą:*	*wakpá*	*wą*	*hé*
true	that	story	DEF	from there	river	IDF.SG	that

opháya	*ithánųg*	*makhíyuthapi*	*nų́m-nųm*	*wahéchetuya*	*wígli*
along	on both sides	mile*	two-RED	about that far	oil

yąká	*kéyá-pi*	*héchel*	*oyáka-pi*	*cha*	*tokháš*	*hé*	*é*	*cha*
sit	say that-IPS	so	tell-IPS	so	maybe	that	IP	QL

ų́	*lé*	*wą-ˀų́-yąka-pi*	*séce.*
because of	this	ST-1PL.AG-see-PL	maybe

Long ago when people went to ease themselves at night they eased themselves on the ground [during the day they used an outside toilet]. I don't know why they did that. Even though they had put up an outhouse they still did that. My mother wanted to ease herself one time, and was waiting on me to go with her. When I saw her sit down something shiny, exactly like what is called [a] gas lamp, that the white people have and which gives a hissing sound when it is lit, was passing by, producing a hissing sound [it was one foot in diameter, and moving about one yard from the ground]. I looked at it. Before me a light like a blue ball was passing by, not too high above the ground, producing a hissing sound, and moved on. Long ago my grandfathers and my fathers [father's brothers counted as fathers in Lakota kinship terminology] reported what this incident was all about: wherever there is mineral oil in the ground [and thus, gas as well] something like that can be observed. I don't know what it is, but I think this might be true. Now I am elderly and can't do anything, but from time to time, when I'm sitting there, I sit remembering the events of the past, and I always wonder what that could have been. Now that I have reached that age I realize it's true, from this rumor: people say that on a stretch about two miles long on both sides of a river [White River, South Dakota], there is [mineral] oil. Maybe this is the reason why we saw that.

Note: Neva Standing Bear adds that such objects were called *phéta yuhá-la* (fire have-DIM) 'carries fire'. To the Lakota, the *phéta yuhála* are in the same category as the *wiwíla wicháša* or 'spring men' (cf. 2.8, 2.23); they are spirits that play around with people. When they bump into you, you will have bad luck. One time Neva encountered a *phéta yuhála* on the reservation. First she saw a bluish flame on top of a hill two to three miles away, which was bouncing up and down. It approached her and landed on top of a tombstone. At that time, it was not bouncing up and down any more, and it had the shape of a ball that emitted bluish flames. It was about eight inches in diameter. Then the *phéta yuhála* quickly moved toward Neva's house. Neva got into the house and slammed the door shut. When the *phéta yuhála* hit the door the whole house vibrated and all the mud plaster was knocked loose. Only direct contact with a *phéta yuhála* is harmful.

2.23. Spring Men

FLORINE RED EAR HORSE

Tape recorded September 1, 1995

lé	*wichó'oyake*	*kihą*	*héchel*	*lekší-wa-ye*	*wąží*	*lé*
this	story	DEF	so	uncle-1SG.AG-have as	one	this

o-má-ki-yake.	*yųkhą́*	*makhá*	*théhą*	*héchel*	*ománi.*	*átaya-š*
ST-1SG-BEN-tell	then	distance	long	so	travel	INT-EMPH

makhíyuthapi	*wikcémna*	*záptą*	*wahéchetu*	*nachéce,*	*wahéchetu-ya,*
mile*	ten	five	about	maybe	about-ADV

iyótiyékiya	*makhá*	*máni*	*héchiya.*	*wašícu*	*ki*	*lé*	*wówaši*
with difficulty	land	walk	there	white man	DEF	this	work.N

echákichų	*s'a*	*cha*	*héchi*	*í*	*na*	*héchi*	*okó*	*nų́m*	*ú*	*na*	*héchi*
do for	HAB	so	there	go	and	there	week	two	come	and	there

wówaši	*echákichų.*	*yųkhą́*	*wókažužu*
work.N	do for	then	paycheck

kicú-'.	*ho*	*cha*	*akhé*	*héchiya-tąhą*
give to one what belongs to him-ASS	well	so	again	there-from

hįhąniyela-ȟci	*mní*	*i-glúha*	*na*	*héchiya-tą*
in the morning-INT	water	L-POSS.hold on to	and	there-from

kú	*kéye.*	*wótį*	*na*	*héchel*	*kú*	*kéye*	*yųkhą́*
come home	QT	eat.NSP.PAT	and	so	come home	QT	then

waná mní iyúha hená glatką́-hą cha waná áta
now water all those POSS.drink-PRG so now all

glaȟépa kéye. yųkhą́ khą́šnišniyela héchel wiwíla wą él
POSS.drink up QT then unexpectedly so spring IDF.SG at

glihų́ni kéye. cha hél glihų́ni ho héhą waná mní ki, wiwíla
arrive QT so there arrive well then now water DEF spring

mní ki, lená líla o-yátke wašté nahą́ líla mní ki sní
water DEF this INT L-drink good and then INT water DEF cold

héchel. hé wichóthawachį ki él hiyú kéye yųkhą́ táku
so that mind DEF to come QT then something

wąží kiksúya-hįgle kéye: wiwíla ki hé tuwéni héchel
IDF.SG remember-suddenly QT spring DEF that nobody so

ígmuha yatkį́-kte-šni. héchų s'e oyáka-pi ki hé kiksúya
sip.VI drink-FUT-NEG that way* tell-IPS LK that remember

kéye. chąkhé lé žąžą́ wą ogná mní i-glúha hé waná
QT then this bottle LK inside water L-POSS.have that now

henála cha ipágmųg icú na ožúla cha yuhá íyutakį na mní
gone so dip in take and full so have sit down and water

hé yatką́ kéye. mní hé yatką́ yųkhą́ héchel wiwíla ki óhuta
that drink QT water that drink then so spring DEF beach

etą́ héchel tuwá khį'į́ kéye yųkhą́ hú akąl aphá kéye,
from so someone throw at QT then leg on hit QT

huchóǧį hé wahétuktel aphá kéye. yųkhą́ hé glí
calf of the leg that about there hit QT then that come home

na ihį́hąni yųkhą́ héchel hú él aphá-pi hé héchel yazą́
and in the morning then so leg at hit-IPS that so hurt

kéye. na po-yá híyutaka kéye nahą́ héchel pó ų́
QT and swell-ADV sit down QT and then so swell CNT

hé naphópa kéye. ho hé oȟlógyahe ki hé tóhąni
that burst QT well that hole DEF that never

naˀókhiyuthe-šni kéye. ho hé thąká-tąhą iglóˀi kéye,
heal-NEG QT well that outside-from take one's own to QT

héchiya héchel hená asní-wicha-ya-pi okíhi-pi cha ho
there so those recover-3PL.PAT-CAU-IPS can-IPS so well

hé Nebraska na lé South Dakota él ithímahetu cha héchetu.
that Nebraska and this South Dakota in inside QL so

yųkhą́ phežúta wą kˀú-pi yųkhą́ lé hú él oȟlógyahą
then medicine* IDF.SG give-IPS then this leg in hole

hé naˀókhiyutha kéye. ho hé táku wąží oyáka-pi ki
those heal QT well that something IDF.SG tell-IPS DEF

hé wiwíla ki hená mní óhuta él wicháša eyá cik-cíkˀala
that spring DEF those water shore at man IDF.PL RED-small

ų́-pi, héchų sˀe oyáka-pi kéye na hená tohą́l wí mahíyaye hé
be-PL that way* tell-IPS QT and those when sun set that

ithókab	*hená*	*thą́ į-ʔicʔi-ya-pi.*	*héchų sʔe*	*oyáka-pi*	*cha*
before	those	visible-3RFL-CAU-PL	that way*	tell-IPS	LK

kiksúya	*kéye.*	*na*	*hé*	*wí*	*mahíyayį-kte-hą*	*hél*	*glíyutakį*	*na*
remember	QT	and	that	sun	set-FUT-PRG	there	sit down	and

mní	*ipágmųg*	*icú*	*na*	*yatké*	*éyaš*	*tuwá*	*khįʔį́*	*kéye,*	*hé*
water	dip in	take	and	drink	but	who	throw at	QT	that

wicháša	*hená*	*wą-wícha-yąke-šni*	*kéye.*	*ho*	*hé*	*įšé*	*wichóʔoyake*
man	those	ST-3PL.PAT-see-NEG	QT	well	that	just	story

héchų sʔe	*akhípha*	*na*	*wąyą́kį*	*na*	*slolyá*	*cha*	*hená*	*ogláka*
that way*	encounter	and	see	and	know	QL	those	POSS.tell

cha	*mi-thá-mother*	*ki*	*hé*	*kichí-wichowe*	*cha*	*lená*	*wichóʔų*
QL	1SG.POR-ALP-mother	DEF	that	REC-siblings	so	these	relatives

táku	*slolyé*	*kʔų*	*hená*	*o-kí-yake.*	*cha*	*etą́*	*lená*	*na-wá-ȟʔų.*
what	know	DEF	these	ST-BEN-tell	so	from	these	ST-1SG.AG-hear

ho	*hé*	*é*	*cha*	*įšé*	*lé*	*ąpétu*	*ki*	*obláki-kte.*
well	that	IP	QL	just	this	day	DEF	tell.1SG.AG-FUT

This story was told to me by one of my uncles. He was on a long trip. It may have been about fifty miles, about that much. He had a hard time traveling. He was on his way to the white man [a rancher] he was always working for. He stayed over there for two weeks and worked there for him. Then he received his paycheck. Again, he got some water ready quite early in the morning and got on his way home. He ate and got on his way. At some point he had used up all his water. He had consumed all of it. Then, unexpectedly, he arrived at a spring. He got there, and the water, the spring water, was very good to drink. The water was very cool. Then something crossed his mind, he suddenly remembered something: nobody is supposed to drink from a spring without using a vessel. He remembered people saying that. So he took the bottle he carried his water supply with, which was now gone, and dipped it in. When it was full he sat down with it and drank that water. He drank the water. Then somebody threw something at him from the edge of the water. It hit him on the leg, around the calf. He went on his way home again, and the next morning the spot where he had been hit hurt. And it swelled up, and when it had been swollen for a while it burst open. That wound never healed. He consulted a doctor from outside [of the reservation], where people could be cured. This was in Nebraska [Chadron], and the accident had happened in South Dakota [on Pine Ridge Reservation]. He was given medicine. The wound in his leg healed. What people report is that there are small men living by the sides of springs; that's what people tell. Before sunset they show themselves. He remembered people talking about that. Right around sunset he sat down there, dipped out water, and drank it, but he didn't see the ones who tossed [something] at him, those men. He experienced that story this way, and he told what he knew to my mother; they were siblings. He told his family what he knew. From them I heard it. This is what I was going to talk about today.

2.24. Indian Doctoring

FLORINE RED EAR HORSE

Tape recorded September 1, 1995

lé	*wichóˀoyake*	*ki*	*lé*	*até-wa-ye*	*kihą*
this	story	DEF	this	father-1SG.AG-have as	DEF

o-má-ki-yake.	*yųkhą́*	*ehą́ni*	*théca*	*ho*	*héhą*	*šųg-wáthogla*
ST-1SG-BEN-tell	then	long ago	young	well	then	horse-wild

aką́yąka	*kéye*	*eyášna.*	*naˀį́š*	*tuktélšna*	*šų-káˀųspe-ši-pi*	*kéye.*
ride*	QT	always	or	sometimes	break horses*-ask-IPS	QT

chą́	*hená*	*echų́*	*kéye.*	*yųkhą́*	*othų́wahe*	*wą*	*South Dakota*
then	those	do	QT	then	town	IDF.SG	South Dakota

ithímahel	*yąké*	*Edgemont*	*eyá-pi*	*cha*	*hél*	*rodeo*	*cha*	*héchiya*	*í*
inside	sit	Edgemont	say-IPS	QL	there	rodeo	so	there	go

kéye.	*yųkhą́*	*šųg-wáthogla*	*aką́yąka-pi*	*él*	*ópha*	*kéye.*	*yųkhą́*	*iyéˀicˀiyį*
QT	then	horse-wild	ride*-PL	in	join	QT	then	mount*

na	*šų́kawakhą́*	*ki*	*lé*	*tókhi*	*líla*	*yeˀícˀiyį*	*na*	*agláskil*
and	horse*	DEF	this	quite	INT	buck*	and	POSS.press on

gliȟpáyį	*na*	*até-wa-ye*	*kihą*	*héchel*	*tˀá*	*kéye.*
fall down	and	father-1SG.AG-have as	DEF	so	unconscious	QT

tókhi	*tohą́*	*tˀá*	*nachéce*	*yųkhą́*	*icígnuniyą*	*ókawįta*	*é*	*hé*	*ki*	*él*
maybe	then	dead	maybe	then	meanwhile	crowd	IP	that	DEF	in

Lakhóta	*ki*	*héchi*	*w-i-wą́yąg*	*a-ˀí*	*na*	*é-thi-pi*	*ki*
Indian	DEF	there	NSP.PAT-L-see	COLL-go to	and	L-camp.VI-PL	DEF

hél wąží héchel Lakhóta waphíya kéye yųkhą́ Lakhóta waphíye ki
there one so Lakota doctor* QT then Lakota doctor* DEF

lé mathó waphíye eyá-pi hécha kéye. yųkhą́ hé phi-yį́ na
this bear doctor* say-IPS COP QT then that good-CAU and

phežúta kʔú yųkhą́ phi-yį́-kta cha phežúta khal-khíya
medicine* give then good-CAU-FUT so medicine* hot-CAU

yųkhą́ hé icígnuniyą táku wą wąyą́ke ki hé tʔá
then that meantime something IDF.SG see DEF that dead

ȟpáye ichų́hą héchel chąʔógnaka wą ȟpáya ki cha étkiya
lie during so casket* IDF.SG lie DEF so toward

paslóhą áya-pi kéye. yųkhą́ hé chąʔógnaka ki hé ogná
push along PRC-IPS QT then that casket* DEF that inside

é-ʔųpa-pi-kta cha hé ų́ chąʔógnaka paslóhą áya-pi
L-place-IPS-FUT so that because of casket* push along PRC-IPS

kéye. wahéhąl phežúta ki lé kʔú yųkhą́ kiní kéye.
QT by that time medicine* DEF this give then revive.VI QT

ho hé wį́yą cha hé Lakhól-waphíya, mathó waphíya cha,
well that woman QL that Lakota-doctor* bear doctor* QL

hé até-wa-ye ki lé phežúta ki lé ni-yá
that father-1SG.AG-have as DEF this medicine* DEF this live-CAU

cha hé eyášna ų́ phikíla wį́yą ki lé kiksúya.
so that always because of appreciate woman DEF this remember

cha lé obláke.
so this tell.1SG.AG

This story was told to me by my father. Long ago, when he was young, he used to ride mustangs. Sometimes he was asked to break horses. So he did that. One time he went to a rodeo in a town in South Dakota called Edgemont. He joined the bronc riders. He mounted, and the horse bucked quite a lot and fell on him. My father was unconscious. It seemed like he was dead. Meantime, in the crowd of Indians who were looking on and camping there, they found a Lakota healer; this Lakota healer was a bear doctor, people said [i.e., her spiritual helpers were bears]. She cured him. She gave him medicine in order to cure him. She heated the medicine, and while he was lying there dead he saw something [in a dream, a hallucination]: a casket was being pushed toward him while he was lying there. He was going to be put into that casket, that was why the casket was being pushed toward him. By that time she gave him this medicine, and he came back to life. That woman's, that Lakota healer's, that bear doctor's medicine saved my father. For that reason he always remembered this woman with gratitude. This is what I wanted to tell.

The Old Ways 3

3.1. Life in the Old Days

MARY LIGHT

Tape recorded May 18, 1994

Mary Light e-má-ciya-pi. cha lehą́l héktakiya líla táku
Mary Light ST-1SG.PAT-say to-IPS so now back.AV INT things

ehą́ni echų́k'ų-pi ki hená o-wá-glakį-kte. ehą́ni
long ago do.1PL.AG-PL DEF those ST-1SG.AG-POSS.tell-FUT long ago

šų́kawakhą́ wichá-'ų-yuha-pi na hená ų́ w-ígni
horse* 3PL.PAT-1PL.AG-have-PL and those with NSP.PAT-hunt

ųk-ómani-pi. na tuktél-šna pte-kté-pi na-šna
1PL.AG-travel-PL and where-HAB buffalo-kill-IPS and-HAB

pus-'ų́-ki-ya-pi nahą́ waníyetu ópta-šna hená
dry.A-1PL.AG-PSS-CAU-PL and then winter through-HAB those

ų-yúta-pi. nahą́ nakų́ chąphá na táku yušpí-pi ki hená
1PL.AG-eat-IPS and then also cherry and things pick-IPS DEF these

pus-yá-pi na hená nakų́ ų́ waníyetu ópta hená yúl
dry.A-CAU-IPS and those also using winter through those eat

ų-yą́ka-pi. waná pté kté-pi na hená thaló ki óhįniya
1PL.AG-CNT-IPS now buffalo kill-IPS and these meat DEF always

tąyą́ kablá-pi na pus-yá-pi na nakų́ waníyetu ópta-šna
well slice-IPS and dry.A-CAU-IPS and also winter through-HAB

hená yúl ų-yą́ka-pi. nahą́ ptąyétu chą́na-šna hehą́l į́š
these eat 1PL.PAT-CNT-PL and then autumn then-HAB then they

tókhiškhiya blo-páhi-pi na'į́š táku héchel igní ománi-pi
wherever potato-gather-IPS and things so hunt travel-PL

nahą́ waníyetu ópta hená oyáte ki iyúha tąyą́ ų́
and then winter through these people DEF all well this way

ní yąká-pi. na akhé ptąyétu chą́na-šna hená hé iyúha echų́-pi.
live CNT-PL and again fall then-HAB those that all do-PL

kichí-co-pi na hená iyópteya wóyute kihą ų-kíchi-c'u-pi.
REC-invite-PL and these passing on food DEF 1PL.AG-REC-give-PL

hená héchel o-blákį-kte.
those so ST-1SG.AG.tell-FUT

I am Mary Light. I will now talk about the things our people did a long time ago. Long ago we had horses. With them, we went hunting. And wherever buffalo were killed we made dried provisions. That is what we ate throughout the winter. And wherever there were [choke]cherries and other fruit that could be picked, people dried them. We ate that, too, throughout the winter. When buffalo were killed, they [the meat] were always sliced well, too, and dried, and we ate that, too, all through the winter. In fall, people would gather potatoes everywhere, and they were out hunting. People all survived the winter in good condition this way. And next fall they would do all that again. They invited each other, sharing the food. This is what I wanted to tell.

3.2. Jerky

MARY LIGHT

Tape recorded May 18, 1994

ho hehą́l tókheškhe pápa káǧa-pi ki hé oblákį-kte.
well then how dried meat make-IPS DEF that tell.1SG.AG-FUT

hé thokéya ptebléška ki wichá-kte-pi na wa-pháta-pi
that first cattle* DEF 3PL.PAT-kill-IPS and NSP.PAT-butcher-IPS

na hehą́l thaló ki hé kablá-pi na tąyą́ pus-yá-pi na
and then meat DEF that slice-IPS and well dry.A-CAU-IPS and

hehą́l púza chą́na-šna pápa ki hé tókhel hená
then dry.A then-HAB dried meat DEF that somehow those

waštų́kala hé icáhiya ohą́-pi naʼį́š tókhel bló
dried sweet corn that mix cook.VT-IPS or somehow potato

naʼį́š wašį ikcéka icáhiya ų́ wahą́pi káǧa-pi. ho nahą́
and tallow grease* mix by soup make-IPS well and then

ho hé nakų́ pápa ki hé ų́ tókhel wasná
well that also dried meat DEF that with somehow pemmican

káǧa-pi-kte ki hé pápa ki hé púze hą́tąhąš tąyé-laȟci
make-IPS-FUT SYP that dried meat DEF that dry.A when well-INT

kaphá-pi na hehą́l wašį ikcéka hé šlo-yá-pi nahą́
pound-IPS and then tallow grease* that melt.VI-CAU-IPS and then

hená	*ų́*	*wasná*	*káǧa-pi.*	*nahą́*	*hé*	*waná*	*wasná*	*ki*
that	with	pemmican	make-IPS	and then	that	now	pemmican	DEF

hehą́yela.	*nakų́*	*hé*	*pápa*	*ki*	*tókhel*	*bló*	*owás'į*
that is all	also	that	dried meat	DEF	somehow	potato	all together

nahą́	*wagmú*	*waskú-pi*	*na*	*waštų́kala*	*na*	*pápa*	*ki*	*hená*
and	squash	peel.VT-IPS	and	dried corn	and	dried meat	DEF	those

iyúha	*owás'į-yą*	*iȟ'ą́-pi.*	*cha*	*hé*	*pápa*	*ki*	*hehą́yela*
all	together-ADV	boil.VT-IPS	so	that	dried meat	DEF	that is all

obláki̜-kte.
tell.1SG.AG-FUT

Next I will tell about how jerky was made. First cows were killed and butchered. Then the meat was sliced thin, and left to dry. When it was dry, the meat, the jerky, was cooked together with dried sweet corn, or stew was made by mixing it with potatoes and tallow grease. In order to make pemmican with dried meat, the jerky was pounded very fine when it was dry. [Before that it was roasted until it became crisp.] Then tallow fat was melted, and with it pemmican was made. That is all [there is to say] about pemmican. Jerky was also boiled together with potatoes and sliced squash, and dried corn. That is all I wanted to tell about jerky.

3.3. Corn

MARY LIGHT

Tape recorded May 18, 1994

lehą́l wagmíza skuyá ki hé ų́ tókheškhe iȟʔą́-pi ki hé
now corn sweet DEF that with how boil.VT-IPS LK that

oblákį-kte. thokéya wagmíza ki hená owátohąyela
tell.1SG.AG-FUT first corn DEF those a little while

lolób-ya-pi na thąkál mniȟúha šóka wąží él hená
tender-CAU-IPS and outside cloth thick IDF.SG on those

yu-bláya-pi na pus-yá-pi na ho hehą́l púza chą́na hená
INS-flat-IPS and dry.A-CAU-IPS and well then dry.A then those

ų́ waštų́kala káǧa-pi. hehą́l wagmíza wasná nakų́ hé
with dried corn make-IPS then corn pemmican also that

káǧa-pi. wagmíza ki hená yukpą́-pi na wígli ikcéka nahą́
make-IPS corn DEF those grind-IPS and tallow grease* and then

chąhą́pi hená icáhiya-pi. ho nahą́ hé waštų́kala ki
sugar* those mix-IPS well and then that dried corn DEF

iȟʔą́-pi na tha-níǧa khó icáhiya-pi na hená
boil.VT-IPS and ruminant-tripe also mix-IPS and those

waštų́kala wahą́pi káǧa-pi. ho cha hená hehą́yela
dried corn soup make-IPS well so those that is all

oblákį-kte.
tell.1SG.AG-FUT

Next I will tell how people cooked with sweet corn. First the corn [only the kernels] was simmered a little, and then it was spread out outside on a heavy piece of cloth, and left to dry. When it was dry the final product was dried corn. People also made corn pemmican. The corn was pounded fine and mixed with tallow grease and sugar. And then the dried corn was cooked and mixed with tripe and made into dried corn stew. That is all I wanted to tell.

3.4. Wild Berries

MARY LIGHT

Tape recorded May 18, 1994

hehą́l chąphá yušpí-pi nahą́ wasná káǧa-pi ki hená
then cherry pick-IPS and then pemmican make-IPS DEF those

oblákį-kte. thokáheya chą-yáta í-pi na chąphá ki hená
tell.1SG.AG-FUT first woods-to go-IPS and cherry DEF those

yušpí-pi na aglí-pi na hehą́l yužáža-pi na hehą́l
pick-IPS and take home-IPS and then wash-IPS and then

kaškí-pi. į́yą chąphá i-cáški-pi ų́ chąphá ki kaškí-pi
pound-IPS stone cherry L-pound-IPS with cherry DEF pound-IPS

na hehą́l yu-bláya pus-yá-pi na ohákab púza chą́na-šna
and then INS-flat dry.A-CAU-PL and afterwards dry.A then-HAB

ho hehą́l wóžapi ų́ káǧa-pi. wóžapi ki aǧúyapi blú
well then berry soup using make-PL berry soup DEF flour*

cónala icáhiya-pi na chąhą́pi héchų s'e káǧa-pi. ho na hehą́l
few mix-IPS and sugar* that way* make-IPS well and then

hé wóžapi kéye. na hehą́l hé wašį́kceka cha hená
that berry soup QT and then that tallow QL those

šlo-yá-pi nahą́ wígli ki hé é na chąhą́pi icáhiya-pi
melt.VI-CAU-IPS and then grease DEF that IP and sugar* mix-IPS

héchų s’e henà wasná ki káǧa-pi. cha hená wóyute ki
that way* those pemmican DEF make-IPS so those food DEF

hé waníyetu wóyute hécha. waná hehą́l khą́ta ki hé nakų́
that winter food COP now then plum DEF that also

į́š iyéchel-ya pus-yá-pi nahą́ hená wóžapi káǧa-pi.
they like that-ADV dry.A-CAU-IPS and then those berry soup make-IPS

maštįca phuté ki hená nakų́ į́š iyéchel-ya tąyą́
buffalo berry* DEF those also they like that-ADV well

kaslí-sli-pi nahą́ yu-míme-yela pus-yá-pi nahą́
smash-RED-IPS and then INS-round-ADV dry.A-CAU-IPS and then

púze ki cha į́š eyá héchų s’e wóžapi káǧa-pi na
dry.A SYP so they also that way* berry soup make-IPS and

héchų s’e į́š eyá hená waníyetu ópta yúta-pi. chųwíyaphehe
that way* they also those winter through eat-IPS grapes*

ki hená į́š eyá chą-yáta yušpí-pi nahą́ hé iyéchel-ya
DEF those they also woods-in pick-IPS and then that like that-ADV

yužáža-pi nahą́ pus-yá-pi na waníyetu ektá wóžapi
wash-IPS and then dry.A-CAU-IPS and winter in berry soup

káǧa-pi nahą́ hená héchų s’e waníyetu wóyute hécha.
make-IPS and then those that way* winter food COP

Next I will tell about picking chokecherries and making pemmican. First people went to the woods, picked the chokecherries, and took them home. Then they washed and pounded them [together with the seeds]. The chokecherries were pounded with a cherry pounding stone [which consisted of a big flat stone and a smaller, conical stone which was flat at the base and served as a pestle]. Then flat patties [two to four inches in diameter] were made from the cherry pulp. They were dried this way. When they had dried, berry soup was made from them. Berry soup was made by mixing in a little flour [corn starch or ordinary flour] and sugar [after the patties had been soaked and boiled]. That was berry soup. In order to make pemmican, tallow fat [i.e., kidney fat] was melted. Then, by mixing the fat with some sugar [and with the chokecherries], pemmican was made. This food was winter food. Plums were dried the same way, too, and made into berry soup. Buffalo berries, too, were smashed well and dried, after they had been formed into round patties. When they were dry, they were made into berry soup the same way, and they were also eaten throughout the winter. Grapes were also picked in the woods, washed the same way, dried, and made into berry soup in winter. They, too, were winter food.

3.5. Old-Time Food

NEVA STANDING BEAR

Tape recorded September 9, 1994

lé ą́pétu ki tókhel Lakhóta ki wóyute káǧa-pi na waníyetu
this day DEF how Lakota DEF food make-PL and winter

ektá hená é-ki-gnaka-pi na waníyetu yúta-pi. lená wóyute ki
in those ST-PSS-put-PL and winter eat-PL these food DEF

é cha obláki̜-kte. cha thokáheya thaló pus-yá-pi na
IP QL tell.1SG.AG-FUT so first meat dry.A-CAU-PL and

pápa káǧa-pi na'į́š wa-pús-ya-pi ki lená
dried meat make-PL and NSP.PAT-dry.A-CAU-PL DEF these

tha-níǧa na tha-šúpa na'į́š phí na
ruminant-stomach and ruminant-intestines and liver and

tha-cháǧu na tha-chą́ta ki lená kablá-pi na'į́š
ruminant-lungs and ruminant-heart DEF these slice-PL and

chosyá-pi. cha ptebléška ki lé kté-pi na átaya thaló
cook.VT a little-PL so cattle* DEF this kill-PL and INT meat

ki hená okhį́yąke hená ogná waksá-pi na hená é cha
DEF those race track those along cut off-PL and those IP QL

kablá-pi na wa-kábla-pi ki líla hą́ska-ska káǧa-pi na
slice-PL and NSP.PAT-slice-PL DEF INT long-RED make-PL and

sáta cha glakįyą tuktél a-ˀíyakaška-pi nahą́ hél aką́n
pole QL across somewhere L-tie-PL and then there on top

pápa ki lená a-ˀíyaȟpeya-pi na chąphá-hu sákala
dried meat DEF these L-throw over-PL and chokecherry bush stick

cha lená hél ipáthake thų́-pi na pus-yá-pi héchų-pi na
QL these there stretcher put in-PL and dry.A-CAU-PL do that-PL and

yuptą́-ptą iȟpéya pus-yá-pi cha. yu-phí-ya púze
turn over-RED throw dry.A-CAU-PL QL INS-good-ADV dry.A

hą́tąhąš hená icú-pi nahą́ lé tha-há wókaphą
if those take-PL and then this ruminant-skin parfleche

héchiya mahél iyéya-pi na hená waníyetu wa-ˀé-ki-gle-pi.
there inside send-PL and those winter NSP.PAT-L-PSS-put-PL

waná tha-níǧa ki hé į́š áta yužáža-pi na
now ruminant-stomach DEF this it INT wash-PL and

tha-šúpa ki hų́ȟ hená paˀéciya-pi nahą́
ruminant-intestines DEF some those turn inside out-PL and then

owóhe wąží él chéǧa wąží ektá hená piȟ-yá-pi nahą́
stove IDF.SG on kettle IDF.SG in those boil.VI-CAU-PL and then

šˀé-šˀe-ya ǧéǧe-ya otké-ya-pi cha hená
drip-RED-ADV dangle-ADV hang.VI-CAU-PL so those

chosyá-pi cha. púze hą́tąhąš hená ošíce-šni cha
cook.VT a little-PL QL dry.A when those spoil-NEG so

héchel pus-yá-pi na mahél iyéya-pi. ho na
so dry.A-CAU-PL and inside send-PL well and

tha-šúpa ki hé į́š hų́ȟ kšą-kšą́ cha hená
ruminant-intestines DEF that they some bend.VI-RED QL those

póğą-pi na ithánųg iyákaška-pi cha héchel póğą-pi
blow up-PL and on each side tie-PL so so blow up-PL

na héchena púze chą́-šna iyáya-pi nahą́ hená chą́ cha
and thus dry.A then-HAB go-PL and then those wood QL

kaˀíyapehą-pi nahą́-š cheˀų́pa-pi, phéta ki iwą́kab
wrap around-PL and then-EMPH roast-PL fire DEF above

cheˀúpa-pi na hé yúta-pi. na tha-cháğu ki hé į́š
roast-PL and that eat-PL and ruminant-lungs DEF that they

paȟlóka-pi na héchiya wašį́kceka mahél iyéya-pi chą́-š
pierce-PL and there tallow inside send-PL then-EMPH

chéˀųpa-pi chą́ líla o-yúl wašté. na tha-phí ki hé į́š
roast-PL then INT L-eat good and ruminant-liver DEF that it

makhá kˀá-pi na phetáğa ektá o-ˀíȟpeya-pi na lé
earth dig-PL and coal there L-throw-PL and this

tha-phí ki lé áta héchi mahél o-ˀíȟpeya-pi na
ruminant-liver DEF this INT there inside L-throw-PL and

phetáğa akšú-pi na áta yu-phí-ya cˀokˀį-pi
coal pile on-PL and thoroughly INS-good-ADV bake.VT-PL

chą́-šna ikcéya waslé-sle-l icú yúta-pi na ošíce-šni héchel
then-HAB just ST-RED-slice take eat-PL and spoil-NEG so

íȟ'ą-pi hą́tąhąš. na tha-chą́ta ki hé į́š waslé-sle-ca-pi
boil.VT-PL if and ruminant-heart DEF that it ST-RED-slice-PL

na héchel pus-yá-pi cha tohą́n iȟ'ą́-pi-kte hą́tąhąš hená
and so dry.A-CAU-PL so when boil.VT-PL-FUT when those

yuȟpá-pi na tókhel waslé-sle-ca-pi hená icú-pi na
pull out-PL and how ST-RED-slice-PL those take-PL and

iyóȟpeya-pi. na'į́š ló ki héchena hų́ȟ thaló
throw into a kettle-PL or fresh SYP still some meat

i-pá'eciya eyá-pi cha héchel thaló cha hą́ske-ya
L-turn inside out say-IPS QL so meat QL long-ADV

só-so-pi na tha-šúpa ki lé
cut into strings-RED-PL and ruminant-intestines DEF this

pa'éciya-pi ki okhíyakaška-pi na mní
turn inside out-IPS DEF tie through the middle-IPS and water

o-káštą-pi. tónakiya hé iyákaška-pi na héchel hená
L-pour-PL in a few places that tie-PL and so those

iyóȟpeya-pi chą́na-šna mní mahél ų́ ki hená wahą́pi
throw into a kettle-PL then-HAB water inside be DEF those soup

káğa-pi cha hená yatką́-pi na iyáyustag i-yáksa yúta-pi. na
make-PL so those drink-PL and together mouth-bite eat-PL and

hohú ki hená ékayeš icú-pi na hú hohú ki hená
bone DEF those even take-PL and leg bone DEF those

kašléca-pi chą́-šna hená tha-cúpa eyá-pi cha hená
split.VT-PL then-HAB those ruminant-marrow say-PL QL those

he-tą́ wígli hená icú-pi na hená aǧúyapi i-ká-šluta-pi
that-from grease those take-PL and those bread* L-INS-slippery-PL

na yúta-pi. naˀį́š ųgná pápa káǧa-pi ki lená kaphá-pi
and eat-PL or perhaps dried meat make-PL DEF these pound-PL

chą́-šna ektá icáhiya-pi na hé yúta-pi na lé hohú ókhihe
then-HAB there mix-PL and that eat-PL and this bone joint

ki hená kašlé-šle-ca-pi na hená piȟ-yá-pi chą́-šna
DEF those ST-RED-split.VT-PL and those cook.VI-CAU-PL then-HAB

wígli ki hená aką́n hiyú hą́tąhąš hená al-ˀátaya kaǧé-pi
grease DEF those on top come when those RED-INT strain-PL

na ipáyeȟ o-gnáka-pi na héchel i-píȟ-ya-pi ho na echél
and away L-put-PL and so L-boil.VI-CAU-PL well and so

wígli waníce hą́tąhąš hená iȟpéya-pi nahą́ wígli ki hená
grease lack when those throw-PL and then grease DEF those

waȟpé wašté-mna icáhiya-pi chą́-šna hená ų́ phehį
leaf good-smell mix-PL then-HAB those with hair

sla-kí-ya-pi. na phá ki į́š hé icú-pi na
greasy-PSS-CAU-PL and head DEF it that take-PL and

tha-chéži na iyóȟa ki lená nakų́ hená piȟ-yá-pi
ruminant-tongue and jaw DEF these too those boil.VI-CAU-PL

na pus-yá-pi cha tohą́n waníyetu ki theȟí kˀéyaš tókhel
and dry.A-CAU-PL so when winter DEF hard but somehow

ní yąká-pi-kte. hená i-kí-ȟˀą-pi na į́š héchel
live CNT-PL-FUT those ST-PSS-cook.VT-PL and they so

o-wól-ya-la sˀe yąká-pi. na wagmíza nakų́ hená
L-eat.NSP.PAT-ADV-DIM like.AV CNT-PL and corn too those

chosyá-pi chą́-šna pus-yá-pi cha hų́ȟ wagmíza ki
cook.VT a little-PL then-HAB dry.A-CAU-PL so some corn DEF

héchena choǧį́ ikhóyag-ya sų́-pi na ǧéǧe-ya pus-yá-pi
still husk adhere-ADV braid-PL and dangle-ADV dry.A-CAU-PL

tohą́n iȟˀą́-pi hą́tąhąš. naˀį́š hé íyohakab-šna yugná-pi na
then boil.VT-PL when and that after-HAB pull off-PL and

ųmá hená į́š waštų́kala káǧa-pi cha hená wagná-pi nahą́
other those they dried corn make-PL so those cut off-PL and then

iyóȟpeya-pi nahą́ líla špą́-šni-ya
throw into a kettle-PL and then INT cooked until tender-NEG-ADV

iyóȟpeya-pi nahą́ wágleyutapi aką́n yu-bláya iȟpéya-pi
throw into a kettle-PL and then table* on top INS-flat throw-PL

chą́-šna hená pus-yá-pi na hená waštų́kala káǧa-pi. cha
then-HAB those dry.A-CAU-PL and those dried corn make-PL so

hená į́ š eyá waní wa-ˀé-ki-gnaka-pi. naˀį́š wagmú-ˀ.
those also winter NSP.PAT-L-PSS-put-PL and squash-ASS

wagmú zí chąhá šóka hé é cha hená átaya kaskú-sku-pi
squash yellow bark* thick that IP QL those INT peel.VT-RED-PL

na lé wagmú kihą waslé-sle-ca-pi na į́š eyá héchel
and this squash DEF ST-RED-slice-PL and also so

wágleyutapi ak ą́n pus-yá-pi. naˀį́š wąží hená į́š átaya
table* on top dry.A-CAU-PL or one those they INT

okáwįȟ wa-só-so-pi na wíkhą wąží icú-pi
go round NSP.PAT-cut into strings-RED-PL and rope IDF.SG take-PL

na choką́ oyáza-pi na yu-bláya-pi chą́-šna hená
and in the middle string up-PL and INS-spread.VI-PL then-HAB those

héchel pus-yá-pi. cha hená echékche wóyute káǧa-pi naˀį́š
so dry.A-CAU-PL so those exactly so food make-PL and

waná waníyetu ektá hená ikíȟˀą-pi-kte hą́tąhąš hená yu-ˀákąn
now winter in those starve-PL-FUT when those INS-on top

i-kí-k-cu-pi na hená ochéthi ki hél ak ą́n hená
ST-PSS-EI-take-PL and those fireplace DEF there on top those

iȟˀą́ glé-pi cha iyéchįkala lolópela. cha hená tóhąni tákuni
boil.VT put-PL so by itself soft so those never nothing

yu-sóta-pi-šni. na hená nakų́ wóšpi-pi. blokétu
INS-wasted-PL-NEG and those also pick.NSP.PAT-PL summer

hą́tąhaš wóšpi-pi na chąphá hená áta yušpí-pi na
when pick.NSP.PAT-PL and cherry those INT pick-PL and

kaškí-pi na pus-yá-pi nahą́ į́š eyá hená mahél iyéya-pi.
pound-PL and dry.A-CAU-PL and then also those inside send-PL

áta yu-bláska-ska hená é-gnaka-pi chą́-šna púze, naˀį́š khą́ta
INT INS-flat-RED those L-put-PL then-HAB dry.A and plum

ki hená icú-pi na ehą́ni įšé wakhą́heza ki khą́ta hená
DEF those take-PL and long ago just child DEF plum those

yaškíl-wicha-khiya-pi. na sú ki hená
make burst with the mouth-3PL.PAT-CAU-PL and seed DEF those

ȟeyáb iyéya-pi ehą́tąhąš sú chóla hená pus-yá-pi. éyaš
away send-PL when seed without those dry.A-CAU-PL but

įšé lehą́n hená chéǧa yukhą́ cha chéǧa ektá o-ˀíȟpeya-pi na
just now those kettle exist QL kettle into L-throw-PL and

iyé tohą́n píǧį na áta naphópe hą́tąhą-šna kazé-pi
they when boil.VI and entirely burst when-HAB ladle out-PL

na sú ki ȟeyáb iȟpéya-pi na héchena hená pus-yá-pi.
and seed DEF away throw-PL and that way those dry.A-CAU-PL

pus-yá-pi cha įšé hená wóyute. waníyetu chą́ hená wóyute
dry.A-CAU-PL so just those food winter when those food

káǧa-pi. yužá-pi. éyaš įšé ehą́ni chąhą́pi waníce cha wóyute
make-PL mash-PL but just long ago sugar* lack QL food

ki lená káǧa-pi hą́tahąš óta icáhiya-pi-šni. hená ehą́ni
DEF these make-PL when much mix-PL-NEG those that

héchų-pi-šni na ehą́ni hená aǧúyapi blú icáhiya-pi éyaš hená
do that-PL-NEG and long ago those flour* mix-PL but those

hé é cha waníce ehą́ni cha lé tha-há kaȟʼú-pi
that IP QL lack long ago so this ruminant-skin scrape-IPS

hená é cha ų́ wóžapi káǧa-pi. na į̨šé hehą́n tuwéni
those IP QL using stew make-PL and just then nobody

aǧúyapi yuhá-šni cha į̨šé lená lechála wašícu ki
bread* have-PL so just those recently white man DEF

ah-íyuweǧa-pi hehą́n nakéš aǧúyapi blú na khukhúše
arrive-cross over-PL then finally flour* and pig

wašį́ na wínakapo na haʼípažaža ki lená
fat and baking powder* and soap* DEF these

wichá-kʼu-pi-ʼ. éyaš hená táku ki slolyá-pi-šni cha
3PL.PAT-give-PL-ASS but those things DEF know-PL-NEG so

ų́-pi-šni. ho éyaš ehą́ni Lakhóta ki hená táku itéšniya
use-PL-NEG well but long ago Lakota DEF those what truly

wašté cha hená yúta-pi na tákuni ikcéya íchi-cahiya-pi-šni.
good QL those eat-PL and nothing ordinary REC-mix-PL-NEG

na táku yúta-pi ki hé tháȟca naʼį̨́š thathą́ka na
and what eat-PL DEF those deer* and buffalo bull* and

wahútopa	*cik-cík'ala*	*hená*	*é*	*tóna*	*hená*	*wichá-yuta-pi.*
quadruped*	RED-small	those	IP	so many	those	3PL.PAT-eat-PL

hená	*é-'e,*	*táku*	*ųmá*	*hená*	*šíca*	*cha*	*yúta-pi-šni.*	*ho*	*tkhá*
those	IP-RED	things	other	those	bad	QL	eat-PL-NEG	well	but

lehą́n	*táku k'éyaš*	*áta*	*íchižena*	*káğa-pi*	*na*	*Lakhóta*	*ki*
now	anything	entirely	mixed	make-IPS	and	Indian	DEF

o-yúl-wicha-khiya-pi	*cha*	*iyúha*	*khúža-pi.*	*wichókhuže*
L-eat-3PL.PAT-CAU-IPS	so	all	sick-PL	sickness

echécha-pi	*na*	*akísni-pi*	*okíhi-pi-šni.*	*ho*	*na*	*hé*	*tókhel*
affected with-PL	and	recover-PL	can-PL-NEG	well	and	that	that way

pápa	*káğa-pi*	*ki*	*le-tąhą*	*wakáphapi*	*eyá-pi*	*cha*
dried meat	make-PL	DEF	this-from	pounded meat	say-IPS	QL

hená	*wašį́kceka*	*cha*	*hená*	*icáhiya-pi*	*hé*	*káğa-pi.*	*ho*
DEM.PL.SG	tallow	QL	those	mix-PL	that	make-PL	well

nahą́	*wasná*	*cha*	*hé*	*į́š*	*pápa*	*cha*	*kaphá-pi*	*nahą́*
and then	pemmican	QL	that	it	dried meat	QL	pound-PL	and then

hé	*chąphá*	*cha*	*hé*	*į́š eyá*	*íchi-cahiya-pi*	*nahą́*	*wašį́kceka*	*na*
that	cherry	QL	that	also	REC-mix-PL	and then	tallow	and

héchel	*wasná*	*káğa-pi,*	*íchi-cahiya.*	*éyaš*	*lehą́n*	*tuwéni*	*hená*
so	pemmican	make-PL	REC-mix	but	now	nobody	those

echų́-šni,	*hená*	*iyúha*	*chąhą́pi*	*icáhiya-pi.*	*táku*	*káğa-pi*	*ki*	*lená*
do-NEG	those	all	sugar*	mix-PL	what	make-PL	DEF	these

iyúha chąhą́pi icáhiya-pi na wíyukpą cha ų́ hená yukpą́-pi.
all sugar* mix-PL and grinder* QL with those grind-PL

į̇šé henáehą́ni íyą eyá gmigméla cha él aką́n
just those long ago stone LK round QL on on top

wa-káški-pi nahą́ íyą imás'iyapha s'e léchecha
NSP.PAT-pound-PL and then stone hammer* like.AV like this

henáų́ kaškí-pi. éyaš lehą́n henáiyúha wíyukpą yukhą́ cha
those using pound-PL but now those all grinder* exist so

hé yukpą́ iyéya-pi na wágleyutapi-la ki aką́n ihpéya-pi
that pulverize send-PL and table*-DIM DEF on top throw-PL

na'į́š wípusye yukhą́ cha hąhépi ópta henáiyúha pus-yá-pi
and dryer* exist so night through those all dry.A-CAU-PL

na mahél iyéya-pi. į̇šé lehą́n wichó'ų ki líla oȟ'ą́kho.
and inside send-PL just now way of life DEF INT fast

ehą́ni henáiyótiyékiya henákáǧa-pi cha henáiyúha
long ago those have a hard time those make-PL so those all

wochékhiye echų́-pi na henáglu'ónihą-yą mahél
prayer do-PL and those POSS.respect.VT-ADV inside

iyé-ki-ya-pi. hechél oyáte ki akíȟ'ą-pi-šni. éyaš lehą́n líla
ST-PSS-send-PL so people DEF starve-PL-NEG but now INT

oyáte kihą wašícu wichó-'ų. cha akíȟ'ą-pi na'į́š líla
people DEF white man COLL-exist so starve-PL and INT

wichókhuže	*cha*	*šíca.*	*ho*	*lé*	*isą́m*	*oblákį-kte*	*éyaš*	*hų́ȟ*
sickness	so	bad	well	this	more	tell.1SG.AG-FUT	but	some

wéksuye-šni,	*hų́ȟ*	*lehą́n*	*cha*	*hé*	*tohą́n*
remember.1SG.AG-NEG	some	now	QL	that	when

wéksuye	*ki*	*akhé*	*hų́ȟ*	*oblákį-kte.*
remember.1SG.AG	when	again	some	tell.1SG.AG-FUT

Today I will talk about how the Lakota prepared food, stored it for winter use, and how they ate it in winter. This food is what I am going to tell about. First, they dried meat and made jerky. In order to make dried provisions, people sliced buffalo or cattle stomachs, intestines, livers, lungs, and hearts, and cooked them a little. After killing a cow, they cut the meat loose along the race tracks [some grooves in the tissue] and sliced it. The sliced pieces were made to be very long. They tied poles together and threw the meat over them. They inserted chokecherry sticks as stretchers. So they let the meat dry. They dried it, turning it over from time to time. When it was thoroughly dry, they took it and packed it into rawhide parfleches and stored that for winter use. The stomach was washed thoroughly. Some of the intestines were turned inside out, boiled on a stove in a kettle, and hung up, dripping and dangling as they were. They were cooked a little [when they were to be eaten]. When they were dry they didn't spoil, so they were dried like that and packed away. And some of the intestines, the curly ones, were blown up and tied together on both ends. When they were dry after they had been blown up that way, people went and wrapped them around a stick, roasted them above a roasting fire, and ate them. And the lungs were pierced, and right there [where the holes had been made] grease was stuffed in; this was roasted, and it tasted very good. As for the liver, a pit was dug in the ground, burning coals were thrown into it, the liver was thrown in, and coals were piled up on top of it. When it was thoroughly done it was cut into small strips and eaten, and it didn't spoil if it was prepared that way. And the heart was cut into small strips and dried like this. When it was to be boiled, people removed it from the storage containers, took it, sliced as it was, and threw it into the kettle.

Or they prepared some meat, while it was still fresh, in a way referred to as "meat turned inside out." The meat was cut into long strips; the intestines which had been turned inside out were tied across at regular intervals [after the meat had been stuffed in], and water was poured over them. They were tied across many times, and when they were thrown into the kettle like this, soup was made from the water in there. People drank it, and ate it [the sausage] with it, biting off pieces from it. And they even used the bones. They split the leg bones and removed the grease, which is called *thachúpa*; they spread it on bread and ate it. Or perhaps they pounded the dried meat they had made, mixed that with it, and ate that. And they split the joints, the joint bones; when they boiled them the fat came to the top. People strained the fat that came to the top, put it separately, and let it cook like this. When they ran out of grease, they threw them [the bones] into the kettle. They also mixed the fat with aromatic leaves and greased their hair with it. And they took the head, the tongue, and the jaw, and cooked and dried them as well. Even when the winter was hard they survived somehow. They boiled that, and they had something to eat all the time that way. Corn was brought to a boil. After that it was dried. Some corn was braided with the husks still on. People let it dry by hanging it up when they had boiled it. After that they took it off. From some other [corn] they made [another kind of] dried corn. People removed them [the kernels from the fresh cob] and threw them into a cooking pot. They boiled them just a bit so they were slightly cooked and spread them on a table. By drying that, dried corn [hominy] was made. This was also stored for winter. About squash: yellow squash with thick rind was peeled; this squash was sliced and dried. It was also dried on a table. Some [squash] were cut spirally; then people took a rope, strung them up on it, pulled them apart, and let them dry like this. That way food was prepared. When people would be starving in winter they would take these things out and bring them to a boil over the fireplace so they turned soft. Nothing was ever wasted. And people went picking [berries], too. In summer they went picking [berries]; they picked cherries, pounded and dried them, and stored them as well. They were formed into flat cakes and put up to dry; the same thing was done with plums. Long ago people had the children chew them up. And when they had discarded the stones, they let them dry without the stones. But now there are kettles, so people throw them into a cooking pot. When they are boiling and have popped open, they are ladled out; the stones are thrown away, and they [the plums] are left to dry. When they have been dried they serve as food. In winter food was prepared from them. They were mashed. But in the old times there was no sugar. When people prepared food, they didn't mix it with many other ingredients. That was not done in the past. There was no flour to mix it [the food] with, either. People used hide scrapings to make stew [to thicken it]. And nobody had bread until recently, when the white people came over [from Europe]. Then people finally received flour, pork fat, baking powder, and soap. But they didn't know about these things, so they didn't use them [at first]. But long ago the Lakota ate what was really good, and they didn't mix anything impure into their food. What they ate were deer, buffalo, and small quadrupeds. All these they ate. Those were the ones, the others were bad, so they didn't eat them. But today everything is being mixed together, and the Indians are forced to eat it, so they are all sick. They catch diseases, and are unable to recover. And from the jerky they [the old-time people] also made what is called pounded meat, when they mixed it with grease. In order to make pemmican they pounded jerky and mixed in chokecherries and grease; pemmican was made that way, by mixing everything together. But nobody does that any more—they all mix in sugar. What they all do is mix in sugar and use a grinder for grinding. In the past the grinding was done on round stones, and the pounding was done with stones that were used like hammers. But now people all have grinders to grind with, and they spread everything on tables, and they have dryers, so they dry everything during the night, and put it away. Today's life is very fast. Long ago people had a hard time making these things, so they all made prayers and packed things away with respect. That way people didn't starve. But today's life is very much like that of the white man. People are starving, and diseases are widespread, which is bad. I want to tell more about this but I cannot remember some of the things, so when I remember some more things I will tell another story.

3.6. Buckskin

NEVA STANDING BEAR

Tape recorded September 9, 1994

ho lé icí-nų̨pa ki lé tha-há káğa-pi ki hé é
well this ORD-two DEF this ruminant-skin make-IPS DEF that IP

naʾį̨́š tókhel wóʾilagya-pi ki hená obláki̧-kte. ho waná pté
and how use-IPS LK those tell.1SG.AG-FUT well now cow

kté-pi hą́tąhąš hená wóyute káğa-pi. ho na tha-há ki
kill-IPS when those food make-IPS well and ruminant-skin DEF

hé ptebléška ki hé há yúza-pi na thahú ki ognáyą
that cattle* DEF that skin take-IPS and neck DEF alongside

thakhą́ ȟpáya cha hé yuslúta-pi nahą́ yužáža-pi na
sinew* lie QL that pull off-IPS and then wash-IPS and

pakʾóğa-pi na chą́ wąží ka-ʾíyaskab-ya pus-yá-pi. na
scrape and wood IDF.SG INS-stick to-ADV dry.A-CAU-IPS and

tha-há ki hé icú-pi na áta kašképa-pi nahą́
ruminant-skin DEF that take-IPS and entirely scrape-IPS and then

yuzíl okátą-pi na pus-yá-pi hą́tąhąš hechél hį́ ki
stretch.VT stake down-IPS and dry.A-CAU-IPS when so fur DEF

hená katkú-pi. nahą́ hé tohą́n katkú-pi yuštą́-pi
those peel.VT off-IPS and then that when peel.VT off-IPS finish-IPS

ehą́tąhąš yuptą́yą iȟpéya-pi nahą́ ųmáchiyatąhą thaló
when turn over.VT throw-IPS and then on the other side meat

echíyatahą įš eyá áta katkú-pi na thakhą́ naˀį́š thaló
from this side also entirely peel.VT off-IPS and sinew* and meat

táku él iyáskape ki hená iyúha ka-ȟláya-pi na ho
things there stick to DEF those all INS-fall off-IPS and well

yuštą́-pi hą́tąhąš iyáya-pi na tha-há ki hé áta
finish-IPS when go-IPS and ruminant-skin DEF that entirely

tha-násu-la cha iyų́-pi na átaya ipáthą-thą-pi na
ruminant-brain-DIM QL apply-IPS and entirely smear-RED-IPS and

yu-spáya-pi ho na tohą́n hé áta kakpá iyáye hą́tąhąš
INS-wet-IPS well and when that entirely through go when

ho hehą́n icú-pi na yužáža-pi ho na yuškíca-pi ho
well then take-IPS and wash-IPS well and wring out-IPS well

na hé phežíkakse héchacha chą́ ektá iyákaška-pi na ho hé
and this sickle* like that tree to tie-IPS and well that

é cha ų́ yuȟų́ta-pi. iwáštegla yuȟų́n áya-pi na
IP QL with rub until soft carefully rub until soft PRC-IPS and

ohómni okáwįȟ yuȟų́ta-hą-pi na ithánųgya áta
around go round rub until soft-PRG-IPS and on each side entirely

ákhilechel-ya yuȟų́ta-pi chą́-šna hécheš tukténi
equal-ADV rub until soft-IPS then-HAB so nowhere

suk-súta-šni, áta héchel íyakhilechel-ya phąphą́la. ho cha
RED-hard-NEG entirely so all the same-ADV soft well so

héchų-pi na héhą hé thakhą́ ki hé púze hą́tąhąš yuȟláya
do that-PL and then that sinew* DEF that dry.A when pull off

icú-pi na ho hená é cha yuslél icú-pi na haȟų́ta
take-IPS and well those IP QL split.VT take-IPS and thread

kǧ́a-pi. thakhą́ ki kazá-pi na hená óta
make-IPS sinew* DEF tear off and twist-IPS and those many

kǧ́a-pi ho na hé é-gnaka-pi na hená é cha ų́
make-IPS well and that L-put-IPS now those IP QL with

áta pšithó kšú-pi na'į́š
entirely small glass beads embroider-IPS or

w-óska-pi. phahį́ óska-pi. na tohą́n
NSP.PAT-do quillwork-IPS porcupine quill do quillwork-IPS and when

hená aką́n tha-há-cik-cik'a hená akáb'iyaye ki hená
those on top ruminant-skin-RED-small those leftovers* DEF those

į́š eyá táku cik-cík'ala kǧ́a-pi na wókaphą na'į́š míyožuha
also what RED-small make-IPS and container or knife sheath

na héchekchekel táku cik-cík'ala hená kǧ́a-pi. na ptebléška
and just like this things RED-small those make-IPS and cattle*

sįté ki hé icú-pi na pabláza-pi na yu-bláya yu-t'į́s
tail DEF that take-IPS and cut open-IPS and INS-flat INS-tight

pus-yá-pi	*cha*	*hená*	*áta*	*hį́*	*ki*	*katkú-pi*	*nahą́*
dry.A-CAU-IPS	so	those	entirely	fur	DEF	peel.VT off-IPS	and then

héchel	*phahį́*	*óska-pi*	*blaská-ya*	*watókhetuya*
there	porcupine quill	do quillwork-IPS	flat-ADV	so big

óska-pi	*chą́-šna*	*ho*	*hél*	*wíyaka*	*nų́m*	*a-ʔíyakaška-pi*	*cha*
do quillwork-IPS	then-HAB	well	there	feather	two	L-tie-IPS	so

hé	*waphégnaka*	*ecíya-pi.*	*na*	*ųmá*	*ki*	*lená*	*chuwígnaka*
that	headgear	say-IPS	and	other	DEF	these	dress*

káǧa-pi	*naʔį́š*	*tha-há-ʔogle,*	*wicháša itháchą*	*tha-ʔógle*	*eyá-pi*
make-IPS	or	ruminant-skin-shirt	chief	ALP-shirt	say-IPS

cha	*héchacha*	*káǧa-pi*	*naʔį́š*	*hųská*	*tha-há-hųska*
QL	like that	make-IPS	or	leggings	ruminant-skin-leggings

naʔį́š	*eyá*	*hé*	*wį́yą*	*tha-hų́ska*	*nahą́*	*hą́pa*	*naʔį́š*
and	also	that	woman	ALP-leggings	and then	moccasin	and

eyá	*há*	*thókecha*	*cha*	*hená*	*átaya*	*sag-yéla*	*pus-yá-pi*	*na*
also	skin	different	QL	those	INT	stiff-ADV	dry.A-CAU-IPS	and

púze	*hą́tąhąš*	*hená*	*é*	*cha*	*waksá-pi*	*nahą́*	*hąp-sícu*
dry.A	when	those	IP	QL	cut-IPS	and then	moccasin-sole

káǧa-pi.	*sicúha*	*hená*	*káǧa-pi.*	*naʔį́š*	*ųgnáš*	*hąké*	*chą́ceǧa*
make-IPS	sole	those	make-IPS	and	perhaps	part	drum

káǧa-pi.	*į́š*	*eyá*	*táku*	*héchel*	*wóʔilake*	*ų́*	*káǧa-pi.*	*cha*
make-IPS	they	also	things	so	commodity	with	make-IPS	so

hé tha-há-saka ki nakų́ hų́ȟ icú-pi nahą́
that ruminant-skin-stiff DEF also some take-IPS and then

só-so-pi nahą́ yu-spáya-pi na líla yu-tˀís-ya
cut into strings-RED-IPS and then INS-wet-IPS and INT INS-tight-ADV

sų́-pi chą́-šna wíkhą káǧa-pi. hená ų́
braid-IPS then-HAB rope make-IPS those with

šų-khóyag-ya-pi ho naˀį́š šų-káška é-gle-pi. na hé é cha
horse-stick to-CAU-IPS well or horse-tie L-put-IPS and that IP QL

wíkhą káǧa-pi kštó. cha hená táku ki iyúha há ki hená
rope make-IPS ASS.F so those things DEF all skin DEF those

wóˀilagya-pi cha Lakhóta ki tóhąni tákuni iȟpéya-pi-šni.
use-IPS QL Lakota DEF never nothing throw away-IPS-NEG

táku ptebléška na wamákhašką etą́ ú ki iyúha
things cattle* and animal* from come DEF all

wóˀilagya-pi nahą́ lé šaké ki hená ékayeš piȟ-yá-pi
use-IPS and then this hoof DEF those even boil.VI-CAU-IPS

na hená waskú-pi na wanápˀį káǧa-pi. hená
and those shave off-IPS and necklace make-IPS those

šla-šlá-yela napˀį-pi cha hená héchel káǧa-pi.
tinkle-RED-ADV wear around the neck-IPS so those so make-IPS

wicháša ki nąpˀį-pi. cha táku Lakhóta
man DEF wear around the neck-PL so things Lakota

wamákhašką etą́ ú ki lená tákuni ikcéya
animal from come DEF these nothing just

iȟpéya-pi-šni, hená iyúha wóˀilake káğa-pi cha
throw away-IPS-NEG those all commodity make-PL so

lehą́tu éyaš ųgnáš takún tuwá wąyáke hą́tąhąš šíca
now but perhaps something someone see when bad

kéchį na iȟpéya-pi éyaš hená héchecha-šni. lená
think that and throw away-IPS but those like that-NEG these

iyúha wóˀilake cha ų́-hą-pi. na hená įšé ehą́ni
all commodity QL use-PRG-IPS and those perhaps long ago

thahį́špa ų́-pi. cha hená thahį́špa ki hohú cha káğa-pi. cha
awl use-IPS so those awl DEF bone QL make-IPS so

hená nakų́ ų́ wakšú-pi. thahį́špa cha į́š ų́
those also using do beadwork-PL awl QL they with

wa-káyeğe-pi éyaš hená šikšílˀiya-pi cha hená obláka
NSP.PAT-sew-IPS but those talk dirty-IPS so those tell.1SG.AG

o-wá-kihi-šni. cha ųmá ki lená é-ˀe tha-há
ST-1SG.AG-can-NEG so other DEF these IP-RED ruminant-skin

ki hená ųgnáš wamákhašką cíkˀala ki lená há ki
DEF those perhaps animal* small DEF these skin DEF

icú-pi nahą́ wa-hį́-šma ki lená ų́ hų́ȟ hą́pa
take-IPS and then NSP.PAT-fur-deep DEF these using some moccasin

káǧa-pi na ógle na'į́š waphóštą na'į́š wahą́'owįžapi cha hená
make-IPS and coat and cap and comforter* QL that

héchel káǧa-pi. hená phąš-phą́žela cha hé ų́ hená
so make-IPS those RED-soft so that in order to those

héchekchel káǧa-pi. cha Lakhóta ki táku óta wa-'échų-pi
so make-IPS so Lakota DEF things many NSP.PAT-do-IPS

na hená lehą́n waníca áye. cha lená iyúha thokhą́-tąhą
and those now lack PRC so these all elsewhere-from

slolyá-pi chį́-pi na lená okáȟniǧa-pi héci Lakhóta ki
know-IPS want-IPS and these understand-IPS if Indian DEF

tókheškhe eháni wichó'ų hená slolyá-pi-kte. lé Lakhóta
how long ago way of life those know-IPS-FUT this Indian

wichó'ų ki lé ąpétu ki ítokha-pi-šni. cha lé waná táku
way of life* DEF this day DEF care-IPS-NEG so this now things

tha-há ų́-pi kihą hé wahéhą.
ruminant-skin use-PL DEF that that far

Next, I will tell how the buckskin that people made was used. When cows [or buffalo] had been killed, people made food of them. They skinned the animal and pulled off the sinews running alongside the neck. Then they washed them, scraped them clean, and dried them by plastering them against a piece of wood. And the hide was taken, all scraped off, stretched and staked down, and when it was dry the hair was shaved off. After the shaving was done, it was turned over and entirely scraped clean on the flesh side as well, so the sinew or bits of meat that were still adhering, and anything else, was removed. When this had been done people went and applied brains all over the hide, rubbed it in thoroughly, and wetted it [the hide]. When it [the brain substance] had been absorbed completely people took it [the hide], washed it, and wrung it out. Then they fastened [the blade of] a sickle to a tree, and rubbed it [the hide] with it until it was soft [by pulling it back and forth over the blade]. They rubbed it well for a while, turning it around and around, until both sides were thoroughly tanned. This way no hard spot was left and it was soft all over. When they had done that, people pulled the sinew [off the tree] when it was dry and made thread by separating it into fine strands. They tore the sinew apart and twisted it [after wetting it in the mouth]. They made many of these threads, and stored them. With them they did all their beadwork or embroidering. They did porcupine quillwork. And from the small leftover pieces of hide small things were made, such as rawhide containers or knife sheaths, and whatever other small things like these there were. And people took the cow's tail, cut it open, stretched it out to dry, and shaved off all the hair. Then they embroidered it with quillwork, across its whole width, and tied two feathers to it. This was called *waphégnaka*. The other things people made were dresses or leather shirts, which were called chief's shirts. Such things they made, and also leggings–buckskin leggings–and women's leggings, and moccasins. Some other hides were dried completely, and when they were so dry that they were stiff, they were cut and made into moccasin soles. People made soles of them. Part [of the hide] could perhaps be made into drums. All kinds of commodities were made from them [hides]. People also took some rawhide, cut it into strips, wetted them and braided them very tightly, and made ropes that way. With these they roped horses or tied horses to a pole. That's what they made ropes from. For all these things hides were used. The Lakota never threw anything away. Whatever came from cattle and [other] animals was used for commodities. Even the hooves were boiled, carved, and made into necklaces. They were made in such a way that they gave a tinkling sound when they were worn around the neck. The men wore them. The Lakota never just threw away anything that comes from the animals. They made them all into commodities. When one of them [non-Indians] sees something [a piece of Indian art] today he may think it's worthless, and that it should be discarded, but it's not like that. People used all these things for commodities. In the old times people used awls. They made those awls from bones. They also used them to do beadwork. They sewed with the awls. But they talked dirty of them. I cannot talk about that. As for the other hides, such as the hides of the small animals, people took them and made moccasins from some of the fur. Coats, caps, and comforters were made that way. They were made to be soft. The Lakota made many things, and they are disappearing today. So people want to know about all that from elsewhere, and if they understood it, the Indians would learn about their way of life long ago. Today people don't care about the Indian way of life. That much about the use of hides.

3.7. Prairie Turnips

NEVA STANDING BEAR

Tape recorded September 9, 1994

thį́psila	*ki*	*lená*	*o-k'á-pi*	*na*	*hená*	*átaya*	*há*	*yuğápa-pi*
prairie turnip	DEF	these	L-dig-IPS	and	those	INT	skin	strip off-PL

na	*sų́-pi*	*na*	*pus-yá-pi*	*cha*	*hená*	*nakų́*	*wóyute*	*káğa-pi.*
and	braid-IPS	and	dry.A-CAU-IPS	so	those	also	food	make-IPS

cha	*hé*	*June*	*wiyáwapi*	*ki*	*él*	*káğa-pi*	*na*	*hená*	*lé*
so	that	June	month*	DEF	in	make-IPS	and	those	this

Lakhóta	*lol'íȟ'ą-pi*	*ki*	*hená*	*hél*	*ikhóyake*	*kštó.*
Lakota	boil.VT-IPS	DEF	those	there	adhere	ASS.F

People dug up the prairie turnips, stripped off the skin, braided them together, and dried them. They were also made into food. This was done in June. They are part of the Lakota style of cooking.

3.8. Puberty Rites

NEVA STANDING BEAR

Tape recorded September 12, 1994

lé tókhel wéksuye ki héchųs'e obláki̜-kte.
that how remember.1SG.AG. LK that way* tell.1SG.AG-FUT

išnáthi a-kí-lową-pi eyá-pi na ų́
have the menses* L-BEN-sing-IPS say-IPS and therefore

hųká-pi. cha wichį́cala ki lé othókaheya
perform a ceremony-IPS so girl DEF this for the first time

waná thąkáyąki̜-kte hą́tąhąš khų́ši-tku ki é
now have the menses*-FUT when grandmother-3POR DEF IP

nahą́ hų́-ku ki iyáya-pi nahą́ thípi wą
and then mother-3POR DEF go-PL and then tipi IDF.SG

é-ki-gle-pi na'į́š ųgná iníyothi cha é-gle-pi nahą́
L-BEN-put-PL or maybe sweatlodge QL L-put-PL and then

héchiya wichį́cala ki thohą́yą thąkáyąke hą́tąhąš
there girl DEF as long as have the menses* when

winúȟcala ki, khų́ši-tku ki kichí yąké. héchiya yąká-pi
old woman DEF grandmother-3POR DEF with sit there sit-PL

na echél wichį́cala ki iglúštą hą́tahąš iyáya-pi na
and so girl DEF POSS.finish when go-IPS and

azílthų-pi na wakpála ektá nakų́ osní éyaš wakpála ektá

burn incense-IPS and river to also cold but river to

aʔí-pi na nųwé-khiya-pi na héktakiya aglí-pi na lé

take to-IPS and swim-CAU-IPS and back.AV take back-IPS and this

oʔínikaǧe ki lél thimá é-ya-ya-pi na

sweatlodge DEF here inside L-go-CAU-IPS and

iní-ki-caǧa-pi na pakhį́ta-pi nahą́

ST-BEN-perform sweatlodge ceremony-IPS and wipe-IPS and then

ho hé él hų́-ku ki i-glú-wįyeya cha héchel áta

well that at mother-3POR DEF ST-POSS.INS-ready so so INT

wóyute ki tókhel okíhi-pi-ka hená iȟʔą́-pi nahą́

food DEF how can-IPS-kind of those cook.VT-IPS and then

wakšúpi eyála sʔe wíȟpeya-pi. ho cha hé

beadwork a lot of practice give away*-IPS well so that

akhí-pi hą́tąhąš lé thi-ʔíkceya pa-wóslal iyéya-pi

bring back-IPS when this house-common INS-upright send-IPS

cha héchi thimá aglí-gnaka-pi. cha héchi wichį́cala tóna

so there inside take back-put-IPS so there girl so many

išnáthi iglúštą-pi kʔų hená é cha iyúha héchi

have the menses* POSS.finish-PL DEF those IP QL all there

thimá yąká-pi cha hená khohą́ thąkál i-glú-wįyeya-pi

inside sit-PL so those meanwhile outside ST-POSS.INS-ready-IPS

hą́tąhąš hé waná waphíya wicháša wą thimá iyáya cha į́š
when that now medicine man* IDF.SG inside go so he

hé ųgnáš wį́yą na'į́š wicháša waphíye hécha. cha thimá iyáyį
that maybe woman or man healer* COP so inside go

nahą́ lená w-ó-wicha-ki-yakį nahą́ chąphá hąpí
and then these NSP.PAT-ST-3PL-BEN-tell and then chokecherry juice

cha yatké-wicha-khiye. hená okáwįȟ yatké-wicha-khiya-pi
QL drink-3PL.PAT-CAU those go round drink-3PL.PAT-CAU-IPS

nahą́ wasná i-y-ó-gną-g-wicha-khiya-pi. héchų-pi
and then pemmican mouth-EI-L-put-3PL.PAT-CAU-IPS do that-PL

nahą́ hé iglúštą-pi hą́tąhąš ho thápa wą
and then that POSS.finish-IPS when well ball LK

kšú-pi cha yuhá hiną́pha-pi na hená ókšą
do beadwork-IPS QL have go outside-PL and those in a circle

nážį-pi cha hé thápa ki hé wąkál ye-yá-pi. wąkál
stand-PL so that ball DEF that up go-CAU-IPS up

ye-yá-pi na hená iyúha wachékhiya-pi na wąkál ye-yá-pi
go-CAU-IPS and those all pray-IPS and up go-CAU-IPS

chą́-šna ho hé tuwá yukhápe hé į́š eyá
then-HAB well that who catch that he also

hųká-kte. cha hená hų́-ku nahą́
perform a ceremony-FUT so those mother-3POR and then

khų́ši-tku ki lená wąží tuwá kaȟníǧa-pi na hé

grandmother-3POR DEF these one someone choose-PL and that

wichį́cala ki lé thokátakiya wíyaksapa-pi na táku

girl DEF this in the future teach-PL and things

wa-ˀų́spe-khiyį-kte. táku echų́-kte ki hená iyúha-ȟci

NSP.PAT-know-CAU-PL what do-FUT DEF those all-INT

ųspé-khiyį́-kte. lolˀíȟˀą nahą́ wakšú-kte na

know-CAU-FUT cook.VI and then do beadwork-FUT and

wóska-kte nahą́ wakábla-kte naˀį́š waphátį-kte na thípi

embroider-FUT and then dry.VT meat-FUT and butcher-FUT and tipi

hená kayéǧį-kte. naˀį́š tókhel thahá kpąyį na tókhel thakhą́ hená

those sew-FUT and how hide tan and how sinew* those

kazá na ų́ wa-káyeǧį-kte héci hená iyúha-ȟci ųspé-kte.

shred and with NSP.PAT-sew-FUT SUB those all-INT know-FUT

hą́pa naˀį́š wichá tha-háyake káǧį-kte. hená iyúha ųspé-kte:

moccasin and man ALP-clothes make-FUT those all know-FUT

ho héchel oyáte étkiya wówaˀųšila na

well so people toward love.N and pity.N and

ų́ši-ˀicˀi-la-kte cha lená hená iyúha-ȟci ųspé-khiya-pi

ST-3RFL-humble.VT-FUT QL these those all-INT know-CAU-IPS

cha. tohą́n hiną́phe hą́tąhąš wáchįhį wą,

QL when go outside when eagle's chest plume IDF.SG

iyá-kici-caška-pi. *ho* *cha* *hé* *waníyetu* *tóna* *yuhá*
ST-PSS-fasten on-IPS well so that year so many have

ú-kte *na* *akhé* *ų̀gnáš* *hųká-kte* *hą́tąhąš* *akhé*
come-FUT and again maybe perform a ceremony-FUT when again

wąží *k'ú-pi.* *cha* *tuwéni* *otúyachį* *wíyaka* *ki* *lená*
one give-IPS so nobody for nothing feather DEF these

phégnake-šni. *ho* *cha* *héchel* *lená* *wichį́cala* *kihą*
wear on the head-NEG well so so these girl DEF

wa-'ų́spe-pi *nahą́* *w-ókaȟniǧa-pi.* *lená*
NSP.PAT-know-PL and then NSP.PAT-understand-PL these

winúȟcala *na'į́š* *wicháȟcala* *lená* *iyótą-ȟci*
old woman and old man these most-INT

ų́ši-wicha-la-ka-pi-kte. *héchel* *hená* *ecéla*
ST-3PL.PAT-love.VT and respect.VT-kind of-PL-FUT so those only

wa-'ų́spe-pi *cha* *héchel* *echų́-pi.* *cha* *lená* *átaya* *oyáte*
NSP.PAT-know-PL so that way do-PL so these INT people

ki *yu-míme-ya* *é-wicha-gnaka-pi* *na* *hená*
DEF INS-round-ADV L-3PL.PAT-put-IPS and those

wól-wicha-khiya-pi *na* *wíȟpeya-pi.* *na* *ų̀gná*
eat.NSP.PAT-3PL.PAT-CAU-IPS and practice give away*-IPS and maybe

šų́kawakhą́ *óta* *wichá-yuha-pi* *hą́tąhąš* *šų́kawakhą́* *khó* *kaȟáb*
horse* many 3PL.PAT-have-PL when horse* also drive

iyé-wicha-ya-pi *cha* *hená* *tuwá* *okíhi* *hą́tąhą*
ST-3PL.PAT-send-PL QL those someone can if

o-wícha-yuspį *nahą́* *wó'ilag-wicha-ye.* *ho* *cha* *táku*
ST-3PL.PAT-grab and then ST-3PL.PAT-use well so things

Lakhóta *étkiya* *wa-'échų-pi* *ki* *lená* *líla* *othéȟike.* *éyaš*
Lakota toward NSP.PAT-do-IPS DEF these INT difficult but

lehą́n *otúyachį* *iná-'ų-piškąyą-pi* *chąkhé* *wašícu*
now senselessly ST-1PL.AG-play around-PL then white man

wichó'ų *ki* *ognáyą* *ųk'ų́-pi* *cha* *átaya* *lehą́n*
way of life DEF according to 1PL.AG.exist-PL so INT now

wichį́cala *ki* *otúyachį* *heyókha* *sékse* *igluzá-pi* *na*
girl DEF senselessly clown like.AV dress up-PL and

wachí-pi. *kawíyakpa-kpa-yela* *mniȟúha* *ocháže* *iyúha* *khoyáka-pi*
dance-PL shiny-RED-ADV fabric all kinds all wear-PL

na *nagwág* *iyéya* *wachí-pi.* *tuwéni* *ehą́ni* *héchel* *wachí-šni.*
and kick send dance-PL nobody long ago so dance-NEG

éyaš *lehą́n* *héchų s'e* *wachí-pi.* *cha* *lená* *tuwéni-ȟci*
but now that way* dance-IPS so these nobody-INT

okáȟniğe-šni. *cha* *lená* *oyáte* *kihą* *lehą́n* *hená* *okáȟniğa-pi*
understand-NEG so these people DEF now those understand-PL

hą́tąhąš *líla* *wichó'ų* *thókecha* *na* *ehą́ni* *líla*
if INT way of life different and long ago INT

wa-náȟʼų-ka-pi, wakȟą́yeža ki. ho na hehą́n waná
NSP.PAT-hear-kind of-PL child DEF well and then now

wikhóskalaka ki lená ichášǧa-pi na thą́kake ki lená abléza-pi
girl DEF these grow-PL and older DEF these notice-PL

na ablés ų́-pi nahą́ ųgnáš chįchá khoškálaka-pi wichį́cala
and notice CNT-PL and then maybe child young man-PL girl

wąží theȟíla-pi hą́tąhąš hiyú-pi na wį́yą ki lé,
IDF.SG love.VT-PL when come-PL and woman DEF this

wichį́cala ki lé, lá-pi. chą́-šna hų́-ku na
girl DEF this ask for-PL then-HAB mother-3POR and

at-kúku ki nųphį́ i-w-óglaka-pi nahą́ echél
father-3POR DEF both L-NSP.PAT-POSS.tell-PL and then so

iyó-kichi-phi-pi hą́tąhąš hokšíla ki lé wichį́cala ki lé
ST-REC-please-PL if boy DEF this girl DEF this

ithánųgya wichá-kichi-cʼu-pi. chą́-šna slol-kíchi-ya-pi-šni
on both sides 3PL.PAT-REC-give-PL then-HAB ST-REC-know-PL-NEG

éyaš takómni hų́-ku na at-kúku-pi ki héchel
but at all costs mother-3POR and father-3POR-PL DEF so

chį́-pi cha. ųgnáš wichį́cala ki hokšíla ki waȟtélašni séce
want-PL so maybe girl DEF boy DEF dislike maybe

kʼéyaš takómni hįgnáye. ho éyaš he-tą́ táku
but nevertheless marry* well but that-from things

wówa'ųšila *na* *táku* *wašté* *etą́* *ú-kta* *héci* *héhą*
love.N and pity.N and things good from come-FUT SUB then

hená *héchel* *i-wícha-kichi-yukcą-pi* *cha* *héchų-pi* *cha*
those so ST-3PL.PAT-REC-think of-PL so do that-PL so

otúyachį *tuwéni* *hųká-šni.* *hųká-pi*
senselessly nobody perform a ceremony-NEG perform a ceremony-PL

ki *lé* *takómni* *Thųkášila* *étkiya* *w-íyukcą-pi* *cha*
DEF this at all costs God* toward NSP.PAT-think of-PL so

tuwá *hųká* *nahą́* *waná* *thoká* *thąkáyąke*
who perform a ceremony and then now first have the menses*

hą́tąhąš *hé* *ohó-ki-la.* *įchį́* *he-tą́* *wakhą́yeža*
when that ST-PSS-respect.VT because that-from child

icháǧa-pi *na* *táku* *etą́hą-š* *hená* *wakhą́yeža*
grow-PL and something from-EMPH those wakhą́yeža

e-wícha-kiya-pi, *sacred,* *eyá-pi.* *hená* *wakhą́yeža* *ki*
ST-3PL.PAT-say to-IPS sacred say-IPS those child DEF

wakhą́yeža *e-wícha-kiya-pi* *ki* *lená* *į́š eyá* *wakhą́-pi* *cha.*
wakhą́yeža ST-3PL.PAT-say to-IPS DEF these also sacred-PL so

wakhą́yeža *hená* *makhá* *etą́* *icháǧa-pi.* *cha* *tuwéni*
child those earth from grow-PL so nobody

otúyachį-šni. *lé* *lehą́n* *wašícu* *ki* *hiyú-pi* *na* *hená*
act senselessly-NEG this now white man DEF come-PL and those

i-wícha-cu-pi	*na*	*žąžą́*	*ogná*	*é-wicha-gle-pi*	*na*
ST-3PL.PAT-take-PL	and	glass jar	inside	ST-3PL.PAT-put-PL	and

icháȟ-wicha-ya-pi	*cha*	*hécha-pi-šni.*	*lená*	*įšé*	*wakhą́-yą*	*hená*
grow-3PL.PAT-PL	QL	COP-PL-NEG	these	just	holy-ADV	those

Thųkášila	*wakhą́yeža*	*wichá-kʼu*	*cha*	*hé*	*ų́*	*héchel*
God*	child	3PL.PAT-give	so	that	because of	so

icháǧa-pi.	*cha*	*hená*	*waná*	*icháǧa-pi*	*hą́tąhąš*	*hokší oʼų́papi*	*eyá-pi.*
grow-PL	so	those	now	grow-PL	when	infant*	say-IPS

cha	*hená*	*cik-cíkʼala-pi*	*cha*	*hé*	*ų́*	*héyá-pi.*	*ho*	*he-tą́*
so	those	RED-small-PL	so	that	while	say that-IPS	well	that-from

icháȟ	*áya-pi*	*chą́-šna*	*hená*	*wakhą́yeža*	*e-wícha-kiya-pi.*	*cha*
grow	PRC-PL	then-HAB	those	child	ST-3PL.PAT-say to-IPS	so

hená	*táku*	*iyá-pi*	*nahą́*	*máni-pi*	*na*	*slohą́-pi,*	*lená*	*į́š eyá*
those	things	speak-PL	and then	walk-PL	and	crawl-PL	these	also

hená	*ųspé*	*ú-pi*	*cha*	*hą́tąhąš,*	*hená*	*wakhą́yeža*
those	know	come-PL	QL	when	those	wakhą́yeža

e-wícha-kiya-pi.	*na*	*hená*	*tuwá*	*a-ʼí-wicha-šįk-šįkcį*
ST-3PL.PAT-say to-IPS	and	those	someone	L-ST-3PL.PAT-RED-angry

chą́-šna	*wakhą́yeža*	*ki*	*khúža-pi*	*cha*	*tuwéni*	*hená*	*íšįkcį*
then-HAB	child	DEF	sick-PL	so	nobody	those	angry

o-wícha-khuwa-šni.	*ų́šika-pi,*	*hená*	*wakhą́yeža*	*ki.*	*cha*	*lehą́n*
L-3PL.PAT-pursue-NEG	dear-PL	those	child	DEF	so	now

éyaš otúyachį iȟpé-wicha-ya-pi na?įš tuktéktel eš
but for nothing ST-3PL.PAT-throw away-IPS and somewhere indeed

iȟpé-wicha-ya-pi, wichá-kte-pi-la na
ST-3PL.PAT-throw away-IPS 3PL.PAT-kill-IPS-DIM and

iȟpé-wicha-ya-pi. lená oyáte ki lená ų́
ST-3PL.PAT-throw away-IPS these people DEF these because of

ų-kákiža-pi éyaš slol-?ų́-yą-pi-šni cha iníhąšni
1PL.PAT-suffer-PL but ST-1PL.AG-know-PL-NEG so nevertheless

héchel ųk?ų́-pi. cha lé hųká ki lé
so 1PL.AG.exist-PL so this ceremony DEF this

tohą́n okíhilaka wakhą́. cha hená wakhą́-yą ųk-íchağa-pi.
as much as can be* sacred so those sacred-ADV 1PL.PAT-grow-PL

éyaš lehą́n hená otúyachį inápiškąyą-pi cha waná Lakhóta
but now those senselessly play around-PL so now Indian

ki sóta áya-pi. na ehą́ni šų́kawakhą́ wą chéyį na eyá
DEF gone PRC-PL and long ago horse* IDF.SG cry and say

škhé "wó?ilag-?ų-ya-ya-pi yųkhą́ oyáte kįhą wąží
QT ST-1PL.PAT-2AG-use-PL then people DEF one

ų-yá-kte-pi na ų-yá-luta-pi cha le-tą́
1PL.PAT-2AG-kill-PL and 1PL.PAT-2AG-eat.2AG-PL QL this-from

thokátakiya šų́kawakhą́ waníca-pi-kte" eyá kéye yųkhą́ lehą́n
in the future horse* lack-PL-FUT say QT then now

iyéchetu, enágna-la šýkawakhá yukhá. cha lená táku eyá-pi
like this scarcely-LIM horse* exist so these things say-PL

ki wakhá. cha tuwéni hená inápiškąye-šni. cha íš eyá tohán
DEF sacred so nobody those play around-NEG so also when

lená wichícala ki slolyá ichháǧa-pi na échel wíyą-pi ehátąhąš
these girl DEF know grow-PL and so woman-PL when

waná chįchá yukhį́ na íš eyá chįchá hená héchecha-pi.
now child exist and also child those like that-PL

hųká-pi-kte hátąhą íš eyá héchų s'e ópha-pi. éyaš
perform a ceremony-IPS-FUT when 3 too that way* join-PL but

lehán hená waníce. cha lená é cha lehán hená lechá icháǧe
now those lack so these IP QL now those recently grow

ki lená ųspé-pi wa-chí, wašícu óhą ú-pi éyaš
DEF these know-PL 1SG.AG-want white man among exist-PL but

takómni lená ųspé-pi hátahąš ųgnáš ka-'éktahe-yela s'e
at all costs these know-PL if maybe INS-moderate-ADV like.AV

witkó-tko-ka-pi-kte. cha hé ú lená eyášna
crazy-RED-kind of-PL-FUT so that because of these always

obláke. na wichícala ki lé lená oyákį nahá oyáte
tell.1SG.AG and girl DEF this these tell and then people

óhą lená wówapi ki lená yawá-pi-kta héchel líla wóphila
among these book DEF these read-PL-FUT so INT thanks

thą́ka hécha.
big OBL

I will tell about this the way I remember it. It [the ceremony] is called "singing over the first period"; that's why there is a ceremony. The grandmother and the mother of the girl who was going to have her first period went and put up a tipi, or maybe a sweatlodge, for her. The girl stayed in there for the length of her period, together with the old woman, her grandmother. They were sitting in there. When the girl's period was over people went and burned incense, and took her to the river, even when it was cold, and had her bathe. Then they took her back again. She was sent into the sweatlodge, and a sweatlodge ceremony was performed for her. Then she was wiped off, and right at that point her mother started to make her preparations. All the food that was available was cooked, and many pieces of beadwork were given away. When she was brought back [from the sweatlodge] she was taken to a tipi which had been put up. In there all the girls who had had their first period [within the past twelve months] were sitting. While the people outside were getting ready a medicine man came in. It was either a medicine woman or a medicine man. [S]he went inside, talked to them [the girls], and gave them chokecherry juice to drink. It [the beverage] was passed around, and they were given pemmican to eat. They did that, and when they were through with it they [the girls] went outside. They went outside. They had a beaded ball with them, and lined up in a circle. Then the ball was thrown in the air [by the medicine man/woman]. [S]he threw it in the air, and they all prayed. The one who caught it when it had been thrown would also perform a ceremony in the near future [i.e., the family of the person who caught the ball]. The mother and grandmother [of the girl for whom the ceremony was being held] chose one [of the other girls]. They instructed that girl in the time to come, and taught her all kinds of things. They would teach her everything she would have to do. Cooking, doing beadwork, embroidering, drying meat, butchering, and sewing tipis. And how to tan hides, how to shred sinew and sew with it, all that she would learn. Making moccasins, and making men's clothing. All that she was supposed to know about: love and pity for everyone, humbling oneself and being kind, all that she was taught. When she went outside a plume [an eagle's chest plume], was fastened on her [head]. She would have that feather with her for many years, and when she would go through another ceremony she would receive another. Nobody wore feathers without having done anything for it. So these girls learned and understood. They would love and respect especially old women and old men. This was the only way they learned to act. The people [at the ceremony] formed a circle. They were given food, and a give-away was performed. And those people who owned many horses would maybe release some of them in the crowd, too. Whoever could get a hold of them grabbed them and used them for work. Doing things the Lakota way was very difficult. But today we waste things foolishly, just for fun, living according to the white man's way of life. Today the girls dress up and dance without meaning, like clowns. They dress up in all kinds of shiny fabrics [especially at powwows] and kick up their heels while they are dancing. Nobody danced like that in the old days. But today people dance like this. Absolutely nobody understands that. If people understood it [the old way of life] today the situation would be all different. In the past they were very well-behaved, the kids. The girls grew up, and the elders watched them. They watched them all the time. When the young boys loved a girl they [the parents] went and asked for the woman, the girl. Then [the girl's and the boy's] mother and father both talked it over, and if they [the respective young man and the respective young woman] liked each other the boy and the girl were given to one other [in marriage]. [But] usually they didn't know each other, but like it or not, their mothers and fathers made the decision. Maybe the girl didn't like the boy, but she married him nevertheless. But they both thought of the affection and the good things that would come out of it [the relationship]; that's what they did. Nobody performed a ceremony for nothing. Those who performed a ceremony were thinking of God wholeheartedly, and whoever performed a ceremony over having the first period was filled with reverence. Because children sprang from that. There is a reason why they [the children] are called *wakhą́yeža*, why they are called sacred [the word *wakhą́yeža* contains the root *wakhą́* 'sacred']. The children, who were called *wakhą́yeža*, were sacred indeed. The children sprang from the earth. Nobody acted senselessly. They [the children] are not like today, now that the white men have come, who take them [sperm and egg], put them into a glass jar and make them grow there. They grew in a sacred way, since they were a gift from God. When they just started to grow they were called *hokší o'ų́papi*. When they were still small they were called that. When they were growing older they were called *wakhą́yeža*. When they started to speak a little, and when they walked and crawled, when they had mastered that, too, they were called *wakhą́yeža*. And when somebody acted angrily toward them the children became sick, so nobody treated them in a mean way. They were raised with affection, these kids. Today they are thrown away for nothing, thrown away somewhere, they are killed and thrown away. We, the [Indian] people, are suffering because of that, but we don't know any better, so we live that way nevertheless. This ceremony [which is described above] is as sacred as can be. We grew up in a sacred way. But now people play around foolishly. The Native Americans are becoming extinct. Long ago, it is said, a horse cried and spoke: "If you people kill and eat one of us after using our labor there won't be any horses any more." Today it is like that. There are hardly any [wild] horses left. What they [the horses] say is sacred. Nobody just played around. If the girls [today] also grew up knowing about these things, turned into women, and had children, these children would be like that, too. When a ceremony is being held, they would also join in. But today these things are gone. I want the new generation to know about these things. They live among white people, but if they really knew about these things, maybe they would act a little less crazy. This is the reason why I talk about these things. And if the girls passed these things on, and if the books [which describe all this] were read by the people, this would be a reason for great appreciation.

Note: The family hosting the ceremony chooses one of the invited girls [not the one who caught the ball] for further instructions on the Lakota way of life. Being chosen on that occasion is considered a great honor. This process is more or less symbolic because the girls have already learned most of what they need to know by that age. In Neva's case, the lectures she received when she was chosen extended over three years.

3.9. Tobacco

NEVA STANDING BEAR

Tape recorded October 14, 1994

ehą́ni	*waphíya wicháša*	*wą*	*él*	*ma-hí-ˀ.*
a while ago	medicine man*	IDF.SG	to	1SG.PAT-come-ASS

Joe Eagle Elk	*ecíya-pi.*	*yųkhą́*	*o-má-ki-yakį*	*na*	*chąšáša*	*ki*
Joe Eagle Elk	call-IPS	then	ST-1SG-BEN-tell	LK	red willow*	DEF

lená	*tákuwe*	*Lakhóta*	*ki*	*ų́-pi*	*ki*	*slolyé-šni*	*kéye.*	*yųkhą́*
these	why	Lakota	DEF	use-PL	LK	know-NEG	QT	then

ihą́mnį	*na*	*ihą́bla*	*yųkhą́*	*chąšáša*	*ki*	*lená*	*Lakhóta*	*kihą*
dream	and	dream	LK	red willow*	DEF	these	Lakota	DEF

wóˀilagya-pi	*ki*	*lé*	*šˀag-yáhą*	*wóˀilagya-pi*	*kéye.*	*chąšáša*
utilize-PL	DEF	this	strong-ADV	employ-PL	QT	red willow*

ki	*lé*	*táku*	*líla*	*óta*	*él*	*a-ˀíkhoyaka*	*kéye*	*yųkhą́*
DEF	this	things	INT	much	there	L-adhere	QT	then

chąšáša	*ki*	*lé*	*chąkú*	*lúta*	*eyá-pi*	*cha*	*hé*	*ogná*	*Lakhóta*
red willow*	DEF	this	road	red	call-IPS	so	that	along	Lakota

ki	*máni-pi-kta*	*kéye.*	*ho*	*hé*	*chąšáša*	*kihą*	*Ųcí*
DEF	walk-PL-FUT	QT	well	that	red willow*	DEF	Grandmother

Makhá	*etą́*	*icháǧe.*	*Ųcí*	*Makhá*	*etą́*	*icháǧį*	*nahą́*
Earth	from	grow	Grandmother	Earth	from	grow	and then

chąšáša ki lená hená ų́pa-pi. waníyetu waná líla
red willow* DEF these those smoke tobacco-IPS winter now INT

osní na iwóblu wahéhąn chąšáša ki lená kaksá-pi
cold and blizzard just then red willow* DEF these cut-IPS

chą́-šna héchel phá-šni kéye. ho cha chą́ ki hená
then-HAB so bitter-NEG QT well so wood DEF those

kaksá-pi nahą́ há ki kakʼóǧa-pi nahą́ hehą́n hél
cut-IPS and then skin DEF scrape off-IPS and then then there

iyókogna chąhá ki hél iyóȟlathe wąží coǧį cha ikhóyake. cha
between bark* DEF there under one pith QL adhere so

hé é cha icú-pi na kakʼóǧa-pi na pus-yá-pi na
that IP QL take-IPS and scrape off-IPS and dry.A-CAU-IPS and

waksá-ksa-pi na lé chąlí icáhiye cha iwákpą-pi
cut off-RED-IPS and this tobacco mix QL cut into small pieces-IPS

na ų́ ų́pa-pi. ho hé é cha chąnų́pa ki lé él
and with smoke tobacco-IPS well that IP QL pipe DEF this in

opáǧi-pi nahą́ ų́pa-pi. ho cha hé chąlí ki
fill pipe-IPS and then smoke tobacco-IPS well so that tobacco DEF

hé tohą́n icú-pi nahą́ chąnų́pa ki hé él opáǧi-pi
that when take-IPS and then pipe DEF that in fill pipe-IPS

hą́tąhąš hená tóna akhígle opáǧi-pi ki hé iyéna
when those so many times fill pipe-PL SYP that each time

wochékhiye káǧa-pi. ho héchel Lakhóta kihą tąyą́ máni-pi na
prayer make-IPS well so Lakota DEF well walk-PL and

wichókhuže wąžíni él hí-pi-kte-šni. tkhá wichózani na
sickness none to come-PL-FUT-NEG but health and

wichóni ki lená ų́ hé chą́šáša ki hé é ephé.
life DEF these exist that red willow* DEF that IP say.1SG.AG

ho yųkhą́ hé tuwéni slolyé-šni yųkhą́ héchų sʼe ihámnį na
well then that nobody know-NEG then that way* dream and

o-kí-yaka-pi na ho hé Ųcí Makhá etą́
ST-BEN-tell-IPS LK well that Grandmother Earth from

Wakhą́thąka ektá iyóȟlogya. tohą́n hé luhá
Great Spirit* to connection when that have.2SG.AG

ma-yá-ni kihą héchel oʼų́ wąží wašté ya-káǧį-kte.
ST-2SG.AG-walk if so living IDF.SG good 2SG.AG-make-FUT

héchel Wakhą́thąka tókhel táku ya-kí-la éyaš
so Great Spirit* how what 2SG.AG-BEN-ask for but

ó-ni-ciyį-kta kéye. ho cha hé héchų sʼe
ST-2SG.PAT-help.VT-FUT QT well so that that way*

įšé hé waná wichášа ki hé ehàke okáȟniǧe. wówapi wą
just that now man DEF that end.N understand book LK

káǧa cha hé é cha ká Osní Makhóche héchiya cha hé
make QL that IP QL over there Alaska* there QL that

eháke hé él é-kihųni-kta yųkhą́ hé héchų s'e o-kí-yaka-pi.
end.N that at L-arrive-FUT then that that way* ST-BEN-tell-IPS

wó'ihąble él o-kí-yaka-pi. ho cha hé icú nahą́
vision in ST-BEN-tell-IPS well so that take and then

ablézį-kta kéye ho yųkhą́ hená héchų s'e waná
get insight-FUT QT well then those that way* now

o-kí-yaka-pi cha ho hé eháke wówapi wą káǧa-pi ki él
ST-BEN-tell-IPS so well that end.N book LK make-IPS DEF in

o-'éhake-ta hená él owá-pi-kte, wichó'oyake ki. yųkhą́ hé
L-end.N-at those there write-IPS-FUT story DEF then that

íyohakab hé o-má-ki-yake. Lakhóta ki tąyą́ ų́-pi chį́
after that ST-1SG-BEN-tell Lakota DEF well exist-PLwant

yųkhą́ oyáte ki są́m líla wa-yátką-pi na itómni-pi na él
then people DEF more INT NSP.PAT-drink-PL and drunk-PL and in

é-'ic'i-k-tųwą-pi-šni kéye. iyókiphi-šni kéyé-'. kéyá
L-3RFL-EI-look-PL-NEG QT happy-NEG say that-ASS say that

o-má-ki-yake "ho cha le-tą́ thokátakiya nakų́ él
ST-1SG-BEN-tell well so this-from in the future also there

wa-'ų́-šni éyaš táku ki lená oláke hą́tąhąš
1SG.AG-exist-NEG but things DEF these tell.2SG.AG when

tókša él wa-'ų́-šni éyaš
after a while there 1SG.AG-exist-NEG but

ó-chi-ci-yį-kte	*k'ų"*	*eyé*	*yųkhą́*	*iyéchetu.*	*cha*
ST-1SG.AG.2SG-BEN-help.VT-FUT	ASS	say	then	like this	so

othéȟike	*éyaš*	*takómni*	*hená*	*é*	*cha*	*obláktkte.*	*na*
terrible	but	at all costs	those	IP	QL	tell.1SG.AG-FUT	and

ų́	*Lakhóta*	*kihą*	*ksápa-pi-kta*	*cha*	*hená*	*obláke.*	*cha*
therefore	Lakota	DEF	wise-PL-FUT	so	those	tell.1SG.AG	so

wa-héhąyela	*hé*	*chąšáša*	*ki*	*oblákįkte.*
NSP.PAT-that is all	that	red willow*	DEF	tell.1SG.AG-FUT

A while ago a medicine man came to me. His name was Joe Eagle Elk. He told me that at one time he didn't know why the Lakota use red willow. Then he had a dream, and he dreamed that the Lakota used the red willow they used in a powerful way. There is a lot connected with red willow. Red willow is called the "red road" [i.e., the good road]; on it the Lakota will walk. Red willow grows out of Grandmother Earth. It grows out of Grandmother Earth, and people smoke the red willow. Red willow is cut in winter when it is very cold and when there are blizzards, since it is not that bitter at that time. People cut the wood and scrape off the [outer] bark. In between, under the bark, some soft pith adheres. People take it, scrape it off, dry it, and cut it. This tobacco mixture they cut into small pieces, and with it they smoke. They fill the pipe with it and smoke. When they take the tobacco and fill the pipe, each time they fill the pipe, they make a prayer. That way the Lakota walk well [on life's road], and not a single disease will come to them. I say that the source of health and life is red willow. Nobody knew about those things until he [Joe Eagle Elk] had that dream, and was told that it [red willow] is a passage from Mother Earth to the Great Spirit. If you walk with this knowledge you will make yourself a good living. Whenever you ask something of the Great Spirit, he will help you. That's the way he [Joe Eagle Elk] understood it. Right now the man up there in Alaska [from Alaska University] who is writing the final chapter of a book [about Joe Eagle Elk] will complete his work; that's what he [Joe Eagle Elk] was told. He was told that in his dream. He took it [the power of his dream] to get wise. Now he has been told that. At the end of the final part of the book being made it will be written down [by the ethnologist from Alaska], the story [of Joe Eagle Elk's dream]. After that [being interviewed by the ethnologists] he told it to me. He wants the Lakota to have a good life. People are drinking even more, they get drunk, and they don't care for themselves. He said he was unhappy. He told me: "From now on, in the future, even if I will not be around any more, if you talk about these things, even if I am not around any more, I will help you." It is true. It is hard, but I will talk about these things nevertheless. And because of that [Joe Eagle Elk's vision] the Lakota will be wise. That is why I talk about these things. That is all I want to say about red willow.

3.10. Powwows and Rodeos

MARY LIGHT

Tape recorded October 25, 1994

lehą́l	*ehą́ni*	*šųkˀákąyąka-pi*	*naˀį́š*	*khiˀíyąka-pi*	*naˀį́š*	*hechékche*
then	long ago	ride*-IPS	and	race-IPS	and	like that

pteˀákąyąka-pi	*nahą́*	*wachí*	*é-wicho-thi*	*chą́-šna*	*nakų́*	*lé*
ride bulls*-IPS	and then	dance	L-COLL-camp.VI	then-HAB	also	this

rodeo	*yuhá-pi.*	*thąkál*	*waȟpé*	*wakhéya*	*káǧa-pi*	*nahą́*	*ho*
rodeo	have-IPS	outside	leaf	tent	make-IPS	and then	well

hél	*áta*	*oyáte*	*kihą*	*ptáyela*	*hél*	*yá-pi*	*nahą́*	*ho*	*hél*
there	INT	people	DEF	together	there	go-IPS	and then	well	there

tónachą-šna	*wachí-pi.*	*na*	*nakų́*	*isákhibya*	*rodeo*	*yuhá-pi.*
so many days-HAB	dance-IPS	and	also	together	rodeo	have-IPS

chą́na-šna	*pteˀákąyąka-pi*	*naˀį́š*	*šųgwáthogla*	*aką́yąka-pi*	*naˀį́š*
then-HAB	ride bulls*-IPS	and	bronc*	ride*-IPS	and

khiˀį́yąka-pi.	*hená*	*iyúha*	*héchų-pi.*	*na*	*wíȟpeya-pi*
race-IPS	those	all	do that-IPS	and	practice give away*-IPS

naˀį́š	*héchekche*	*hená*	*oˀíyokiphi-phi-ya*	*é-wicho-thi.*	*éyaš*	*líla*
and	like that	those	happy-RED-ADV	L-COLL-camp.VI	but	INT

wówąyąke	*na*	*líla*	*oˀíyokiphi*	*yuhá-pi.*	*éyaš*	*tóhąni*
sight	and	INT	fun	have-IPS	but	never

wiwą́yąg wachípi hé é tákuni slol-wá-ye-šni. hená į́š eyá
sundance* that IP nothing ST-1SG.AG-know-NEG those also

hehą́l-šna tónachą wachí-pi éyaš hé é tókhel echų́-pi ki
then-HAB many days dance-IPS but that IP how do-IPS DEF

héhą slol-wá-ye-šni. ho éyaš Lakhóta ki hél
then ST-1SG.AG-know-NEG well but Lakota DEF there

ptáye-la-šna o'íyokiphi-ya-šna wichó-thi. cha į́šé hé
together-DIM-HAB happy-ADV-HAB COLL-camp.VI so just that

ųgnáhąšna hél iyúha ptáye-la ų́-pi nahą́ nakų́
sometimes there all together-DIM be at-PL and then also

wól-kichi-ya-pi. cha nakų́ hená slol-wá-ye cha
NSP.PAT.eat-REC-CAU-IPS so also those ST-1SG.AG-know QL

obláke.
1SG.AG.tell

In the old times people rode horses, had horse races, and rode bulls. Whenever they camped together to dance they also had a rodeo. They constructed a shade out of poles and branches in the open, and all the people got together there and danced there for several days. At the same time, there also was a rodeo. People rode bulls and broncs and had horse races. All that they did there. And they had give-aways. They had a good time camping like that. It was quite a sight to see, and they had lots of fun. But I don't know anything about the sundance. People also danced for many days there, but I don't know how it was done. The Lakota camped there together [at the powwow], having fun. People just all got together there sometimes, and there also were feasts [potlatchs]. Now I've told what I know about that, too.

3.11. Spirituality

NEVA STANDING BEAR

Tape recorded October 31, 1994

ehą́ni	*Lakhóta*	*kihą*	*lená*	*Lakhól-wichó-w-ichaǧe.*	*ho*	*na*	*lená*
long ago	Lakota	DEF	these	Indian-COLL-EI-grow	well	and	these

ų́	*wówahokųkhiye*	*ų-kʔú-pi.*	*ho*	*na*	*lé*	*wachékhiya-pi*
exist	education	1PL.PAT-give-IPS	well	and	this	pray-IPS

ki	*lé*	*iyótą-ȟci*	*líla*	*iyótą*	*ki-lá-pi.*	*ho*	*chąkhé*	*lehą́n*
DEF	this	most-INT	INT	most	PSS-consider-IPS	well	then	now

wichóʔichaǧe	*ki*	*lená*	*slolyá-pi-šni*	*na*	*hé*	*é*	*táku*
generation	DEF	these	know-PL-NEG	and	that	IP	things

ipáyeȟ	*echų́-pi*	*na*	*hená*	*táku*	*wašté*	*echų́-pi*
the wrong way	do-PL	and	those	things	good	do-PL

kéchį-pi.	*ho*	*tohą́n*	*Lakhól-ʔiyá*	*lená*	*wachékhiya-pi*	*hą́tąhąš*
think that-PL	well	when	Indian-speak	these	pray-IPS	when

lená	*wanáǧi*	*ki*	*spirits*	*e-wícha-kiya-pi.*	*wanáǧi*	*ki*	*lená*
these	ghost	DEF	spirits	ST-3PL.PAT-call-IPS	spirit	DEF	these

į́š	*eyá*	*makhá*	*ki*	*lél*	*aką́n*	*ų́-pi*	*cha*	*hená*
they	also	earth	DEF	here	on top	be-PL	QL	those

ó-ʔų-kiya-pi.	*ho*	*cha*	*tohą́n*	*wicháša*	*wąží*	*wichóni*
ST-1PL.PAT-help.VT-PL	well	so	when	man	one	life

é-ki-gnakį na makhá mahél iyéya-pi hą́tąhą̨š hená wochékhiye

L-PSS-put and earth inside send-IPS when those prayer

ų-kí-cağa-pi héchel tha-wóniya ki lená makhá aką́n

1PL.AG-BEN-make-PL so ALP-spirit DEF these earth on top

ų́-pi na hená ó-ˀų-kiya-pi. ho cha hehą́n lená

be-PL and those ST-1PL.PAT-help.VT-PL well so then these

héchel wochékhiye ų-káğa-pi cha tákuni tóhąni

so prayer 1PL.AG-make-PL so nothing never

ųk-éya-pi-šni na héchetu ųk-éya-pi ųk-ókihi-pi-šni.

1PL.AG-say-PL-NEG and that way 1PL.AG-say-PL 1PL.AG-can-PL-NEG

lená į́š eyá ehą́ni hų́-ku na at-kúku-pi na

these also long ago mother-3POR and father-3POR-PL and

khų́ši-tku-pi na thųkáši-tku-pi ki lená wóˀoyake

grandmother-3POR-PL and grandfather-3POR-PL DEF these lesson

o-wícha-ki-yag a-wícha-ˀu-pi kˀéyaš takómni hená

ST-3PL-BEN-tell ST-3PL.PAT-CNT-PL but by no means those

abléza-pi-šni na hená nah̆ˀų́-pi-šni chąkhé líla oˀíyokišice. ho

notice-PL-NEG and those hear-PL-NEG so INT sad well

chąkhé lehą́n ųkˀ-ų́-pi ki lé ská makhóche ektá

then now 1PL.AG-exist-PL DEF this white land in

ųkˀ-ų́-pi, othų́wahe thą́ka wą ektá ųkˀ-ų́-pi. ho

1PL.AG-exist-PL city big IDF.SG in 1PL.AG-exist-PL well

na	*ektá*	*óhą*	*ųkˀ-ų́-pi*	*cha*	*lé*	*Lakhól-ˀiyá*
and	there	among	1PL.AG-exist-PL	QL	this	Indian-speak

wochékhiye	*ki*	*lená*	*othéȟike.*	*tukténi*	*manį́n*	*ų-yą́-pi*
praying	DEF	those	difficult	nowhere	outdoors	1PL.AG-go-PL

na	*waché-ˀų-khiya-pi-kta*	*waníce.*	*hená*	*áta*	*oyáte*	*ki*
and	ST-1PL.AG-pray-PL-FUT	lack	those	INT	people	DEF

thi-káȟ	*áya-pi,*	*hená*	*ská*	*oyáte*	*ki,*	*na*	*tukténi*
house-make	PRC-PL	those	white	people	DEF	and	nowhere

manį́tu	*waníce-šni.*	*ho*	*chąkhé*	*wamákhašką*	*ki*	*ékayeš*	*lená*
wilderness	lack-NEG	well	then	animal*	DEF	even	these

manį́n	*ų́-pi*	*yųkhą́*	*lená*	*othų́wahe*	*étkiya*
in the wilderness	exist-PL	then	these	city	toward

a-ˀú	*chąkhé*	*kahį́ȟpe-wicha-ya-pi,*	*iyéchįkyąke*	*óta.*	*cha*
COLL-come	then	ST-3PL.PAT-run over-IPS	car*	many	so

ų́ši-ši-ya	*hená*	*tˀá-pi.*	*hená*	*ų́ši-ši-ya*	*wichóni*
pitiable-RED-ADV	those	die-PL	those	pitiable-RED-ADV	life

é-ki-gnaka-pi.	*ho*	*chąkhé*	*tohą́n*	*wochékhiye*	*ų-káǧa-pi*
L-PSS-put-PL	well	then	when	prayer	1PL.AG-make-PL

hą́tąhąš	*oˀíyokišice*	*na*	*othéȟike.*	*lená*	*ų́*	*wochékhiye*
when	sad	and	terrible	these	because of	prayer

wichá-ˀų-ki-caǧa-pi.	*héchel*	*wichóni*	*é-ki-gnaka-pi*	*ki*	*lená*
3PL-1PL.AG-BEN-make-PL	so	life	L-PSS-put-IPS	SYP	these

wiyóȟpeyata-kiya na waziyata-kiya na wiyóhiyąpata na itókaǧa
west*-to and north-to and east* and south

hená wanáǧi kihą khiglá-pi hą́tąhąš héktakiya wí hiną́phe
those spirit DEF go home-PL when back.AV sun come out

héchiya-tą, wiyóhiyąpha-tąhą gliyáhą-pi kéyá-pi. ho na
there-from east*-from come back up-PL say that-IPS well and

hehą́n aˀíyokpaze, hąhépi ektá wazíyata nahą́ itókaǧata wanáǧi
then darkness night in north and then south spirit

tha-chą́ku wą eyá-pi cha maȟpíya ektá glakį́yą ȟpáya cha hé
ALP-road LK say-IPS QL sky there across lie QL that

ogná máni-pi kéyá-pi. cha hé ogná-šna hená iyúha máni-pi
along walk-PL say that-IPS so that on-HAB those all walk-PL

na tókhel hukhúta wa-ˀéchųkˀų-pi ki lená
and how down NSP.PAT-do.1PL.AG-PL DEF these

wą-ˀų́-yąka-pi cha takómni waché-ˀų-khiya-pi-šni hą́tąhą hená
ST-1PL.PAT-see-PL so at all ST-1PL.AG-pray-PL-NEG if those

chąté šíca-pi kéyá-pi. cha ú-pi na ó-ˀų-kiya-pi
sad*-PL say that-IPS so come-PL and ST-1PL-help.VT-PL

okíhi-pi-šni. héchel tohą́n
can-PL-NEG so when

iní-ˀų-kaǧa-pi na waché-ˀų-khiya-pi
ST-1PL.AG-perform sweatlodge ceremony-PL and ST-1PL.AG-pray-PL

chą́-šna henáektá hí-pi chą́-šna hená wanáǧi
then-HAB those there come-PL then-HAB those spirit

w-ó-wicha-ˀų-ki-cˀu-pi. héchel okáblaya tókhiya
NSP.PAT-L-3PL-1PL.AG-BEN-give-PL so unhampered anywhere

ománi-pi-kte. na tohą́n wóˀokiye ų-lá-pi hą́tąhąš
travel-PL-FUT and when help.N 1PL.AG-ask for-PL when

ó-ˀų-kiya-pi. héchel ų-kákiža-pi-kte-šni na
ST-1PL.PAT-help.VT-PL so 1PL.PAT-suffer-PL-FUT-NEG and

wichóni wašté ų-yúha-pi-kte nahą́ wichózani wašté
life good 1PL.AG-have-PL-FUT and then health good

ų-yúha-pi-kte. ho cha hé lehą́n táku wą líla iyótą-ȟci
1PL.AG-have-PL-FUT well so that now things LK INT most-INT

iyótą ų-lá-pi ki hé wówaȟwala eyá-pi na
most 1PL.AG-consider-PL DEF that gentleness say-IPS and

wówaˀųšila eyá-pi cha henáos takómni wašˀág-yahą
kindness say-IPS so both at all costs strong-ADV

gluhá na-ˀų́-žį-pi hą́tąhąš héchel táku
POSS.hold on to ST-1PL.AG-stand-PL when so things

Thųkášila ų-kí-la-pi ešą́š hená
God* 1PL.AG-BEN-ask for-PL if . . . then perhaps those

ó-ˀų-kiya-pi-kte. héchel wóphila ųk-éya-pi na ho
ST-1PL-help.VT-PL-FUT so gratitude 1PL.AG-say-PL and well

akhé	*takún*	*ų-lá-pi*	*cha*	*ešáš*	*akhé*
again	something	1PL.AG-ask-PL	so	if . . . then perhaps	again

ó-ˀų-kiya-pi-kte.	*ho*	*tkhá*	*áyecechola*	*táku*
ST-1PL.PAT-help.VT-PL-FUT	well	but	without	things

ų-lá-hą-pi	*hą́tąhąš*	*tóhąni*	*hená*
1PL.AG-ask-PRG-PL	when	never	those

ųk-ókihi-pi-kte-šni.	*hé*	*é*	*cha*	*ų́*	*Lakhóta*
1PL.AG-accomplish-PL-FUT-NEG	that	IP	QL	because of	Lakota

oyáte	*ki*	*lehą́n*	*núni*	*sˀe*	*wichó-ˀų*	*na*	*wa-yátką-pi*
people	DEF	now	lost	like.AV	COLL-be	and	NSP.PAT-drink-IPS

ki	*líla*	*šˀag-yáhą*	*į́yąke.*	*ho*	*na*	*tákuni*	*él*
DEF	INT	strong-ADV	run	well	and	nothing	to

é-wa-chį-pi-šni	*na*	*él*	*é-ˀicˀi-k-tųwą-pi-šni.*	*hená*	*iyúha*
L-NSP.PAT-want-PL-NEG	and	to	L-3RFL-EI-look-PL-NEG	those	all

hógna	*ecéla,*	*wa-yátką*	*hé*	*ecéla*	*ų́,*	*zaní-ya*
that way*	only	NSP.PAT-drink	that	only	by means of	healthy-ADV

ų́-pi-kta	*kéchį-pi*	*éyaš*	*héchetu-šni.*	*hená*	*ehą́ni*
exist-PL-FUT	think that-PL	but	true-NEG	those	long ago

wówahokųkhiye	*ki*	*lená*	*ų-kˀú-pi*	*cha.*	*hená*	*miyé*	*é*
lessons	DEF	these	1PL.PAT-give-IPS	QL	those	I	IP

wicákhe-yahą	*glús*	*na-wá-žį.*	*héchel*	*iná*	*é*	*na*
truthful-ADV	POSS.hold	ST-1SG.AG-stand	so	mother	IP	and

até na thųkášila na ųcí-wicha-wa-ye
father and grandfather and grandmother-3PL.PAT-1SG.AG-have as

ki lená héchel wanáği o-ˀómani káğa-pi kˀų hená iyókiphi-ya
DEF these so spirit L-travel make-IPS DEF those happy-ADV

máni-pi-kta chąkhé miyé é makhá ki lél akąn kakíš-ya
walk-PL-FUT then I IP earth DEF here on top suffer-ADV

wa-ˀų́ tkhá takómni oyáte ki ó-wicha-wa-kiya
1SG.AG-exist but at all costs people DEF ST-3PL.PAT-1SG.AG-help.VT

cha į́š eyá héktakiya hená ó-ma-kiya-pi. cha hená
so also backwards those ST-1SG.PAT-help.VT-PL so those

ų́ wóphila ephį́ nahą́ héchel
because of gratitude say.1SG.AG and then so

wichá-wa-gluˀonihą. hógna ecéla ma-záni-kte na
3PL.PAT-1SG.AG-honor that way* only 1SG.PAT-healthy-FUT and

hógna ecéla oyáte ki záni-pi-kta cha ų́ lená
that way* only people DEF healthy-PL-FUT so therefore these

echámų. ho chąkhé tohą́n okíhilaka iyó-ma-kiphi-šni
do.1SG.AG well then as much as can be* ST-1SG.PAT-happy-NEG

tohą́n oyáte kihą wachékhiye yá-pi-šni, nakų́ ská owáchekiye
then people DEF pray go-PL-NEG also white church

cha ektá wachékhiya-pi éyaš hé tókha-šni įchį́ į́š eyá
QL in pray-PL but that matter.VI-NEG because also

hená Thųkášila chékhiya-pi cha. į́š eyá hé wašícu iyápi
those God* pray to-PL QL also that white man language

chékhiya-pi cha tókha-šni, ho tkhá Lakhól-ˀiyá-hą
pray to-PL so matter.VI-NEG well but Indian-speak-PRG

wachékhiya-pi hą́tąhą ųkí-tha-thitakuye-pi ki lená
pray-PL when 1PL.POR-ALP-relative-PL DEF these

naˀ-ų́-ȟˀų-pi-kta cha ó-ˀų-kiya-pi-kta cha hé
ST-1PL.PAT-hear-PL-FUT so ST-1PL.PAT-help.VT-PL-FUT so that

ų́ Lakhól-ˀiyá-hą waché-ˀų-khiya-pi. hógna táku
because of Indian-speak-PRG ST-1PL.AG-pray-PL that way* things

ki lená ųk-ókihi-pi-kte. ho cha iyótą-š iyáya-pi nahą́
DEF these 1PL.AG-can-PL-FUT well so most-EMPH go-PL and then

wa-yátką-pi na phežúta šíca icú-pi ki lená ayų́štą-pi
NSP.PAT-drink-PL and drugs* take-PL DEF these finish-PL

nahą́ oˀínikağe wą él thimá iyáya-pi na
and then sweatlodge IDF.SG into inside go-PL and

ikpákhįta-pi hą́tąhąš tohą́n okíhilaka hé wóphila
purify one's own-PL when as much as can be* that gratitude

thą́ka hécha. na hé ogná máni-pi hą́tąhąš lé chąkú wą
big OBL and that along walk-PL when this road IDF.SG

lúta eyá-pi ki lé hé ogná ma-ˀų́-ni-pi-kte. ho tkhá
red call-IPS DEF this that along ST-1PL.AG-walk-PL-FUT well but

tuwá chąkú wą sápa cha ogná iyáya ešáš wa-yátkį na
who road LK black QL along go indeed NSP.PAT-drink and

thíwichakte na wa-mánų na táku šíca lená iyúha įyąke.
murder.VI* and NSP.PAT-steal and things bad these all run

hená ská wichó'ų ki ogná wichó-'ų-pi cha hé
those white way of life DEF inside COLL-exist-1PS QL that

ų́. hé ogná othápha-pi hątąhąš ųkíye ųk-íchağa-pi
because of that along follow-PL if we 1PL.PAT-grow-PL

kihą thąkake ki lená o'íye na-wícha-'ų-ȟ'ų-pi cha
when elder DEF these word ST-3PL.PAT-1PL.AG-listen-PL so

tąyą́ ųk'-ų́-pi éyaš lehą́n icháğe ki héchų-pi-šni cha
well 1PL.AG-exist-PL but now grow DEF do that-PL-NEG so

wókakiže thąka ikhóyaka. cha eyášna ų́ chąté ma-šíce
misery big adhere so sometimes because of ST 1SG.PAT-sad

tohą́n Lakhóta ki hená iyúha itómni-pi na él
when Indian DEF those all drunk-PL and in

é-'ic'i-wa-chį-pi-šni. na hųȟ iyótą-š lechála icháğe
L-3RFL-NSP.PAT-want-PL-NEG and some most-EMPH recently grow

ki lená líla hųȟ ową́yąg wašté-šte-pi éyaš áta ité ki
DEF these INT some good looking*-RED-PL but INT face DEF

šló a'ú sékse ománi-pi, kacék-ceg, šab-yéla. cha
melt.VI IGR like.AV walk about-PL stagger-RED dirty-ADV so

lená ehą́ni hų́-ku na at-kúku-pi ki
these long ago mother-3POR and father-3POR-PL DEF

the-wícha-ȟila-pi yųkhą́ léchiya él é-ʔicʔi-k-tųwą-pi-šni cha
ST-3PL.PAT-love.VT-PL then here in L-3RFL-EI-look-PL-NEG so

ų́-pi kʔų ephé. ho cha le-tą́ thokátakiya lená
exist-PL ASS say.1SG.AG well so this-from in the future these

oyáte kihą tąyą́ ų́-pi hą́tąhąš héchel wóphila thą́ka hécha-kte.
people DEF well be-PL when so gratitude big OBL-FUT

ho.
well

Long ago the Lakota grew up the Indian way. And along these lines we received our education. Praying was held in highest, highest esteem. Today's generations do not know about these matters; they do things the wrong way and think they are doing something good. When people pray the Indian way they call the ghosts "spirits" [*wanáǧi* can be translated both by 'ghost' and 'spirit']. The spirits, who also exist on this earth, help us. When one man puts down his life and is sent back into the earth we make prayers for him, so their [the dead people's] spirits remain on this earth and help us. For this reason, we make prayers. We never say anything without a reason [i.e., without meaning it]; we simply cannot say such things. Also, in the past people were continuously given lessons by their mothers, fathers, grandmothers, and grandfathers, but today people don't pay any mind at all and don't listen to them. This is very sad. We who live today live in a white world, we live in a big city. And since we are living in this environment it is difficult to pray the Indian way. There is no way for us to go to some place in the wilderness and pray. People are building more and more houses, the white people, and nowhere is there any wilderness left. Even the animals that live in the wilderness wander into the city and get run over, since there are so many cars. They die pitifully. They put down their lives pitifully. So when we make prayers they [the prayers] are sad and desperate. For this reason, we make prayers for them [the animals]. When people, after they have put down their lives, have gone home to the west, the north, the east, and the south, being spirits, they come back up from where the sun rises, from the east. In the darkness, at night, to the north and the south, there stretches across the sky what is called "spirit road" [the Milky Way]. On it they travel. On it they all travel, and watch what we are doing down below. If we don't pray at all, they are sad. They cannot come and help us. When we perform a sweatlodge ceremony and pray, they come here. Then we feed the spirits. They move about freely to any place. And when we ask them for help, they help us. That way we will not suffer, and have a good life, and be in good health. The things we consider most important of all are called *wówaȟwala* ['gentleness'] and *wówa'ų̌šila* ['kindness']. So if we stand up for these two things with all our determination, they [the spirits] will perhaps help us with the things we ask from God. We express our gratitude, and they will perhaps help us again when we ask for something again. But if we keep asking for things just so, we will never accomplish anything. For this reason, the Lakota people are now lost, and drinking is going on very strongly. They don't care for anything, and they lack self-criticism. They all think that that way only, only by drinking, they will be doing alright, but this is not true. Long ago we were given these preachings. I am the one who defends them faithfully. My mother, father, grandfathers, and grandmothers, who have all been made to travel among the spirits, will travel happily. I am the one who is living on this earth suffering, but I help people as much as I can, so they help me in return. For this reason, I express my gratitude, and honor them [the ancestors]. Only that way I will be doing alright. Only that way the people will be doing alright, and this is why I do these things [healing, preaching etc.]. I am as unhappy as can be when people don't go to pray. They may pray in a white church as well. It does not matter because they, too [the white people] pray to God. Even if they pray to Him in the white man's language that does not matter, but when they pray in Indian our [deceased] relatives will hear us, and help us. This is why we pray in Indian. That way we will be able to accomplish things. If only people went and quit drinking, stopped taking drugs, and went into a sweatlodge and purified themselves, this would be a reason for great appreciation. And if they followed this direction we would walk on what is called the red road. But someone who walks the black road drinks, murders, and steals. All these bad things are going on. This is because people are all living the white way of life. If they followed this direction [the old way of life] (we did pay attention to what the elders said when we were growing up) we would have a good life, but today's people do not do that, so the great misery remains. Sometimes I am sad because of that, when the Indians are all drunk and don't take care of themselves. And some of today's generation are extremely good-looking, but they walk around as if their faces were starting to melt, staggering, dirty. In the old times their mothers and fathers loved them [their children]. I say that today they are living without self-criticism. If these people have a good life in the future this would be a reason for great appreciation. That's the way it is.

3.12. Praying

NEVA STANDING BEAR

Tape recorded October 31, 1994

ho cha lehą́n lechála icháǧe ki lená táku ų́ wochékiye
well so now recent grow DEF these things with prayer

káǧa-pi nahą́ ų́ lená wicála-pi-kte ki hé wąblí wíyaka
make-PL and then with these believe-PL-FUT DEF that eagle feather

wą hé é nahą́ chąnų́pa wą hé é nahą́
IDF.SG that IP and then pipe IDF.SG that IP and then

iníkaǧa-pi ki hé é nahą́ chąglėška
perform sweatlodge ceremony-PL DEF that IP and then wheel

wą thatúye tópa cha eyá-pi. cha hé wichóni hécha. ho
IDF.SG direction four QL say-IPS so that life COP well

hé é nahą́ phežíȟota nahą́ wachą́ǧa nahą́ ȟąté
that IP and then sagebrush* and then sweetgrass and then cedar

nahą́ lená iyúha naʾį́š Lakhóta phežúta ki lená ų́
and then those all or Indian medicine* DEF these with

wochékhiye eyášna ų-káǧa-pi. ho cha hé é wąblí wíyaka
prayer always 1PL.AG-make-PL well so that IP eagle feather

ki lé ehą́ni Lakhóta ki hená ihą́bla-pi na hų́ȟ
DEF this ancient Lakota DEF those dream-PL and some

wakhą́-ȟʔą-pi yųkhą́ zįtkála waȟúpakoza eyá-pi. cha hé wąblí
sacred-act-PL then bird wing flapper* say-PL so that eagle

ki hé iyótą-ȟcį wąkátuya yawá-pi. ho hé é cha wíyaka ki
DEF that most-INT above rate-PL well that IP QL feather DEF

hé icú-pi na yuhá wachékhiya-pi nahą́ wąblí ki hé
that take-PL and have pray-PL and then eagle DEF that

wicháša iyéchecha-pi éyaš héchų-pi-šni ithókab lé zįtkála ki
man like that-PL but do that-PL-NEG before this bird DEF

lé iníyothi thimá éyaya-pi na wachékhiya-pi na pakhį́ta-pi
this sweatlodge inside send-PL and pray-PL and purify-PL

na ho yuhá glinápha-pi hą́tąhąš ho hehą́n wíyaka ki
and well have go outside-PL when well then feather DEF

hená yužų́-pi nahą́ sitúpi ki hená icú-pi na hená
those pull out-PL and then tail feather DEF those take-PL and those

wóʔilagya-pi nahą́ nakų́ ȟupáhu ki hená. ho na wáchįhį
utilize-PL and then also wing DEF those well and plume

ki hená nakų́ wóʔilagya-pi. hená iyóhi-la Lakhóta ki
DEF those also utilize-PL those each-DIM Lakota DEF

táku ų́ wóʔilagya-pi. chąkhé hená ohó-ki-la-pi.
something for utilize-PL then those ST-3AG.POR-respect.VT-PL

éyaš lehą́n otúyachį hų́ȟ wichá-ʔų-pi na wichá-kte-pi
but now for no reason some 3PL.PAT-use-PL and 3PL.PAT-kill-PL

chą́ sni-yą́ wichá-ˀųpa-pi. ho nahą́ hehą́n chąnų́pa ki
then cool-ADV 3PL.PAT-put-PL well and then then pipe DEF

lé makhá etą́, Ųcí Makhá etą́ hí. cha hé į́yą
that earth from Grandmother Earth from come so that stone

ki hé ká wiyóhiyąpata-kiya į́yą šá oˀókˀe cha
DEF that over there east*-in stone red mine.N QL

héchiya-tąhą icú-pi na chąnų́pa káğa-pi nahą́ hená ų́
there-from take-IPS and pipe make-PL and then those with

ų́pa-pi nahą́ hé pséȟtį ki icú-pi nahą́
smoke tobacco-PL and then that ash DEF take-IPS and then

našléce-šni hą́ni kaksá-pi na kağápa-pi nahą́ pus-yá-pi
split.VI-NEG before cut-IPS and peel.VT-IPS and then dry.A-CAU-IPS

na yu-ˀówothą khuwá-pi na echél púze. ho cha hé iyókogna
and INS-straight treat-IPS and so dry.VI well so that between

ki hél ogná ehą́ni tókhel léchų-pi ki
DEF there inside long ago how do this-IPS LK

slol-wá-ye-šni éyaš hená coğį́ wą chokną́ ikhóyaka cha
ST-1SG.AG-know-NEG but those pith LK middle adhere QL

hená ğu-yá-pi chą́ oȟlóka cha hé chąnų́pa káğa-pi. cha
those burned-CAU-IPS then hole QL that pipe make-IPS so

hé é iyúha opáği-pi nahą́ Thųkášila wóˀokiye
that IP all load a pipe-IPS and then God* help.N

ki-lá-pi *na'į̨š* *wóphila* *ekíya-pi.* *ho* *hé* *ų́*
BEN-ask for-IPS or gratitude say to-IPS well that by means of

hená *w-í-y-okihi-pi.* *ho* *nahą́* *hé* *ichų́hą* *lená*
those NSP.PAT-L-EI-accomplish-IPS well and then that during these

ųgnáš *iyó-ni-kiphi-šni* *na'į̨š* *táku* *i-ní-cakiže*
maybe ST-2SG.PAT-happy-NEG or something ST-2SG.PAT-suffer

hą́tąhąš *lená* *phežíȟota* *ki* *lé* *é* *na'į̨š* *wachą́ǧa* *ki* *lé*
if these sagebrush* DEF this IP or sweetgrass DEF this

é *na'į̨š* *ȟąté* *ki* *lená* *zil-yá-yį-kte.*
IP or cedar DEF these burn.VI-2SG.AG-CAU-FUT

zil-yá-yį *na* *ų́* *waché-ya-khiyį-kte.* *héchel* *ehą́ni*
burn.VI-2SG.AG-CAU and with ST-2SG.AG-pray-FUT so long ago

otákuye *ki* *lená* *hí-pi* *na* *ó-'ų-kiya-pi-kte.* *hená*
relatives DEF these come-PL and ST-1PL.PAT-help.VT-PL-FUT those

táku *ų-lá-pi* *k'ų* *hená* *echél* *héchų-pi.* *ho*
something 1PL.AG-ask-PL SYP those so do that-IPS well

ųkí-ci-yusu-pi-kta *cha* *ų́* *hená* *cha* *Lakhóta* *kihą*
1PL-BEN-make ready-PL-FUT so therefore those so Lakota DEF

tóhąni *otúyachį* *makhá* *ki* *lél* *aką́n* *ų́-pi-šni.* *táku*
never thoughtlessly earth DEF here on top be-PL-NEG something

kté-pi *hą́tąhąš* *hená* *iyáya-pi* *na* *chąlí* *wa-'é-ki-gnaka-pi*
kill-PL when those go-PL and tobacco NSP.PAT-L-PSS-put up-PL

na a-wáchekhiya-pi na ho hená yúta-pi. ho chąlí ki lé
and L-pray-PL and well those eat-PL well tobacco DEF this

chąšáša ki hé etą́ ú cha hé ų́ Ųcí
red willow* DEF that from come so that because of Grandmother

Makhá etą́ hiyú na Thųkášila wąkáta mahpíya ektá yąké ki
Earth from come and God* above sky in sit DEF

ektá étkiya šóta ki lé izíte hą́tąhąš ho hená
to toward smoke DEF this burn.VI when well those

ų́ wó'okiye cha hé ų́ hená héchel wachékhiya-pi.
because of help.N so that because of those so pray-PL

ho cha táku ki lená otúyachį-šni éyaš hų́h otúyachį
well so things DEF these meaningless-NEG but some senselessly

wó'ilagya-pi. ho na hehą́n hé chąglėška wą ikhóyaka cha
utilize-PL well and then that wheel IDF.SG adhere QL

hé phežúta chąglėška eyá-pi ho cha hé chąglėška ki
that medicine wheel say-IPS well so that wheel DEF

miméla cha phahį lul-yá-pi na ohómni óska-pi. na
circular QL porcupine quill red-CAU-IPS and around apply-IPS and

chą'íchipaweğa wą choką́ ikhóyake cha hé į́š eyá lé
cross.N* IDF.SG middle adhere QL that also this

wašícu wachékhiya-pi ki hé chą'íchipaweğa wą ų́
white man pray-IPS when that cross.N* IDF.SG with

wachékhiya-pi ki lé į́š eyá iyéchecha. ho éyaš ųkíye hé

pray-PL DEF this also like that well but we that

chą'íchipaweğa ki wiyóȟpeyata na wazíyata na wiyóhiyąpa na

cross.N* DEF west* and north and east* and

itókağa ho na chokį́ wíyaka wą ikhóyaka cha hé ų́

south well and middle feather IDF.SG adhere QL that with

Ųcí Makhá nahą́ Thųkášila Até Wakhą́thąka

Grandmother Earth and then God* Father Great Spirit*

maȟpíya ektá hená ų́ wochékhiye ų-káğa-pi. cha hená

sky in those with prayer 1PL.AG-make-PL so those

otúyachį wó'ilag-'ų-yą-pi-šni. cha Lakhóta oyáte ki lená

senselessly ST-1PL.AG-utilize-PL-NEG so Lakota people DEF these

lená wichó'ų ki miméyela cha okáwįȟ wachékhiya-pi hé

these way of life DEF circular QL go round pray-IPS that

įthó wiyóȟpeyata-kiya na he-tą́ wazíyata-kiya na

and so west*-in and that-from north-to and

wiyóhiyąpata-kiya na itókağata-kiya o-káwįȟ héchel yį́

east*-to and south-to L-turn around.VI so go

na héchel héktakiya wiyóȟpeyata-kiya khihų́ni. ho na

and so back.AV west*-to come back to well and

thípi, thi-'íkceya o-thí-pi ki, lená nakų́ miméyela. ho cha

tipi house-common L-live-IPS DEF these also circular well so

tóhąni tákuni oblóthų-šni. cha héchel hé iníyothi ki hená
never nothing angular-NEG so so that sweatlodge DEF those

nakų́ miméla. cha hená Lakhóta kihą tóhąni oblóthų-yą
also round so those Lakota DEF never angular-ADV

thí-pi-šni kéyá-pi. héchetu wichóʼų ki lé okáblaya
live-PL-NEG say that-IPS so existence DEF this unhampered

okáwįȟ-ya hiyáya-pi na echél glihų́ni-pi-kte.
go round-ADV pass.VI-PL and so arrive at the beginning-PL-FUT

hé é cha ų́ táku ki iyúha miméyela. naʼį́š nakų́ zįtkála
that IP QL therefore things DEF all round or also bird

ki hená hoȟpí tháwa-pi hená nakų́ chągléška. miméyela
DEF those nest its-PL those also wheel round

wichó-thi. naʼį́š táku óta chągléška hé Lakhóta wóʼilagya-pi,
COLL-dwell and things many wheel that Lakota utilize-PL

hená tóhųweni wąžíni oblóthų-šni. cha hé ų́ hená
those never none angular-NEG so that because of those

ohó-ki-la-pi cha. Lakhóta kihą hená ablés-ya ų́-pi
ST-PSS-respect.VT-PL QL Lakota DEF those notice-ADV exist-PL

hą́tąhąš líla tayą́ ų́-pi-kte. ho, henákecha.
when INT well exist-PL-FUT well enough

It is said that the things that today's generation make prayers with and trust in [when practicing spirituality] are an eagle feather, a pipe, the sweatlodge, and the [medicine] wheel that indicates the four directions. It symbolizes life. With it, as well as with sagebrush, sweetgrass, cedar, with all that, or with Indian medicine [certain herbs], we always make prayers [these plants serve as incense or medicine]. About eagle feathers, the old-time Lakotas had visions, and some performed sacred acts [with them]. The birds they called wing flappers [*wah̆úpakoza* is a sacred word that is used mainly in prayers]. They rated the eagles the highest. They took the feathers and prayed with them. The eagles were like human beings [because people understand eagles—the eagle is the mediator between man and God]. But they didn't do that [take the feathers] before bringing the bird into the sweatlodge, before praying and purifying it [with incense]. Then, when they took it outside again, they pulled out the feathers. They took the tail feathers and used them, and also the wings. The plumes were also used. The Lakota used each and every one [of the feathers, except for the smallest ones which were left on the body] for something. They respected them. But now some people [mostly white people] use them senselessly, kill them [the eagles] and store them in a cool place [freezer]. Next is the pipe. It comes from the earth, from Grandmother Earth. As for that stone [catlinite], over there in the east there is a red stone quarry. People take these stones, make pipes, and smoke with them. They use ash trees [for the pipe stems]. Before they crack they are cut, peeled and dried. [After the blizzards in January and February ash trees crack when they are cut and dried, and cannot be used any more.] They are straightened out, and they dry like this. As for the core [of the piece of wood]—how people did that in the old times I don't know—at any rate, they burn out the pith that is stuck fast at the center, and when there is a hole in it [the pipe stem], they make a pipe. They load the whole construction with tobacco, and either ask God for assistance, or express their gratitude to Him. That way people are powerful. During this ceremony, if you are maybe unhappy or suffering from anything, you burn either sagebrush or sweetgrass or cedar. You burn it and pray with it. This way our long-gone relatives come and help us. When we ask anything of them they make things ready for us beforehand; this is why people do these things. The Lakota never lived here on this earth thoughtlessly. When they killed something they went and put up tobacco and prayed over it [the dead animal]; then they ate it. The tobacco comes from the red willow, and therefore it comes from Grandmother Earth. When the smoke rises to God up in Heaven there will be help; that is why people pray this way. These things do have meaning, but some people practice them senselessly. In addition, there is a wheel connected [with spiritual customs]. It is called medicine wheel. This wheel is circular; porcupine quills are dyed red and wrapped around it. And in the middle a cross is attached. It is like the cross the white people also pray with when they pray. But we [Indians] make prayers with a cross that symbolizes the west, the north, the east, and the south, and has a feather attached in the middle. With it we make prayers to Grandmother Earth and God, the Father, the Great Spirit in the Heavens. We don't use these things senselessly. The Lakota way of life is like a circle, so people pray in a circle [i.e., addressing the four directions]. From the west it turns to the north, and then to the east and the south, and then comes back to the west. The tipis, traditional shelters people lived in, are also circular. [In the natural world] there never is anything with sharp corners. The sweatlodges are also circular. It is said that the Lakota never lived in an environment with corners. So people's existences went round smoothly in a circle, and would come back to where they had started. Thus everything was round. Moreover, birds' nests are also shaped like wheels. People camped in a circle [i.e., they arranged the tipis in a circle]. The Lakota used many circular things, none of them ever had corners. For these reasons they respected them. If the Lakota live wisely they will have a very good life. Well, that's enough.

3.13. Making Fire

NEVA STANDING BEAR

Tape recorded November 4, 1994

tókheškhe	*phéta*	*káǧa-pi*	*ki*	*hé*	*é*	*cha*	*oblákį-kte.*	*phéta*
how	fire	make-IPS	DEF	that	IP	QL	1SG.AG.tell-FUT	fire

ilé-ya-pi	*ki*	*hé*	*wáǧachą*	*há*	*iyókogna*	*haȟų́ta*	*sˀe*
burn.VI-CAU-IPS	SYP	that	cottonwood	skin	between	string	like.AV

swaká	*cha*	*hená*	*é*	*cha,*	*chą-pų́pų*	*cha*	*icú-pi*	*na*	*yuptá*
shredded	QL	those	IP	QL	wood-rotten	QL	take-IPS	and	pile up

é-gnaka-pi	*na*	*lé*	*chąhá*	*ki*	*héchacha*	*áta*	*ohómni*
L-put up-IPS	and	this	bark*	DEF	like that	entirely	around

é-gnaka-pi	*na*	*lé*	*wahį*	*héchacha*	*ų́*	*íchi-y-apha-pi*	*na*
L-put up-IPS	and	this	flint	like that	using	REC-EI-strike-IPS	and

ka-ˀíle-ya-pi	*chą́-šna*	*ilé*	*cha*	*kitą́la*	*ilé*	*hą́tąhą*
INS-burn.VI-CAU-IPS	then-HAB	burn.VI	so	a little	burn.VI	when

chąsákala	*nahą́*	*są́m*	*chą́*	*thąkį́kiyą*	*akšú-hą-pi*	*na*	*hé*
twig*	and then	more	wood	huge	pile up-PRG-IPS	and	that

phéta	*ki*	*líla*	*thą́ka*	*hą́tąhąš*	*chą́*	*thą́ka*	*cha*	*hená*
fire	DEF	INT	big	when	wood	big	QL	those

yu-wósla-sla-l	*é-gle-pi*	*hą́tąhą*	*líla*	*phéta*	*ki*	*thą́ka*	*ilé.*
INS-ST-RED-upright	L-put-IPS	when	INT	fire	DEF	big	burn.VI

cha héchų s'e phéta ki káǧa-pi. tohą́n phéta
so that way* fire DEF make-IPS when fire

ilé-ya-pi-kte hą́tąhąš hená héchų s'e echų́-pi na'į́š
burn.VI-CAU-IPS-FUT when those that way* do-IPS or

ųgnáš manį́n tuktél hą́tąhąš lé phežíšaša cha
maybe in the wilderness somewhere when this buffalo grass* QL

hená buffalo grass ecíya-pi cha héchacha hená icú-pi nahą́
those buffalo grass say to-IPS QL like that those take-IPS and then

ptáya é-gnaka-pi nahą́ lé tha-thų́kce púza cha áta
together L-put up-IPS and then this ruminant-manure dry.A QL all

ohómni égnaka-pi na ilé-ya-pi hą́tąhąš héchel ilé
around put up-IPS and burn.VI-CAU-IPS when so burn.VI

cha hená é cha ų́ chethí-pi nakų́ manį́n
QL those IP QL with build a fire-IPS also in the wilderness

thí-pi éyaš hená tuwéni tóhųweni oyáke-šni. éyaš Lakhóta
camp.VI-IPS but those nobody never tell-NEG but Indian

thókecha ki hená thogyé phéta káǧa-pi. éyaš ųkíye hógna
different DEF those differently fire make-PL but we that way*

ecéla echų́k'ų-pi.
only do.IPL.AG-PL

The topic of this story is how people made fire [in the old times]. In order to make fire people took the shredded, string-like inner bark of cottonwood trees, of rotten trees, and piled it up in a [little] heap. They put the [thick outer] bark around it and struck two flints together. When there was a spark it [the tinder] caught fire. When it was just barely burning people piled twigs or larger pieces of wood up on it. Then, when the fire was really big, and people added big pieces of wood, placing them in an upright position, the fire gave big flames. That way people made fire. Whenever people wanted to build a fire they did it that way. Or, when [they were] somewhere out in the wilderness, they took *phežíšaša,* which goes by the name of buffalo grass. They put it up in a pile, placed dry buffalo chips all around it, and when they set it on fire it started burning. With these things people started a fire, even if they lived in the wilderness. But nobody ever talked about that [one just knew that]. Other tribes have other ways of making fire. But we did it only that way.

3.14. How Wood Was Used

NEVA STANDING BEAR

Tape recorded November 16, 1994

lé	*ho*	*hehą́n*	*táku*	*chą́*	*ų́*	*wíphe*	*naˀį́š*	*táku*	*thušú*
this	well	then	things	wood	using	weapon	or	things	lodge pole

thípi	*thušú*	*naˀį́š*	*wahįkpe*	*ki*	*káǧa-pi*	*ki*	*tókhel*
tipi	pole	or	arrow	DEF	make-IPS	LK	how

weksúya	*héci*	*lé*	*oblákį-kte.*	*thokéya*	*wahįkpe*
remember.1SG.AG	SUB	this	1SG.AG.tell-FUT	first	arrow

káǧa-pi	*ki*	*hé*	*lé*	*chąsákala*	*cha*	*willow*	*naˀį́š*	*ųgnáš*
make-IPS	SYP	that	this	stick*	QL	willow	or	maybe

chąpháhu	*nachéce*	*cha*	*hená*	*icú-pi*	*nahą́*	*owóthąla*	*ki*
chokecherry	maybe	QL	those	take-IPS	and then	straight	DEF

Hená	*icú-pi*	*na*	*yu-ˀówothą*	*khuwá-pi*	*na*	*pus-yá-pi.*
Those	take-IPS	and	INS-straight	treat-IPS	and	dry.A-CAU-IPS

héchų-pi	*na*	*thakhą́*	*cha*	*icú-pi*	*nahą́*	*yu-spáya-pi*	*nahą́*
do that-PL	and	sinew*	QL	take-IPS	and then	INS-wet-IPS	and then

lé	*wíyaka*	*ki*	*hé*	*yusléca-pi*	*nahą́*	*sįté*	*ektá*	*iyápehą-pi.*
this	feather	DEF	that	splice-IPS	and then	tail	to	wrap around-IPS

cha	*hé*	*ihą́ke*	*ektá*	*wíyaka*	*iyápehą-pi*	*cha*	*hél*	*ihą́ke*	*él*
so	that	end.N	in	feather	wrap around-IPS	QL	there	end.N	in

waškíta-pi na hél ogná thakhą́ ki lená yu-spáya-pi
make notches-IPS and there along sinew* DEF those INS-wet-IPS

na iyápemni-pi na hená lé ųgnáš wazí chąší naʾį́š táku
and wrap around-IPS and those this maybe pine gum or things

tha-šáke lolób-ya-pi héchacha iyų́-pi chą́-šna séce
ruminant-hoof tender-CAU-IPS like that apply-IPS then-HAB dry.A

na sáka cha. héchel naglá-šni. cha hená él iyápemni-pi
and stiff QL so unravel-NEG so those there wrap around-IPS

nahą́ ithánųgya wíyaka ki hená iyápemni-pi. ho na
and then on both sides feather DEF those wrap around-IPS well and

hehą́n lé chą́ kitą́la thą́ka ki echíyatąhą cha hé iyų́-pi
then this wood a little big DEF from there QL that apply-IPS

na choką́ wasléca-pi nahą́ lé wahį́ ki hé
and middle split.VT-IPS and then this arrow point DEF that

iyókogna iyéya-pi na hehą́n tohą́n iyéya-pi nahą́ hél
in between send-IPS and then when send-IPS and then there

waškíta-pi cha hógna į́š eyá hé thakhą́ iyápemni-pi
make notches-IPS QL that way* also that sinew* wrap around-IPS

naʾį́š iyéchel iyáskab-ya-pi. ho chą́-šna hená é cha tuwá
and so stick to-CAU-IPS well then-HAB those IP QL someone

wayúphike hą́tąhąš hená owóthąla ikhóyag-ya cha ų́
skilful* if those straight adhere-CAU QL therefore

wątą́yeya keyá-pi. na hená wayé yá-pi na hená ų́
sharp-shooter* say that-IPS and those hunt go-IPS and those with

wamákhašką wichá-kte-pi na thaló ki aglí-pi. ho
animal* 3PL.PAT-kill-IPS and meat DEF bring home-IPS well

na hehą́n íyokhiheya hél į́š ehą́ni į́yą ka-pémni-pi
and then next there it long ago stone INS-twirled-IPS

eyá-pi cha hená į́š į́yą cha lé íyą šlušlúta cha hų́ȟ
say-IPS QL those they stone QL this stone smooth so some

sápį naˀį́š hų́ȟ ská. cha hená į́yą ki icú-pi nahą́
black or some white so those stone DEF take-IPS and then

tókheškhe chokʹą́-yą yu-ȟlóka-pi nahą́ chą́
somehow middle-ADV INS-hollow-IPS and then wood

ihúpa-ya-pi. na į́yą wą choką́ yu-ȟlóka-pi cha hél
handle-use as-IPS and stone LK middle INS-hollow-IPS QL there

opázą-pi na he-tą́ lená táku thakhą́ é cha hená
push onto-IPS and that-from those something sinew* IP QL those

icú-pi nahą́ hená į́yą ki opémni icú-pi nahą́
take-IPS and then those stone DEF wrap take-IPS and then

khútakiya lé chą́ ki ogná iyáskab-ya-pi chą́-šna hé
downwards this wood DEF along stick to-CAU-IPS then-HAB that

líla sutá cha hená ų́ kašlóka-pi-šni cha héchel
INT hard so those because of knock out-IPS-NEG so so

káğa-pi. na'įš hųh̆ tha-há cha įyą ki hél
make-IPS or some ruminant-skin QL stone DEF there

a-'ópemni-yą a-káyeğe-pi nahą́ sutá-ya káğa-pi chą́-šna
L-wrap-ADV L-sew-IPS and then hard-ADV make-IPS then-HAB

hená įyą ka-pémni-pi ki ų́ na'íc'ižį-pi na
those stone INS-twirled-IPS DEF with defend oneself-IPS and

okíchize chą́ hená ų́-pi, wicháša ki. thóka ki kah̆pá
battle then those use-PL man DEF enemy DEF knock down

wichá-yąka-pi kéye. ho cha hená héchel įyą ka-pémni-pi
3PL.PAT-sit-IPS QT well so those so stone INS-twirled-IPS

eyá chažeyáta-pi. ho nahą́ he-tą́ táku isą́m
say call-IPS well and then that-from things in addition

káğa-pi ki hé ocháže iyúha-h̆ci cha hų́h̆ pšithó ihúpa
make-IPS DEF that kind all-INT so some glass bead handle

káğa-pi. éyaš įšé hená wópazo ų́ káğa-pi. nahą́ wahįkpe
make-IPS but maybe those show.N for make-IPS and then arrow

wahįkpe eyá-pi-šni, tókhel eyá-pi, wéksuye-šni éyaš hená
arrow say-IPS-NEG how say-IPS remember.1SG.AG but those

įš eyá hé táku wíphe cha hená káğa-pi cha. įš eyá hé
also that something weapon QL those make-IPS QL also that

é cha líla ihúpa hą́ske na wahįkpe wą thą́ka cha įkpa ektá
IP QL INT handle long and flint LK big QL point at

ikhóyag-ya-pi	*cha*	*hé*	*wahúkeza*	*eyá*	*chažéyata-pi.*	*naˀį́š*
adhere-CAU-IPS	so	that	spear	say	call-IPS	or

tuwá	*khuwá-pi*	*hą́tąhąš*	*ų́*	*chaphá-pi*	*naˀį́š*	*hená*	*ų́*	*į́š eyá*
someone	chase-IPS	when	with	stab-IPS	or	those	with	also

napíkceya	*chaphá-pi,*	*khuté-pi-šni,*	*hé*	*é*	*ų́*	*hená*
by hand*	stab-IPS	shoot-IPS-NEG	that	IP	with	those

wamákhašką	*wichá-kte-pi.*	*cha*	*hená*	*héchel*	*ką́ğa-pi*	*nahą́*
animal*	3PL.PAT-kill-IPS	so	those	so	make-IPS	and then

hehą́n	*hél*	*thípi*	*thušú*	*ką́ğa-pi.*	*cha*	*hená*	*į́š eyá*	*kaksá-pi*	*na*
then	there	tipi	pole	make-IPS	so	those	also	cut-IPS	and

tohą́	*chą́*	*ki*	*hená*	*nahą́ȟcį*	*spáye*	*hą́tąhąš*	*hená*	*áta*	*há*
when	wood	DEF	those	still	wet	when	those	entirely	skin

ki	*yuȟláya-pi.*	*tóhąni*	*kaskú-sku-pi-šni,*	*hé*	*é*	*napíkceya*
DEF	peel.VT off-IPS	never	peel.VT-RED-IPS-NEG	that	IP	by hand*

yuȟláya-pi	*cha*	*áta*	*há*	*yu-šlóka-hą*	*cha*
peel.VT off-IPS	so	entirely	skin	INS-pull off-PRG	so

šlušlúl-yela-šna	*áta*	*yuȟlá*	*yuštą́-pi*	*hą́tąhąš*	*hená*
smooth-ADV-HAB	entirely	peel.VT off	finish-IPS	when	those

yuptą́yą	*khuwá-pi*	*na*	*púze*	*hą́tąhąš*	*héchel*	*wążíni*	*kawį́že-šni*
turn over	treat-IPS	and	dry.A	when	so	none	bent-NEG

cha	*héchel*	*ką́ğa-pi.*	*cha*	*hená*	*ų́*	*thi-ˀíkceya*
so	so	make-IPS	so	those	by means of	house-common

pa-wóslal iyéya-pi cha káğa-pi na'į̨š hená tohą́n yuȟpá-pi
INS-upright send-IPS so make-IPS and those when take down-IPS

hą́tąhąš hená tohą́n ehą́ni iglág wich-ómani hą́tąhąš
when those when long ago move camp COLL-travel when

hená šų́ka na'į̨š šų́kawakhą́ hená ithánųg
those dog or horse* those on both sides

iyá-wicha-kaška-pi. cha šų́ka ki hená wakhą́yeža hená
ST-3PL.PAT-tie to-IPS so dog DEF those child those

wichá-yu-sloha-pi na'į̨š táku wókaphą hená yu-slóhą-pi na
3PL.PAT-INS-slide-IPS or things parfleche those INS-slide-IPS and

šų́kawakhą́ ki lená į̨š hená thušú ki él iyá-wicha-kaška-pi
horse* DEF these they those pole DEF at ST-3PL.PAT-tie to-IPS

cha hená į̨š wakhą́yeža na'į̨š tuwá hų́kešni ehą́tąhąš
so those they child or someone weak when

hékta-tą yąká-pi. cha thi-'ákaȟpe ki hená é cha átaya
back.AV-from sit-PL so tipi-cover.N DEF those IP QL INT

pagmų́-pi na hékta-tą oyą́ke s'e káğa-pi cha hé é
roll up-IPS and back.AV-from seat like.AV make-IPS QL that IP

cha wichá-yu-slohą-pi. cha į̨šé hená echékche wa-'échų-pi.
QL 3PL.PAT-INS-slide-IPS so just those like this NSP.PAT-do-IPS

nahą́ tohą́n i-thí-kağa-pi hą́tąhąš hená chą́ ki
and then then L-house-make-IPS when those wood DEF

wakhą́-yą ki-chúwa-pi cha wąžíni kawéǧe-šni líla théhą-hą
respectful-ADV PSS-treat-IPS so none break.VI-NEG INT distant-RED

yu-slóhą ománi-pi. cha hená tuwá thípi ki tąyą́ káǧa-pi-šni
INS-slide travel-IPS so those someone tipi DEF well make-PL-NEG

na chą́ hená a-wą́glaka-pi-šni hą́tąhąš kawéǧa kéye.
and wood those L-POSS.see-PL-NEG if break.VI QT

I will talk about what people made from wood—weapons or things such as poles, tipi poles, or arrows, the way I remember it. First, in order to make an arrow, people took a sapling, willow or maybe chokecherry. They took the straight ones and treated them [i.e., they took off the bark and the limbs and straightened them by bending them in the hand] until they were [totally] straight, and dried them. When they had done that they took sinew, wetted it, spliced feathers, and tied them to the end of the shaft. Then they made notches in that end, in the end at which the feathers were fastened [in order to keep the sinew from slipping off]. At that point they wrapped the wetted sinew around [the shaft], and applied either boiled pine gum or boiled hoofs [both substances made good glue] to it. It became dry and stiff. That way it [the sinew] did not unravel. They wrapped it around [the shaft], wrapping the feathers on both ends. Then they applied it [the glue] to that end of the shaft which was a bit thicker [the front end]. They split it in the middle and inserted the arrow point in between. After inserting it they made notches right there. That [end] was also wrapped with sinew. That way people made sure that it [the point] remained in place. If a person was skillful he fixed them [the points and feathers] straight, and therefore people called him a sharp-shooter. When people went hunting, and killed animals with these [arrows], they brought the meat home. The next thing [that was made from wood] in the old times was called twirling stone [war club]. These [clubs] were made of stones, smooth stones. Some of them were black, others white. People took these [more or less egg-shaped] stones and pierced them in the middle somehow. They used a piece of wood for a handle. And the stone that was pierced in the middle was pushed onto it. Then they took some kind of sinew and wrapped it around the stone. They fixed this stone [by wrapping the sinew around the wood] at the bottom [i.e., at the handle]. This was [a] very strong [construction]. Therefore, they didn't knock it [the stone] loose. That way they made it. Some people wrapped the stone with rawhide and sewed it on. They made these things to last. With those war clubs people defended themselves. They used them at war, the men. They knocked the enemies off their horses while riding next to them. These [clubs] were called twirling stones. In addition to this, people made all kinds of other things. Some were made with beaded handles. But those were perhaps made for show purposes. Besides, there were, they were not called arrows, I don't remember what they were called. These things also served as a kind of weapon. They also had a very long handle, and there was a large piece of flint fastened to them at the end. This was a spear. When people chased somebody they stabbed him with it. With these [spears] they also killed animals, with their hands by stabbing, not by shooting. That's the way they did it. Besides [that], people made tipi poles. They, too, were cut, and while the wood was still moist they were peeled entirely. They were never peeled by hacking, they were peeled with the hands only. When the bark was all peeled off they were very smooth, and when the peeling was all done people kept turning them over and over [while they were drying]. When they had dried not a single one was bent. That's the way it was done. By means of these [poles] tipis were put up. When they were dismantled when people moved camp in the old times they were tied to the flanks of a dog or a horse. The dogs dragged the children and things such as parfleches. And behind the horses to which those poles were tied [this construction was called "travois"], the children and whoever was weak were sitting. The tipi covers were all rolled up and made into seats behind [the horses]. That way people were dragged. That's the way it was done. When the tipis were pitched the poles were treated with care. So not a single one of them broke, even though they were dragged around over great distances. If someone didn't pitch the tipi well and didn't look after the poles they broke.

3.15. How to Make Bows and Arrows

NEVA STANDING BEAR

Tape recorded November 16, 1994

ho hehą́n lé itázipa nahą́ wahį́kpe káǧa-pi ki lená įšé
well then this bow and then arrow make-IPS DEF these just

wichá tha-wóʾechų. cha hé pséȟtį cha ų́ itázipa káǧa-pi.
man ALP-work.N so that ash QL using bow make-IPS

pséȟtį théca cha icú-pi nahą́ kaksá-pi nahą́ lé alétka
ash young QL take-IPS and then cut-IPS and then this branch

waníca cha. tuktél alétka waníce hétu cha kaksá-pi na chą́ ki
lack QL where branch lack there QL cut-IPS and tree DEF

lé wa-žípa-pi na yuktą́-pi na púza áya. echél
this INS-smooth-IPS and bend.VT-IPS and dry.A PRC so

pus-yá-pi cha héchel oyúspe ki hél héchena gmigméla na
dry.A-CAU-IPS QL so handle DEF there thus round and

ithánųg wa-zízipela-pi cha hé ų́ yuktą́-pi okíhi-pi.
on both sides INS-thin-IPS QL that because of bend.VT-IPS can-IPS

cha icú-pi nahą́ lé thakhą́ cha hená íchi-yugmų-pi na
so take-IPS and then this sinew* QL those REC-twist-IPS and

hená ikhą́ káǧa-pi. ho nahą́ wahį́kpe ki hená įš
those string make-IPS well and then arrow DEF those they

lé, táku, chąšáša hé é cha éyaš thókecha chąšáša éyaš
this what red willow* that IP QL but different red willow* but

šá-šni, zí-ˀ, cha hená icú-pi nahą́ wahį́kpe káǧa-pi.
red-NEG yellow-ASS so those take-IPS and then arrow make-IPS

na hená į́š eyá há yuǧápa-pi nahą́ yu-ˀówothą khuwá-pi na
and those also skin pull off-IPS and then INS-straight treat-IPS and

lé thą́ka echíyatąhą wahį́ ki hé ikhóyag-ya-pi na hehą́n
this big from there flint DEF that stick to-CAU-IPS and then

ųmá echíyatąhą, sįté echíyatąhą, hé wíyaka wą yuzá-pi
other from there tail from there that feather IDF.SG split.VT-IPS

nahą́ kakˀóǧa-pi cha thakhą́ ų́ iyáskab-ya a-ˀíyapehą-pi
and then scrape off-IPS QL sinew* with apply-ADV L-wrap-IPS

nahą́ ųgnáš wazí chąšį́ naˀį́š tha-šáke pih̆-yá-pi
and then perhaps pine resin or ruminant-hoof boil.VI-CAU-IPS

héchacha iyúthą-thą-pi cha héchel naglá-šni na líla sutá
like that apply-RED-IPS so so unwind-NEG and INT hard

kéyá-pi. cha héchų-pi na hená ų́ hų́h̆ wątą́yą
say that-IPS so do that-IPS and those with some aim straight

ye-yá-pi cha hená į́š eyá chą́ ki owóthąla-h̆ci káǧa-pi cha
go-CAU-IPS so those also wood DEF straight-INT make-IPS QL

tuwéni hená otúyachį káh̆ iyéye-šni. lená i-wą́yąka-hą-pi na
nobody those carelessly make CEL-NEG these L-see-PRG-IPS and

echél	*tąyą́*	*wa-khúte-pi-kta*	*héchel*	*hená*	*káǧa-pi*	*na*
so	well	NSP.PAT-shoot-IPS-FUT	so	those	make-IPS	and

yuštą́-pi.	*cha*	*lé*	*ų́,*	*wahį́kpe*	*na*	*itázipa*	*ki*	*lená*	*ų́,*	*wayé*
finish-IPS	so	this	with	arrow	and	bow	DEF	these	with	hunt

yá-pi	*naˀį́š*	*tohą́n*	*kichíza-pi*	*hą́tąhąš*	*hená*	*él*	*ų́-pi.*	*cha*	*lená*
go-IPS	and	when	fight-IPS	when	those	there	use-IPS	QL	these

ehą́ni	*wicháša*	*ki*	*líla*	*wašˀáka-pi*	*cha*	*thathą́ka*	*ki*
old time	man	DEF	INT	strong-PL	so	buffalo bull*	DEF

kaˀísakhibya	*wichá-ˀįyąka-pi*	*na*	*wichá-ˀo-pi.*	*na*
beside	3PL.PAT-run-PL	and	3PL.PAT-shoot-PL	and

wichá-ˀo-pi	*chą́*	*lé*	*hél*	*khą́*	*thą́ka*	*wą*	*ȟpáya*	*cha*	*hé*
3PL.PAT-shoot-PL	then	this	there	string	big	LK	lie	QL	that

é	*cha*	*wo-psáka-pi*	*chą́-šna*	*iyáya-pi*	*okíhi-pi-šni.*	*cha*	*į́yąka-pi*
IP	QL	INS-broken-PL	then-HAB	go-PL	can-PL-NEG	so	run-PL

na-šna	*loté*	*ki*	*él*	*o-chá-wicha-pha-pha-pi*	*chą́-šna*
and-HAB	throat	DEF	in	L-ST-3PL.PAT-stab-RED-PL	then-HAB

éna	*tˀá-pi*	*kéyá-pi.*	*na*	*héchel*	*wichóˀoyake.*	*henákecha.*
right there	die-PL	say that-IPS	and	so	story	that is all

Making bows and arrows was exclusively men's work. Bows were made from ash. People picked a young ash tree and cut it down, one that didn't have too many branches. They cut out the part that was without branches. This [piece of wood] was whittled until it was smooth, and bent [in order to shape it]. It dried out. People let it dry that way. The handle was round, and both sides [the shoulders] were scraped thin. Thus people could bend it. They took it [the finished bow], and then twisted sinew [buffalo and deer, later cattle] together, and made them into a bowstring. As for the arrows, people took—what was it?—red willow, but it was another type of red willow, it was not red, but yellow [real willow], and made arrows. The bark was peeled off of them [the sticks], too, and they were treated until they were straight. On the large end the arrow point was fastened. Then people wrapped [one half of] a feather which had been split [lengthwise along the quill] and scraped [i.e., the quill had been scraped thin] tightly to the other end [of the shaft] with sinew. Then they applied either pine gum or boiled hoofs [both substances produced glue], so it did not unwind. This [construction] was very strong. People did that, and with these [arrows] some could shoot very accurately. Also, straightening the sticks completely was a job that nobody did carelessly and in a hurry. People looked at the wood over and over. That way they would be able to shoot well. They made them that way, and finished them. With this, with these arrows and bows, people went hunting. And they used them when they went to war. These old-time men were very strong. They raced along next to the buffalo [on horseback], and shot them. When they had shot them they cut the main tendon located there [at the lower leg]. So they [the animals] could not run away. Then they [the men] ran and stabbed them in the throat. They died on the spot. That's the way the story goes. That's all.

3.16. Games

NEVA STANDING BEAR

Tape recorded November 16, 1994

khą-sú-khute-pi eyá-pi hé hená khą́ta sú cha hená
plum-seed-shoot-IPS say-IPS that those dice* QL those

khá-pi. cha hená khą́ta sú ki hená icú-pi nahą́
mean.VT-IPS so those plum seed DEF those take-IPS and then

ošté-šte-ya ǧu-yá-pi. ho na hená é cha napé él
well-RED-ADV burned-CAU-IPS well and those IP QL hand in

o-kí-gnaka-pi na ka-slóhą ye-yá-pi chą́-šna tuwá ohíye
L-PSS-put-IPS and INS-slide go-CAU-IPS then-HAB who win

hą́tąhąš tókhetu cha ųgnáš pšithó oyáza-pi cha hená
when how QL maybe glass bead string.VT-IPS QL those

ų́ ahí-gle-pi. cha hená ahí-gle-pi chą́ winų́ȟcala cha
using bring-put-IPS so those bring-put-IPS then old woman QL

ptáyela yąká-pi na hená khą-sú khuté-pi. cha hená hé
together sit-PL and those plum-seed shoot-PL so those that

oškáte ki wąží. ho na hehą́n hél wąží pa-slóhą-pi eyá-pi
game DEF one well and then there one INS-slide-IPS say-IPS

cha hená į́š lé pséȟtį sakála cha įšé hé tohą́kca-kca cha
so those it this ash sapling QL just that so long-RED QL

hą́ska-ska cha hená lé chą́ kihą lé thą́ka echíyatąhą
long-RED QL those this wood DEF this big from there

ka-phésto-pi cha hé é cha tókheškhe yu-ˀówothą pus-yá-pi
INS-pointed-IPS so that IP QL somehow INS-straight dry.A-CAU-IPS

cha hé é cha sí ki aką́n é-ki-gnaka-pi nahą́ wohˇtáka-pi
QL that IP QL foot DEF on top L-PSS-put-IPS and then hit-IPS

na wo-slóhą iyéya-pi chą́-šna wąkátakiya kįyį́ na
and INS-slide send-IPS then-HAB upwards fly and

tókhiyab-šna kaˀótą gli-hé cha. hená
somewhere-HAB pound tight fall-stand QL those

a-kíchi-ya-pi cha hená hé pa-slóhą iyéya-pi. ho na
ST-REC-challenge-IPS so those that INS-slide send-IPS well and

hehą́n hél thápa kakhápa-pi eyá-pi cha hé į́š thápa kihą
then there ball strike a ball-IPS say-IPS QL that it ball DEF

tha-há cha kayéǧe-pi nahą́ pséhˇtį chą́ cha hená
ruminant-skin QL sew-IPS and then ash wood QL those

nahą́hˇcį théca wą héhą icú-pi na yuktą́-pi na
still fresh IDF.SG then take-IPS and bend.VT-IPS and

ki hél aˀíyopteya a-chéthi-pi chą́-šna héchena
SYP there right there L-build a fire-IPS then-HAB thus

yuktą́-yą púze cha héchel nasléce-šni cha tohą́n púze
bend.VT-ADV dry.A so that way split.VI-NEG QL when dry.A

hą́tąhąš héchena sagyé s'e púze cha hená há yuǧápa-pi
when thus stick like.AV dry.A QL those skin take off-IPS

nahą́ hená é cha ų́ thápa yukháb icú į́yąka-pi cha hená
and then those IP QL with ball catch take run-IPS so those

thápa kakhápa-pi eyá-pi. cha ithánųg nážį-pi na
ball strike-IPS say-IPS so on both sides stand-IPS and

a-kíchi-ya-pi. tuwá lúzahe hą́tąhąš áta thápa ki
ST-REC-challenge-IPS someone fast when INT ball DEF

ikhóyag-yį na yu-psíl iyéya į́yąkį na ųmáchiyatą chą́ nų́m
adhere-CAU and INS-jump send run and on both sides wood two

pa-slál hą́ cha choką́ iyéya-pi. cha hená ohíya-pi cha hé
INS-upright stand so middle send-IPS so those win-IPS so that

ų́ héchų-pi. ho na hehą́n akhé chą-ká-wachi-pi eyá-pi
with do that-IPS well and then again wood-INS-dance-IPS say-IPS

cha hé į́š chą́ cha gmigmé-ya paskú-pi nahą́ hená átaya
so that it wood QL round-ADV carve-IPS and then those INT

pa-šlúšluta-pi na ho hé phésto-ya káǧa-pi. cha hé le
INS-slippery-IPS and well that pointed-ADV make-IPS so that this

tha-há cha hé yusléca-pi na iyápehą-pi na cháǧa
ruminant-skin QL that tear-IPS and wrap around-IPS and ice

ektá aką́n ka-wáchi-pi. ka-psíl iyéya-pi na-šna áta
on on top INS-dance-IPS INS-jump send-IPS and-HAB INT

yusáksaka-pi	*chą́-šna*	*hé*	*chą́*	*ki*	*hé*
hit from a distance-IPS	then-HAB	that	wood	DEF	that

ka-wáchi-pi.	*cha*	*hé*	*įšé*	*hokšíla*	*wóškate*	*hécha.*	*na*	*chąglėška*
INS-dance-IPS	so	that	just	boy	toy	COP	and	hoop

pa-gmíyą-pi	*eyá-pi*	*cha*	*hé*	*lé*	*chąsákala*	*cha*	*mimé-ya*
INS-round-IPS	say-IPS	QL	that	this	stick*	QL	round-ADV

iyákaška-pi	*na*	*héchel*	*pus-yá-pi*	*na*	*chą́*	*wą*
tie to-IPS	and	so	dry.A-CAU-IPS	and	wood	IDF.SG

tohą́kecha-kecha	*kaksá-pi*	*na*	*hé*	*é*	*cha*	*ų́*	*pa-gmíyą*	*į́yąka-pi*
so long-RED	cut-IPS	and	that	IP	QL	with	INS-round	run-IPS

chą́-šna	*tuwá*	*hé*	*kaʔų́ke*	*hą́tąhąš*	*hé*	*ohíya*	*kéye.*	*cha*	*įšé*
then-HAB	who	that	cut down	when	that	win	QT	so	just

hé	*hokšíla*	*wóškate*	*cha,*	*hená*	*echél*	*káğa-pi.*
those	boy	game	QL	those	so	make-IPS

[The game] called "shooting plum seeds" is like playing dice. People took the plum seeds and burned in nice designs. Then they took them in the hand and tossed them. They put up bead strings, for example, [as a prize] for the one who won. After putting them up, the old women sat together and played shooting plum seeds. That was one of the games. Besides, there was one [game] called "making it slide." An ash sapling of about that length [six feet], this [piece of] wood was carved into a point at the thick end. Using some kind of procedure, it was straightened while it was being dried. Then people placed it on the foot [across the instep, with the thick end pointing upwards], and when they gave it a shove it shot upwards through the air and pierced into the ground somewhere. People competed with each other by having throwing matches. Besides, there was a game called "striking the ball." The ball was composed of leather pieces which were sewn together. Then people took a piece of ash wood which was still fresh and bent it. While bending it they heated it over the fire right there [where they were bending it]. That way it [one end] dried in a curved shape and didn't split [which tends to happen when wood is drying]. When it was dry, dry like a cane, the bark was peeled off [in the places that had not undergone the bending procedure]. With that they caught the ball and ran. [The racket was about four feet long, and the sharp curve at the end enabled the player to hook the ball.] This [game] was called striking the ball. People formed two teams and competed with each other. A fast player was able to keep the ball close to him while it was bouncing up and down, as he was running. People [tried to] hit right between the two upright poles [which marked the goal] that were located on both sides [of the field]. That way they scored. [This is usually referred to as "shinny game."] Besides, there was another [game] called "making the wood dance." A [piece of] wood [four to five inches by two to three inches] was carved to a round shape, polished and tapered so that it had a point. A piece of leather was cut into a string, wrapped around it, and then people made it spin on the ice. By making it bounce and whipping it [with the string] that piece of wood was given a spinning motion. That was a toy for boys only. The [game] called "rolling the hoop" was made by tying a sapling so that it formed a circle, and letting it dry that way, so that it kept its circular shape. Then people cut a stick of about this length [two to three feet], and ran while rolling it [the hoop] with it. The person who made it tip over [with the hands or feet] scored. This was only a boys' game. That's the way it was done.

3.17. Marriage

FLORINE RED EAR HORSE

Tape recorded September 19, 1995

ho	*hehą́l*	*táku*	*wąží*	*oblákį-kte*	*ki*	*hé*	*ehą́ni*
well	then	something	IDF.SG	tell.1SG.AG-FUT	DEF	that	long ago

ųcí-wa-ye	*wą*	*lé*	*wichóʔoyake*	*ki*
grandmother-1SG.AG-have as	IDF.SG	this	story	DEF

o-má-ki-yake	*yųkhą́*	*ehą́ni*	*wikhóškalaka*	*wąží*	*thiwáhe*	*él*
ST-1SG-BEN-tell	then	long ago	young woman	IDF.SG	family	in

yuhá-pi	*chą́-šna*	*héchel*	*a-wą́-ki-glaka-pi*	*kéye*	*nahą́*	*tąyą́*
have-IPS	then-HAB	so	L-ST-PSS-POSS.see-PL	QT	and then	well

héchel	*hįgnáthų-khiya-pi*	*chį́-pi*	*kéye.*	*cha*	*héchel*
so	marry*-CAU-PL	want-PL	QT	so	so

kpağą́-pi-šni	*kéye*	*yųkhą́*	*héchel*	*echų́-pi*	*hą́tąhą*	*ąpétu*
give away easily-PL-NEG	QT	then	so	do-PL	when	day

wąží	*él*	*khoškálaka*	*wąží*	*wikhóškalaka*	*ki*	*lé*	*waštélakį*
IDF.SG	on	young man	IDF.SG	young woman	DEF	this	love.VT

naʔį́š	*iyókiphi*	*hą́tąhąš*	*hiyóʔu*	*kéye.*	*yųkhą́*	*šų́kawakhą́*	*wąží*
and	like.VT	if	come after	QT	then	horse*	IDF.SG

héchel	*aką́yąkį*	*na*	*wąží*	*héchel*	*kašká*	*yús*	*aʔú*	*kéye.*	*yųkhą́*	*hé*
so	ride*	and	one	so	tie	hold	bring	QT	then	that

šų́kawakhą́ ki hé thiwáhe él yuhá hí na hų́-ku na
horse* DEF that family to have come and mother-3POR and

at-kúku ki o-wícha-ki-yake na wikhóškalaka ki hé
father-3POR DEF ST-3PL-BEN-tell and young woman DEF that

chųwį́-tku ki hé wichá-ki-la kéye. ho hé
daughter-3POR DEF that 3PL-BEN-ask for QT well that

šųkawakhą́ ki hé akąyąke-khiya kéye. ho nahą́
horse* DEF that ride*-CAU QT well and then

šų́kawakhą́ wą akábya ahí hé thiwáhe ki él wichá-kʔu
horse* LK extra bring that family DEF to 3PL.PAT-give

kéye. ho chą́ lé akąyąke-khiyį na kašká yús héchel aglá
QT well then this ride*-CAU and tie hold so take home

kéye. ho hé waná thiwáhe tháwa-pi ektá héchel waná kichí
QT well that now family his-PL there so now with

ų́-kta cha héchel akhí kéye. akhí nahą́
be-FUT QL so come home with QT come home with and then

ho hé íyohakab hél wóʔechų yąká kéye éyaš hená héhą
well that after there feast be QT but those then

wi-má-chįcala cha tąyé-kel táku ki lená
ST-1SG.PAT-girl so well-kind of things DEF these

o-wá-kaȟniğe-šni na a-wá-bleze-šni cha hehą́l
ST-1SG.AG-understand-NEG and ST-1SG.AG-notice-NEG so then

wichóʔoyake ki hé é wa-gnúni. ho hehą́yela obláką-kte.
story DEF that IP 1SG.AG-lose well that is all tell.1SG.AG-FUT

What I will talk about is this: long ago, one of my grandmothers told me this story. When they had a young woman in the family in the old times, they closely watched over her. They wanted her to have a good marriage. They did not give her away easily. When they did that it would be when someday a young man came after the young woman, if he loved her and liked her. He would ride a horse and would lead another. He would come to the family with the horse and talk to her mother and father, and would ask for the young woman, their daughter. He would make her ride the horse [the one he was riding]. And the extra horse he brought he would give to the family. He would make her ride the horse, taking her home by leading her. From then on she would live with his family; he took her back [to where he lived]. After he had taken her back there would be a feast, but since I was a little girl back then [when I witnessed such feasts] I did not really understand and pay any attention to these things. That is why I have lost that story [about the feasts]. That is all I wanted to say.

3.18. Cocklebur (*Xanthium echinatum*)

FLORINE RED EAR HORSE

Tape recorded September 19, 1995

hehą́n táku wąží obláki̜-kte ki hé winą́wizitkhą
then something IDF.SG tell.1SG.AG-FUT DEF that cocklebur

hú ki hé ehą́ni Lakhóta ki phežúta-ya-pi yu̜khą́
root DEF that long ago Lakota DEF medicine*-use as-PL then

táku hé wą líla o-wášte ki hé ažų́tka wóyazą ki hé
what that IDF.SG INT L-good DEF that kidney pain DEF that

ihéya-pi okíhi-pi-šni, ihéya-pi oglúspa-pi, na
discharge-PL can-PL-NEG discharge-PL POSS.catch-PL and

ihéya-pi okíhi-pi-šni ki hé ų́ lé phežúta kihą
discharge-PL can-PL-NEG SYP that because of this medicine* DEF

húta kihą apé kihą hą́ske-ya átaya ithánųg léchel apé
bottom DEF leaf DEF long-ADV all over on each side so leaf

kihą cik-cík'ala a-'íchi-yupte-ya hą́ske-ya ikhóyaka cha
DEF RED-small L-REC-take turns-ADV long-ADV adhere QL

chokį́ táku wítka s'e léchecha phe-phé ikhóyake. ho
middle things egg like.AV like this pointed-RED adhere well

hé o-'íyeya-pi okíhi-pi, phežúta ki lé. ųgnáhąšna mayá
that L-find-IPS can-IPS medicine* DEF this sometimes river bank

aglágla icháǧe. ho hé yužų́-pi ehą́tąhąš hutkhą́ líla
along grow well that pull out-IPS if root INT

hą́ska-ska. hutkhą́ ki hé zi-zí s'e léchecha. ho hé
long-RED root DEF that yellow-RED like.AV like this well that

líla hą́ske-ya yužų́-pi hą́tąhąš ho hé waksá-ksa-pi na
INT long-ADV pull out-IPS when well that cut-RED-IPS and

kaskú-sku-pi nahą́ tohą́hą waksá-ksa-pi na ho
peel.VT-RED-IPS and then at regular intervals cut-RED-IPS and well

hé é cha mní ų́ pilȟ-yá-pi na mní waná tąyą́
that IP QL water with boil.VI-CAU-IPS and water now well

píǧa-hą hená ȟeyáb icú-pi na hehą́l waná mní ki lé
boil.VI-PRG those away take-IPS and then now water DEF this

ka-sní-pi nahą́ ho t'ecá hą́tąhąš ho wakšíca ogná
INS-cold-IPS and then well lukewarm when well dish inside

tuwé ki lé k'ú-pi ehą́tąhąš ho hé lé ihéye-šni
someone DEF this give-IPS when well that this discharge-NEG

na'į́š ažų́tka yazą́ hé ų́ akísni. cha héchel-ya phežúta
or kidney ache that because of recover so so-ADV medicine*

ki lé ilágya-pi. yųkhą́ winá́wizitkhą ecíya-pi Lakhótiya,
DEF this utilize-PL then cocklebur say to-IPS in Lakota

winá́wizitkhą phežúta ki lé. cha tukté'el yukhé hą́tąhąš ųgná
cocklebur medicine* DEF this so wherever exist when maybe

chąphá naʼį́š khąthúhu ožú eyá hą́ska-ska-ke
cherry or plum tree bunch IDF.PL long-RED-kind of

héchecha-ke sʼe, hú kihą thąį́yą-hį-kte. ho yųkhą́ lé
like that-kind of like.AV stem DEF visible-PRG-FUT well then this

phežúta hé é cha ų́ ažų́tka wichókhuže ki lé iyókihi.
medicine* that IP QL with kidney disease DEF this cure

eyášna asní-pi. hé ų́ akísni-pi. yųkhą́ ąpétu wą
always recover-IPS that by means of recover-IPS then day IDF.SG

él wicháša wą į́š lé phežúta ki lé aką́-tąhą
on man IDF.SG he this medicine* DEF this on top-from

chąwáphe nahą́ táku eyá wítka sʼe gmigmé-la cha
leaf and then something LK egg like.AV round-DIM QL

phe-phé ki hená é-ʼe, hená é ilágya-pi-šni yųkhą́ lená
pointed-RED DEF those IP-RED those IP utilize-IPS-NEG then these

é cha áta pahí kéye. na yuhá chąkú okhížata wą él
IP QL lots of gather QT and have road junction IDF.SG at

nážį kéye. ho hél ogná wich-ómani cha wicháša hená
stand QT well there along COLL-travel so people those

éna o-wícha-yuspį-kta cha slolyá kéye. yųkhą́
right there ST-3PL.PAT-catch-FUT LK know QT then

héchecha-kta waná iyéchįkyąke wą í na kaslóhą hinážį
like that-FUT now car* IDF.SG come and park*

kéye. ho cha o-kí-yaka kéye “lená phahį́ wítka cha,
QT well so ST-BEN-tell QT these porcupine egg QL

wíyopheya yeló” eyá kéye. éyaš tóna igláwa kihą
sell ASS.M say QT but how much price DEF

oyáka-pi-šni éyaš héchų sʔe wichóʔoyake ki lé oyáka-pi. yųkhą́
tell-IPS-NEG but that way* story DEF this tell-IPS then

waná héchel inážį áyį na hąkéya líla wich-óta-pi kéye.
now so stop PRC and finally INT person-many-PL QT

yųkhą́ hená átaya wicákhela-pi na hená iyúha tónana áta
then those all believe-PL and those all several INT

ophéthų-pi kéye. ho yųkhą́ lé wicháša wą slolyá cha iyáya
buy-PL QT well then this man IDF.SG know QL go

kéye táku tókha sʔe léchecha cha į́š eyá él inážį yųkhą́
QT what happen like.AV like this so also there stop then

hé wicháša kihą héchel wichášašni yųkhą́ héchecha. lé
that man DEF so tricky then like that this

wináwizitkhą eyá táku ikhóyaka lená cha áta óta pahí na
cocklebur IDF.PL what adhere these QL INT many gather and

wašícu ki lená wichá-gnayą cha lé áta ophéthų-pi kéye.
white man DEF these 3PL.PAT-trick so this all buy-PL QT

ho hená tókhi wítka hená ogná etą́ phahį lená
well those maybe egg those inside from porcupine these

ikpákpi-kta kéchį-pi nachéce. wašícu kihą hųȟ táku ki
hatch-FUT think that-PL perhaps white man DEF some things DEF

lená héchetu kéchį-pi na wicákhela-pi na ophéthų-pi éyaš
these true think that-PL and believe-PL and buy-PL but

hé ikpákpi-kta kéchį-pi kéye. ho héchetu-šni škhá hená
that hatch-FUT think that-PL QT well true-NEG but those

wichá-gnayą kéye. ho hé i-wá-yu-phi-ya įšé
3PL.PAT-trick QT well that L-NSP.PAT-INS-good-ADV just

taktókhų kéyá-pi na oyáka-pi. ho hé lé obláke.
figure out say that-IPS and tell-IPS well that this tell.1SG.AG

So I will tell something about cocklebur root. Long ago the Lakota used it as medicine. One thing it is very good for is kidney pain, when people cannot urinate, when they hold their urine and cannot urinate. This medicine has small leaves attached all over in a long row starting at the bottom [of the stem] on both sides, arranged opposite each other [like a fern]. In the center [next to the stem] prickly things which are shaped like eggs adhere. That is where it can be found, this medicine. Sometimes it grows along riverbanks. When it is pulled out, the root is very long. The root is yellowish. When a very long piece has been pulled out, it is cut it off and peeled, and cut it into uniform pieces [about three inches long]. This is boiled with water, and when the water is boiling nicely it is set aside. Then the water is allowed to cool off, and when it is lukewarm it is given to the person who cannot urinate, or has kidney pain, in a cup, and he recovers from it. That's how this medicine was used. It is called *wináwizitkhą* in Lakota, this cocklebur medicine. Wherever it grows, they are pretty long, the stems, about that long [two feet], there may also appear some clumps of chokecherry or plum bushes. With this medicine kidney disease can be cured. The patients always recover. They recover from it. One day a man gathered a lot of the leaves growing on top of this medicine plant, which are somewhat round like eggs and prickly; they are not used [as medicine]. With them he waited at an intersection. At that place a lot of traffic was passing through. He knew he would get a hold of people right there. He was right. A car came and parked. He said: "These are porcupine eggs, they are on sale!" It is not reported what the price was; that's the way the story is told. Now more and more people stopped, and finally there was a big crowd. People all believed him and they all bought some eggs. Then a man who knew him [the vendor] went [to check things out] because something seemed to be going on. He also stopped there [to put an end to this]. That man [who sold the eggs] was really tricky. He collected a lot of the things that adhere to the cocklebur plant and tricked the white people, who bought them all. They thought that perhaps porcupines would hatch from those eggs. Some of the white people thought that this was true, and they believed him and bought them because they thought that they would hatch. It was not true, he had tricked them. People say that this was nicely figured out, and pass the story on. This is what I wanted to tell.

3.19. Yucca (*Yucca glauca*)

FLORINE RED EAR HORSE

Tape recorded September 19, 1995

ho lé táku wąží oblákį-kte ki hé
well this something IDF.SG tell.1SG.AG-FUT SYP that

hú ki hé ehą́ni oyáte— kihą wį́yą ki é cha— lená
root DEF that long ago people DEF woman DEF IP QL these

huphéstola hú ki lé o-kʼá-pi nahą́ hé táku wą
yucca* root DEF this L-dig-PL and then that something IDF.SG

hé tuktógna kéyá-pi éyaš líla-ȟcį
that some way say that-IPS but INT-INT

o-wá-kaȟniǧe-šni. yųkhą́ huphéstola hú wąží o-kʼá-pi
ST-1SG.AG-understand-NEG then yucca* root IDF.SG L-dig-IPS

ehą́tąhąš húta ki hé oȟlóǧa cha hą́tąhąš hé táku
when base DEF that hole QL when that something

khá-pi kéyá-pi. ho hená ilágya-pi-šni kéyá-pi. éyaš
mean.VT-IPS say that-IPS well those utilize-IPS-NEG say that-IPS but

hé táku-ȟca héci slol-wá-ye-šni. éyaš huphéstola hú ki
that what-INT SUB ST-1SG.AG-know-NEG but yucca* root DEF

lé héchacha-šni hená yužų́-pi nahą́ hutkhą́ ki hená
this like that-NEG those pull out-IPS and then root DEF those

kaskú-pi nahą́ héchel piȟ-yá-pi kéye. piȟ-yá-pi na
peel.VT-IPS and then so boil.VI-CAU-IPS QT boil.VI-CAU-IPS and

ų́ héchel natá kihą glužáža-pi hą́tąhą phehį́ hą́ska-ska-pi
with so head DEF POSS.wash-IPS when hair long-RED-IPS

naʔį́š phehį́ wašté-šte. héchų sʔe oyáka-pi. ho na icí-nųpa ki
and hair good-RED that way* tell-IPS well and ORD-two DEF

hé huphéstola hú ki lé táku wą líla héchel
that yucca* root DEF this something IDF.SG INT so

o-wášte: tuwá thezí-yazą hą́tąhąš ho hé į́š eyá hú
L-good someone stomach-ache.VI when well that also root

ki hé yužų́-pi nahą́ kaskú-pi nahą́ hé hená
DEF that pull out-IPS and then peel.VT-IPS and then that those

waksá-ksa-pi na hé wąží héchel mní icáhi piȟ-yá-pi
cut-RED-IPS and that IDF.SG so water mix boil.VI-CAU-IPS

na iyásni hą́tąhąš ho hehą́l wakšíca ogná ožúla héchel
and cool off when well then dish inside full so

kʔú-pi hą́tąhąš ho hé yatké hą́tąhąš ho hé wą́cagna
give-IPS when well that drink when well that at once

kakpíya ki lé héchel natháka kéyá-pi. ho owénųpkiya
diarrhea DEF this so stop.VT say that-IPS well in two ways

huphéstola hú ki lé ilágya-pi. héchų sʔe ehą́ni
yucca* root DEF this utilize-IPS that way* long ago

ųcí-wa-ye *ki* *lená* *o-má-ki-yake.* *cha* *hé* *é*
grandmother-1SG.AG-have as DEF these ST-1SG-BEN-tell so that IP

cha *lé* *obláke.*
QL this tell.1SG.AG

So I will tell something about soapweed root. Long ago people—actually, the women—dug up these soapweed roots. There is something to it, but I absolutely don't remember it. When the soapweed root they were digging up had a hole in it at the bottom that meant something. It was not used. But I don't know what that was all about. But the soapweed roots that were not like that they pulled out. The roots were peeled and boiled. They were boiled, and when people washed their hair with it [the suds] they got very long hair, and very beautiful hair. That's what people say. The second thing soapweed root is very good for is this: when somebody had a stomachache, people also harvested out that root. They peeled it, cut it into pieces, and boiled one [piece of about two inches] mixed with water. When it had cooled off and the patient was given a cupful and drank it, that stopped the diarrhea at once. Soapweed root was used in two ways. Long ago my grandmother told me so. This is what I wanted to tell.

3.20. Mushrooms

FLORINE RED EAR HORSE

Tape recorded September 19, 1995

ho	*lé*	*į́š*	*wichóˀoyake*	*ki*	*lé*	*chą́*	*él*	*táku*	*eyá*
well	this	it	story	DEF	this	tree	on	something	IDF.PL

ska-ská	*cha*	*icháǧe.*	*ho*	*hená*	*ehą́ni*	*oyáte*	*ki*
white-RED	QL	grow	well	those	long ago	people	DEF

wóyute-ya-pi.	*yųkhą́*	*Lakhótiya*	*chąnákpa*	*ecíya-pi.*
food-use as-PL	then	in Lakota	mushroom*	say to-IPS

wašícu-ya	*mushrooms*	*eyá-pi.*	*yųkhą́*	*hená*	*táku*	*ki*
white man-ADV	mushrooms	say-IPS	then	those	things	DEF

akhí-pi	*na*	*líla*	*tąyą́*	*yužáža-pi*	*na*	*mní*	*icáhi*	*héchel*
take back-IPS	and	INT	well	wash-IPS	and	water	mix	so

piȟ-yá-pi	*nahą́*	*él*	*wašį́*	*o-gnáka-pi.*	*ho*	*į́š*
boil.VI-CAU-IPS	and then	there	fat	L-place-IPS	well	it

lolób-ya-pi	*chą́*	*líla*	*wahą́pi*	*wašté-ˀ.*	*ho*	*héchel*	*įšé*
tender-CAU-IPS	then	INT	soup	good-ASS	well	so	just

ehą́ni	*wichóˀų*	*ki*	*lená*	*táku*	*ki*	*lená*	*yúta-pi*	*na*
long ago	generation	DEF	these	things	DEF	these	eat-PL	and

ilágya-pi.	*hé*	*ų́*	*tókhi*	*ųgná*	*héhą*	*oyáte*	*ki*	*tąyą́*
utilize-PL	that	because of	maybe	maybe	then	people	DEF	well

ų́-pi nachéce. ehą́ni oyáte kihą wį́yą ki thachą́

be-PL perhaps long ago people DEF woman DEF body

cik-cík'ala-pi na phehį́ ki líla sap-sápa-pi nahą́ tuwéni

RED-small-PL and hair DEF INT RED-black-PL and then nobody

į̌šé ehą́ni ištámaza ų́-šni s'e léchecha na wichášá ki

just long ago glasses* use-NEG like.AV like this and man DEF

į́š eyá iyéchecha-pi, hená thachą́ cik-cík'ala-pi na waš'áka-pi cha

also alike-PL those body RED-small-PL and strong-PL so

hé ehą́ni oyáka-pi na hená wichášá kihą tháȟca wąží

that long ago tell-IPS and those man DEF deer IDF.SG

héchel kté-pi ehą́tąhąš nakų́ tohą́ makhá théhą éyaš héchel

so kill-PL when also when distance long but so

k'į́-pi na kú-pi kéyá-pi. ho lehą́l tuwá

carry on the back-PL and come-PL say that-IPS well now someone

héchų-wachį-kta kéchį éyaš okíhi-kte-šni. įchį́ ehą́ni

do that-try-FUT think that but can-FUT-NEG because long ago

oyáte kihą wóyute eyá yúta-pi ki hená ąpétu ki lé lehą́l

people DEF food IDF.PL eat-PL DEF those day DEF this now

wóta-pi ki kichí íchi-thokecha. ehą́ni líla bliheca-pi

NSP.PAT-eat-PL DEF from REC-different long ago INT energetic-PL

na waš'áka-pi éyaš lehą́l oyáte ki héchecha-pi-šni. lehą́l

and strong-PL but now people DEF like that-PL-NEG now

tha-wóyute	*ki*	*thok-thókecha*	*cha*	*líla*	*chep-chépa-pi*	*na*
ALP-food	DEF	RED-different	so	INT	RED-fat-PL	and

hų́ka-pi-šni.
ST-PL-weak

This story is about the whitish things which grow on trees. In the old times people used them as food. In Lakota they are called *chąnákpa*. In English they are called mushrooms. People took these things home, washed them very thoroughly, and boiled them with water. Then they added fat. This was boiled until tender. It made a very good soup. The people of the past ate these things and used them [for food]. For that reason, people were probably doing well back then. The women of the old-time people had very slim bodies and really black hair, and it seems like nobody needed glasses back then. The men were the same, they had very slim bodies and were strong. At least this is what was reported in the past. When those men killed a deer they carried it home even when it was far. If somebody thought of trying to do that today he would not be able to. This is because the food that the old-time people ate is different from what people eat today. In the old times people were very active and strong, but today people are not like that. Today their food is all different, so people are extremely fat and weak.

3.21. Chewing Gum

FLORINE RED EAR HORSE

Tape recorded September 19, 1995

ho	*hehą́l*	*táku*	*wąží*	*oblákį-kte*	*ki*	*hé*	*ȟé*	*ektá*
well	then	what	IDF.SG	tell.1SG.AG-FUT	SYP	that	mountain	in

wazízi	*ožú*	*ki*	*hé*	*héchiya*	*chą-húta*	*ki*	*ųgnáš*
pine	bunch	DEF	that	there	tree-bottom	DEF	maybe

ikhą́-khą-yela	*táku*	*zí*	*cha*	*a-ˀíyaskape.*	*yųkhą́*	*hená*
ST-RED-close to	something	yellow	QL	L-adhere	then	those

ehą́ni	*paȟláya-pi*	*na*	*hená*	*chéğa*	*ogná*	*paȟláya-pi*	*hená*
long-ago	peel.VT off-IPS	and	those	kettle	inside	chip off-IPS	those

o-gnáka-pi	*na*	*chą́*	*yuhá*	*khí-pi*	*na*	*chethí-pi*	*na*	*ho*
L-place-IPS	and	wood	have	go back-IPS	and	build a fire-IPS	and	well

hé ogná	*mní*	*icáhiya*	*piȟ-yá-pi.*	*ho*	*héchel*	*įšé*	*į́š eyá*
that way*	water	mix	boil.VI-CAU-IPS	well	so	just	also

ehą́ni	*Lakhóta*	*ki*	*chą́šį*	*icˀí-cağa-pi.*	*ho*
old-time	Lakota	DEF	chewing gum	3RFL-make-PL	well

chą́šį	*ki*	*lé*	*ųgná*	*į́š*	*yathá-pi*	*thachą́-pi*	*él*	*táku*
chewing gum	DEF	this	maybe	it	chew-IPS	body-PL	in	something

ókiya	*nachéce-lakha-š,*	*ehą́ni*	*oyáte*	*ki*	*líla*	*hí*
help.VT	maybe-kind of-EMPH	long ago	people	DEF	INT	tooth

wašté-šte-pi.	*ho*	*hé*	*é*	*cha*	*į̀šé*	*obláka*	*wa-chį́.*
good-RED-PL	well	that	IP	QL	just	tell.1SG.AG	1SG.AG-want

hehą́yela.
that is all

What I will talk about then is this: there is something yellow that adheres close to the bottom of the pines [in little dips] that grow abundantly in the mountains. In the old times people scraped it off and put the lumps into a pot. Then they took home some wood and built a fire and they boiled them mixed with water. Just that way the old-time Lakota, too, made chewing gum. Maybe chewing this gum did something good to their bodies, since the old-time people had very good teeth. That is what I wanted to tell. That's all.

3.22. Cottonwood

FLORINE RED EAR HORSE

Tape recorded September 19, 1995

hehą́l táku wąží oblákį-kte ki hé ehą́ni oyáte kihą,
then thing IDF.SG tell.1SG.AG-FUT SYP that long ago people DEF

wį́yą kihą, ehą́ni wáǧachą hé é cha há ki
woman DEF long ago cottonwood that IP QL skin DEF

paȟláya-pi nahą́ hená é cha ų́ na mní é cha ų́
peel.VT off-PL and then those IP QL with and water IP QL with

na wagmíza ikcéka hená ų́ wanášlogyapi káǧa-pi. ho hé
and squaw corn* those with hominy* make-PL well that

chaȟóta ki hé é cha ų́ mní ki piȟ-yá-pi na lená
ashes DEF that IP QL use water DEF boil.VI-CAU-PL and these

wagmíza kihą o-gnáka-pi hą́tąhą į́š eyá há ki hená
corn DEF L-place-PL when also skin DEF those

na-ȟlá-ȟla-ye. ho hé nazéya-pi hą́tąhąš ho hé
INS-ST-RED-peel.VI well that strain-PL when well that

wanášlogyapi káǧa-pi. tohą́l pte-kté-pi hą́tąhąš tha-síha
hominy* make-PL when cattle-kill-PL when ruminant-foot

ho hená į́š wašlóka-pi na hená kakʼóǧa-pi na hená
well those they take off-PL and those scrape off-PL and those

yužáža-pi na pus-yá-pi. ho hená wanášlogyapi kihą
wash-PL and dry.A-CAU-PL well those hominy* DEF

icáhiya	*héchel*	*piȟ-yá-pi*	*chą́*	*ho*	*hé*	*líla*	*ihą́keya*
mix	so	boil.VI-CAU-PL	then	well	that	INT	extremely

wahą́pi	*wašté*	*kéye.*	*ho*	*héchų-šna*	*ehą́ni*	*wį́yą*	*ki*	*lená*
soup	good	QT	well	do that-HAB	long ago	woman	DEF	these

wahą́pi	*káğa-pi.*	*ho*	*éyaš*	*lehą́l*	*hená*	*waná*	*waníce.*	*nahą́*
soup	make-PL	well	but	now	those	now	lack	and then

tuwá	*Lakhóta*	*wį́yą*	*wąží*	*lehą́l*	*hená*	*echų́-ši-pi*	*hą́tąhą*
someone	Indian	woman	IDF.SG	now	those	do-ask-IPS	if

ųgná	*slolyį́-kte-šni*	*tókheškhe*	*káğa-pi*	*héci.*	*į́šé*	*hená*	*waná*
maybe	know-FUT-NEG	how	make-IPS	SUB	just	those	now

Lakhóta	*oyáte*	*ki*	*wichóȟʔą*	*ki*	*gnúni*	*ųk-áya-pi.*	*ho*
Indian	people	DEF	traditions	DEF	lose	1PL.PAT-PRC-PL	well

líla	*lé*	*táku*	*kihą*	*mahétu-ya*	*o-wá-kaȟniğe-šni*
INT	this	something	DEF	inside-ADV	ST-1SG.AG-understand-NEG

yųkhą́	*į́šé*	*ehą́ni*	*ųcí-wa-ye*	*wą*	*táku*	*ki*
then	just	long ago	grandmother-1SG.AG-have as	IDF.SG	things	DEF

lená	*echų́-pi*	*lená*	*o-má-ki-yake.*	*cha*	*héhą*	*ma-théca*	*na*
these	do-IPS	these	ST-1SG-BEN-tell	so	then	1SG.PAT-young	and

hená	*tókheškhe*	*ąpétu*	*lehą́l*	*į́še*	*táku*	*o-má-ki-yake*	*ki*	*hená*
those	somehow	day	now	just	things	ST-1SG-BEN-tell	DEF	those

wąžígži	*wéksuye*	*cha*	*hé*	*lé*	*wichóʔoyake*	*ki*
certain ones	remember.1SG.AG	so	that	this	story	DEF

obláke.
tell.1SG.AG

The thing I will talk about, then, is this: the old-time people, the women, peeled off the [inner] bark off cottonwood trees and made hominy with it, by adding water and squaw corn [they just used the kernels, not the cobs]. Using the ashes [of the bark], the water was brought to a boil. When the corn was put in, the [outer] skin [of the kernels] came off [it disappeared completely]. By draining that [in order to remove the ashes], hominy was made. When a cow was killed the [interiors of the] hooves were taken off; they were scraped off [i.e., off the hooves], washed, and dried. That was boiled together with hominy [to thicken it]. It made a really delicious soup. Doing that, the women always made soup in the old days. But now these things are gone. If some Indian woman were asked to do that today, she would maybe not know how it is done. Now we are in the process of losing the traditions of the Indian people. I don't really have a deep understanding of these things. It's just that long ago one of my grandmothers told me how to do these things. Back then I was young, and I somehow just remember certain details of what she told me to this day. So this is the story I wanted to tell.

Note: Neva Standing Bear adds that ashes from ash trees worked even better because ash yields white and very smooth ashes. The particles are smaller and cleaner. The ashes were boiled with water. The liquid was poured into a cloth and strained that way, and then boiled with corn. The corn pops a bit, and the shells around the kernels come off. The corn is washed and dried. By blowing on it, the shells are removed. Instead of ashes, soda can be used. The water must be renewed twice. The hooves are cleaned thoroughly. The tendons are scraped off the bones. The hooves and tendons are boiled with water for one day, together with the corn and seasoning like salt, pepper, and maybe some herbs. The hooves serve to thicken the stew. The meat inside them is eaten, as well as the tendons which are soft by then. Both the corn and the hooves should be dried before that meal is prepared. Neva says: "It's ugly, it's cheap, but it is a delicacy."

3.23. Swelling Weed

FLORINE RED EAR HORSE

Tape recorded September 19, 1995

heh̨ál	*táku*	*w̨ąží*	*obláki̜-kte*	*ki*	*hé*	*Lakhóta*
then	something	IDF.SG	tell.1SG.AG-FUT	DEF	that	Lakota

phežúta	*lé*	*po[?]íphiye*	*eyá-pi.*	*yu̜khá̜*	*hé*	*phežúta*	*kiha̜*
medicine*	this	swelling weed*	say-IPS	then	that	medicine*	DEF

tóha̜ni	*miyé*	*mi-[?]íšta*	*ú̜*	*wa̜bláke-šni*	*éyaš*	*oyáka-pi*
never	I	1SG.POR-eye	with	see.1SG.AG-NEG	but	tell-IPS

echíya-ta̜ha̜	*wanáȟca*	*kiha̜*	*kitá̜la*	*héchel*	*thosá̜*	*kéyá-pi.*
there-from	flower	DEF	a little	so	light purple*	say that-IPS

nahá̜	*hú*	*kiha̜*	*makhá-ta*	*i-wá̜kata*	*tohá̜ha̜-ke*	*yu̜khá̜*
and then	stalk	DEF	earth-on	L-above	that far-kind of	then

táku-la	*gmigméla*	*s[?]e*	*léchecha*	*swéla*	*s[?]e*
something-DIM	round	like.AV	like this	packed tight	like.AV

léchecha	*apé*	*s[?]e*	*ikhóyaka*	*kéye.*	*ho*	*hé*	*ú̜*
like this	leaf	like.AV	adhere	QT	well	that	by means of

i-slólya-pi-kte,	*hé*	*ú̜*	*oyáka-pi*	*okíhi-pi*	*kéye.*	*yu̜khá̜*
L-know-PL-FUT	that	by means of	tell-IPS	can-IPS	QT	then

wichá̜ša	*otówas[?]i̜*	*lé*	*táku*	*ki*	*slolyá-pi-šni*	*tkhá*	*wichá̜ša*
man	every single	this	what	DEF	know-PL-NEG	but	man

cónala lená ilágya-pi cha hená slolyá-pi. yųkhą́ hé
few these utilize-PL QL those know-PL then that

tha-wó'ophe wą yukhą́ kéyá-pi tohą́l phežúta ki hé
ALP-rule IDF.SG exist say that-IPS when medicine* DEF that

o-k'á-pi-kte hą́tąhąš o-k'á ki hétu nachéce į̨šé tuktétu cha
L-dig-IPS-FUT when L-dig DEF there maybe just where QL

chąlí él okála-pi kéye. ho na icú-pi kéye. ho na
tobacco there sprinkle-IPS QT well and take-IPS QT well and

hé hutkhą́ kihą íš eyá kak'óğa-pi nahą́ waksá-ksa-pi na
that root DEF also scrape off-IPS and then cut-RED-PL and

pus-yá-pi kéye. ho púzį na ohákab lé tuwá
dry.A-CAU-IPS QT well dry.A and after this someone

tukté'el pó hą́tąhąš lé piȟ-yį́ na hé tókhi yatką́
somewhere swell when this boil.VI-CAU and that maybe drink

ųgná oyáka-pi na-wá-ȟ'ų-šni tkhá tókhi ų́
maybe tell-IPS ST-1SG.AG-hear-NEG but maybe with

glužáža-pi na'į́š takún opútką na él a-'íyustak
POSS.wash-IPS or something dip.VT and there L-apply against

tókhi glúza-pi nachéce ehą́tąhąš hé líla wašté kéyá-pi,
maybe POSS.hold-PL maybe if that INT good say that-IPS

pó ki hé ahúkhul iyáya kéyá-pi. įšé lé po'íphiye
swell DEF that down go say that-IPS just this swelling weed*

cha	*hená*	*phežúta*	*ki*	*ehą́ni*	*Lakhóta*	*kihą*	*hé*	*phežúta*
QL	those	medicine*	DEF	ancient	Lakota	DEF	that	medicine*

ilágya-pi	*ki*	*hé*	*wąží.*	*ho*	*hehą́yela.*
utilize-PL	DEF	that	one	well	that is all

What I will tell something about now is the Lakota medicine called swelling plant. I have never seen that medicine with my own eyes, but according to the descriptions the flowers are somewhat purplish. And about that high from the ground [three feet] little round things, which seem to be composed of little petals which are packed tight [as in a sunflower] adhere to the stem. By that it [the plant] will be recognized, by that it can be identified. Not everyone knows what it is, but a few people who use those [plants] know them. There is a rule to that plant, it is said: when that medicine is to be dug up people sprinkle some tobacco around the digging hole. Then they remove it. [The root is three to four feet long and one and a half inches thick.] They scrape off the root [the scraps are not used as medicine], cut it into pieces [two inches long], and dry it. It dries up, and afterwards anyone who has a swelling somewhere boils it. I haven't heard it said that this is taken internally, but it is probably used for washing [wounds] or for pads. When they are held against the wound this is very good, the swelling goes down. This swelling plant, this medicine, was one of the medicines the old-time Lakota used. That's all.

3.24. Purple Cone Flower (*Brauneria angustifolia*)

FLORINE RED EAR HORSE

Tape recorded September 19, 1995

lehą́l táku wąží obláki̧-kte ki hé icáȟpe hú
now something IDF.SG tell.1SG.AG-FUT DEF that purple cone flower

eyá-pi Lakhótiya. ho hená wanáȟca kihą šamná. éyaš wanáȟca
say-IPS in Lakota well those flower DEF pink but flower

eyá zi-zí cha icháǧe. ho héchecha-ke s'e
IDF.PL yellow-RED QL grow well like that-kind of like.AV

léchecha éyaš lená cík'ala na hú ki hé makhá-ta hą́ska
like this but these small and stalk DEF that earth-on long

icháǧe-šni éyaš wanáȟca ki lená šamná s'e léchecha. ho
grow-NEG but flower DEF these pink like.AV like this well

héchecha o-wą́yąke na pahá hepíya icháǧe hą́tąhąš hé é cha
like that L-see and hill hillside grow if that IP QL

na choką́ ǧí. yųkhą́ hé é cha o-k'á-pi na ho hé
and middle brown then that IP QL L-dig-IPS and well that

hutkhą́ kihą kak'óǧa-pi na pus-yá-pi ehą́tąhąš ho hé į́š
root DEF scrape-IPS and dry.A-CAU-IPS when well that it

mahél kitą́la ȟo-ȟóte s'e léchecha, hutkhą́ ki. ho éyaš
inside a little RED-gray like.AV like this root DEF well but

hená é cha į́š eyá yuksá-ksa-pi na pus-yá-pi. ho hé
those IP QL also cut-RED-IPS and dry.A-CAU-IPS well that

tuktél yazą́-pi hą́tąhąš, ho hé ugnáš hí yazą́-pi hą́tąhą
where ache-IPS when well that maybe tooth ache-IPS when

hé i-y-ó-gnaka-pi-kte, pus-yá-kel, hą́tąhą hé
that mouth-EI-L-place-IPS-FUT dry.A-ADV-kind of when that

ó-wicha-kiye. na ųmáchetkiya į́š eyá-š tuktéˀél
ST-3PL.PAT-help.VT and in another place also-EMPH somewhere

thachą́ mahél yazą́-pi hą́tąhą ho hé į́š mní icáhi
body inside ache-IPS when well that it water mix

piȟ-yá-pi nahą́ hé į́š wíyatke ogná yatką́-pi. ho hé
boil.VI-CAU-IPS and then that it cup* inside drink-IPS well that

nų́pa-kiya héchų sˀe ilágya-pi, lená icáȟpe hú ki, na
two-ways that way* utilize-IPS these purple cone flower DEF and

lé w-í-y-okihi. Lakhóta ki ehą́ni lená makhá-tąhą
this NSP.PAT-L-EI-can Lakota DEF ancient these earth-from

phežúta ki héchų sˀe ilágya-pi na ų́ tókheca-pi ki
medicine* DEF that way* utilize-PL and with not alright-PL when

lená asní-ˀicˀi-ya-pi. ho hehą́yela hé obláką-kte.
these recover-3RFL-CAU-PL well that is all that tell.1SG.AG-FUT

What I will tell something about now is what is called *ichǎȟpe hú* in Lakota. Those plants have pink flowers. However, there are some plants which grow with yellow flowers [sunflowers]. They [purple cone flowers] look very much like them, but they are small, and the stem does not grow high from the ground [just about one foot]. The flowers are pink. They look like that. A characteristic feature of these plants is that they grow on hillsides. They are brown in the center [of the flower]. People dig them up and scrape [the bark off] the root, and when they dry it [the root, not the scrapings] it turns somewhat grayish, the root. It is cut into pieces and dried. When people have a pain somewhere, when they maybe have a toothache, they put it in their mouth, dried as it is. It helps [it numbs the toothache]. And when people have a pain somewhere else in the body they boil it mixed with water, and drink a cupful. These *ichǎȟpe hú* plants are used like that, in two ways, and they help. The old-time Lakota used these earth medicines like that, and when there was anything wrong with them they cured themselves with them. This is all I wanted to tell.

3.25. Courtesy

FLORINE RED EAR HORSE

Tape recorded September 27, 1995

hehą́l	*táku*	*wąží*	*obláki̜-kta*	*hé*	*ehą́ni*	*Lakhóta*
then	something	IDF.SG	tell.1SG.AG-FUT	that	long ago	Lakota

oyáte	*ki*	*wichóʔų.*	*hé*	*thiwáhe*	*él*	*hų́-ku-pi*	*nahą́*
people	DEF	way of life	that	family	in	mother-3POR-PL	and then

at-kúku-pi	*nahą́*	*thųkáši-tku-pi*	*nahą́*
father-3POR-PL	and then	grandfather-3POR-PL	and then

khų́ši-tku-pi	*na*	*wakhą́yeža*	*hél*	*ich※ǧa-pi.*	*hená*
grandmother-3POR-PL	and	child	there	grow-PL	those

takú-kichi-ya-pi	*lená*	*líla*	*kichí-yuʔóniha̜-pi.*	*yųkhą́*
something-REC-have as-PL	these	INT	REC-respect.VT-PL	then

tuwá	*wichį́cala*	*wąží*	*icháȟ-ya-pi*	*nahą́*	*hi̜gnáthų*	*hą́ta̜ha̜š*
someone	girl	IDF.SG	grow-CAU-PL	and then	marry*	when

wichį́cala	*ki*	*lé*	*hi̜gná-ku*	*ki*	*hé*	*thakóš*	*eyá-pi-kta*
girl	DEF	this	husband-3POR	DEF	that	son+in+law	say-PL-FUT

škhé.	*hé*	*yusúta-pi,*	*hé*	*wówahechų*	*hécha*	*škhé.*	*nahą́*
QT	that	legalize-PL	that	relative	COP	QT	and then

wicháwoȟa	*ki*	*eyá-pi*	*hą́ta̜ha̜š*	*hé*	*wówicakhe-šni*	*škhé,*	*hé*
boyfriend	DEF	say-PL	when	that	truth-NEG	QT	that

įȟąhą thakóš-ya-pi, ųgná héchų sˀe wichóˀiye ki
not seriously son in law-have as-PL maybe that way* word DEF

hé ekíya-pi-kta škhé. ho hehą́l wicháwoȟa ki lé
that say to-PL-FUT QT well then boyfriend DEF this

thųką́-ku na khų́-ku ki lená
father in law-3POR and mother in law-3POR DEF these

wichá-kağí-kte. kağí-šni itóžu
3PL.PAT-respect.VT-FUT respect.VT-NEG in the face

a-wícha-yuta-kte-šni. na kağí-šni
ST-3PL.PAT-look-FUT-NEG and respect.VT-NEG

chažé-wicha-yatį-kte-šni. takú-wicha-ya héci
ST-3PL.PAT-call by name-FUT-NEG something-3PL.PAT-have as SUB

hél ognáyą ché-wicha-kiyį-kte. hé
there according to ST-3PL.PAT-call by term of relationship-FUT that

wókağí hécha. ho hé lé wó-kichi-cağí, wichóˀiye,
respect.N COP well that this ST-REC-respect.N word

wichóȟˀą cha lená thiwáhe él gluhá-pi. yųkhą́
tradition QL these family in POSS.hold on to-PL then

wicháwoȟa ki lé, wicháwoȟa eyá-pi ki, hé įȟąhą
boyfriend DEF this boyfriend say-PL SYP that not seriously

thakóš-ya-pi cha khá-pi škhé na
son in law-have as-IPS LK indicate-PL QT and

mi-thákoš eyá-pi ki lé itéšniya héchel wówahechų
1SG.POR-son in law say-PL SYP that truly so in law

hécha cha eyá-pi. itéšniya thakóš-ya-pi hél ognáyą.
COP LK say-PL truly son in law-have as-IPS there that way

yųkhą́ thakóš-ku-pi ki, lé thakóš-wicha-ya-pi
then son in law-3POR-PL DEF this son in law-3PL.PAT-have as-PL

ki lená tha-wícu ki hé ób wichówe hená é-ʔe héchel
DEF these ALP-wife DEF that with sibling those IP-RED so

él hóye-wicha-ye okíhi ówehąhą. ówehąhą ób
there ST-3PL.PAT-call* can joke.VI joke.VI with

w-ó-kichi-yaka okíhi-pi nahą́ tha-wícu ki hé thųwį́-cu
NSP.PAT-ST-REC-tell can-IPS and then ALP-wife DEF that aunt-3POR

na lekší-tku na hų́-ku na at-kúku, khų́ši-tku,
and uncle-3POR and mother-3POR and father-3POR grandmother-3POR

thųkáši-tku ki lená wichá-glaǧi-kta hécha,
grandfather-3POR DEF these 3PL.PAT-POSS.respect.VT-FUT OBL

hená tákuni héchetu-šni e-wícha-kiyį-kte-šni naʔį́š tuktél
those nothing right-NEG ST-3PL.PAT-say to-FUT-NEG and where

yąká-pi kʔų wich-íthokab ki iyáyį-kte-šni. naʔį́š
sit-PL DEF 3PL.PAT-before DEF go-FUT-NEG and

ų́ši-wicha-la-kte. héchų sʔe thiwáhe ehą́ni lená
ST-3PL.PAT-love.VT-FUT that way* family long ago these

kichí-cağì-pi, wichóȟˀą hécha. na lehą́l į̨šé wichóˀichağe na
REC-respect.VT-PL tradition COP and now just generation and

thiwáhe ų́-pi lená Lakhól-wichóȟˀą, hená tąyą́ wichóˀų hená
family be-PL these Lakota-tradition those well way of life those

nasól áye. na lehą́l wókağì ki hé yuhá-pi-šni. na
fade away PRC and now respect.N DEF that have-PL-NEG and

chažé-kichi-yata-pi. ehą́ni thiwáhe él tuwá él wichá-ˀi
ST-REC-call by name-PL long ago family to who to 3PL.PAT-go

chą́na-šna w-ó-wicha-kˀu-pi, lená ékayeš
then-HAB NSP.PAT-L-3PL.PAT-give-PL these even

chékiciya hé ecíya "hél íyutakį na wakhálapi
call by term of relationship that say to there sit down and coffee*

yatką́ yé, šicˀéši" éyį-kte. ho hé
drink IMP.SG.F woman's male cousin say-FUT well that

šicˀéši-tku ki hé wóta-hį na
woman's male cousin-3POR DEF that eat.NSP.PAT-PRG and

iglúštą hą́tąhą ho hehą́l į́š ehákela "lé i-kí-k-cu
POSS.finish when well then he finally this ST-PSS-EI-take

wó, hąkáši, wakšíca ki, philámayaye ló"
IMP.SG.M man's female cousin dish DEF thank you* ASS.M

eyį́-kte. ho hená wókağì wichóˀiye hécha. na chažé yukhą́-pi
say-FUT well those respect.N language COP and name there is-PL

éyaš henáchažé-kichi-yata-pi-šni. táku i-kíchi-yųǧa-pi
but those ST-REC-call by name-PL-NEG things ST-REC-ask-PL

yųkhą́ takú-kichi-ya-pi héci hél ognáyą héchel
then something-REC-have as-PL SUB there according to so

eyá-pi na hehą́l w-í-kichi-yųǧa-pi táku slolyá-pi-šni naʔį́š
say-PL and then NSP.PAT-ST-REC-ask-PL things know-PL-NEG and

táku slolyá-pi chį́-pi naʔį́š héchetu hená i-kíchi-yųǧa-pi. ho
things know-PL want-PL and so those ST-REC-ask-PL well

hená wókaǧi thiwáhe él ehą́ni hé líla a-wą́glaka-pi na hé
those respect.N family in long ago that INT L-POSS.see-PL and that

líla gluhá ų́-pi. ho oyáte ehą́ni wichóʔų ki
INT POSS.hold on to CNT-PL well people long ago way of life DEF

líla wašté. lehą́l héchetu-šni. chąkhé théca ki, lená Lakhóta-pi
INT good now SO-NEG then young DEF these Indian-PL

hé é cha Lakhóta wichá-chaže yuhá-pi éyaš wašícu-ya
that IP QL Indian person-name have-PL but white man-ADV

ų́-pi na Lakhóta wichóʔiye hé éktųža-pi na Lakhóta
exist-PL and Indian language that forget-PL and Indian

wichóȟʔą hé nakų́ éktųš áya-pi. na Lakhóta iyá hé
tradition that also forget PRC-PL and Indian speak that

kiksúya wa-chį́-pi khéš iyé wa-chį́-pi khéš
remember NSP.PAT-want-PL but speak NSP.PAT-want-PL but

okíhi-pi-šni. tkhá hų́ȟ naȟˀų́-pi. naȟˀų́-pi hą́tąhąš wašícu-ya
can-PL-NEG but some hear-PL hear-PL if white man-ADV

wa-ˀáyupta-pi-kta. ho į̀šé Lakhóta wichóˀiye ki na
NSP.PAT-answer-PL-FUT well just Lakota language DEF and

wichóȟˀą na wichóˀų ki hená líla wašté. cha hená įšé
tradition and way of life DEF those INT good so those just

thą́ka ki lená chįchá na thakóžakpaku ki lená
elderly DEF these child and grandchild DEF these

o-wícha-ki-yaka-pi iyé-kapį-šni. o-wícha-ki-yaka-hą-pi hą́tąhąš
ST-3PL-BEN-tell-PL say-tired of-NEG ST-3PL-BEN-tell-PRG-PL if

watóhąl ihų́ni-pi hą́tąhą lená él éwachį-pi-kte. cha
some time arrive-PL when these to pay attention-PL-FUT so

wahéhąl ihų́ni-pi hą́tąhą lená kiksúya-pi-kte na lená
by that time arrive-PL when these remember-PL-FUT and these

wašté ki abléza-pi-kte. hé ogná ų́-pi-kte na héchel
good LK realize-PL-FUT that according to be-PL-FUT and so

éwachį-pi-kte ki hé líla wašté-kte. ho héchetu.
pay attention-PL-FUT if that INT good-FUT well so

So I will tell something about the way of life of the old-time Lakota people. In the family, the children grew up together with their mothers, fathers, grandfathers, and grandmothers. People who were related to each other respected each other very much. The ones who raised a girl would call the girl's husband, when she got married, *thakósh* [son-in-law]. It [the relationship] was legalized, he was a relative. As long as he was called *wicháwoȟa* [boyfriend], it [the relationship] was not legal, he was not really a son-in-law, although he might be addressed by that word. A *wicháwoȟa* had to respect his [prospective] father-in-law and mother-in-law. He was not supposed to look them in the face disrespectfully. And he was not supposed to call them by their names disrespectfully. He had to use the appropriate term of relationship. That was respect. These rules of conduct—that is, mutual respect, the forms of address, and the traditions—were strictly observed in the family. By *wicháwoȟa*, by saying *wicháwoȟa*, people indicated that a person was not legally a son-in-law. By saying *mitȟákoš* they indicated that he was really an in-law. That way [when they called him *mitȟákoš*] he truly was a son-in-law. A son-in-law, someone who was a son-in-law, could communicate with his wife's brothers and sisters teasingly. They could talk to each other jokingly, and his wife's aunts, uncles, mothers [i.e., mother's sisters], fathers [i.e., father's brothers], grandmothers, and grandfathers he had to treat respectfully; he was not supposed to say anything wrong to them and he was not supposed to go by in front of where they were sitting. And he had to love them. That way the members of the old-time family treated each other respectfully. That was the tradition. For today's generation, and for the families living now, those Lakota traditions, those good ways of life, are disappearing. And today people don't have respect. And they call each other by their names. In the old times, someone who came to visit a family was given food. One was even supposed to address him or her by a term of relationship, and say: "Sit down and have some coffee, cousin." The cousin would eat, and after finishing his meal he would finally say: "Take them back, the dishes, cousin, thank you." That was the language of respect. People did have names, but they did not use them for addressing each other. When they asked each other questions they used the address required by their degree of relationship, and then they asked each other what they did not know and what they wanted to know; that way they asked each other questions. In the old-time family, people always took those rules of respect very seriously and stuck to them in any case. The old-time people's way of life was very good. Today it is different. Even though the young ones, if they are Indians, have Indian names, they nevertheless live the white man's way of life and forget the Indian language, and they also forget the Indian traditions more and more. They try to remember the Indian language, but when they try to speak it they cannot. But some of them understand it. Even if they understand it they will answer in the white man's language. The Lakota language and culture and way of life are very good. The elders are not tired of telling their children and grandchildren [about the old language, culture etc.] If they keep on telling them about it they [the young ones] will think of it when they reach a certain age. By the time they reach a certain age they will remember these things and realize that they are good. If they live according to them, and pay attention, that will be very good. That's the way it is.

Mythology 4

One of the most prominent figures in Lakota mythology is Iktomi, the trickster. A "real" Iktomi story usually contains elements that violate taboos both for the Native American as well as for the white listener.

4.1. Iktomi Meets the Prairie Chicken and Blood Clot Boy

NEVA STANDING BEAR

Tape recorded September 12, 1994

yųkhą́	*ehą́ni*	*Iktómi*	*kákhena*	*yá-hą*	*kéye.*	*yųkhą́*	*ųgnáhelakha*
then	long ago	Iktomi	about	go-PRG	QT	then	suddenly

tuktél	*lową́-pi*	*na*	*wachí-pi*	*cha*	*na-wícha-ȟ'ų*	*kéye*	*cha.*
somewhere	sing-IPS	and	dance-IPS	so	ST-3PL.PAT-hear	QT	QL

pahá	*ektá*	*iyáhą*	*yųkhą́*	*echél*	*hukhúta*	*ųmáchiyatą*
hill	on	climb a hilltop	then	so	down below	on the other side

átaya	*šiyó*	*wachí-pi*	*kéye*	*átaya-š*	*šiyó*	*ki*
INT	prairie chicken	dance-PL	QT	INT-EMPH	prairie chicken	DEF

mimé-ya	*nážį-pi*	*na*	*átaya*	*wachí-pi*	*chąkhé*	*anáǧoptą*
round-ADV	stand-PL	and	INT	dance-PL	then	listen

nážį-hą	*yųkhą́*	*lé*	*šiyó-bloka*	*ki*	*iyáya-pi*	*na*
stand-PRG	then	this	prairie chicken-male	DEF	go-PL	and

wį́yela	*ki*	*a-'ó-wicha-kawįǧa-pi*	*na*	*"mambú"*	*eyá*
female	DEF	L-ST-3PL.PAT-circle around-PL	and	mambu	say

chą́-šna wį́yą akíšʔa-pi "mi-šą́" eyá wachí-pi kéye.
then-HAB woman shout-PL 1SG.POR-vagina say dance-PL QT

chąkhé étkiya yá-hį na hukhúta ihų́ni kéye ho cha
then toward go-PRG and down below arrive QT well so

"wą́ mi-sų́ na thąkší, táku
IJ.M 1SG.POR-younger brother and younger sister what

wa-yá-chi-pi hųwó?" eyá kéye, Iktó é cha. chąkhé "wą́
ST-2AG-dance-PL QS.M say QT Iktomi IP QL then IJ.M

lé šiyó wa-ʔų́-chi-pi yeló" eyá kéye yųkhą́
this prairie chicken ST-1PL.AG-dance-PL ASS.M say QT then

"áta ipáyeȟ echánųpe ló" eyá kéye. "átaya yu-míme-ya
INT wrong 2AG.do-PL ASS.M say QT INT INS-round-ADV

i-nážį-pi nahą́ išt-ógmus wachí pó" eyá kéye. chąkhé
L-stand-PL and then eye-close dance IMP.PL.M say QT then

átaya ohómni mimé-ya é-nažį nahą́ke kaʔíhąkeya
INT go round and round round-ADV L-stand and then at the end

i-nážį nahą́ke lową́ kéye. na héyá kéye, Iktó: "išt-ógmus
L-stand and then sing QT and say that QT Iktomi eye-close

wachí pó! ya-tų́wą-pi ki ištá ni-šá-ša-pi-kte
dance IMP.PL.M 2AG-look-PL if eye 2SG.PAT-red-RED-PL-FUT

ló" eyá kéye. eyá lową́ chąkhé hená iyúha áta išt-ógmus
ASS.M say QT say sing then those all INT eye-close

wachí-pi *kéye* *c'éyaš* *ųgnáhelakha* *wąží* *tųwą́-hįgla* *yųkhą́*
dance-PL QT but suddenly one look-suddenly and then

áta *Iktómi* *é* *cha* *aglágla* *ka-t'á* *a-wícha-'u* *chąkhé* *eyá*
INT Iktomi IP QL along INS-dead ST-3PL.PAT-IGR then say

kéye *"wą́* *tųwą́* *pó,* *Iktó* *ka-t'á* *ųk-á'u-pe* *lő"*
QT IJ.M look IMP.PL.M Iktomi INS-dead 1PL.PAT-IGR-PL ASS.M

chąkhé *iyúha* *tųwą́-pi* *na* *kįyą́* *éyaya-pi* *kéye.* *yųkhą́* *áta* *hená*
then all look and fly CEL-PL QT then INT those

iyúha *ištá-ša-ša-pi* *kéye* *cha.* *hehą́tą* *šiyó* *kihą*
all eye-red-RED-PL QT QL from that time prairie chicken DEF

ištá-ša-ša-pi *kéyá-pi.* *ho* *hé* *Iktó* *tóna* *wichá-kte*
eye-red-RED-PL say that-IPS well that Iktomi many 3PL.PAT-kill

cha *hé* *wichá-yuha* *na* *wichá-k'į* *na* *yá-hį* *na* *áta* *chą́*
so that 3PL.PAT-have and 3PL.PAT-carry and go-PRG and INT tree

o'íyohązi *ową́šteca-ka* *kaȟmí* *cha* *ektá* *wichá-yuha*
shade pleasant-kind of river bend QL at 3PL.PAT-have

íyutakį *na* *áta* *chethí* *nahą́* *lé* *šiyó-la* *k'ų*
sit down and INT build a fire and then this prairie chicken-DIM DEF

hená *é* *cha* *wichá-yu-šla* *na* *pa-slá-slal*
those IP QL 3PL.PAT-INS-bald and ST-RED-put upright

é-wicha-gle *kéye.* *cho-wícha-k'į* *kéye.* *chąkhé* *líla* *óta-pi*
L-3PL.PAT-put QT ST-3PL.PAT-roast QT then INT many-PL

cha átaya a-ché-wicha-thi cha átaya hená iyúha
QL INT L-ST-3PL.PAT-build a fire so INT those all

sí-la ki thąį́-yą cho-wícha-k'į kéye. o'íyohązi-ya
foot-DIM DEF visible-ADV ST-3PL.PAT-roast QT shade-ADV

Iktó yąkį́ nahą́ke Iktó wąyą́g yąkį́ na "hųhé,
Iktomi sit and then Iktomi see sit and well

yu-phí-ya-š wayé wa-'í" eyá kéye. Ȟcehą́n chą́
INS-good-ADV-EMPH hunt 1SG.AG-go to say QT just then tree

nų́m íchi-ka-kis-kiza-ke thaté chą́-šna kéye.
two REC-ST-RED-squeak-kind of wind then-HAB QT

"mi-sų́, ową́ži yąká pó" eyá kéye. "ową́ži
1SG.POR-younger brother quiet sit IMP.PL.M say QT quiet

yąká pó, héchų-pi-šni yó, wi-ní-chowe-pi-'." cha
sit IMP.PL.M do that-PL-NEG IMP.M ST-2PAT-siblings-PL-ASS so

thaté ki akísni cha hé ų́ ka-kís-kize-šni cha.
wind DEF subside QL that because of ST-RED-squeak-NEG QL

chą́-šna w-óglag yąká-hą kéye. chą́-šna akhé thaté
then-HAB NSP.PAT-POSS.tell sit-PRG QT then-HAB again wind

hiyú cha lé chą́ ki lenáos íchi-ka-kis-kiza cha
come so this tree DEF both REC-ST-RED-squeak so

"mi-sų́, héchų-pi-šni yó, hená héchetu-šni
1SG.POR-younger brother do that-PL-NEG IMP.M those right-NEG

yeló" eyá kéye. ȟcehą́n šugmáyetu wą hiyáhį na
ASS.M say QT just then coyote IDF.SG appear on a hilltop and

glakį́yą hiyáya kéye. chąkhé ektá é-tųwį na "hé::, thahénakiya
across go by QT then at L-look and hey to this place

ya-ʾú kilo, lél wa-chó-wa-kʾį ki ųgnáš
2SG.AG-come don't you here NSP.PAT-ST-1SG.AG-roast DEF maybe

hé ya-ʾú kilo, akhóketkiya iyáya yő" eyá
that 2SG.AG-come don't you the other way go IMP.SG.M say

chąkhé šųgmáyetu ki hená cha iyúkcą kéye. "ho lé
then coyote DEF those QL think about QT well this

wóyute káǧa héci įthó ektá é-wąblakį-kte" eyá kéye.
food make SUB in that case at L-see.1SG.AG-FUT say QT

eyį nahą́ke yá kéye. étkiya iyáya yųkhą́ "hé lél khiyéla
go and then go QT toward go then that here near

ú-šni yő" eyá kéye. ȟcehą́n thaté hiyú na lé chą́
come-NEG IMP.SG.M say QT just then wind come and this tree

ki íchi-ka-kis-kiza chąkhé "wą́ iyó-chi-chi-pi-šni
DEF REC-ST-RED-squeak then IJ.M ST-1SG.AG.2PAT-forbid-PL-NEG

wą, héchų-pi-šni yő" na lé chą́ ki hé é cha alí na
ASS do-PL-NEG IMP.M and this tree DEF that IP QL climb and

napé ki khušéya iyé-ki-ya kéye, lé ka-kís-kise ki
hand DEF in between ST-PSS-send QT this ST-RED-squeak DEF

hé él. cha ichų́hą thaté ki ayúštą cha napé ki choką́
that at so meanwhile wind DEF finish so hand DEF middle

ikhóyakį na hé chą́ ki iyókognayą. chąkhé šųgmáyetu ki hé
adhere and that tree DEF in between then coyote DEF that

é cha étkiya yá chąkhé “hé::, él é-tųwe-šni, él ú-šni
IP QL toward go then hey at L-look-NEG here come-NEG

yó, hél iyúha wa-chó-wa-kˀį cha hená ųgnáš
IMP.SG.M there all NSP.PAT-ST-1SG.AG-roast QL those maybe

theb-má-ya-ki-ye kilo” eyá chąkhé wą-kál-kata-kiya
ST-1SG-2SG.AG-BEN-eat up don't you say then ST-RED-up-toward

šiyó hená áta sí thąį́-yą ȟpáya-pi chąkhé hé
prairie chicken those INT foot visible-ADV lie-PL then that

áta yąkį́ na íphi-ˀicˀi-ya kéye. íphi-ˀicˀi-ya
INT sit and full of food-3RFL-CAU QT full of food-3RFL-CAU

chąkhé Iktó é cha “wą́, theȟí-ya o-má-ya-ki-ȟˀą
then Iktomi IP QL IJ.M terrible-ADV L-1SG-2SG.AG-BEN-act

yeló, hená-š wa-glútį-kte kˀų” eyá kéye. cha éyaš
ASS.M those-EMPH 1SG.AG-POSS.eat-FUT ASS say QT so but

sí-la ki hená ecéla hékta-kta-kiya wichá-paslatį na
foot-DIM DEF those only back.AV-RED-to 3PL.PAT-put upright and

ųmá ki thebyį́ na héchena iyáya kéye chąkhé “tókša,
other DEF eat up and thus go QT then just wait

waȟtéšni inítˀe ló, tókša o-chí-yuspe kihą tókša
doggone you* just wait ST-1SG.AG.2SG.PAT-catch when just wait

níš eyá héchų sˀe i-chí-ȟˀą-kte ló” eyé. eyá
you too that way* L-1SG.AG.2SG.PAT-act-FUT ASS.M say say

chąkhé lé šųgmáyetu ki hé hóyekhiye ki ho héhą thaté
then this coyote DEF that call to* SYP well then wind

hiyú na chą́ ki hená kakhínųkhą iyáya cha héchiya-tą
come and tree DEF those separate.VI go so there-from

hįȟpáya kéye. Iktómi hįȟpáya na chąkhé “wą́ lél
fall QT Iktomi fall and then IJ.M here

wa-chó-wa-kˀį-la kˀų theȟí-ya
NSP.PAT-ST-1SG.AG-roast-DIM DEF terrible-ADV

o-má-ya-ki-ȟˀą yeló. waȟté-šni inítˀe ló,
L-1SG-2SG.AG-BEN-act ASS.M doggone you*

tókša o-chí-yuspe kįhą
just wait ST-1SG.AG.2PAT-catch when

táku-chi-yį-kte ló” eyé. eyį nahą́ke
something-1SG.AG.2SG.PAT-CAU-FUT ASS.M say say and then

yá-hą kéye. yá-hą yųkhą́ echél šųgmáyetu ki hé é cha
go-PRG QT go-PRG then so coyote DEF that IP QL

íphi-ˀicˀi-yį na okásniyą hą́ cha ektá óhązi
full of food-3RFL-CAU and cool breezy place stand QL there shade

wą́ él ištíma-hą chąkhé Iktómi ektá ihų́ni nahą́ke éyaš áta
IDF.SG in sleep-PRG then Iktomi there arrive and then but INT

ka-tˀé-šni. ayúta nážį nahą́ke "wą́ lé tókha
INS-dead-NEG look at stand and then IJ.M this what

wécˀų-kta hųwó?" eyá-hą chąkhé áta ųgnáhelakha makhú
1SG.AG.do with QS.M say-PRG then INT suddenly chest

ki él naȟtákį na héchena iyáyekiya kéye. iyáyekiya kéye
DEF in kick and thus run away QT run away QT

chąkhé "wą́ theȟí-ya wa-ˀéchanų welő" eyá kéye
then IJ.M terrible-ADV NSP.PAT-do.2SG.AG ASS.M say QT

nahą́ke yá-hą kéye. yá-hą yųkhą́ ųžį́žįtka eyá ptáyela hą́
and then go-PRG QT go-PRG then rose LK together stand

cha él ihų́ni. lochį́ chąkhé lé ųžį́žįtka-la kˀų hená é cha
QL at arrive hungry then this rose-DIM DEF those IP QL

yušpí nahą́ke eyá kéye "wą́, lená mi-sų́, táku
pick and then say QT IJ.M these 1SG.POR-younger brother what

e-ní-ciya-pi só?" eyá yųkhą́ "ųžį́žįtka e-má-ciya-pi
ST-2PAT-say to-IPS QS say then rose ST-1SG.PAT-say to-IPS

kˀų" eyá kéye. yúta-pi chą́ ųzé o-yášpuya-pi
ASS say QT eat-IPS then rectum L-itch-IPS

e-má-ciya-pi kˀų eyá kéye. chąkhé "ų́, lená-š
ST-1SG.PAT-say to-IPS ASS say QT then oh these-EMPH

wátį na-š ųzé o-má-yašpuye-ka" eyį nahąke
eat.1SG.AG and-EMPH rectum L-1SG.PAT-itch-kind of say and then

lé ųžį́žįtka k'ų hená é cha yútį na yúl yá-hą yųkhą́
this rose DEF those IP QL eat and eat sit-PRG then

ųgnáhelakha ųzé o-yášpuya cha héchena áta ųzé
suddenly rectum L-itch so thus INT rectum

o-glúk'eȟ yá-hą kéye. yá yųkhą́ akhé lé omníca eyá
L-POSS.scratch go-PRG QT go then again this bean LK

ptáyela hą́ cha wąyą́ka chąkhé icú na "wą́ lél wóyute-la
together stand LK see then take and IJ.M here food-DIM

eyá wašté yeló, lená níš táku e-ní-ciya-pi hé?"
IDF.PL good ASS.M this you what ST-2PAT-say to-IPS QS

yųkhą́ "yúta-pi chą́ ų́kche-pi e-má-ciya-pi k'ų" eyá kéye
then eat-IPS then fart-IPS ST-1SG.PAT-say to-IPS ASS say QT

chąkhé "lená-š wátį na ų́-wa-kche-ka" eyį
then these-EMPH eat.1SG.AG and ST-1SG.AG-fart-kind of say

nahą́ke yúta kéye yųkhą́ áta ų́kche na nité ki
and then eat QT then INT fart and lower back DEF

na-psí-psil iyáya kéye. máni kéye. héchel na-psí-psil iyáya
ST-RED-jump go QT walk QT so ST-RED-jump go

máni nahą́ke chąkhé "wą́ ową́ži yąká pó, wą́ waná
walk and then then IJ.M quiet sit IMP.PL.M IJ.M now

wicá-chi-la-pe	*ló”*	*eyé.*	*éyaš*	*iníhąšni*	*ųzé*
ST-1SG.AG.2PAT-believe-PL	ASS.M	say	but	nevertheless	rectum

o-yášpuya	*chąkhé*	*ųzé*	*o-glúkˀeȟ*	*yá-hą*	*yųkhą́*	*lé*
L-itch	then	rectum	L-POSS.scratch	go-PRG	then	this

thą-máhel	*wašį́*	*wą*	*zizípela*	*cha*	*thezí*	*ki*	*a-ˀówį*
body-inside	grease	LK	thin	QL	stomach	DEF	L-cover.VT

ikhóyaka	*yųkhą́*	*hé*	*é*	*cha*	*gluslúta*	*kéye*	*chąkhé*	*“hųhųhé,*
adhere	then	that	IP	QL	POSS.pull out	QT	then	IJ.M

theȟí-ya	*o-wá-ȟˀą*	*yeló”*	*eyá*	*kéye.*	*“áta*	*lé*
terrible-ADV	ST-1SG.AG-act	ASS.M	say	QT	INT	this

tókhamų-kta	*hųwó?*	*wą́*	*lé*	*échuȟci-š*
do what.1SG.AG-FUT	QS.M	IJ.M	this	at least-EMPH

phe-wá-gnakį-kte	*ló.”*	*líla*	*o-kháta*	*cha*	*lé*
ST-1SG.AG-wear as headgear-FUT	ASS.M	INT	L-hot	so	this

thachéžįgžįgca	*ki*	*gluslútį*	*na*	*hé*	*é*	*cha*
fat on the outside of the stomach	DEF	POSS.pull out	and	that	IP	QL

phégnakį	*na*	*yá-hą*	*kéye.*	*yáhą*	*yųkhą́*	*wichóthi*	*cha*	*él*
wear as headgear	and	go-PRG	QT	go-PRG	then	camp.N	QL	at

ihų́ni	*kéye.*	*wichóthi*	*cha*	*él*	*ihų́ni*	*nahą́ke*	*áta*	*thą́kal*
arrive	QT	camp.N	QL	at	arrive	and then	INT	outside

wakhą́yeža	*ki*	*škáta-pi*	*cha*	*pahá*	*aką́n*	*yąká-hą*	*kéye.*	*héchena*
child	DEF	play-PL	so	hill	on top	sit-PRG	QT	thus

nahą́ke khútakiya ohómni iyóȟpaya kéye yųkhą́ wicháša
and then downwards go around go down QT then man

wą chįchá, hokšíla wą, kichí-la thí kéye. hokšíla ki lé
IDF.SG child boy IDF.SG with-DIM live QT boy DEF this

líla wicháša wašté cha, chąkhé ektá í kéye. ektá í na
INT good looking* QL then there go QT there go and

wą-wícha-yąka-hą kéye éyaš khiyéla yé-šni kéye yųkhą́ lé
ST-3PL.PAT-see-PRG QT but near go-NEG QT then this

wicháša ki lé tokhíyothą wayé iyáya kéye yųkhą́
man DEF this somewhere hunt go QT then

théhą glí-šni chąkhé hokšíla ki lé išnála
for a long time come home-NEG then boy DEF this alone

yąká cha. at-kúku ki le yá yųkhą́ héchena glí-šni
sit QL father-3POR DEF this go then thus come home-NEG

kéye. ho yųkhą́ wicháša ki glí nahą́ke chįchá ki
QT well then man DEF come home and then child DEF

él ų́-šni chą́ líla chąté šíca kéye cha. lé heȟáka wą
there be-NEG then INT sad* QT QL this elk IDF.SG

k'į na glí kéye cha waphátį na wéyotha cha icú
carry and come home QT so butcher and blood clot QL take

nahą́ é-gnakį na héyá kéye "ešá hokšíla
and then L-put and say that QT DES boy

i-ní-chağe-šni. hokšíla mitháwa wa-gnúni cha hehą́n
ST-2SG.PAT-grow-NEG boy my 1SG.AG-lose QL then

icínųpani. mi-chį́cha waníce na mi-thá-wicu khó
never again 1SG.POR-child lack and 1SG.POR-ALP-wife also

waníce yelő" eyá kéye, "cha o'íyokišice yelő" eyá kéye,
lack ASS.M say QT so sad ASS.M say QT

"chąté ma-šíce yelő" eyá kéye. héchi óhą ų́ kéye, aglágla
ST 1SG.PAT-sad* ASS.M say QT there among be QT along

ománi kéye, yųkhą́ lé thahá wą yu-bláya é-gnakį na
walk about QT then this buckskin IDF.SG INS-flat L-put and

lé wéyotha ki lé aką́n é-gnaka yųkhą́ hokšíla bébe-la
this blood clot DEF this on top L-put then boy baby-DIM

wą wé etą́ icháğa kéye. chąkhé hokšíla ki lé éyaš
IDF.SG blood from grow QT then boy DEF this but

hehą́yą-š tókhaȟ'ą kéye. yųkhą́ hokšíla ki lé é cha
at that time-EMPH disappear QT then boy DEF this IP QL

waná icháğį na lé líla wa-khúl wayúphika kéye. yųkhą́
now grow and this INT NSP.PAT-shoot skillful* QT then

Iktómi Wéyotha Hokšíla khį́ nahą́ke "wą́ léchiya wį́yą
Iktomi Blood Clot Boy say to and then IJ.M here woman

wą líla o-wą́yąg wašté cha ų́ cha ektá wąyą́g lá
LK INT L-see good QL be so there see go.2SG.AG

wašté-ke lő” eyá kéye. yųkhą́ lé wikhóškalaka ki hé
good-kind of ASS.M say QT then this young woman DEF that

wicháša itháchą cha chųwį́-tku. chąkhé ektá í nahą́ke
chief QL daughter-3POR then there go and then

waná khoškálaka ki okhíya kéye. yųkhą́ wicháša itháchą ki
now young man DEF court QT then chief DEF

hé waštélakį nahą́ke eyá kéye “ho lé mi-chų́kši
that like.VT and then say QT well this 1SG.POR-daughter

lúzį-kte lő” eyá kéye. “ho éyaš táku nų́m
take hold of.2SG.AG-FUT ASS.M say QT well but things two

wichá-ya-khute-kte lő” eyá kéye. “cha hé ópta
3PL.PAT-2SG.AG-shoot-FUT ASS.M say QT so that through

iyáya-pi kihą le-tą́ wahį́kpe ų́ wichá-ya-ˀo-kte
go-PL when this-from arrow with 3PL.PAT-2SG.AG-shoot-FUT

lő” eyá kéye. chąkhé thokéya lé šųğíla cha ópta iyáyį-kta
ASS.M say QT then first this fox QL through go-FUT

kéye. “ya-khúte-kte yeló” eyá kéye. “na hé é nahą́
QT 2SG.AG-shoot-FUT ASS.M say QT and that IP and then

chetą́ wą héchų sˀe wichá-ya-kte hą́tąhąš wichį́cala ki
hawk IDF.SG that way* 3PL.PAT-2SG.AG-kill when girl DEF

lé lúzį-kte yeló” eyá kéye. ho chąkhé le Iktó
this take hold of-FUT ASS.M say QT well then this Iktomi

hená waná naȟˀų́ chąkhé étkiya yá-hą kéye. iyáyį nahą́ke
those now hear then toward go QT go and then

chą-máheta-kiya yá-pi yųkhą́ wąkáta-kiya é-tųwį nahą́ke "wą́
woods-inside-to go-PL then up-toward L-look and then IJ.M

lél kákhiya wąkáta chą́ ki lená kichíza-hą-pi cha ektá
here yonder up tree DEF these fight-PRG-PL QL to

mnį́ nahą́ iyó-wicha-wa-khi-kte-šni yelő" eyá
go.1SG.AG and then ST-3PL.PAT-1SG.AG-forbid-FUT-ST ASS.M say

kéye. héchel nahą́ke chą́ ki hená étkiya wąkáta-kiya óskapį
QT so and then tree DEF those toward up-toward climb

na wąkáta ihų́ni nahą́ke "khóla, híyu na ó-ma-kiya
and upwards arrive and then friend come and ST-1SG.PAT-help.VT

yó, theȟíya o-má-tke yeló," eyá kéye chąkhé
IMP.SG.M terribly ST-1SG.PAT-hang.VI ASS.M say QT then

Wéyotha Hokšíla wąkáta-kiya yį́ na wąkáta iyáhą kéye
Blood Clot Boy up-toward go and up reach the top QT

yųkhą́ Iktómi é cha héyá kéye "iyáskapa yó, iyáskapa
then Iktomi IP QL say that QT stick to IMP.SG.M stick to

yő" eyį́ na iȟátˀį na hiyú-ˀicˀi-ya kéye chą́ hokšíla
IMP.SG.M say and laugh and come-3RFL-CAU QT then boy

ki glicú-kta yųkhą́ Wéyotha Hokšíla ektáni ka-ˀį́yaskab
DEF get off-FUT then Blood Clot Boy there INS-stick to

ihą́ chąkhé tókhani glicú-šni kéye cha. he-tą́ Iktómi

remain then cannot get off-NEG QT QL that-from Iktomi

hokšíla ki lé, Wéyotha Hokšíla é-ˀicˀi-cağį nahą́ke

boy DEF this Blood Clot Boy L-3RFL-make and then

wichóthi étkiya ya-hą́ kéye. étkiya yá-hį nahą́ akhé

camp.N toward go-PRG QT toward go-PRG and then again

ektá ihų́ni nahą́ héyá kéye "wą́ lé wikhóškalaka ki

there arrive and then say that QT IJ.M this young woman DEF

hé ų́ thą́tahą wa-hí yeló" eyá kéye. "ho

that because of for the sake of 1SG.AG-come ASS.M say QT well

cha waná mi-glú-wįyeya yeló" eyá kéye. "cha waná

so now 1SG.AG.PSS-POSS.INS-ready ASS.M say QT so now

ȟtáyetu kihą héchiya lé táku ki hená

evening when there this things DEF those

wichá-wa-khute-kte ló" eyá kéye. chąkhé waná

3PL.PAT-1SG.AG-shoot-FUT ASS.M say QT then now

i-glú-wįyeya-pi na áta wichášą ithąchą ki thi-ˀíkceya

ST-POSS.INS-ready-IPS and INT chief DEF house-common

etą́ thąkáta-kiya éyokasˀį yąká-pi kéye yųkhą́ waná áta šųǧíla

from outside-to peep at sit-IPS QT then now INT fox

wą ópta hiyáya chąkhé khuté éyaš wošná kéye chąkhé "wą́

IDF.SG through go by then shoot but miss QT then IJ.M

tuwá ma-ȟmų́ǧa cha tąyą́ wa-ˀó

somebody 1SG.PAT-bewitch so well 1SG.AG-shoot

o-wá-kihi-šni" eyá kéye. eyį́ nahą́ke akhé waná lé zįtkála

ST-1SG.AG-can-NEG say QT say and then again now this bird

kˀų hé ópta kįyą́ yųkhą́ akhé wošná chąkhé "wą́ lená-š

DEF that through fly then again miss then well these-EMPH

tuwá šil-ˀá-w-i-ma-yukcą cha wa-ˀó

somebody bad-L-NSP.PAT-ST-1SG.PAT-think of so NSP.PAT-shoot

o-wá-kihi-šni kˀų" eyá kéye chąkhé waléhąn lé

ST-1SG.AG-can-NEG ASS say QT then by that time this

Wéyotha Hokšíla iglúšpu na yį́ nahą́ akhé waná

Blood Clot Boy POSS.pick off and go and then again now

wichóthi ki ektá él ihų́ni na héyá kéye "wichášá wą hé

camp.N DEF at at arrive and say that QT man LK that

thimá yąké ki hé Iktómi é-ˀe yelő" eyá kéye. "ma-gnáyį

inside sit DEF that Iktomi IP-RED ASS.M say QT 1SG.PAT-trap

na hé hiyú welő" eyá kéye chąkhé wą́cagna wichášá itháchą

and that come ASS.M say QT then at once chief

ki hé é na hų́-ku, wichį́cala hų́-ku ki, henáos

DEF that IP and mother-3POR girl mother-3POR DEF both

áta khuwá iyáya-pi kéye nahą́ "lé Iktó é cha akhé hí

INT chase IGR-PL QT and then this Iktomi IP QL again come

cha hé ų-gnáyą-pe lő" eyá-pi kéye. "kté pő" eyá-pi
QL that 1PL.PAT-trap-PL ASS.M say-PL QT kill IMP.PL.M say-PL

kéye chąkhé áta khuwá-pi kéye, áta aˀíyakapteya khuwá-pi kéye
QT then INT chase-IPS QT INT uphill chase-IPS QT

cha. Iktó é cha áta themní pakį́n iyéya istó-kos į́yąka
QL Iktomi IP QL INT perspire wipe CEL arm-swing run

kéye. áta į́yąke éyaš "hé miyé é-šni, lé hokšíla ki lé
QT INT run but that I IP-NEG this boy DEF this

ni-gnáyą-pe lő" eyá chąkhé waná kawį́ȟ iyáya-pi
2PAT-deceive-PL ASS.M say then now turn around.VI go-PL

na Wéyotha Hokšíla oyúspa-pi nahą́ akhé waná
and Blood Clot Boy grab-PL and then again now

yu-ˀákağal otké-ya-pi kéye. chąkhé héyá kéye
INS-spread eagle hang.VI-CAU-PL QT then say that QT

"tókheškhe eháke táku ehį́-kta héci" eyá-pi kéye. "ho
how end.N what say.2SG.AG-FUT SUB say-PL QT well

thó éyaš thokéya wa-lówą-kte lo" eyá kéye, Wéyotha
first but first 1SG.AG-sing-FUT ASS.M say QT Blood Clot

Hokšíla hé é cha. "kholá, kholá, wí ki lé ékayeš kichí
Boy that IP QL friend friend sun DEF this even with

wéchize kˀų, háųw, háųw" eyá kéye. na ho
fight.1SG.AG ASS IJ.M IJ.M say QT and well

"mi-glúštą yelṓ" eyá kéye. "waksá
1SG.AG.PSS-POSS.finish ASS.M say QT cut

wa-má-sota pṓ" eyá chąkhé áta Lakhóta ki
INS-1SG.PAT-destroyed IMP.PL.M say then INT Lakota DEF

ókšą iyaya-pi na áta míla gluhá-pi na áta
around go-PL and all knife POSS.have-PL and INT

wašpá icú-pi khéš na'ókhiyutha kéye cha isą́m áta
cut into pieces take-PL but heal QT so beyond INT

tohą́yą wąkátuya thaló ki áya chąkhé wąží héyá kéye "wą́
so far high flesh DEF PRC then one say that QT IJ.M

lé Wéyotha Hokšíla ki hé é škhá wa-sól
this Blood Clot Boy DEF that IP but INS-destroyed

wa-chį́ ya-khúwa-pe ló, tóhąni
NSP.PAT-want 2AG-chase-PL ASS.M never

wa-yá-sota-pi-kte-šni yelṓ" eyá kéye. chąkhé áta Iktómi
INS-2AG-destroyed-PL-FUT-NEG ASS.M say QT then INT Iktomi

hél ohíti-ya šką́ k'ų héchel akhé é-khuwa-pi na ho
there busy-ADV move SYP so again L-chase-PL and well

waná oyúspa-pi-kta yųkhą́ héyá kéye "ho, thakóža, héchetu
now catch-PL-FUT then say that QT well grandchild right

welṓ" eyá į́yąka kéye. "héchetu weló. hená héchekche
ASS.M say run QT right ASS.M those that way

wa-'échų-pi chą́-šna šil-wá-chį-pi khéš léchekche
NSP.PAT-do-PL then-HAB bad-NSP.PAT-want-PL but this way

otké-ya-pe lǫ́" eyá kéye. ho héyá kéye "thųkášila,
hang.VI-CAU-IPS ASS.M say QT well say that QT grandfather

ų́ši-ma-la pǫ́" eyá kéye. na "thakóža, héchų-šni
ST-1SG.PAT-pity.VT IMP.PL.M say QT and grandchild do that-NEG

pǫ́" eyé éyaš waná oyúspa-pi na į́š eyá yu-ˀákağal
IMP.PL.M say but now catch-PL and also INS-spread eagle

otké-ya-pi kéye. yu-ˀákağal otké-ya-pi nahą́ke
hang.VI-CAU-PL QT INS-spread eagle hang.VI-CAU-PL and then

"ho níš waná Iktó táku ehį́-kta hųwó?" eyá-pi yųkhą́
well you now Iktomi what say.2SG.AG-FUT QS.M say-PL then

Iktó é cha "ho míš eyá wa-lówą-kte lǫ́" eyá kéye.
Iktomi IP QL well I too 1SG.AG-sing-FUT ASS.M say QT

chąkhé waná Iktó lową́-khiya-pi kéye chąkhé Iktó é cha
then now Iktomi sing-CAU-PL QT then Iktomi IP QL

į́š eyá olówą ki hé ahíyaye kéye. "kholá, kholá, wí
also song DEF that sing QT friend friend sun

ki lé ékayeš kichí wéchize kˀų" eyá kéye. "ho,
DEF this even with fight.1SG.AG ASS say QT well

wahų́ wa-má-sota pǫ́" eyá chąkhé áta kákhel
slash INS-1SG.PAT-destroyed IMP.PL.M say then INT about to

wahų́ icú-pi yųkhą́ átaya ų́kche-kche na héchena tˀá kéye.
slash take-PL then INT fart-RED and thus faint QT

A long time ago Iktomi was traveling around. Suddenly he heard that there was singing and dancing going on somewhere. He climbed a hill. Down below, on the other side, there was a prairie chicken dance going on. The prairie chickens had formed a circle and were dancing. He stood there listening for a while. The male prairie chicken went and circled around the female ones, hollering *mambú* [the sound male pheasants make], and the female ones answered by saying *mišą́* [my vagina] as they were dancing. He approached them, and when he arrived down there he—Iktomi—said: "Well, my younger brothers and sisters, what kind of dance are you dancing?" They replied: "Well, we are dancing the prairie chicken dance." He said: "You're doing it all wrong. Get in a circle and dance with your eyes closed." They got in a circle, and he joined them at the end and sang. Iktomi sang, and the words [of his song] were: "Dance with your eyes closed! If you open your eyes you will get red eyes!" That way he sang. They all danced with their eyes closed. But suddenly one of them opened his eyes [and saw that] Iktomi had started killing them one after the other. "Look, Iktomi is slaughtering us one after the other!" he yelled. They all opened their eyes and flew away in a hurry. They all had red eyes. From this incident, it is said, the prairie chickens have red eyes. Iktomi had killed many of them, and now he had them with him, carrying them. He went on and sat down with them in a pleasant, shady forest by a [river] bend. He built a fire, plucked the prairie chickens, and stuck them upright in the ground [on skewers]. He roasted them. There were a lot of them. He put coals on top of them and roasted them all, with their feet sticking out [because the feet are not eaten anyway]. Iktomi was sitting in the shade, looking on, and said: "Well, I had a pretty good hunt." Just then two trees started to produce a squeaking sound whenever there was some wind blowing. "My younger brothers, be quiet," he said. "Be quiet, don't do that, you are brothers, after all." Then the wind stopped blowing, so there was no squeaking any more. He sat there for a while, soliloquizing. Then the wind rose again. The two trees started squeaking. "My younger brothers, don't do that, it's not right," he said. Just then a coyote was coming over the hill, and was about to pass by. He [Iktomi] looked in his direction and said:

"Don't even think of coming here, don't even think of getting close to my roastings, get lost." The coyote started thinking about it. "If he is preparing food I will have a look at it," he said. He said that and got on his way. He went in his [Iktomi's] direction. He [Iktomi] said: "Don't get near me." At that time the wind started blowing, and the trees were squeaking. He [Iktomi] said: "I told you not to do that, don't do that!" and climbed up the trees. He inserted his hand between them, at the point where they were squeaking. Meantime the wind had stopped blowing, and his hand was stuck right in the middle, caught between the trees. The coyote went near him. He [Iktomi] said: "Hey, don't look inside, don't come here, don't you think of eating all my roastings in there!" The prairie chickens were lying with their bellies turned up, with their feet showing, so he [the coyote] sat down and got his fill. He ate until he was full, and Iktomi said: "You have done a terrible thing to me, I was going to eat them." But he [the coyote] put only the feet back in the ground in an upright position [to make fun of Iktomi], and ate the rest, too. When he left, he [Iktomi] said: "Doggone you, just wait till I catch you, soon I'll do the same thing to you!" As he was hollering that at the coyote, the wind started blowing. The trees separated, and he [Iktomi] fell down. Iktomi fell down and shouted: "You have done a terrible thing to my roastings. Doggone you, just wait and see what I'll use you for as soon as I catch you!" He said that and got on his way. He went on for a while, and then there was the coyote, stuffed with food and sleeping in a cool, breezy place. Iktomi got there, but he didn't kill him at all. He stood there watching him, wondering: "What should I do with him?" All of a sudden he [the coyote] kicked him [Iktomi] in the chest and ran away. He ran away, and he [Iktomi] said: "You have done a terrible thing." Then he went on his way. He went on for a while, and then stopped in front of a rose bush. Since he was hungry he picked them [the rose hips], asking: "My younger brothers, what is your name?" It [the bush] replied: "My name is rose. I am called 'When people eat me their rectum itches'." He said: "Oh, so I eat them and then my rectum itches." He ate the rose hips. He kept on eating for a while. Then, all of a sudden, his rectum started itching. He was scratching his rectum as he was going on. He went on, and this time he discovered some beans growing in a bunch. He picked them and said: "There is some good little food, what is your name?" It [the plant] replied: "'When people eat me they fart', this is my name." He said: "So I eat them and then I fart." He ate them, and then started farting. His behind went jumping up and down. He went on. He was bouncing up and down as he went on. Then he said [to the beans]: "Hey, be quiet, now I believe you!" But his rectum was itching nevertheless, so he kept on scratching his rectum. Then he pulled out the thin layer of fat covering the stomach and said: "Alas, I have done a terrible thing, what am I going to do with it? Well, at least I can wear it on my head." It was very hot, so he put the fat from the outside of his stomach that he had pulled out on his head and went on. He went on, and then he arrived at a camp. He arrived at a camp, and the children were playing outside. He sat down on top of a hill for a while. On his way down he went around it [the hill, so people didn't see him]. A man was living there with his young son. This boy was very handsome. He got there. When he was there he watched them for a while, but didn't go near them. [What had happened before was this:] This man had gone hunting and didn't return for a long time. So the boy was alone. His father had gone and didn't return. Then the man did come back. At that time his son was not there [not alive] anymore [he had been killed out in the woods], so he was very sad. He [the man] was carrying an elk as he was coming home. He butchered it, and then he took a blood clot, put it down in front of him, and said: "May you grow up to be a boy. I have lost my boy, and there will not be another. I don't have children any more, and I don't have a wife, either. That's sad. I'm unhappy." Then he joined the village people. He was walking about. Then he spread a piece of leather and put the blood clot on it. Then a baby boy grew out of the blood. The boy [the original boy] was already gone at that time. The boy [Blood Clot Boy] grew up now, and he was a very skilled marksman. Iktomi said to Blood Clot Boy: "A very beautiful woman lives over there, it would be good if you went to see her." [Iktomi had big ears and therefore always knew what was going on.] This girl was a chief's daughter. So he [Blood-Clot Boy] went to visit her and courted her. The chief liked him. He said: "You will marry my daughter. But [before that] you'll shoot two things. When they are passing through you will shoot them with an arrow from here [from inside the chief's tipi]." First a fox would be passing through. "You will shoot it," he [the chief] said. "When you will have killed it, and a hawk, that way you will marry the girl," he [the chief] said. Now Iktomi heard about that. He got on his way there [to the girl's camp]. He went there. Then they [Iktomi and Blood Clot Boy] went to the woods [hunting]. He [Iktomi] looked up and said: "I'll go up there to where these trees are fighting, and tell them how to behave." So he climbed up on the trees, and reached the top. He said: "Friend, come and help me, I'm hanging up here in a terrible way!" So Blood Clot Boy climbed up to the top. Iktomi shouted: "Get stuck, get stuck," laughed, and jumped off. The boy tried to get off [the tree]. Blood Clot Boy remained stuck there, unable to get off. After that Iktomi transformed himself into the boy, into Blood Clot Boy, and headed for the camp. He went there, and got back there again. He said: "I've come because of the girl. I'm getting ready now. When evening comes I will shoot these things." So people got ready and sat down in the chief's tipi, looking outside. Then a fox passed through, so he shot at it but missed it. He said: "Somebody has bewitched me, so I am not able to shoot well." As he said that the bird came flying by. He missed it, too, and said: "Somebody is sending me bad thoughts, so I cannot shoot well." By that time Blood Clot Boy had freed himself and was on his way back. He arrived at the camp and said: "The man inside there is Iktomi! He trapped me and then came here." Immediately the chief and the mother, the girl's mother, both started chasing him [Iktomi]. "It is Iktomi who has come back, he has tricked us!" they said. "Kill him!" they [the parents] said. People chased him. They chased him up the hill. Iktomi ran, wiping off the sweat in a hurry, swinging his arms. He ran fast, but then he said: "It's not me, it's this boy who has deceived you!" They turned around, grabbed Blood Clot Boy, and hung him spread-eagle. They asked him: "What will be your last words?" Blood Clot Boy replied: "But first I will sing." He sang: "Friends, friends, I even fought the sun [this refers to another story], oh well, oh well." Then he said: "I'm through. Put an end to me by cutting me up." So the Lakota gathered around him with their knives in their hands and cut him into pieces. But his wounds healed again. The flesh [they had cut off] piled up higher and higher. Then someone said: "This is Blood Clot Boy, but you are after him, trying to kill him! You'll never kill him!" Iktomi was moving about anxiously as people were chasing him again. When they were about to catch him he said: "That's alright, grandchildren." That he said while he was running. "That's alright. Whenever people do such things and have bad intentions they are hung up this way," he said. He added: "Grandfathers [i.e., the spirits above], pity me! Grandchildren, don't do that!" But they caught him now and hung him up spread-eagle, too. When they had hung him spread-eagle they asked him: "What will you say now, Iktomi?" Iktomi replied: "I will sing, too!" So they let Iktomi sing, and Iktomi sang the same song. "Friends, friends, I even fought the sun!" [which was not true in his case], he sang. "Go ahead, put an end to me by slashing me!" he said. Just when they were about to slash him he farted very much and fainted [he didn't die, because he is immortal]. [And the story goes on and on forever.]

4.2. Iktomi Meets Two Women and Iya

NEVA STANDING BEAR

Tape recorded September 19, 1994

Iktómi	*kákhena*	*yá-hą*	*kéye.*	*yųkhą́*	*áta*	*ȟtayétu*	*echíyatahą.*
Iktomi	about	go-PRG	QT	then	INT	evening	toward

ȟtayétu	*owášteca-kį*	*na*	*wiyóȟpeyata*	*áta*	*maȟpíya*	*ki*
evening	pleasant-kind of	and	west*	INT	sky	DEF

zi-yá	*na*	*šá-yela*	*áta*	*iyóyąm-ya*	*ȟpáya*	*chąkhé*	*ektá*	*é-tųwą*
yellow-ADV	and	red	INT	shine-ADV	lie	then	at	L-look

yá-hą	*yųkhą́*	*lé*	*wį́yą*	*nų́m*	*thí-pi*	*cha*	*él*	*ihų́ni*	*kéye.*	*cha*
go-PRG	then	this	woman	two	live-PL	QL	at	arrive	QT	so

lená	*táku-kichi-ya-pi*	*kéye,*	*wichį́cala*	*ki*	*nųphį́,*	*wį́yą*
these	something-REC-have as-PL	QT	girl	DEF	both	woman

ki	*nųphį́,*	*na*	*nųphį́*	*hokšícala*	*wichá-yuha-pi*	*kéye*	*chąkhé*
DEF	both	and	both	baby	3PL.PAT-have-PL	QT	then

étkiya	*yá-hį*	*na*	*ektá*	*ihų́ni*	*kéye*	*yųkhą́*	*lol'íȟ'ą-pi*	*kéye.*
toward	go-PRG	and	there	arrive	QT	then	cook.VI-PL	QT

lol'íȟ'ą-pi	*nahą́ke*	*héyá*	*kéye*	*"ahą́,*	*má*	*yu-phí-ya*
cook.VI-PL	and then	say that	QT	look!	IJ.F	INS-good-ADV

ya-hí	*kštó"*	*eyá*	*kéye,*	*yųkhą́*	*ųmá*	*"thimá*	*hiyú*	*wé,*
2SG.AG-come	ASS.F	say	QT	then	other	inside	come	IMP.SG.F

w-ó-ˀų-ni-cˀu-pi-kte" eyá kéye yųkhą́ "ho lé
NSP.PAT-L-1PL.AG-2SG.PAT-give-PL-FUT say QT then well this

į̨šé hé w-óyag wa-ˀú weló" eyá kéye, Iktómi é
just that NSP.PAT-tell 1SG.AG-come ASS.M say QT Iktomi IP

cha. chąkhé ųmá "hą́, táku oyág ya-hí hé?"
QL then one of them yes what tell 2SG.AG-come QS

héyá yųkhą́ "ká átaya wiyóȟpeyata-kiya iyóyąm-ya
say that then over there INT west*-to shine-ADV

ša-yéla ȟpáye ki héchiya khą́ta ožú cha hé áta iyóyąm-yela
red-ADV lie DEF there plum full so that INT shine-ADV

ȟpáye ló" eyá kéye. "cha į̨šé ųgná wóšpi
lie ASS.M say QT so just maybe pick.NSP.PAT

lá-pi-kte séca cha hé ų́ wa-ú." "ohą́,
go.2SG.AG-PL-FUT maybe so that because of 1SG.AG-come okay

héchųkˀų-pi ųk-ókihi-pi éyaš tuwéni hokší a-wą́yąke-šni
do that.1PL.AG-PL 1PL.AG-can-PL but nobody child L-see-NEG

kˀų" eyá kéye. chąkhé Iktó é cha "ho iyáya pó,
ASS say QT then Iktomi IP QL well go IMP.PL.M

tókša ób makį́-kte, iyáyį na wóšpi pó"
for a while with sit.1SG.AG-FUT go and pick.NSP.PAT IMP.PL.M

eyá kéye chąkhé ų́šˀųmakeci waná wóšpi
say QT then one being as silly as the other now pick.NSP.PAT

iyáya-pi kéye. étkiya wóšpi iyáya-pi na théhą
go-PL QT toward pick.NSP.PAT go-PL and for a long time

glí-pi-šni kéye yųkhą́ waná ȟta'íyokpaze ehą́n
come back-PL-NEG QT then now grow dark about that time

glihų́ni-pi. nahą́ke kú-pi kéye chąkhé éyaš ichų́hą
arrive at home-PL and then come-PL QT then but meanwhile

lol'íȟ'ą-ke kštó. yųkhą́ lé hokšícala ki hená é cha nųphį́
cook.VI-kind of ASS.F then this baby DEF those IP QL both

wichá-kte na iyóȟpe-wicha-ya kéye. iyóȟpe-wicha-yį
3PL.PAT-kill and ST-3PL.PAT-cook.VT QT ST-3PL.PAT-cook.VT

nahą́ke lolób-ya wichá-gle chąkhé lé hų́-ku-pi ki
and then tender-CAU 3PL.PAT-put then this mother-3POR-PL DEF

glihų́ni-pi cha héyá kéye "ho lé tháȟca wą lél
come back-PL QL say that QT well this deer IDF.SG here

iyáya cha wa-kté na lé átaya chéǧa thą́ka ki ogná
go so 1SG.AG-kill and this INT kettle big DEF inside

iyóȟpe-wa-ye ló" eyá kéye. "ho cha tąyą́ lochį́
ST-1SG.AG-cook.VT ASS.M say QT well so well hungry

ya-glí-pi cha wa-yáta-pi-kte ló" eyá kéye
2AG-come back-PL so NSP.PAT-eat.2AG-PL-FUT ASS.M say QT

chąkhé įšé wį́yą ki nųphį́ líla w-íyuškį-pi kéye.
then just woman DEF both INT NSP.PAT-happy-PL QT

héchų-pi éyaš ų́šˀųmakeci pąȟyá áta khą́ta ki
do that-PL but one being as silly as the other a lot INT plum DEF

iyúha yušpí-pi na glí-pi kéye. chąkhé waná íyutaka-pi
all pick-PL and come back-PL QT then now sit down-PL

na wóta-pi-kta yųkhą́ lé Iktómi é cha khiną́phį
and eat.NSP.PAT-PL-FUT then this Iktomi IP QL go outside

nahą́ke eyá kéye "é, wą-wícha-yąka pó, wį́yą nų́m
and then say QT IJ ST-3PL.PAT-see IMP.PL.M woman two

chįchá wicha-glúta-pi" eyá chąkhé wį́yą ki nųphį́ chéya
child 3PL.PAT-POSS.eat-PL say then woman DEF both cry

iyáya-pi na khuwá éyaya-pi kéye. khuwá éyaya-pi chąkhé átaya
IGR-PL and chase CEL-PL QT chase CEL-PL then INT

į́yąkį nahą́ke lé wašų́-ˀoȟloka wą ektá mahél iyáya
run and then this hole in the ground-hole IDF.SG to inside go

kéye. mahél iyáyį na áta i-glúšpa-špa na
QT inside go and INT L-POSS.scratch off-RED and

i-glú-ȟla-ȟlatį na áta wé eyála sˀe gliną́phį na eyá
L-POSS.ST-RED-scratch and INT blood full of come out and say

kéye "tókha hųwó?" eyá kéye, "thakóža,
QT what's the matter QS.M say QT grandchild

tókha hųwó?" eyá yųkhą́ wį́yą ki é cha "lé
what's the matter QS.M say then woman DEF IP QL this

Iktómi lél hiyú na hokší glul-ˀų-khiya-pi kštó” eyá
Iktomi here come and child POSS.eat-1PL.PAT-CAU-PL ASS.F say

kéye cha “hél mahél iyáye” héyá yųkhą́ “wą́, hé é cha áta
QT QL there inside go say that then IJ.M that IP QL INT

ma-khízį na átaya léchel ihą́g-ma-ye ló” eyá
1SG.PAT-fight and INT so end.VI-1SG.PAT-CAU ASS.M say

kéye, iyé cha hécha i-ˀícˀi-ˀų nahą́ke iyáyekiyį na akhé
QT he QL such ST-3RFL-do to and then run away and again

oȟlóka wą héchiya mahél iyáyį nahą́ iȟátˀį na héyá
hole IDF.SG there inside go and then laugh and say that

kéye “áta lená wį́yą ki hokší glúta-pi cha. tókša oyáte
QT INT these woman DEF child POSS.eat-PL QL soon people

ki na-wícha-ȟˀų-pi-kte ló” eyá chąkhé héchena “í::,
DEF ST-3PL.PAT-hear-PL-FUT ASS.M say then thus IJ.F

šícelaȟ” eyá-pi na áta lé oȟlóka ki ithánųgya pheží
no good say-PL and INT this hole DEF on both sides grass

pa-ˀo-tˀįza-pi na ilé-ya-pi cha akhé ųmáchiyatą
INS-L-dense-PL and burn.VI-CAU-PL so again from the other side

glinąphį na akhé átaya iyáyekiya kéye éyaš líla lúzahą cha
go outside and again INT run away QT but INT fast so

oyúspa-pi okíhi-pi-šni. cha lé wašų́-ˀoȟloka he-tą́
catch-PL can-PL-NEG so this hole in the ground-hole that-from

gliną́phį na héchena iyáyekiyį na yá-hį na akhé wichóthi
come out and then run away and go-PRG and again camp.N

wą ektá ihų́ni kéye. ektá ihų́ni yųkhą́ átaya táku
IDF.SG at arrive QT there arrive then INT something

okʼó-kį na átaya táku i-w-óglaka-pi cha
uproar-kind of and INT something L-NSP.PAT-POSS.tell-PL so

yá-hį na ektá ihų́ni yųkhą́ héyá kéye “wą́ lé táku
go-PRG and there arrive then say that QT IJ.M this what

i-w-ó-ya-glaka-pi hųwó?” éya kéye chąkhé “hą́, lé
L-NSP.PAT-ST-2AG-POSS.tell-PL QS.M say QT then well this

Íya wą lél hí cha. lél wakhą́heža ų́-pi ki hená
Iya IDF.SG there come QL there child be-PL DEF those

hų́ȟ tókhaȟʔą-hą-pi yųkhą́ Íya wą thi-y-óhą hiyú
some disappear-PRG-PL then Iya IDF.SG house-EI-among come

na átaya wa-ʔíhąg-ye kštó” eyá o-kí-yaka-pi kéye
and INT NSP.PAT-end.VI-CAU ASS.F say ST-BEN-tell-IPS QT

yųkhą́ “wą́ tókša o-wá-le-kte ló” eyá kéye “na
then IJ.M at once ST-1SG.AG-seek-FUT ASS.M say QT and

étkiya mnį́ nahą́ ektá wa-ʔí na Íya
toward go.1SG.AG and then there 1SG.AG-go to and Iya

iyé-wa-ye ki tókša o-chí-ci-yaka-pi-kte ló”
ST-1SG.AG-find when at once ST-1SG.AG.2-BEN-tell-PL-FUT ASS.M

eyá kéye. chąkhé yá-hį na pahá a-ˀíną m yá yųkhą́ léchel-ya
say QT then go-PRG and hill L-beyond go then so-ADV

hé é cha w-íphi-ˀicˀi-ye-laȟcakį na ištį́ma-hą kéye.
that IP QL NSP.PAT-full of food-3RFL-CAU-INT and sleep-PRG QT

ištį́ma-hą chąkhé a-ˀíyokasˀį naháke yuȟíca kéye yųkhą́
sleep-PRG then L-look at and then wake up.VT QT then

"mi-sų́," eyá kéye, "tókheškhe lél ya-ȟpáya-hą
1SG.POR-younger brother say QT how come there 2SG.AG-lie-PRG

hé?" eyá kéye chąkhé "ho hé lél įšé wichóthi cha
QS say QT then well that there just camp.N QL

kaˀísakhibya wa-ˀų́" eyá kéye "lél wóyute óta cha" eyá.
beside 1SG.AG-be say QT there food much QL say

yųkhą́ eyá kéye "mi-sų́, owíchota él lá
then say QT 1SG.POR-younger brother crowd in go.2SG.AG

chą́na-šna táku kho-yá-kipha hé?" eyá kéye chąkhé "táku
then-HAB what ST-2SG.AG-fear.VT QS say QT then things

ka-ȟlá-ȟla-pi chą́ hé kho-wá-kiphe" yųkhą́ "hą́, miš
INS-rattle-RED-IPS then that ST-1SG.AG-fear.VT then yes I

eyá-š" eyá kéye. "míš eyá-š átaya táku ȟlá-ȟla
too-EMPH say QT I too-EMPH INT things rattle-RED

kho-wá-kiphe yeló" eyá kéye. chąkhé "na nakų́ táku
ST-1SG.AG-fear.VT ASS.M say QT then and also what

kho-yá-kipha hé?" yų̨khą́ hé "lé išnáthi-pi
ST-2SG.AG-fear.VT QS then that this have the menses*-IPS

tha-chegnáke ki hená kho-wá-kiphe k'ų́" eyá chąkhé
ALP-breechcloth DEF those ST-1SG.AG-fear.VT ASS say then

"ohą́, míš eyá he-má-checha yeló" eyá kéye. "ho istį́ma
yes I too ST-1SG.PAT-like that ASS.M say QT well sleep

yó, tókha-šni yeló, tókša
IMP.SG.M not alright-NEG ASS.M just wait

a-wą́-chi-yą-kį-kte ló" eyá kéye. eyį́ nahą́ke isákhib
L-ST-1SG.AG.2SG.PAT-see-FUT ASS.M say QT say and then beside

íyutake. ho cha lé Íya hé héktakiya ištį́ma chąkhé nah̆má
sit down well so this Iya that back.AV sleep then hide

iyáyį na lé wichóthi él šil-w-óyaka kéye. "wą́ Íya lé
go and this camp.N in bad-NSP.PAT-tell QT IJ.M Iya this

pahá akhótąhą h̆páya cha hé táku h̆lá-h̆la na
hill on the other side lie QL that things rattle-RED and

chą́chega ka-bú-pi ki lená khokípha kéyé ló," ho
drum INS-sound.VI-IPS DEF these fear.VT say that ASS.M well

é na táku wą iyótą-h̆ci khokíphe ki hé išnáthi
IP and thing IDF.SG most-INT fear.VT DEF that have the menses

tha-chégnake cha khokípha kéyé ló eyá kéye. "ho hé
ALP-breechcloth QL fear.VT say that ASS.M say QT well that

é cha lená héchel a-yá-lową-pi na átaya chą́cheǧa
IP QL these so L-2AG-sing-PL and INT drum

a-yá-ka-bu-pi na táku ya-ka-ȟlá-ȟla-pi kihą
L-2AG-INS-sound.VI-PL and things 2AG-INS-rattle-RED-PL when

áptąyį-kte lő" eyá kéye chąkhé waná ektá ihų́ni-pi
collapse-FUT ASS.M say QT then now there arrive-PL

nahą́ke áta táku ka-ȟlá-ȟla-pi kéye.
and then INT things INS-rattle-RED-PL QT

cheȟ-ʔá-ka-ȟla-ȟla-pi naʔį́š chą́cheǧa a-ká-bu-pi na lé
kettle-L-INS-rattle-RED-PL and drum L-INS-sound.VI-PL and this

wį́yą tha-chégnake é cha khó ektá aʔí-pi chąkhé áta
woman ALP-breechcloth IP QL also there take to-PL then INT

yukšą́-kšą įyąkį na sniyą́tʔa kéye, Íya ki. chąkhé áta ektá
bend.VT-RED run and faint QT Iya DEF then INT there

ihų́ni-pi na áta lé wíkhą hená istó na hú na natá ki
arrive-PL and INT this rope those arm and leg and head DEF

na thahú él ohómni iyákaška-pi na lé wihų́paspa cha ų́
and neck at around tie-PL and this stake QL with

áta makhá ektá okátą-pi na wíkhą cha ų́ a-ʔíyakaška-pi
INT ground to pin down-PL and rope QL with L-tie-PL

cha iyáya okíhi-šni kéye cha ka-tʔá-pi kéye. ka-tʔá-pi-kta
so go can-NEG QT so INS-dead-IPS QT INS-dead-PL-FUT

yųkhą́ hé Íya ki é cha eyá kéye “wą́ ehą́ʾų Iktómi
then that Iya DEF IP QL say QT IJ.M aha! Iktomi

ma-yá-gnaye lő” eyá kéye cha. “tókša tohą́n
1SG.PAT-2SG.AG-trick ASS.M say QT QL just wait when

áta-chi-ye ki echél chi-cáǧį-kte
ST-1SG.AG.2SG.PAT-meet when right 1SG.AG.2SG.PAT-make-FUT

lő” eyá kéye. éyaš ichų́hą ka-tʾá-pi cha. he-tą́
ASS.M say QT but meanwhile INS-dead-PL QL that-from

Iktó ȟeyáb iyáya kéye. he-tą́ akhé iyáya kéye.
Iktomi away go QT that-from again go QT

Iktomi was traveling about. It was already around evening. It was a pleasant evening, and in the west the sky was yellow and red all over. He was heading in this direction, watching the phenomenon. He went on for a while. He got to a place where two women were living. They were sisters, the two girls, the two women, and they both had babies. He started walking in their direction and arrived there. They were cooking. They were cooking, and one of them said: “Look who’s here! It’s good that you came!” The other one said: “Come inside, we’ll give you food!” Iktomi replied: “I’ve just come to tell you something.” One of them [the women] said: “Alright, so say what you have come to tell us.” He said: “Far to the west, where there is this red glow, there are huge masses of plums [wild plains plums are yellow with a reddish tinge], it’s them that produce the color. [I say that] because maybe you want to go to pick them.” They replied: “Okay, we can do that, but there’s nobody to take care of the babies.” Iktomi said: “Just go ahead, I will babysit them, go and pick them.” So they went picking right away. They went there picking and didn’t return for a long time. It was already getting dark when they came back. They came back, but meantime he [Iktomi] had done some cooking. He had killed the two babies and boiled them. He had boiled them until they were tender. When their mothers returned he said: "A deer passed through here, so I killed it and cooked it in the big kettle. You came back pretty hungry, so you'll probably want to eat." The two women were very happy. They had done it [picking plums], and even though there were so many they had picked all the plums, and had then returned home. As they were sitting down and ready to eat Iktomi went outside and hollered: "Hey, look at them, the two women are eating their children!" The women both started crying, and went to chase him right away. They chased him right away, so he ran as fast as he could. Then he slipped into a hole in the ground. He slipped inside, and scratched and tore off his skin. He came out all bloody and said: "What's the matter? What's the matter, grandchildren?" [addressing the women who didn't recognize him]. The women replied: "Iktomi came here and made us eat our children!" "He has come inside," he said. "Aha! He must be the one who fought with me. He has battered me completely." He had done that to himself, of course. Then ran away. He ran away and slipped into another hole. He laughed and said: "These women have eaten their children. Soon people will hear about them!" They [the women] said: "He's no good." They stuffed the hole with grass on both sides and set it on fire. He escaped again through another exit. He ran away quickly. Since he was very fast, they couldn't catch him. He escaped from this hole in the ground and ran away. He went on for a while, and arrived at another camp. As he got there, there was great excitement and talk. He went there and asked: "What are you talking about?" He was told: "Well, an Iya [a monstrous giant] has come here. Some of the children living here disappeared. Then an Iya came to the village and destroyed everything." He said: "I'll go looking for him right now. I will go there to see him, and when I find this Iya I will let you know immediately." So he got on his way. He went to the other side of the hill. There he [Iya] was, stuffed with food and sleeping. He was sleeping, so he [Iktomi] looked at him, woke him up, and said: "My younger brother, how come you are lying here?" He [Iya] replied: "I'm just hanging around the camp. There is much food here." He [Iktomi] said: "My younger brother, what do you fear when you walk among people?" He [Iya] replied: "When they rattle something, that I fear." He [Iktomi] said: "Yes, so do I. I'm very scared when something is rattling, too." Then he asked: "What else do you fear?" He [Iya] replied: "I am scared of menstruating women's sanitary napkins." He [Iktomi] said: "Yes, I am like that too. Go to sleep, everything is alright, just wait, I will watch over you." He said that, and sat down beside him. After Iya had gone back to sleep he got on his way secretly and gossiped in the camp. "This Iya lying on the other side of the hill said he is afraid of things that rattle, and of drum beating. And he said that what he fears the most is menstruating women's sanitary napkins. So if you sing over him, and beat drums over him, and produce rattling sounds, he will collapse." So they paid him a visit and produced rattling sounds. They rattled kettles and beat drums, and the women brought their sanitary napkins, too. He ran amok and fainted, the Iya. They went back [to the camp] and tied ropes around his arms, legs, head and neck, and pinned him to the ground with stakes. They tied him with ropes and, since he could not escape, they killed him. When they were about to kill him Iya said: "Iktomi, I realize that you have tricked me. Just wait until we meet again, then I'll fix you!" But meantime they killed him. After that Iktomi left. After that he went on his way again.

4.3. The Giant Snake

NEVA STANDING BEAR

Tape recorded Septenber 19, 1994

ehą́ni Lakhóta wichóʔų ki héhą pahá wą Zuzéca Pahá
long ago Lakota existence DEF then hill LK Snake Butte*

eyá-pi cha hél zuzéca wą líla thą́ka ų́ škhé. yųkhą́
say-IPS QL there snake IDF.SG INT big exist QT then

tuwéni ikhíyela yé-šni kéyá-pi cha. tuwá él yá chą́-šna
nobody near go-NEG say that-IPS QL who there go then-HAB

tókhaȟʔą cha. yųkhą́ lé khoškálaka nų́m étkiya yá-pi nahą́ke
disappear QL then this young man two toward go-PL and then

ektá í-pi kéye. ųmá kihą wicálašni éyaš į́š ųmá
there arrive-PL QT one of them DEF refuse but he other

ki thimá yį́-kta kéyá chąkhé iyókhišni éyaš takómni thimá
DEF inside go-FUT say that then prevent but at all costs inside

yį́-kteȟcį cha. kaʔíyuzeya khinážį kéye, ųmá ki.
go-want very much QL a little way off stop QT other DEF

yųkhą́ hiyú-ʔicʔi-yį na héchena thimá iyáya kéye. átaya
then come-RFL-CAU and thus inside go QT INT

bu-yéla hí na átaya makhá ki na-hų́hųza kéye
sound.VI-ADV come and INT ground DEF INS-shake.VI QT

chąkhé héchena ųmá kihą ka'íyuzeya khinážį na ektá é-tųwą
then still other DEF a little way off stop and at L-look

yųkhą́ líla wašté-mna thimá thąkáta-kiya lé wašų́ etą́
then INT good-smell inside outside-to this den from

hinąpha kéye. cha ektá é-tųwą nážį yųkhą́ átaya zuzéca wą
come out QT so to L-look stand then INT snake IDF.SG

ícat'a hinąpha kéye. hinąphį nahą́ke héktakiya thimá
huge come out QT come out and then backwards inside

gli-yų́ke-la kéye. k'éyaš zuzéca ki lé hé yukhą́ kéye.
go back in-lie-DIM QT but snake DEF this horn exist QT

líla ištá thąkį́kįyą. chąkhé lé táku echį ektá é-tųwą nážį kéye
INT eye huge then this what think to L-look stand QT

yųkhą́ átaya thimá héktakiya khignį nahą́ke átaya p'ó
then INT inside backwards go home and then INT fog

hinąphį na íyohakap zuzéca wą hinąpha yųkhą́ lé
come out and behind snake IDF.SG come out then this

thahą́ši-tku hé é cha waná hąké zuzéca chąkhé
cousin-3POR DEM.D IP QL now part snake then

phá'íyuksa zuzéca-šni, héchena wicháša, na thachą́ ki
from head on up snake-NEG still man and body DEF

waná átaya zuzéca áya chąkhé eyá kéye "thahą́ši, theȟí-ya
now entirely snake PRC then say QT cousin terrible-ADV

o-yá-ȟʔą yeló" eyá kéye yųkhą́ "hą́, ehą́ni
L-2SG.AG-act ASS.M say QT then yes before

héchamų-kte-šni tkhá yeló" eyá kéye. chéya kéye.
do that.1SG.AG-FUT-NEG CNF ASS.M say QT cry QT

ištámniğağa ȟpáye. "éyaš ya-khí kihą
tear* fall but 2AG-arrive at home when

iná-wa-ye na até o-wícha-ki-yaka yő" eyá
mother-1SG.AG-have as and father ST-3PL-BEN-tell IMP.SG.M say

kéye. "héchel eyášna waníyetu wąží chą́" eyá kéye. "tókša
QT so always year one then say QT soon

wó-ma-kahi-pi-kte lő" "wó-ma-kahi-pi hą́tąhą
ST-1SG.PAT-bring food-PL-FUT ASS.M ST-1SG.PAT-bring food when

thąkál wa-hí-mųkį-kte na
outside 1SG.AG-come-1SG.PAT-lie-FUT and

wą-má-yąka-pi-kte lő" eyá kéye. "kʔéyaš i-wá-ya
ST-1SG.PAT-see-PL-FUT ASS.M say QT but ST-1SG.AG-speak

o-wá-kihi-kte-šni cha wą-má-yąka-pi-kta hécha. wóyute
ST-1SG.AG-can-FUT-NEG SO ST-1SG.PAT-see-PL-FUT OBL food

ahí-ma-ki-gle-pi hą́tahąš ho hená wátį-kta cha
bring-1SG-BEN-put up-PL when well those eat.1SG.AG-FUT so

aʔú-pi-kte lő" eyá kéye. ho chąkhé héchena thahą́ši-tku
bring-PL-FUT ASS.M say QT well then thus cousin-3POR

ki šųk-ˀákǫ-iye-ˀicˀi-yį na héchena chéya glá kéye.
DEF mount* and thus cry go home QT

héchena wichóthi ektá khí na oyáka cha. ektá éhųni-pi
thus camp.N at come and tell QL there arrive at-PL

éyaš waná khoškálaka ki héchena átaya zuzéca cha. phá ki
but now young man DEF still entirely snake so head DEF

khó áta cha zuzéca wą, áta ícatˀa ahíyokasˀį
also entirely QL snake IDF.SG entirely huge come and look

hiyų́kį na ištámniǧaǧa ȟpáya kéye chąkhé héchegla
lie down and tears* fall QT then right then

hų́-ku na at-kúku ki wašíkhigla-pi na átaya
mother-3POR and father-3POR DEF mourn-PL and INT

wíȟpeya-pi na ektá táku tha-wóyuha ki hená
practice give away*-PL and to things ALP-belongings DEF those

aˀí-pi na ilé-ya-pi kéye. héchų-pi nahą́ke tohą́n hél
bring-PL and burn.VI-CAU-PL QT do that-PL and then when there

ópta wich-ómani chą́šna lé thitákuye ki hená wóyute
through COLL-travel then-HAB this relatives DEF those food

é-ki-gle-pi chą́-šna é-ki-gle-pi na ȟeyáb iyáya-pi
L-BEN-put up-PL then-HAB L-BEN-put up-PL and away go-PL

chą́-šna hiną́phį na hená tókhaȟˀą kéye. chąkhé waníyetu
then-HAB come out and those disappear QT then year

óta	*héchų-hą-pi*	*éyaš*	*hąkéya*	*hinąphe-šni*	*kéye.*	*ho*	*hél*
many	do that-PRG-PL	but	finally	come out-NEG	QT	well	there

hé	*Zuzéca Pahá*	*eyá*	*chažéyata-pi*	*kéyá-pi*	*lehą́n*	*lé*
that	Snake Butte*	say	call-IPS	say that-IPS	now	this

ąpétu	*ki.*
day	DEF

At the time of the old-time Lakota, a very big snake lived by a hill named Snake Butte. Nobody went near it. Whoever went there disappeared. One time, two young men went in this direction and got there. One of them refused [to enter the cave in the hill], but the other one said he would go in. Even though he [his cousin] tried to keep him from doing so, he felt a great desire to go in. The other one was standing a little way off. He jumped down and went inside. There was a big noise coming his way, and the ground was shaking hard. The other one was still standing a little way off, watching; then a very pleasant odor came out of the cave. He stood watching, and then a huge snake came out. It came out, and then crept back in again, and lay down. The snake had horns. Its eyes were gigantic. He was standing there looking at it, wondering what it was, as it was crawling back in again. Then fog emerged [from the cave], and behind it another snake came out. It was his cousin who was now in part a snake. From his head on up he was not a snake, he was still human, but his body had now entirely become a snake's. He [the one who had been waiting outside] said: "Cousin, you have done a terrible thing." He [the snake] replied: "Yes, I shouldn't have done that." He cried. His tears were falling. "But when you arrive at home, tell my mother and father," he said. "Once a year they should bring me food," he said. "When they bring me food I will come out quickly and lie down, and they will see me. But I won't be able to speak, so they can only see me. When they bring and put up food I will eat it, so they should bring some." So his cousin got on his horse and went home crying. He arrived at home, at the camp, and reported the event. People went there [to the snake hill], but now the young man had completely turned into a snake, his head was also a snake's. His huge body came crawling out, he looked and lay down, and his tears were falling. His mother and father were mourning and made a big give-away. They took his belongings to him and burned them. After they had done that, his relatives would put up food there for him whenever they were passing through and would go away after they had put it up. Then he would come out and it [the food] disappeared. They kept doing this for many years, but finally he didn't come out any more. To this day this place is called Snake Butte.

Note: Snake Butte is supposed to be located in eastern South Dakota on a reservation. Giant snakes, as well as bigfoots, still exist on the reservations today, according to what the Native Americans say.

4.4. Star Boy

NEVA STANDING BEAR

Tape recorded October 31, 1994

ehą́ni	*wichóʔoyake*	*ki*	*wį́yą*	*wą*	*maȟpíya*	*ektá*	*yąká*	*škhé.*
ancient	story	DEF	woman	IDF.SG	sky	in	sit	QT

lé	*maȟpíya*	*tho-yá*	*yųké*	*ki*	*héchiya*	*wį́yą*	*ki*	*lé*	*yąká*
this	sky	blue-ADV	lie	DEF	there	woman	DEF	this	sit

škhé.	*cha*	*eyášna*	*wa-wópta*	*ománi*	*škhé.*	*thį́psila*
QT	QL	sometimes	NSP.PAT-dig up	walk about	QT	prairie turnip

kʔá	*ománi*	*na*	*chą́-šna*	*lé*	*wakhą́yeža*	*ihákab-šna*
dig	walk about	and	then-HAB	this	child	behind-HAB

ománi-pi	*cha*	*hená*	*ókiya-pi*	*škhé*	*yųkhą́*	*wąží*
walk about-PL	so	those	help.VT-PL	QT	then	one

wa-sló-slol-ki-ye-ka	*cha*	*ihákab*	*ú*	*na*	*iyų́ǧa-hą*
NSP.PAT-RED-ST-PSS-know-kind of	QL	behind	come	and	ask-PRG

kéye	*“tákuwe*	*cha*	*lená*	*lužų́*	*hé?”*	*eyá*	*kéye.*	*yųkhą́*	*cha*
QT	why	QL	these	pull out.2SG.AG	QS	say	QT	then	so

“ektá	*éyokasʔį-šni*	*yé.*	*ni-hį́ȟpayį-kte*	*kštó”*	*eyá*	*škhé.*
at	look at-NEG	IMP.SG.F	2SG.PAT-fall-FUT	ASS.F	say	QT

“oȟlóka	*he-tą́*	*ni-hį́ȟpaye*	*ki*	*líla*	*théhą*	*ni-hį́ȟpayį-kte*
hole	that-from	2SG.PAT-fall	if	INT	far	2SG.PAT-fall-FUT

kštó,	*héchų-šni"*	*eyá*	*kéye.*	*yųkhą́*	*hokšíla*	*ki*	*léchel*	*iníhąšni*
ASS.F	do that-NEG	say	QT	then	boy	DEF	here	nevertheless

lé	*thį́psila*	*yužų́-pi*	*cha*	*oȟlóka*	*cha*	*ektá-šna*	*éyokasʔį-hą*
this	prairie turnip	pull up-IPS	QL	hole	QL	at-HAB	look at-PRG

škhé	*yųkhą́*	*tókheškhe*	*éyokasʔį*	*yųkhą́*	*pašlúl*	*iyéyį*	*nahą́*	*oȟlóka*
QT	then	how	look at	then	slip	CEL	and then	hole

ki	*ogná*	*hįȟpáya*	*škhé*	*chąkhé*	*hįȟpáya*	*chąkhé*	*ayúta*	*ų́-pi*
DEF	inside	fall	QT	then	fall	then	look at	CNT-PL

yųkhą́	*a-wą́yąg*	*khuwá-pi*	*yųkhą́*	*léchel*	*ú*	*na*	*héchena*
then	L-see	chase-PL	then	so	come	and	continuously

áta	*iléȟ-ya*	*ú*	*na*	*i-y-átakunišni*	*na*	*etą́*
entirely	burn.VI-ADV	come	and	L-EI-destroyed	and	from there

iléȟ-leȟ-ya	*yąká*	*škhé*	*yųkhą́*	*hokšíla*	*ki*	*hé*	*wicháȟpi*	*cha*
burn.VI-RED-ADV	sit	QT	then	boy	DEF	that	star	QL

hé	*maȟpíya*	*ektáni*	*héchena*	*yąká*	*škhé.*	*cha*	*lená*	*įšé*
that	sky	thereafter	still	CNT	QT	so	these	maybe

ehą́ni	*wichóʔoyake*	*hécha.*
ancient	story	COP

This ancient tale is about a woman who lived in the sky. This woman was living where the sky is blue. Sometimes she walked around digging [for edible roots]. Whenever she went to dig prairie turnips some children followed her. They helped her. One of them, a curious one, walked behind her and kept asking: "Why are you pulling them out?" She said: "Don't look at it, you will fall down. If you fall from the hole you will fall very far. Don't do that." But the boy, nevertheless, kept peeping through the holes left when she pulled out the prairie turnips. As he was looking out, he suddenly slipped and fell through the hole. He was falling, and the others stood watching, following him with their eyes. He was falling, falling deeper and deeper, and burst into flames. Then he was gone. Only sparks remained. The boy lives on as the stars in the sky. This is probably a very old story.

4.5. Iktomi

NEVA STANDING BEAR

Tape recorded October 31, 1994

Iktómi	*ecíya-pi*	*ki*	*lé*	*ųgnáyešna*	*wicháša*	*na*	*tókhi*	*wablúška*
Iktomi	call-IPS	DEF	this	sometimes	man	and	maybe	insect

nachéce.	*eyášna*	*wicháša*	*ic'í-cağį*	*na*	*ųgnáš*	*wamákhašką.*
maybe	sometimes	man	3RFL-make	and	maybe	animal*

na	*iyé*	*tókhel*	*ic'í-cağį-kta*	*héci*	*héchų s'e*	*ic'í-cağe.*	*ho*	*na*
and	he	how	3RFL-make-FUT	SUB	that way*	3RFL-make	well	and

lé	*tohą́n*	*wicháša*	*hą́tąhąš*	*wicháša-la*	*cha*	*líla*	*hú*	*cik-cík'a*	*na*
this	when	man	when	man-DIM	QL	INT	leg	RED-small	and

istó	*khó*	*cik-cík'ala.*	*líla*	*niğé*	*thą́ka*	*na*	*natá*	*thą́ka*	*kéyá-pi.*
arm	also	RED-small	INT	belly	big	and	head	big	say that-IPS

ho	*cha*	*phé*	*él*	*aką́n*	*hé*	*yukhé*	*s'e*	*phestó-sto-yela*
well	so	head	on	on top	that	exist	like.AV	pointed-RED-ADV

a-káwįš-wįš-ya	*hą́*	*kéye.*	*táku*	*phé*	*él*	*aką́n*	*icháğa*	*cha*
L-bend.VT-RED-ADV	stand	QT	things	head	on	on top	grow	QL

hená.	*ho*	*cha*	*héhą*	*hé*	*wablúška*	*kéchąmi.*	*ho*	*cha*
those	well	so	then	that	insect	think that.1SG.AG	well	so

hé	*tohą́n*	*iyáyį*	*na*	*Lakhóta*	*óhą*	*iyáye*	*chą́-šna*	*Lakhóta*	*ki*
that	when	go	and	Lakota	among	go	then-HAB	Lakota	DEF

wichá-gnayį̧ naˀį̧́š líla ówakhąkhą nahą́ ų̧gná takún
3PL.PAT-trick or INT tell lies and then maybe something

icˀí-cağį̧ na thi-y-óhą iyáye hą́tąhąš wicákha.
3RFL-make and house-EI-among go when tell the truth

wicála-pi. wicála-pi tohą́n takún waná ówakhąkhą na
believe-PL believe-PL when something now lie and

wa-ˀéchų-kte hą́tąhąš cha hená oyáte ki wichá-gnayį̧
NSP.PAT-do-FUT when so those people DEF 3PL.PAT-trick

nahą́ i-glú-thokecha na tóhųweni tákuni wašté echų́-šni
and then L-POSS.INS-different and never nothing good do-NEG

éyaš hená iyúha Iktómi wa-ˀéchų ki tóhąni tuwéni
but those all Iktomi NSP.PAT-do DEF never nobody

slolyé-šni. ho éyaš wicála-pi na į̧šé waná wa-yúˀižena
know-NEG well but believe-PL and just now NSP.PAT-disturb

chą́na-šna héhą iyáyekiyį̧ na o-ˀí-glake. khéš akhé takún
then-HAB then run away and ST-L-POSS.tell but again something

ipáyeȟ echų́ cha oyáte ki tohą́n thi-y-óhą hiyú chąkhé
wrong do so people DEF when house-EI-among come then

kte-wáchį-pi khéš okhíhi-pi-šni. cha hé táku wablúška
kill-try-PL but can-PL-NEG so that something insect

nachéce cha oȟlóka naˀį̧́š táku kˀéyaš ektá mahél iyáye. táku kˀéyaš
maybe QL hole or whatever to inside go whatever

icˀí-caǧe. *cha* *hé* *isą́m* *tákuni* *slol-wá-ye-šni.* *ho* *hé*
3RFL-make so that more nothing ST-1SG.AG-know-NEG well that

wa-héhąyela.
NSP.PAT-that is all

The being called Iktomi is sometimes a man, and sometimes maybe an insect. Sometimes he turns himself into a man, at other times maybe into an animal. He transforms himself into whatever he wants to transform himself into. When he is a man, he is a midget with very short legs and very short arms, too. He has a very big belly and a big head. On his head there are some things like antennas, waving back and forth. Those are the things that grow from his head. Therefore, I think he is actually an insect. When he travels and walks among the Lakota he tricks the Lakota or tells a lot of lies. When he has transformed himself into something and walks among people he may be honest. People believe him. When they believe him he tells a lie, and when he plans a trick, he fools these people and transforms himself. He never does any good. Nobody ever knows about all the things Iktomi does. But people believe him. And after creating trouble he runs away and reveals his identity. When he visits people to play a prank on them again, they try to kill him, but they cannot [because he is immortal]. Perhaps he is some kind of an insect, so he can slip into holes or anything else. He turns himself into anything. I don't know any more than that. That's all.

4.6. The End of the World

NEVA STANDING BEAR

Tape recorded October 31, 1994

ho	*lé*	*į́šé*	*oyáte*	*thókecha*	*tháwa,*	*tha-wóˀoyake*	*hécha.*
well	this	maybe	people	different	its	ALP-story	COP

yųkhą́	*hé*	*wį́yą*	*wą*	*wąkáta*	*maȟpíya*	*ektá*	*yąká*	*cha*	*hé*	*é*
then	that	woman	LK	high above	sky	in	sit	QL	that	IP

cha.	*wį́yą*	*ki*	*lé*	*šiná*	*wą*	*káğa*	*škhé.*	*šiná*	*wą*	*sų́*
QL	woman	DEF	this	rug	IDF.SG	make	QT	rug	IDF.SG	weave

škhé.	*cha*	*tohą́n*	*sų́*	*áyį*	*na-šna*	*tohą́*	*é-ki-gnaka*	*chą́*
QT	so	when	weave	PRC	and-HAB	when	L-PSS-put	then

šųȟpála	*wą*	*lé*	*šiná*	*ki*	*haȟų́ta*	*ki*	*yaȟtákį*	*na-šna*
puppy	IDF.SG	this	rug	DEF	yarn	DEF	bite	and-HAB

yaglá	*į́yąkį*	*na-šna*	*yaglá*	*iȟpéya*
unravel with the mouth	run	and-HAB	unravel with the mouth	throw

cha	*akhé*	*phi-yá*	*káğa*	*škhé.*	*phi-yá*	*sų́-hą*	*škhé.*
so	again	good-CAU	make	QT	good-CAU	weave-PRG	QT

yųkhą́	*hé*	*oyáka-pi*	*na*	*tohą́n*	*šų́ka*	*ki*	*lé*	*áta*	*yuglá*
then	that	tell-IPS	LK	when	dog	DEF	this	entirely	unravel

ayústą	*hą́tąhąš*	*na*	*wį́yą*	*ki*	*hé*	*šiná*	*wą*	*sų́*	*ki*	*lé*
finish	when	and	woman	DEF	that	rug	LK	weave	DEF	this

yuštą́	*hą́tąhąš*	*hé*	*hehą́yela*	*wichóʼų*	*ki*	*lé*	*ihą́ke-kta*
finish	when	that	that is all	existence	DEF	this	end.N-FUT

kéyá-pi	*škhé.*
say that-IPS	QT

This tale may belong to another tribe. It is about a woman sitting up there in the sky. This woman is making a rug. She is weaving a rug. While she is weaving, whenever she puts down her work, a puppy bites the rug yarn and runs around holding it in its mouth, unraveling it [the rug]. As it is tossing it about, it unravels it, so she fixes it again. She weaves it all over again. People say that when the dog stops unraveling it for good, and the woman finishes the rug she is weaving, this will be the end of creation.

4.7. Iktomi and the Ducks

FLORINE RED EAR HORSE

Tape recorded September 1, 1995

cha	*táku*	*wąží*	*oblákį-kte.*	*yųkhą́*
so	something	IDF.SG	tell.1SG.AG-FUT	then

ųcí-wa-ye	*wąží*	*hé*	*é*	*cha*	*waníyetu*	*óta*	*ní*
grandmother-1SG.AG-have as	one	that	IP	QL	year	many	live

yųkhą́	*ąpétu*	*wą*	*él*	*ųk-áyuštą-pi*	*na*	*iyáya*	*éyaš*
then	day	IDF.SG	on	1PL.PAT-leave behind-PL	and	go	but

héchena	*wichóˀiye*	*ki*	*lená*	*ąpétu*	*wąžígži*	*wéksuye.*
still	word	DEF	these	day	some	remember.1SG.AG

héchel	*ąpétu*	*ki*	*lé*	*él*	*wóˀoyaka*	*wąží*	*oyág-ma-ši-pi*
so	day	DEF	this	on	story	IDF.SG	tell-1SG.PAT-ask-IPS

yųkhą́	*hé*	*wéksuye.*	*yųkhą́*	*iktómi*	*ki*	*lená*
then	that	remember.1SG.AG	then	spider	DEF	these

wicháša-pi-šni	*škhé*	*yųkhą́*	*Iktómi*	*ki*	*lé*	*lochį*	*cha*	*héchel*
tricky-PL-ST	QT	then	Iktomi	DEF	this	hungry	so	so

ąpétu	*wą*	*él*	*olówą*	*wówapi*	*eyá*	*kˀį*	*na*	*héchel*	*yá*	*yųkhą́*
day	IDF.SG	on	song	book	IDF.PL	carry	and	so	go	then

mağáksica	*optáya*	*wąží*	*héchel*	*áta-wicha-ye.*	*yųkhą́*
duck	herd	IDF.SG	so	ST-3PL.PAT-meet	then

wichá-gnaye. "iyúha hiyú pó nahą́ iyúha mimé-ya
3PL.PAT-trick all come IMP.PL.M and then all round-ADV

i-nážį yį́ na chi-cí-lową-pi-kta cha wachí pő"
L-stand go and 1SG.AG.2-BEN-sing-PL-FUT so dance IMP.PL.M

eyá kéye. "nahą́ tuwá ya-tų́wą ki ištá
say QT and then someone 2SG.AG-look if eye

ni-žáka-pi-kte lő" eyá wichá-gnayą cha héchel lową́
2PAT-wide open-PL-FUT ASS.M say 3PL.PAT-trick so so sing

cha áta wachí-pi kéye. yųkhą́ táku wą yuhá cha icú na
so INT dance-PL QT then something LK have QL take and

héchel waná tóna áta wichá-ka-tʔa. wahéhąl wąží tųwą́
so now some INT 3PL.PAT-INS-dead by that time one look

cha hé oyáka kéye "tųwą́ pó, Iktómi waná hų́ȟ
so that tell QT look IMP.PL.M Iktomi now some

ų-ká-tʔa-pi" eyá cha tųwą́-pi yųkhą́ héchų cha
1PL.PAT-INS-dead-PL say so look-PL then do that so

iyáyekiya-pi kéye. ho na wichá-ka-tʔe ų́ hená
run away-PL QT well and 3PL.PAT-INS-dead in order to those

wichá-gnayį na wichá-ka-tʔe hená i-wícha-cu na
3PL.PAT-trick and 3PL.PAT-INS-dead those ST-3PL.PAT-take and

ųmá hená naphá-pi cha héchel lená wichá-yuha na héchena
other those flee-PL so so these 3PL.PAT-hold and thus

khútakiya líla chąté wašté-ya yá kéye. héchiya chethí na
downwards INT happy*-ADV go QT there build a fire and

áta cho-wícha-kʾį eyá-pi cha héchų kéye. na
INT ST-3PL.PAT-roast say-IPS so do that QT and

a-w-íyuškį kaȟyá chą́ nų́m íchi-kakizį na yųkhą́
L-NSP.PAT-rejoice like.AV tree two REC-squeak and then

kakíza-hą chąkhé héchel héyá kéye "héchų-pi-šni yó,
squeak-PRG then so say that QT do that-PL-NEG IMP.M

wi-ní-chowe-pi škhá yéchiza-pi-kteȟci yeló" eyį́
ST-2PAT-relatives-PL but fight.2AG-PL-want very much ASS.M say

na héchel iyáhį na yu-léhą i-wícha-cu
and so climb to the top and INS-apart ST-3PL.PAT-take

wa-chį́ cha héchel sí ki anáǧipį na glicú okíhi-šni.
NSP.PAT-want so so foot DEF hold fast and get off can-NEG

cha héchiya wąkáta yąké ki waléhąl šųgmáyetu ki— į́š eyá
so there up sit SYP by that time coyote DEF also

wicháša-pi-šni škhé ehą́ni— na hél hé į́š eyá lochį́ cha
tricky-PL-ST QT long ago and there that also hungry so

aglágla ú-hą hé wąyą́ka cha lé él hí na ómna-mna
along come-PRG that see so this to come and sniff-RED

yųkhą́ hé maǧáksica ki lená é cha cho-wícha-kʾį cha
then that duck DEF these IP QL ST-3PL.PAT-roast LK

wąyą́ka cha héchel yaslútį na hél áta wótį

see so so pull out with the teeth and there INT eat.NSP.PAT

na wíphi-ˀicˀi-yį na héchel o-mášte cha él

and surfeited-3RFL-CAU and so L-warm QL on

a-mášte-ˀicˀi-ya ȟpáya-hą kéye. héchena glicú kéye. waná lé

L-warm-3RFL-CAU lie-PRG QT then get off QT now this

anáǧipe wą hé tókheškhe echų́ na kaǧą́ cha ki-yúǧą

hold fast IDF.SG that somehow do and open.VI so BEN-open.VI

cha héchel hįȟpáya-ˀicˀi-yį na glicú na wąyą́ke éyaš ehą́ni

so so fall-3RFL-CAU and get off and see but already

iyúha thebyį́ na héchena iyáyekiya kéye. cha ho lé akhé

all eat up and thus run away QT QL well this again

hél wóˀiyukcą wą káǧe ki hé chéǧa wą áta mní

there plan LK make DEF that kettle IDF.SG INT water

o-káštąna piȟ-yá kéye. hé iyéye hą́tąhąš hél o-ˀíȟpeyį

L-pourand boil.VI-CAU QT that find if there L-throw

na ho hé yútį-kta cha héchų na olé éyaš iyéye-šni

and well that eat-FUT so do that and look for but find-NEG

kéye. ho hehą́yela Iktómi wichóˀoyake hé hehą́yela ihą́ke. ho

QT well that is all Iktomi story that that is all end.N well

hé tókhetu. hehą́yela hé ųcí-wa-ye ki lé

that how that far that grandmother-1SG.AG-have as DEF this

o-má-ki-yake.

ST-1SG-BEN-tell

So I will tell a story. One of my grandmothers lived to be very old. One day she left us behind and went [to the spirit world]. But I still remember her words on some days. Today I was asked to tell a story, so that is the one I remember. Spiders are tricky. Iktomi [the trickster] was hungry. One day he was walking about, carrying some song books. He met a flock of ducks. Then he tricked them. [He said:] "Come here, and get in a circle, all of you. I will sing for you, so dance. And if one of you opens his eyes you guys will become pop-eyed," he said, tricking them. So he sang, and they were dancing hard. Then he took something [like a club] that he had with him and killed some of them. By then one of them opened his eyes and told [the others what was going on]. "Look, Iktomi has killed some of us!" he said. They opened their eyes, and [saw that] he had done that, so they ran away. He had fooled them in order to kill them. He took the ones that he had killed. The others escaped. So he grabbed them and went down the hill. He was very happy. There he built a fire and roasted them all, it is said. That's what he did. Just as he was quite happy, two trees started rubbing on each other, which produced a squeaking sound. They kept on squeaking, so he said: "Don't do that, you are brothers, but still you're trying to fight!" He climbed up, trying to pull them apart. His feet got caught [between the trees] and he could not get off. While he was sitting up there a coyote—coyotes were also said to be tricky in the past—that was also strolling along, and hungry, saw [what was going on]. He came there and sniffed. He saw that he [Iktomi] had roasted the ducks. He pulled them off the fire. He ate greedily until he was surfeited. Then he lay down on a sunny spot to warm himself. Then he [Iktomi] got off [the tree]. He had somehow managed to loosen the grip of the trees. They came apart. So he dropped himself off and got down. He looked [at his meal] but he [the coyote] had already devoured everything and had run away. The plan he made this time was to fill a pot with water and boil him [the coyote]. If he found him he would throw him in and eat him. He was going to do that and looked for him, but didn't find him. That is where the Iktomi story ends. That's how it was. That is all my grandmother told me.

4.8. Bean, Grass, and Fire

FLORINE RED EAR HORSE

Tape recorded September 19, 1995

hehą́l wichóˀoyake wąží ptécela cha oblákį-kta yųkhą́ lé
then story LK short QL tell.1SG.AG-FUT then this

ohų́kaką hécha. yųkhą́ wakhą́heža khų́ši-tku kihą
bedtime story COP then child grandmother-3POR DEF

ób yąkį́ na waná iyų́ka-pi-kte ithókab héchel héyá
with sit and now go to sleep-PL-FUT before so say that

kéye: "thakóža, hiyú pé na lél mimé-ya híyutaka
QT grandchild come IMP.PL.F and here round-ADV sit down

pé. hų-chí-ci-kaką-pi-kte" eyá kéye.
IMP.PL.F ST-1SG.AG.2-BEN-tell a bedtime story-PL-FUT say QT

yųkhą́ héyá kéye: "tohą́l wichóˀoyake ki lé
then say that QT when story DEF this

o-chí-ci-yaka-pi hą́tąhąš é-blaštą cha 'hą́'
ST-1SG.AG.2-BEN-tell-PL when L-stop talking.1SG.AG QL yes

eyá pé eyá kéye." ho hé táku ų́ hé wichá-ši héci
say IMP.PL.F say QT well that what for that 3PL.PAT-ask SUB

slol-wá-ye-šni éyaš hé ogná, "hą́" eyá-pi ehą́tąhąš, ho
ST-1SG.AG-know-NEG but that way* yes say-PL when well

patháke-šni o-wícha-ki-yakį-kta héchetu cha khá
stop abruptly-NEG ST-3PL-BEN-tell-FUT so QL mean.VT

kéchąmi. yųkhą́ héyá kéye: “omníca na pheží na
think that.1SG.AG then say that QT bean and grass and

phéta, hená yámni kholá-kichi-ya-pi kéye. ho yųkhą́
fire those three friend-REC-have as-PL QT well then

hená ptáya ománi yá-pi-kta kéye. yųkhą́ yá-pi yųkhą́ wakpála
those together travel go-PL-FUT QT then go-PL then river

wą ȟpáya kéye. yųkhą́ mní ki šmá cha tókheškhe
IDF.SG lie QT then water DEF deep QL somehow

iyúweǧa-pi-kta héci hé óhuta él nážį-pi na
cross.VT-PL-FUT SUB that shore at stand-PL and

i-w-óglaka-pi kéye. yųkhą́ pheží ki lé héyá kéye:
L-NSP.PAT-POSS.tell-PL QT then grass DEF this say that QT

‘tóktu éyaš miyé ma-hą́ska cha įthó wakpála ki lél
whichever way I 1SG.PAT-long so perhaps river DEF here

ópta imų́kį-kte ló’ eyá kéye. ‘kihą wąží
across lie down.1SG.AG-FUT ASS.M say QT and then one

thógthog ogná alí i-má-ya-lala-pi-kte ho
one by one along step on ST-1SG.PAT-2AG-go.2AG-PL-FUT well

tókša khowákatą ilúweǧa-pi ki tókša wékta na
soon across cross.VT.2AG-PL when soon get up.1SG.AG and

ó-chi-pha-pi-kte ló' eyá kéye. chąkhé 'ohą́' eyá-pi
ST-1SG.AG.2PAT-join-PL-FUT ASS.M say QT then okay say-PL

kéye. 'héchel wašté yeló' eyá-pi kéye. ho waná pheží hé áta
QT so good ASS.M say-PL QT well now grass that INT

wakpála ópta iyų́ka kéye. ho omníca į́š thokéya iyáye-šni.
river across lie down QT well bean it first go-NEG

phéta hé é cha thokáheya yá cha. waná alí na
fire that IP QL first go QL now step on and

choką́gnąya yé ki waléhąl phéta áta pheží ki lé
in the middle go SYP by that time fire INT grass DEF this

okséya cha kichí mah-íyayį na ókaȟ iyáya kéye. chąkhé omníca
burn.VT QL with inside-go and float go QT then bean

nážį-hį na wóʔiȟaka-la-ka nážį-hį na iȟátʔa-hį na
stand-PRG and fun-consider-kind of stand-PRG and laugh-PRG and

iȟátʔa-hį na hąkéya chokų́yą nabláza kéye." ho hehą́yela
laugh-PRG and finally in the middle burst QT well that is all

o-w-íhąke kéye.
L-EI-end.N QT

I will tell a short story. It is a bedtime story. When a grandmother was babysitting she would tell such stories before bedtime. "Grandchildren, come, sit down in a circle here, I will tell you a bedtime story," she would say. "When I tell you this story, say 'yes' whenever I finish a sentence," she would say. I don't know exactly why she told them [to do] that, but I think that that way, when they said "yes," it meant that she would keep on talking to them without stopping [because that way she knew if the kids were still awake]. Then she said [on one occasion]: "Bean, grass, and fire, those three were friends. They were planning a trip together. They went on their way, and then there was a river. The water was deep, so they were standing by the riverside, discussing how they might get across. The grass said: 'At any rate, I am tall, so I could lie down across the river. Then you guys walk on me one by one. When you will have gotten across I will get up and join you.' They said: 'Okay, that's a good idea.' Now the grass lay down across the river. The bean refused to go first. The fire was the one who went first. It stepped on it [the grass], and by the time it arrived in the middle, the fire had burned the grass completely, so it fell into [the water] with it and floated away. The bean was standing there, standing there thinking that this was very funny, and laughed and laughed, and finally it burst open in the middle." This is the end of the story.

True Stories 5

5.1. The Deer Spirits

NEVA STANDING BEAR

Tape recorded November 4, 1994

wawíyopheya ománi wą héchacha ká Mission,
salesman* travel IDF.SG like that over there Mission

South Dakota étkiya glá yųkhą́ wichį́cala nų́m máni
South Dakota toward go home then girl two walk

glá-pi kéye. hą́ théhą éyaš máni glá-pi chąkhé inážį
go home-PL QT night long but walk go home-PL then stop

nahą́ héyá kéye "o-chí-gnaka-pi nahą́ Mission
and then say that QT L-1SG.AG.2PAT-put-PL and then Mission

ektá akhí-ȟpe-chi-ya-pi-kte ló" eyá
in arrive at home with-ST-1SG.AG.2PAT-throw-PL-FUT ASS.M say

kéye. eyá chąkhé "ohą́" eyá-pi na nųphį́ mahél íyutaka-pi khéš
QT say then okay say-PL and both inside sit down-PL but

ókowąžila iȟát'a-pi kéye chąkhé o-w-óglag yąkį́ na
all the time laugh-PL QT then L-NSP.PAT-POSS.tell CNT and

waná Mission ki khiyéla glá-pi yųkhą́ ųmá héyá
now Mission DEF near go home-PL then one of them say that

kéye "lél ų-glíyacu-pi-kte" ho eyá kéye chąkhé
QT here 1PL.AG-start going home-PL-FUT well say QT then

"tókša ektá-ȟci éȟpe-chi-ya-pi-kte k'ų" eyá yųkhą́
soon at-INT ST-1SG.AG.2PAT-drop off-PL-FUT ASS say then

"hiyá, lél ų-glíyacu-pi-kte k'ų" ho eyá cha
no here 1PL.AG-start going home-PL-FUT ASS well say so

chąkú él inážį chąkhé nųphį́ glicú-pi kéye. nųphį́ glicú-pi
road on stop and then both get out-PL QT both get out-PL

nahą́ke iyóškokpa étkiya į́yąg iyáya-pi chąkhé
and then ditch* toward run go-PL then

a-wícha-yuta yųkhą́ nųphį́ heȟáka hécha-pi kéye. chąkhé áta
ST-3PL.PAT-look at then both elk COP-PL QT then INT

yuš'į́yeya-pi cha gnį́ na héchena Mission ektá khihų́ni nahą́ke
scare-PL so go on and thus Mission at arrive and then

oyáke k'éyaš tuwéni wicákhela-šni, hená iyúha chet'ų́gla-pi cha
tell but nobody believe-NEG those all doubt-PL so

iyópteya Mission ki khignį́ na othų́wahe ki isą́m
through Mission DEF go on home and town DEF further

khiglá yųkhą́ akhé hená é cha glá-pi cha iníhąšni
go on home then again those IP QL go home-PL so nevertheless

o-wícha-gnaka kéye, akhé įšé "otúyachį héchecha"
L-3PL.PAT-put QT again just it does not matter like that

kéchį na o-wícha-gnakį nahą́ tohą́n glá yųkhą́ iȟátˀa-pi
think that and L-3PL.PAT-put and then when go on then laugh-PL

cha sí ektá a-wícha-yuta yųkhą́ sí ki okhížata-pi kéye.
so foot at ST-3PL.PAT-look at then foot DEF split.A-PL QT

napé ki a-wícha-yuta yųkhą́ okhížata-pi na ištá
hand DEF ST-3PL.PAT-look at then split.A-PL and eye

thąkįkįyą-pi na phuté kihą sap-sápa-pi chąkhé áta inážį
huge-PL and upper lip DEF black-RED-PL then INT stop

nahą́ke thąsák tˀá kéye na "glicú pó, lená wicháša
and then struck with fear* QT and get out IMP.PL.M these man

wicháša he-ní-cha-pi-šni yeló" eyá kéye. "lená wicháša akątu
man ST-2PAT-COP-PL-NEG ASS.M say QT these human being*

he-ní-cha-pi-šni yeló" nahą́ke áta hetą́ni kawį́ğį
ST-2PAT-COP-PL-NEG ASS.M and then INT from there turn around.VI

na héktakiya Mission ektá khihų́ni. thąsák tˀá kéye cha.
and back.AV Mission at arrive at struck with fear* QT QL

chąkhé Lakhóta ki o-kí-yaka-pi nahą́ke eyášna hógna-šna
then Lakota DEF ST-BEN-tell-PL LK always that way*-HAB

héchecha škhá. "tákuwe hél ogná hą-ˀóma-ya-ni hé?"
like that QT why there along night-ST-2SG.AG-travel QS

eyá-pi kéye. "cha hená heȟáka cha eyášna
say-PL QT so those elk QL always

i-glú-thokecha-pi na-šna héchų-pe ló" eyá-pi. eyá
L-POSS.INS-different-PL and-HAB do that-PL ASS.M say-PL say

o-kí-yaka-pi *kéye* *cha* *icínųpani* *hé* *wašícu* *ki* *hé* *hé*
ST-BEN-tell-IPS QT so never again that white man DEF that that

ogná *tóhųweni* *hą-ˀíyopta-šna* *wa-w-íyopheya* *hiyáye-šni*
along never night-through-HAB NSP.PAT-EI-sell pass.VI by-NEG

kéye.
QT

A traveling salesman was on his way home to Mission, South Dakota. Then [he saw] two girls walking there. They were walking there, even though it was late in the evening. He stopped and said: "I'll give you a lift and drop you off in Mission." He said that, and they said "Okay." They both got into his car. But they were giggling all the time. He kept on talking, and when they were approaching Mission one of them said: "We're getting off here." He replied: "I'll drop you off further on." "No, we're getting off here," she [one of the girls] said. So he stopped on the road, and they both got out. They both got out and went running toward the ditch [next to the highway]. He looked at them, and [all of a sudden] both of them were elks. They scared him very much, and so he went on. He arrived at Mission and related his story. But nobody believed him. They all doubted him. He passed through Mission and rode on toward the next town. There they were again [the girls], walking. Nevertheless, he picked them up again, thinking: "There is nothing to it." He picked them up, and when he was driving again, they laughed. He looked at their feet and they had split feet [like deer hooves]. He looked at their hands and they were split. They had huge eyes, and their upper lips were black. He stopped instantly, struck with fear, and said: "Get out, you are not human! You are not human beings!" At this point he turned back, and went back to Mission. He was struck with fear. The Lakota told him that rumor had it that such things were always happening there. "Why do you travel here at night?" he [the one he was talking to] said. "These elks always transform themselves and do that [to people]." People told him that, and after that this white man never again passed through there at night to do business.

5.2. The Fly on the Window

NEVA STANDING BEAR

Tape recorded November 16, 1994

ehą́ni	*até-wa-ye*	*ki*	*khoškálaka*	*kˀų*	*héhą*	*cha*
long ago	father-1SG.AG-have as	DEF	young man	SYP	then	so

théca-ka	*cha*	*héhą*	*líla*	*enágna*	*ománi*	*kéye*	*yųkhą́*
young-kind of	so	then	INT	here and there	travel	QT	then

léchel	*oyáka-pi*	*na*	*hél*	*wicháša*	*wą*	*tha-wícu*	*kichí*	*thí*
so	tell-IPS	LK	there	man	IDF.SG.SG	ALP-wife	with	live

kéye	*yųkhą́*	*wicháša*	*ki*	*tókhi*	*okó*	*wąží*	*naˀį́š*	*ųgnáš*
QT	then	man	DEF	about	week	one	or	maybe

isą́mya-šna	*tókhi*	*iyáyį*	*na-šna*	*glí*	*kéye.*	*chą́-šna*
beyond-HAB	somewhere	go	and-HAB	come home	QT	then-HAB

wíyą	*ki*	*lé*	*líla*	*théhą-hą*	*išnála*	*yąká*	*cha*
woman	DEF	this	INT	for a long time-RED	alone	sit	so

watóhąn	*wicháša*	*wą*	*ektá-šna*	*wąyą́g*	*í*	*kéye*	*cha.*
sometimes	man	IDF.SG.SG	to-HAB	see	go	QT	QL

chąkhé	*éyaš*	*slol-kí-ye-šni.*	*lé*	*wį́yą*	*ki*	*lé*	*wicháša*
then	but	ST-PSS-know-NEG	this	woman	DEF	this	man

yuhá	*šką́*	*slolyé-šni*	*cha.*	*akhé*	*iyáyį-kte.*	*tohą́n*	*iyáyį-kta*	*chą́*	*líla*
with	act	know-NEG	QL	again	go-FUT	then	go-FUT	then	INT

iyáye-khiya ináȟni éyaš ųgnáhą-šna ȟˀąhí-ya-šna šką́-hą
go-CAU hurry but sometimes-HAB slow-ADV-HAB act-PRG

kéye chąkhé įšé lolˀíȟˀą na wakhą́-yą w-ó-kˀu na
QT then just cook.VI and special-ADV NSP.PAT-L-give and

ohíti-ya šką́ kéye yųkhą́ cha waná iyáye-šni hą́ni léchel
hurry.VI-ADV act QT then so now go-NEG before so

pahá echíyatąhą ahíyokasˀį hi-nážį kéye, tha-wíchaša, cha
hill from there come and look come-stand QT ALP-man so

wį́yą ki lé ináȟni hįgná-ku ki iyáye-khiyį-kteȟci
woman DEF this hurry husband-3POR DEF go-CAU-want very much

nahą́ke waná kítąȟci iyáya chąkhé ektá é-tųwą nážį-hą yųkhą́
and then now at last go then at L-look stand-PRG then

yį na héchena waná pahá a-ˀínąm iyáya chąkhé héchena ųmá
go and thus now hill L-beyond go then thus other

wicháša ki lé pahá echíyatąhą ahíyokasˀį ȟpáya-hą cha
man DEF this hill from there come and look lie-PRG so

étkiya šiná kos-kóza chąkhé waná šų́kawakhą́ ki
toward blanket RED-wave then now horse* DEF

iyé-ˀicˀi-yį na étkiya ú-hį na ektá hihų́ni kéye yųkhą́
ST-3RFL-send and toward come-PRG and there arrive QT then

"má lé lolˀí-wa-ȟˀą cha thó éyaš thokéya
IJ.F this ST-1SG.AG-cook.VI so wait a minute first

wa-yátį-kte" eyá cha. "waná iyáye kštó" eyá chąkhé
NSP.PAT-eat.2SG.AG-FUT say QL now go ASS.F say then

thimá hiyú na waná wól íyutakį nahą́ke ožą́glepi
inside come and now eat.NSP.PAT sit down and then window*

etą́ thąkáta-kiya éyokas'į yųkhą́ léchel ųgnáhelakha héktakiya
from outside-to look then so suddenly backwards

šųk'ákąyąka wą ú chąkhé héyá kéye "kú weló" eyá
rider* IDF.SG come then say that QT come ASS.M say

kéye. "kú weló" eyį́ na héchena áta pąȟyá khiną́pha
QT come ASS.M say and thus INT run in panic go outside

kéye cha. áta tohą́n okíhilaka į́yąkį nahą́ke thi-lázata-kiya
QT QL INT as much as can be* run and then house-behind-to

našlóg khignį́-kta yųkhą́ slolyé-šni cha hél ohómni
escape go home-FUT then know-NEG so there around

chąkáškapi chąkhé áta yu-hékta iȟpéye éyaš inážį na
fence* then INT INS-backwards throw but get up and

slohą́-hą ȟpáyį na chų́kaške ki iyóȟlathe iyáyį na
crawl-PRG fall and fence* DEF under go and

tohą́n okíhilaka į́yąkį na héchena áta hél mayá kaksá-ksa-pi
as much as can be* run and thus INT there cliff cut-RED-IPS

wą cha áta į́yąkį na héchena héchi o-hį́ȟpaya kéye. héchena
IDF.SG QL INT run and thus there L-fall QT thus

oníyą ka-thą́kal hiyú-ya cha tókha kiktá-šni ȟpáya yųkhą́
breath INS-outside come-CAU so unable get up-NEG lie then

wíyą ki é cha ektá é-tųwį na "ma éya tákunišni kštó,
woman DEF IP QL at L-look and IJ.F nothing ASS.F

gliyáhą yé, éyaš to-ní-kheca-šni hé?" eyá yųkhą́ "hą́,
come on up IMP.SG.F but ST-2SG.PAT-well QS say then yes

to-má-kheca-šni yelő" eyá kéye. eyá chąkhé "ho cha hiyú
ST-1SG.PAT-well ASS.M say QT say then well so come

wé" éyaš "thóhįyąká yő" eyá chąkhé "tákuwe?
IMP.SG.F but wait a minute IMP.SG.M say then why

éna ų́ hé?" eyá yųkhą́ "iyáya hé?" yųkhą́ "tákunišni
right there be QS say then go QS then nothing

kštó, hé įšé theȟmų́ǧa cha ožą́glepi él alí hiyáya cha hé
ASS.F that just fly QL window* on climb go by so that

wąlákį nahą́ na-yá-phe kštő" eyá chą́ "wą́
see.2SG.AG and then ST-2SG.AG-flee ASS.F say then IJ.M

theȟí-ya micʔí-kte tkhá wą" eyį́ na "icínųpani ožą́glepi
terrible-ADV 1SG.RFL-kill CNF ASS say and next time window*

ki hená ya-glúžaža ki héchel tákuni-š héchel
DEF those 2SG.AG-POSS.wash if so nothing-EMPH so

a-wá-khipha-kte-šni škhá. katʔé-ma-ya-ye kʔų"
ST-1SG.AG-meet-FUT-NEG but fall-1SG.PAT-2SG.AG-CAU ASS.M

eyá kéye. héchegla iglúštą.
say QT that is all POSS.finish

Long ago, when my father was a young man, when he was young, he used to travel around a lot. People related [to him] what follows: A man was living with his wife. The man regularly went out [hunting] for about a week or maybe longer and then he would return. The woman was staying by herself for long periods of time. Sometimes a man would come to see her. But he [her husband] didn't know anything about it, he didn't know that the woman was fooling around with this man. Again he was planning a trip. When he was about to leave she hurried his departure very much, but sometimes he took his time, so she cooked and fed him a lot of food, moving about nervously. Before he left, he—her boyfriend—had arrived and stood peeking from the hill. So the woman was eager to get her husband on his way in a hurry. Then, at last, he left. She was standing there watching him, and he left. While he was disappearing behind the hill the other man was lying [on the ground], watching from the hill. She waved a blanket at him. He mounted his horse and approached her. He got to her, and when he arrived she said, "I've done some cooking, you will eat first, just wait a minute. Now he's gone." So he went inside and sat down to eat. Then he looked out the window. All of a sudden a rider was coming. He yelled: "He is coming! He is coming!" And, panicking, he ran outside. He ran as fast as he could and was going to seek protection behind the house. He didn't know that there was a fence around it, so he was thrown back, but got up again and struggled to get away on his knees. Then he went under the fence and ran as fast as he could. There was a steep cliff. He ran and fell off. He was knocked out of breath and lying there, unable to get up. The woman looked at him and said: "It's nothing, come on up, but are you alright?" He replied: "Yes, I'm alright." She said: "So come on." But he said: "Wait a minute. What's going on? Is he still around? Is he gone yet?" She said: "It's nothing. You just saw a fly walking on the window and you ran away." Then he said: "I almost killed myself in a terrible way. And if you clean the windows next time something like this won't happen to me again. It's your fault that I fell down." Here the story ends.

5.3. How to Become a Father

FLORINE RED EAR HORSE

Tape recorded September 19, 1995

ho	*hehą́l*	*akhé*	*wąží*	*oblákį-kta*	*yųkhą́*	*hé*	*khoškálaka*
well	then	again	one	tell.1SG.AG-FUT	then	that	young man

wą	*tóhąni*	*thawícuthų-šni*	*kéye*	*éyaš*	*wicháša*	*lená*	*ehą́ni*
IDF.SG	never	marry*-NEG	QT	but	man	these	long ago

tˀatˀá	*e-wícha-kiya-pi.*	*tˀatˀá*	*eyá*	*chažé-wicha-yata-pi*
retarded	ST-3PL.PAT-be called-PL	retarded	say	ST-3PL.PAT-call-IPS

yųkhą́	*hé*	*é*	*cha,*	*khoškálaka*	*ki*	*lé.*	*yųkhą́*	*owítaya*	*wą*	*él*
then	that	IP	QL	young man	DEF	this	then	gathering	IDF.SG	in

wítaya-pi	*yųkhą́*	*wikhóškalaka*	*wą*	*líla*	*wį́yą wašté*	*cha*
get together-IPS	then	young woman	LK	INT	beautiful*	QL

chįchá	*yukhą́*	*kéye*	*yųkhą́*	*hé*	*wikhóškalaka*	*ki*	*wicháša*	*wąží*
child	exist	QT	then	that	young woman	DEF	man	IDF.SG

kichí	*ų́-kta*	*cha*	*wakhą́yeža*	*ki*	*lé*	*tuwá*	*até-yį-kta*	*cha*
with	be-FUT	so	child	DEF	this	who	father-have as-FUT	QL

olé-pi	*kéye*	*yųkhą́*	*waná*	*átaya*	*wicháša*	*ki*	*wíyata-pi*
look for-PL	QT	then	now	all	man	DEF	get together-PL

na	*mimé-ya*	*íyutag*	*áya-pi*	*kéye.*	*yųkhą́*	*wakhą́yeža-la*	*ki*
and	round-ADV	sit down	PRC-PL	QT	then	child-DIM	DEF

lé héchel aglágla yeyá-pi kéye cha hená iyúha wicháša hé
this so along send-PL QT so those all man that

icú-pi na yuhá yąká-pi na-šna akhé isákhib yąké hé
take-PL and have sit-PL and-HAB again next to sit that

kˀú-pi hą́tąhąš ho héchel yá kéye. ho hé wakhą́yeža ki
give-PL when well so go QT well that child DEF

hé tuwá a-ˀíheye hą́tąhąš ho hé até-yį-kta cha hé
that who L-urinate when well that father-have as-FUT so that

ų́ héchų-pi kéye. yųkhą́ wakhą́yeža ki lé héchel
because of do that-PL QT then child DEF this so

aglágla yeyá-pi yųkhą́ khą́šnišniyela tˀatˀá wicháša wą hé
along send-PL then unbelievably retarded man IDF.SG that

a-ˀíheye kéye. ho hé lé wį́yą, wikhóškalaka wį́yą wašté
L-urinate QT well that this woman young woman beautiful*

ho hé waná kichí ų́-kta cha ųmá-pi ki hená chįchá
well that now with be-FUT so other-PL DEF those child

tˀatˀá cha kitą́la i-wáȟtela-pi-šni kéye, wikhóškalaka wą
retarded QL a little L-dislike-PL-ST QT young woman LK

wį́yą wašté cha yúzį-kta hé ų́. hehą́yela o-w-íhąke.
beautiful* QL take-FUT that because of that is all L-EI-end.N

I will tell another [story]. There was a young man who never got married. These men were called *t'at'á* [retarded] in the old times. He was one of those who are called *t'at'á,* this young man. One time, people [i.e., the unmarried men] got together at a gathering. A very beautiful girl had given birth to an [illegitimate] child. They were looking for a man who would live with that girl and who would be the child's father. The men all got together and sat down in a circle, one after the other. Then they passed the little child around, and every man took it and sat there holding it, and then handed it on to the one sitting next to him. That's how it went. They did that because the one the child would urinate on would be its father [the mother wanted it so; she thought that the child should choose its father that way]. They passed the child around that way, and the incredible thing happened; it urinated on the retarded man. So he would live with this woman, this beautiful girl, from now on. The others were a bit jealous of the retarded kid, since he would marry a beautiful girl. That is the end of the story.

Note: Neva Standing Bear's comment on this story: "Old-time talk was a bit dirty."

5.4. The Rescued Prisoner

FLORINE RED EAR HORSE

Tape recorded November 1, 1995

lé	*wichóˀoyake*	*kihą*	*ehą́ni*	*Lakhóta*	*kihą*	*igláka*	*ománi-pi*
this	story	DEF	long ago	Lakota	DEF	move camp	travel-PL

na	*tuktél-šna*	*kaȟmí*	*wąží*	*él*	*chą́*	*na*	*mní*	*ikhą́yela*
and	where-HAB	river bend	IDF.SG	at	wood	and	water	near

eyášna	*é-thi-pi.*	*yųkhą́*	*etą́*	*khoškálaka*	*wąží*	*héchel*
always	L-live-PL	then	from there	young man	IDF.SG	so

zuyá	*iyáye.*	*tóna*	*zuyá*	*iyáya-pi*	*na*	*etą́*	*wąží*
go to war	go	some	go to war	go-PL	and	PART	one

glí-šni.	*yųkhą́*	*héchel*	*oyáka-pi*	*na*	*glí-šni*	*ki*
come home-NEG	then	so	tell-PL	LK	come home-NEG	DEF

lé	*wayáka*	*icú-pi,*	*héchų sˀe*	*oyáka-pi.*	*yųkhą́*	*wikhóškalaka*	*ki*
this	captive	take-IPS	that way*	tell-PL	then	young woman	DEF

lé	*khóškalaka*	*ki*	*lé*	*hé*	*tha-wíchaša.*	*yųkhą́*	*héchel*
this	young man	DEF	this	that	ALP-man	then	so

iyókiphi-šni	*na*	*wí*	*hiną́phe-šni*	*hą́ni*	*héchel*	*šųkˀákˀį*
happy-NEG	and	sun	come out-NEG	before	so	saddle horse

iyákaškį	*na*	*khoškálaka*	*wą*	*kašká*	*yus-khíyį*	*na*	*kichí*	*iyáya*
tie	and	young man	IDF.SG	tie	hold-CAU	and	with	go

kéye. na ȟé wą líla wąkátuya cha hé ektá wazí-zi
QT and mountain LK INT high QL that on pine-RED

ožú cha inážį-pi na khútakiya é-tųwą-pi yųkhą́ áta thóka
clump QL stop-PL and downwards L-look-PL then INT enemy

ki yu-mímeya wichó-thi kéye. ho héchel i-wą́yąka-pi kihą
DEF INS-round COLL-camp.VI QT well so L-see-PL when

tuktétu cha wayáka icú-pi ki hé slolyá-pi s'e léchecha
where QL captive take-PL DEF that know-PL like.AV like this

kéye. ho cha waná hiyóȟpaya-pi na echétkiya
QT well so now come down from a hill-PL and toward

ú-pi kéye. yųkhą́ thípi wą él ihų́ni-pi na ųmá
come-PL QT then tipi IDF.SG at arrive-PL and other

glicú na héchel okáǧeǧe ki tókhi lená okó
start going home and so seam DEF where these space

nachéce cha etą́ éyokas'į yųkhą́ héchecha-kta khoškálaka wą
perhaps so from peep in then like that-FUT young man IDF.SG

hé thimá héchel kašká nážį kéye. na othímahe hiyú ki él
that inside so tie stand QT and entrance* DEF at

isákhib wicháša wą a-wą́yąg yąká kéye. ho éyaš ištį́ma kéye.
beside man IDF.SG L-see sit QT well but sleep QT

ho cha héchel míla yuhá-pi cha nážį ki a'íyopteya
well so so knife have-PL so stand DEF opposite

thi-ˀíkceya ki lé héchel wahˇléca-pi kéye. wahˇléca-pi na
house-common DEF this so cut open-PL QT cut open-PL and

kašká nážį ki lená nakų́ áta o-wá-psa-psaka-pi na
tie stand DEF these also entirely L-INS-RED-broken-PL and

yu-thą́kal i-kí-k-cu-pi kéye. ho akˀį́ iyákaška
INS-outside ST-PSS-EI-take-PL QT well saddle horse tie

aˀí-pi kˀų hé aką́l íyutakį na héchiya-tą kichí
take to-PL DEF that on top sit down and there-from with

naphá-pi kéye. áta naˀų́g kú-pi nahą́ pahá wą él
flee-PL QT INT gallop come-PL and then hill IDF.SG on

khútakiya é-tųwą nážį-pi héchiya glihų́ni-pi kéye. na
downwards L-look stand-PL there arrive-PL QT and

opcélyela héchel khútakiya é-tųwą nážį-pi yųkhą́ wicháša
for a short time so downwards L-look stand-PL then man

wą ú na hé khoškálaka wą etą́ yu-thókhąl
IDF.SG come and that young man IDF.SG from there INS-elsewhere

icú-pi ki hé éyokasˀį na héchena áta thóka iyá éyapaha
take-PL DEF that peep in and thus INT enemy talk shout

kéye. aglágla hiyáya kéye. áta hená a-hínapha-pi na
QT along go by QT all those COLL-come out-PL and

echétketkiya į́yąg a-ˀú-pi kéye. yųkhą́ khoškálaka wą
toward run COLL-come-PL QT then young man LK

wayáka icú-pi hé tókahˇˀą. áta lená thóka kihą táku iyá
captive take-PL that disappear INT these enemy DEF what speak

w-ó-kichi-yaka-pi. šų́kawakhą́ akų́yąka-pi lená kašká-ška

NSP.PAT-ST-REC-tell-PL horse* ride*-IPS these tie-RED

wichá-ki-gle-pi cha hé aką́ʾiye-ʾicʾi-ya-pi na áta natą́

3PL.PAT-PSS-put-PL QL that mount*-PL and INT attack

a-híyu-pi kéye. wahéhąl lená átaya khiglékiya-pi kéye.

COLL-come-PL QT by that time these INT go back-PL QT

a-hí-thi-pi wą hé echétkiya khiglékiya-pi kéye. áta

COLL-come-camp.VI-PL LK that toward go back-PL QT INT

naʾų́g glá-pi na glá-pi na echél khihų́ni-pi kéye.

gallop go home-PL and go home-PL and so arrive-PL QT

yųkhą́ a-khíhųni-pi cha áta tha-ʾóyate kihą héchel

then COLL-arrive back-PL so INT ALP-people DEF so

gluhá-ha chéya-pi kéye. na hehą́l wichóʾoyake ki lé

POSS.hold-RED cry-PL QT and then story DEF this

hehą́l héchų sʾe oyáka-pi na-wá-ȟʾų. isą́m tókhetu héci

then that way* tell-IPS ST-1SG.AG-hear more how SUB

slol-wá-ye-šni. éyaš ąpétu lehą́l thóka ki hé kiksúya

ST-1SG.AG-know-NEG but day now enemy DEF that remember

ų́-pi škhé. tókhi wichóʾichaǧe hená kákhel o-kíchi-yag

CNT-PL QT maybe generation that that way ST-REC-tell

aʾú-pi ki ų́ lehą́l lehą́hųniya wichóȟʾą ki hé

CNT-PL DEF because of now to this day deed DEF that

kiksúya-pi héchų sʾe oyáka-pi.

remember-PL that way* tell-PL

This story is about the time long ago when the Lakota were still nomads. They always camped where there was a river bend [steep cliffs offered protection from the wind], where water and wood were within reach. From there [i.e., from such a camp] a young man went to war. Several people were in this war-party, and one of them did not return. They [the members of the war-party] said that the one who had not returned had been taken captive; that's what they said. The young man was a certain young woman's boyfriend. She was unhappy, and before the next sunrise she hired another young man to lead an extra saddle horse and left with him. They stopped on a very high mountain in a thick growth of pines and looked down. Right there was the enemies' camp circle [they were Crows]. From looking on they thought they knew where the captive was held [from the painting on the tipi]. Then they descended from the hill and approached it [the camp]. They came to a tipi [the one they had picked]. One of them got off [the horse] and peeped in through a seam, where there were little holes [from sewing the hides together]. As expected, the young man was standing inside, all tied up. By the entrance, a man was sitting, keeping watch. But he was sleeping. They took out their knives and cut up the tipi right behind where he [the captive] was standing. They cut it open, cut loose the ropes, and took him outside. He got on the extra saddle horse they had brought with them. They escaped with him. They galloped, and then reached a hilltop, stopped, and looked down. When they had stopped for a little while, looking down, a man came to check on the young man who had been rescued. Then he called out in the enemies' language. He was going around [the camp to tell people what had happened]. All the people came out of their tipis and ran to the captive's tipi. The young man they had taken captive was gone. They were disputing the matter in the enemies' language. They got on their saddle horses, which they always kept tied close to their tipis, and rushed forward. By that time, they [the fugitives] were on their way back. They were heading back to where their own people were camping. They galloped all the way and finally arrived at home. When they returned people hugged them and cried. I have heard this story told that way. I don't know any more about it than that. But the enemies are still remembering it to this day. Since every generation passes the story on to the next, that deed is related that way to this day, as people remember it.

5.5. Coyote Woman

FLORINE RED EAR HORSE

Tape recorded November 1, 1995

héchel ehą́ni oyáte kihą igláka ománi-pi kˀų héhą tuktéˀel

so long ago people DEF travel travel-PL SYP then anywhere

é-wicho-thi kéye. yųkhą́ héchel wį́yą wą etą́ héchel

L-COLL-camp.VI QT then so woman LK from there so

yu-wáchįkho-pi cha tókhaȟˀą kéye. ho éyaš tuwéni olé-šni

INS-pout-IPS QL disappear QT well but nobody seek-NEG

kéye. tókša héchel héktakiya khí-kta iyúkcą-pi na olé-pi-šni

QT soon so back.AV come-FUT think-PL and seek-PL-NEG

éyaš éna thí-pi kéye. yųkhą́ héchel tókhi wí wąží

but right there camp.VI-PL QT then so about month one

są́m yá wahéchetu-ya tókhaȟˀą kéye. yųkhą́ lé táku tháwa

more go that long-ADV disappear QT then this what her

hená ki-cˀį na manįta-kiya yá kéye. héchel manįta-kiya

those PSS-pack and wilderness-to go QT so wilderness-to

yį na pahá akąl íyutaka kéye. yųkhą́ léchel šųgmáyetu wą

go and hill on top sit down QT then so coyote IDF.SG

watóhą héchel hinážį kéye. hé hinážį na ayúta

at a certain distance so stop QT that stop and look at

nážį-hį na héchena khiglá kéye cha lé wįyą ki nážį
stand-PRG and then leave QT so this woman DEF stand

iyáyį na ihákab yá kéye. yųkhą́ héchel gnį́ na pahá
IGR and after go QT then so go home and hill

makhóšica s'e léchecha wą égna iyáya yųkhą́ héchel
badlands* like.AV like this IDF.SG among go then so

hél ohlóka wą hą́ yųkhą́ hél mahél khiglá kéye. ho
there hole IDF.SG stand then there inside go home QT well

héhą lé ohlóka ki nakų́ wichó'iye wą él yukhé éyaš
then this hole DEF also word IDF.SG there exist but

wéksuye-šni. éyaš hél mahél šųgmáyetu ki lé hél
remember.1SG.AG-NEG but there inside coyote DEF this there

thimá khiglá cha ihákab thumá iyáya kéye. yųkhą́ šųgmáyetu
inside go home so after inside go QT then coyote

ki hé ecéla-šni kéye. tóna áta hél ptáya thí-pi kéye.
DEF that only-NEG QT some INT there together live-PL QT

éyaš tákuni w-óhitika-pi na'į́š yahtáka-pi na'į́š tákunišni
but nothing NSP.PAT-mean.A-PL and bite-PL and nothing

kéye. ho cha hél ób thí kéye. hél-šna ištį́mį na hį́hąni
QT well so there with live QT there-HAB sleep and morning

kiktá chą́ lená tókhiya iyáya-pi kéye. na-šna
wake up then these somewhere go-PL QT and-HAB

watóhąl-šna a-glí-pi chą́na-šna héchel thaló
sometimes-HAB COLL-come back-PL then-HAB so meat

yaphá a-glí-pi kéye. nahą́ tókhi ithókab
hold in the mouth COLL-come back-PL QT and then maybe before

iȟpé-ki-ya-pi. chą́na-šna lé míla wą yuhá cha héchel
ST-PSS-throw-PL then-HAB this knife LK have QL so

wa-kábla na hená pus-yá kéye. pus-yá-hą ų́
NSP.PAT-slice and those dry.A-CAU QT dry.A-CAU-PRG CNT

waná líla óta yuhá kéye nahą́ théhą ób ų́ ki
now INT much have QT and then for a long time with be SYP

ų́ waná iyé na-wícha-ȟʼų kéye. yųkhą́ waná líla pápa
because of now talk ST-3PL.PAT-hear QT then now INT jerky

óta káǧa kéye. wóžuha wą áta héchel ožú-ya kéye. yųkhą́
much make QT sack IDF.SG INT so full-CAU QT then

wąží tókhi iyáya yųkhą́ glí nahą́ke hél héyá
one somewhere go then come back and then there say that

kéye: "ųci, hį́hąni ki i-glú-wįyeya yó,
QT grandmother tomorrow SYP ST-POSS.INS-ready IMP.SG.M

ųk-á-ni-ya-pi-kte," eyá kéye. "pahá ki lél
1PL.AG-ST-2SG.PAT-take to-PL-FUT say QT hill DEF here

akhótąhą héchi ni-thá-ʼoyate ki hená
on the other side there 2POR-ALP-people DEF those

a-hí-wicho-thi-pi *yeló"* *eyá* *kéye.* *"ho* *cha* *ektá*
L-come-COLL-camp.VI-PL ASS.M say QT well so there

ųk-á-ni-ya-pi-kte *ló,"* *eyá* *kéye.* *ho* *hé*
1PL.AG-ST-2SG.PAT-take to-PL-FUT ASS.M say QT well that

hį̨hąni *él* *tókhi* *waná* *wachįkho* *hé* *chąl-ˀákisni* *nachéce* *ų́*
morning on maybe now pout that heart-recover perhaps be

na *wí* *wąží* *sąm* *yá* *cha.* *ho* *héchel* *waná*
and month one more go QL well so now

i-glú-wįyeya *nahą́* *pápa* *ožúthų* *hé* *ki-cˀį́* *na*
ST-POSS.INS-get ready and then jerky sackful that PSS-carry and

waná *sagyé-ki-thų* *na* *waná* *ób* *iyáya* *kéye.* *yį́* *na* *wąží*
now cane-PSS-take and now with go QT go and one

thokéya *yį́* *na* *hé* *pahá* *akąl* *héchel* *inážį* *na* *khútakiya*
first go and that hill on top so stop and downwards

é-tųwą *nážį* *cha* *iyáhį* *na* *echétkiya* *yį́* *na* *isákhib*
L-look stand so reach a hilltop and toward go and beside

inážį *yųkhą́* *áta* *khúta* *héchel* *tha-ˀóyate* *ki* *yu-mímeya* *héchel*
stop then INT down so ALP-people DEF INS-round so

a-hí-thi-pi *kéye.* *ho* *hé* *é-thi-pi* *wą* *hé* *etą́*
L-come-camp.VI-PL QT well that L-camp.VI-PL LK that from

tókhaȟˀą *hé* *ipáyeȟ* *héchel* *é-thi-pi.* *yųkhą́* *ipáyeȟ*
disappear that away so L-camp.VI-PL then away

é-thi-pi éyaš héchena-š ikhą́yela, oˀų́ye ki hél
L-camp.VI-PL but still-EMPH nearby place to live DEF there

ikhą́yela é-thi-pi kéye. ho cha lená ománi-pi cha slolyá-pi
nearby L-camp.VI-PL QT well so these travel-PL LK know-PL

cha ektá pahá-ta aˀí-pi cha ho he-tą́ išnála
so there hill-to take to-PL so well that-from alone

wa-kí-cˀį na wichóthi ki echétkiya héchel glá
NSP.PAT-PSS-carry and camp.N DEF toward so go home

kéye. gnį́ na waná khąyéla khihų́ni yųkhą́ héchel átaya
QT go home and now nearby arrive then so all

wį́yą hená áta našlóg a-híyu-pi na phóski-ski
woman those all run COLL-come-PL and embrace-RED

oyúspa-pi na gluhá-ha chéya-pi kéye. ehą́ni oyáte
grab-PL and POSS.hold on to-RED cry-PL QT long ago people

kihą tuwá tókhaȟˀą chą́na-šna héchel héktakiya khí
DEF someone disappear then-HAB so back.AV come

chą́-šna į́š héktakiya akhé wągláka-pi cha héchel
then-HAB he back.AV again POSS.see-PL so so

gluhá-ha chéya-pi kéye. yųkhą́ héchų-pi kéye. ho
POSS.hold on to-RED cry-PL QT then do that-PL QT well

hehą́l hehą́yą o-w-íhąke.
then that is all L-EI-end.N

When the old-time folks were still roaming about as nomads, they camped anywhere. From there [i.e., from one of these camps] one time a woman who had been given reason to pout disappeared. But nobody went looking for her. People thought that soon she would come back anyway and did not search for her. But they didn't move the camp [because of her]. She was gone for more than a month. She had packed all her belongings, and gone into the wilderness. She went into the wilderness and sat down on a hilltop. Then, a coyote stopped at some distance from her. He stopped and kept staring at her for a while, then he left. The woman got up and followed him. He was on his way back to his den. He headed for an eroded hill. In it there was a hole [i.e., cave]. He went in. There also is a word for that kind of hole, but I don't remember it. The coyote went in, so she followed him inside. The coyote was not alone. A whole pack was living here together. But they didn't bother her in any way, nor bite her, nothing like that. She lived there with them. She always slept there, and in the morning, when she woke up, they were gone. Sometimes, when they came back, they brought some meat. And many times they dropped it in front of her. Then she would slice it with the knife she had with her and dry it. When she had dried meat for quite a while, she had plenty of it. Since she lived with them for a while, she began to understand their language. By then she had made a lot of jerky. She had enough to fill a sack. One time one of them left, and when he came back, he said: "Grandmother, tomorrow you will have to get ready, we will take you to a certain place. On the other side of this hill your people have arrived, they are camping there. We will take you there." That morning she must have recovered from her pouting, and more than one month had passed. So she got herself ready, took her jerky sack, grabbed her cane, and went with them. One of them was leading. He stopped on the hilltop, and stood looking down. She climbed the hill and went toward them [the coyotes]. She stopped beside them, and right down below, her people had arrived. They were camping in a circle. They were camping a little ways away from the campsite she had disappeared from. They had moved a little, but they were still camping close to the old campsite. They [the coyotes] knew that they [the people] were moving about. So they took her there, to the hill. From there she went on alone, carrying her belongings, and went back to the camp. She went back, and as she was approaching, all the women came running, hugged her, held her, and cried. In the old times, when someone disappeared and came back, people always hugged that person and cried when they saw him or her again. That is what they did. That is the end [of the story].

5.6. The Horse Thief

FLORINE RED EAR HORSE

Tape recorded November 1, 1995

ho *hehą́l* *wąží* *obláki̜-kte* *ki* *hé* *thóka* *kihą,* *Psáloka*
well then one tell.1SG.AG-FUT DEF that enemy DEF Crow

kihą, *hą'íyokpazi̜* *na* *mni'ózą-zą* *chą́* *héchel* *Lakhóta* *wichóthi*
DEF nighttime and drizzle-RED then so Lakota camp.N

ki *echétkiya* *šųg-mánų* *a-'ú-pi* *kéye.* *yųkhą́* *waná*
DEF toward horse-steal COLL-come-PL QT then now

Lakhóta *ki* *slolyá-pi* *cha* *wíchoką* *są́m* *hiyáye* *héhą́ni*
Lakota DEF know-PL so noon* more pass.VI at that time

i-glú-wi̜yeya-pi *kéye.* *chąsákala* *naksá-ksa-pi* *na*
ST-POSS.INS-ready-PL QT stick* break with foot-RED-PL and

thimá *é-ki-gle-pi* *na* *šų́ka* *hé* *kašká* *thimá* *é-ki-gle-pi.*
inside L-PSS-put-PL and dog that tie inside L-PSS-put-PL

nahą́ *héchel* *iyúha* *echą́ni* *héchel* *wóta-pi* *na* *waná*
and then so all early so eat.NSP.PAT-PL and now

éyųka-pi *kéye.* *yųkhą́* *héchecha-kte* *k'ų* *waná* *šųk'ákąyąka*
go to sleep-PL QT then like that-FUT SYP now rider*

wą *ú* *kéye.* *ú* *cha* *óthąi̜* *kéye.* *yųkhą́* *ú* *na*
IDF.SG come QT come so visible QT then come and

héchena *lé* *thípi* *ki* *lél* *isákhib* *hináži̜* *cha* *óthąi̜* *kéye.* *ho*
thus this tipi DEF here beside stop LK visible QT well

héchel khoškálaka wą hé thípi ki hél thumá yąké ki hé
so young man LK that tipi DEF there inside sit DEF that

mázawakhą́ wą yuhá kéye. ho ehą́ni wašícu ób
gun* IDF.SG have QT well long ago white man with

héchel kholá-kichi-ya-pi hená táku-ku wa-há yuhá-pi
so friend-REC-have as-PL those what-RED NSP.PAT-skin have-PL

hená glo'í-pi chą́ į́š eyá ichí-c'u-ya mázawakhą́
those POSS.take to-PL then also REC-give-ADV gun*

iyópheya-pi na'į́š táku wichá-k'u-pi chą́ į́š eyá óštą
buy-PL and what 3PL.PAT-give-PL then also in place of

takų́l héchel wichá-k'u-pi kéye. hé é cha ų́
something so 3PL.PAT-give-PL QT that IP QL because of

mázawakhą́ ki lená yuhá-pi kéye. yųkhą́ sú ki okšú na
gun* DEF these have-PL QT then bullet DEF load and

tuktél hinážį ki a'íyopteya apáha na héchel uthá yųkhą́ ho
where stop DEF opposite aim at and so shoot then well

thóka wą hé lazáta-kiya hįȟpáya kéye. ho kat'íyeya
enemy IDF.SG that behind-to fall QT well kill by shooting

kéye. ho cha lé iną́pha-pi na wąyą́ka-pi yųkhą́ wąyą́ka-pi
QT well so this come out-PL and see-PL then see-PL

na ųmá hená áta o-wícha-ki-yaka-pi cha a-híhųni kéye.
and other those INT ST-3PL-BEN-tell-PL so COLL-arrive QT

yųkhą́ wąží héchel lé Psáloka hécha cha oyáka kéye. o'ígluze
then one so this Crow COP LK tell QT clothing

tháwa	*echíyatahą*	*héchel*	*Psáloka*	*héchel*	*tha-wókhoyake*	*hécha*	*cha*
his	from there	so	Crow	so	ALP-regalia	such	QL

khoyáka	*kéye.*	*yųkhą́*	*táku*	*wą*	*él*	*héchel*	*i-kázo-pi*	*kéye.*
wear	QT	then	things	IDF.SG	there	so	L-mark-IPS	QT

yųkhą́	*tób*	*héchel*	*i-kázo-pi*	*na*	*icí-zaptą*	*ki*	*hé*	*glakį́yą*
then	four	so	L-mark-IPS	and	ORD-five	DEF	that	across

i-kázo-kte	*éyaš*	*hé*	*i-kázo-šni*	*yųkhą́*	*hé*	*é*	*cha*	*hé*	*hąhépi*
L-mark-FUT	but	that	L-mark-NEG	then	that	IP	QL	that	night

kihą	*šų́kawakhą́*	*wąží*	*icú*	*kihą*	*ho*	*hé*	*glakį́yą*
DEF	horse*	IDF.SG	take	when	well	that	across

i-glázo-kta	*cha*	*héchų*	*éyaš*	*manų́-šni*	*hą́ni*	*héchel*
L-POSS.mark-FUT	so	do that	but	steal-NEG	before	so

katʼíyeya-pi	*kéye.*	*ho*	*héchel*	*Lakhóta*	*hená*	*átaya,*
kill by shooting-IPS	QT	well	so	Lakota	those	all

wicháša,	*ho*	*hená*	*a-hí*	*na*	*héchel*	*wókhoyake*	*tháwa*
man	well	those	COLL-come	and	so	outfit	his

hená	*wąžígži*	*khí-pi*	*na*	*héchel*	*hená*	*icú-pi*	*kéye.*	*hená*
those	some	take from-PL	and	so	those	take-PL	QT	those

yuhá-pi-kta	*cha*	*icú-pi*	*kéye.*	*ho*	*hé*	*į́š eyá*	*akhé*	*thóka,*
have-PL-FUT	so	take-PL	QT	well	that	also	again	enemy

Psáloka	*ki,*	*ąpétu*	*lehą́l*	*wichóȟʼą*	*ki*	*hé*	*ši-kí-gla-pi*
Crow	DEF	day	now	deed	DEF	that	ST-PSS-hate-PL

nachéce.	*ho*	*héchel*	*hé*	*kiksúya-pi*	*škhé.*	*hehą́yą.*
perhaps	well	so	that	remember-PL	QT	that is all

The one [story] I will tell, then, is about how the enemies, the Crow, came to steal horses in a Lakota camp, in the night and in drizzling rain. However, the Lakota knew that. They had already made preparations in the afternoon. They had broken off twigs [for firewood] and had put them in the tipis [so nobody would have to leave the camp], and had brought the dogs inside and tied them [to poles]. They had all eaten early and gone to rest. As expected, now a rider came. It was obvious when he came [from the sound his horse made]. He came and stopped next to a tipi, clearly noticeable. The young man who was sitting in that tipi had a gun. In the old times people took whatever types of hides they had to the white men they were friends with. They traded them for guns; for whatever goods they gave away, they received something in return. For that reason, they had guns. So he [the young man] loaded a bullet and aimed straight at where he [the rider] had stopped. He fired, and the enemy fell backwards. He had killed him. They [the inhabitants of the village] came out [of their tipis] and looked. They looked and told the others [what had happened], so they came there [to the place where the enemy had been shot]. One said that this was a Crow. Judging by his clothing, what he wore was a Crow regalia. There were marks [on his shirt, signifying stolen horses]. There were four marks, and he was going to add the fifth mark [that night], but he didn't [get a chance to] add that mark. That night, when he would have taken a horse, he would have added the mark. He would have done that, but before he could steal it he was killed. The Lakota, the men, came and removed some pieces of clothing from him and took them. They wanted to own them, that's why they took them. Again, this deed is one of those that the enemies, the Crow, may resent to this day. This is the way people remember it. That is all.

5.7. Adultery

FLORINE RED EAR HORSE

Tape recorded November 1, 1995

lehą́l	*wichó'oyake*	*wąží*	*obláki̜-kte.*	*yųkhą́*	*ehą́ni*	*oyáte*
now	story	IDF.SG	tell.1SG.AG-FUT	then	long ago	people

kihą	*tąyą́*	*ų́-pi*	*ų.*	*tuwá*	*thawícuthų*	*na*	*thiwáhe*	*yąká*
DEF	well	be-PL	ASS	someone	marry*	and	family	be

chą́-šna	*líla*	*héchel*	*the-kíchi-ȟila-pi*	*na*	*tąyą́*	*ų́-pi*	*yųkhą́*
then-HAB	INT	so	ST-REC-love.VT-PL	and	well	be-PL	then

wicháša	*ki*	*lé*	*tha-wícu*	*ki*	*ųgnáhelakha*	*tókhaȟ'ą*	*kéye.*	*cha*
man	DEF	this	ALP-wife	DEF	suddenly	disappear	QT	so

héchel	*i-kí-gni*	*nahą́*	*éyaš*	*iyé-ki-ye-šni*	*kéye.*
so	ST-PSS-go after	and then	but	ST-PSS-find-NEG	QT

i-kí-gni	*na*	*olé*	*éyaš*	*iyé-ki-ye-šni.*	*yųkhą́*	*waná*
ST-PSS-go after	and	seek	but	ST-PSS-find-NEG	then	now

nat'ų́gya	*kéye.*	*tókhiya*	*iyáye*	*kihą*	*hé*	*tóhąni*	*héchų-šni*
hesitate	QT	somewhere	go	DEF	that	never	do that-NEG

yųkhą́	*héchų*	*chąkhé*	*iyókiphi-šni*	*na*	*héchel*	*akhé*	*olé-kta*
then	do that	then	happy-NEG	and	so	again	seek-FUT

iyúkcą	*na*	*mázawakhą́*	*wą*	*i-kí-k-cu*	*kéye.*	*héchena*
think about	and	gun*	IDF.SG	ST-PSS-EI-take	QT	thus

yá kéye. yá yųkhą́ héchel manį́l šųkʔákąyąka nų́m
go QT go then so in the wilderness rider* two

yá-pi kéye. yųkhą́ tha-wícu ki hé ųmá kéye. na ųmá
go-PL QT then ALP-wife DEF that one of them QT and other

héchel wicháša kéye. yųkhą́ héchel líla chązéka ų́ héchel
so man QT then so INT angry because of so

wicháša ki lé katʔíyeya kéye. ho na hehą́l tha-wícu
man DEF this kill by shooting QT well and then ALP-wife

ki katʔíyeya kéye. ho hé chązéka ų́ ho hé
DEF kill by shooting QT well that angry because of well that

hél táku tha-wícu echų́ ki hé wąglákį na iyókiphi-šni ki
there what ALP-wife do DEF that POSS.see and happy-NEG SYP

ų́ wichóȟʔą ki léchų kéye. ho hehą́yela hé
because of deed DEF do this QT well that is all that

oyáka-pi.
tell-IPS

Now I will tell a story. The old-time folks had a good life. When somebody got married and started a family there was much mutual love, and people had a good life. One time a certain man's wife suddenly disappeared. He went after her, but didn't find her. He went after her, and searched for her, but didn't find her. Then he had a suspicion. Going away was something she had never done before. Now she had done that, and he was unhappy. He considered looking for her again and took his gun. He went on his way. He went, and then there were two riders traveling in the wilderness. One of them was his wife. And the other one was a man. Since he was very furious, he killed the man. Then he killed his wife. Since he was furious because he had realized what his wife had done, and was hurt in his feelings, he committed this deed. This is all that people tell about it.

Jokes 6

6.1. The Holy Man

NEVA STANDING BEAR

Tape recorded November 16, 1994

lé wichó'oyake ki wakhąyeža ki lé ówehąhą w-óyaka-pi
this story DEF child DEF this for fun NSP.PAT-tell-PL

hécha cha lé hokšíla thokápha ki é cha oyákį na wį́yą
COP QL this boy eldest DEF IP QL tell LK woman

wą é na wichášа wą kichícha kéye cha yųkhą́ waná
IDF.SG IP and man IDF.SG together with QT so then now

w-óglaka-hą-pi yųkhą́ yąkáhelakha "wa-má-khą
NSP.PAT-POSS.tell-PRG-PL then suddenly ST-1SG.PAT-holy

yeló" eyá kéye. "wa-má-khą cha wa-kį́yą o-wá-kihi
ASS.M say QT ST-1SG.PAT-holy so 1SG.AG-fly ST-1SG.AG-can

yeló" eyá kéye. "wa-kį́yą o-wá-kihi yeló" eyá kéye cha
ASS.M say QT 1SG.AG-fly ST-1SG.AG-can ASS.M say QT so

"wą-má-yąka yó" eyá kéye. chąkhé lé mayá kaksá-ksa-pi
ST-1SG.PAT-see IMP.SG.M say QT then this cliff cut-RED-IPS

cha kichí héchiya í na átaya waná kįyą́ iyáyį-kta cha iyópsica
QL with there go and INT now fly go-FUT so jump off

yųkhą́ kįyą́ okíhi-šni cha áta hukhúta oníya ka-thą́kal
then fly can-NEG so INT down breath INS-outside

hiyú-ya glihpáya kéye, chąkhé tha-wícu ki ektá é-tųwį
come-CAU fall down QT then ALP-wife DEF at L-look

nahą́ke "to-ní-ktuka hé?" eyá kéye, "to-ní-khašni
and then ST-2SG.PAT-how is it QS say QT ST-2SG.PAT-well

hé?" eyá yųkhą́ "iníla yąká yó. léchiya wakhą́-yą
QS say then silent sit IMP.SG.M here sacred-ADV

mųké" eyá kéye.
lie.1SG.AG say QT

This is the kind of story that the children tell for fun. This one was told by my oldest boy. There was a woman, and she was with a man. They were talking for a while, and all of a sudden he said: "I am holy. I am holy, and therefore I can fly. I can fly. Watch me." So she accompanied him to a steep cliff. Now he was going to fly, so he jumped off. He couldn't fly and dropped down below, which knocked the wind out of him. His wife looked at him and said: "How are you? Are you okay?" He replied: "Shut up. I'm lying here in a sacred manner."

Note: This joke alludes to the common idiom, "In a sacred manner I walk," which is used in the context of Native American spirituality.

6.2. The Turtle in the Microwave

NEVA STANDING BEAR

Tape recorded November 16, 1994

lé	*othų́wahe*	*thą́ka*	*cha*	*héchiya*	*ektá*	*Lakhóta*	*khoškálaka*	*nų́m*
this	city	big	QL	there	in	Lakota	young man	two

ų́-pi	*kéye.*	*yųkhą́*	*tákuni*	*lé*	*Lakhól-wichóȟˀą*	*hená*
be-PL	QT	then	nothing	that	Lakota-culture	those

slolyá-pi-šni	*chąkhé*	*ųmá*	*áta*	*makhú*	*yazą́*	*kéye.*	*makhú*
know-PL-NEG	then	one of them	INT	chest	hurt	QT	chest

yazą́	*na*	*thezí*	*khó*	*yazą́*	*chąkhé*	*othų́wahe*	*étkiya*	*yá-hą-pi*
hurt	and	stomach	also	hurt	then	city	toward	go-PRG-PL

kéye.	*yųkhą́*	*héyá*	*kéye*	*"tókheškhe*	*líla*	*o-má-phi-šni*
QT	then	say that	QT	somehow	INT	ST-1SG.PAT-feel well-NEG

kˀų"	*eyá*	*kéye.*	*"líla*	*thezí*	*ma-yázą*	*na*	*makhú*	*khó*
ASS	say	QT	INT	stomach	1SG.PAT-hurt	and	chest	also

ma-yázą"	*cha*	*yųkhą́*	*"wą́*	*lél*	*Lakhóta*	*wicháȟcala*	*wą*	*thí*
1SG.PAT-hurt	so	then	IJ.M	here	Indian	old man	IDF.SG	live

cha	*él*	*ų-yį́-kte*	*na*	*ųk-íyųǧį-kte*	*ho*	*na*	*takún*
so	to	DU.AG-go-FUT	and	DU.AG-ask-FUT	well	and	something

iyó-ni-cihi	*yuhá*	*séce"*	*eyá*	*kéye*	*chąkhé*	*aˀíyakapteya*
ST-2SG.PAT-help.VT	have	maybe	say	QT	then	uphill

yá-hą-pi nahą́ke waná lé wichášcala wą hél thí cha ektá
go-PRG-PL and then now this old man LK there live QL to

í-pi kéye. ho chąkhé “háo, tókha hųwó?” eyá kéye.
go-PL QT well then hallo what’s the matter QS.M say QT

“tókheškhe ták-eha-pi na ya-ˀú-pi hųwó?” eyá
how something-say.2AG-PL LK 2AG-come-PL QS.M say

chąkhé “hiyá, lé thezí yazą́ na makhú khó yazą́” kéyá
then no this stomach hurt and chest also hurt say that

cha “ųgná takún iyókihi cha ya-kˀú o-yá-kihi
so maybe something help.VT QL 2AG.SG-give ST-2SG.AG-can

séce ló” eyá yųkhą́ héyá kéye “wą́ khéya chąté cha
maybe ASS.M say then say that QT IJ.M turtle heart QL

yáte hą́tąhąš echél i-ní-yayį-kte ló” eyá kéye.
eat.2SG.AG when ST ST-1SG.PAT-get well-FUT ASS.M say QT

chąkhé “tuktél hé cha wąžígži ųk-óyuspa-pi-kte hé?” eyá
then where that QL some 1PL.AG-catch-PL-FUT QS say

yųkhą́ héyá kéye. “ho héhą wąží olúspa-pi hą́tąhąš ho
then say that QT well then one catch.2AG-PL when well

ya-kté-pi nahą́ ya-pháta-pi na chąté ki hé
2AG-kill-PL and then 2AG-butcher-PL and heart DEF that

ihˀą́-šni héchena yátį-kte ló” eyá kéye,
cook.VT-NEG still eat.2SG.AG-FUT ASS.M say QT

"na-ya-pcį-kte lő" eyá kéye. "ki
ST-2SG.AG-swallow-FUT ASS.M say QT in that case

echél i-ní-yayį-kte lő" eyá kéye. eyá chąkhé waná
ST ST-2SG.PAT-get well-FUT ASS.M say QT say then now

glinąpha-pi na chąkú ogná máni glá-hą-pi yųkhą́ léchel
come out-PL and road along walk go home-PRG-PL then so

chąkú ki glakįyą khéya wą hiyáya chąkhé héyá kéye "ho
road DEF across turtle IDF.SG go by then say that QT well

lé wąží hiyáya cha ųk-óyuspį-kte" eyá kéye chąkhé oyúspa-pi
this one go by so DU.AG-catch-FUT say QT then catch-PL

nahą́ke akhí-pi kéye. akhí-pi nahą́ke cha "wą́ lé
and then bring home-PL QT bring home-PL and then so IJ.M this

tókheškhe ų-kté-pi-kte kihą ųk-ó-ki-yaka-pi éyaschį
somehow 1PL.AG-kill-PL-FUT LK 1PL-ST-BEN-tell-IPS but

chéğa thą́ka ų-níca-pi cha tukténi thąkál
kettle big 1PL.PAT-lack-PL so nowhere outside

che-ˀų́-thi-pi ųk-ókihi-pi-šni cha tókheškhe
ST-1PL.AG-build a fire-PL 1PL.AG-can-PL-NEG so how

echų́kˀų-pi-kta hé?" yųkhą́ ųmá ki é cha "wą́
do.1PL.AG-PL-FUT QS then one of them DEF IP QL IJ.M

microwave wą ų-yúha-pi cha héchi mahél
microwave IDF.SG 1PL.AG-have-PL so there inside

iyé-ya-ye ki oȟʔą́kho-ya tʔá iyáyį-kte" eyá cha. eyá
ST-2SG.AG-send when fast-ADV die go-FUT say QL say

chąkhé "ohą́, cha héchųkʔų-pi-kte" nahą́ke lé khéya-la
then okay so do that.1PL.AG-PL-FUT and then this turtle-DIM

kʔų héchena ní kʔéyaš héchena lé microwave ki héchiya
DEF still live but still this microwave DEF there

pa-thímahel iyéya-pi kéye na thiyópa echél iyéya-pi chąkhé áta
INS-inside send-PL QT and door ST lock-PL then INT

mahél na-kʔéȟ-kʔeǧe éyaš thi-y-ų́ma-ta íyutaka-pi na TV
inside ST-RED-scratch but house-EI-other-in sit down-PL and TV

wąyą́g yaká-hą-pi kéye. yųkhą́ léchel tuwá katóto cha thiyópa
see sit-PRG-PL QT then so someone knock so door

yuǧą́-pi éyaš tuwénišni chąkhé "tuwá lé hí séce
open.VT-PL but nobody then someone this come maybe

éyaš" eyá-pi na yąká-hą-pi kéye. akhé thi-lázata thiyópa
but say-PL and sit-PRG-PL QT again house-behind door

ektá tuwá katóto cha ektá é-wąyąka-pi éyaš tuwénišni.
at somebody knock so at L-see-PL but nobody

chąkhé olólʔiȟʔą thimá anáǧoptą nážį-pi yųkhą́ akhé katóto
then kitchen inside listen stand-PL then again knock

kéye chąkhé katóto ki é cha owé othápha-pi yųkhą́ lé
QT then knock DEF IP QL track.N follow-PL then this

microwave	*etą́*	*cha*	*ú*	*chąkhé*	*“wą́*	*lé*	*khéya*	*wą*	*lél*
microwave	from	QL	come	then	IJ.M	this	turtle	LK	here

mahél	*iyé-ˀų-yą-pi*	*kˀų*	*hé*	*é*	*cha*	*na-kˀéȟ-kˀeğe*	*séca*
inside	ST-1PL.AG-send-PL	DEF	that	IP	QL	ST-RED-scratch	maybe

wą”	*eyá-pi*	*yųkhą́*	*thiyópa*	*ki*	*yuğą́*	*icú-pi*	*yųkhą́*	*echél*	*lé*
ASS	say-PL	then	door	DEF	open.VT	take-PL	then	so	this

khéya-la	*kˀų*	*hé*	*é*	*cha*	*khéya*	*há*	*ki*	*é*	*cha*
turtle-DIM	DEF	that	IP	QL	turtle	skin	DEF	IP	QL

aló-ki-ksohį	*na*	*hu-ká-ˀichi-cawįȟ*	*lé*	*thiyópa*	*ki*
ST-PSS-tuck under the arm	and	leg-INS-REC-bend.VI	this	door	DEF

él	*apúthag*	*ahíyokasˀį*	*hi-nážį*	*na*	*“mi-tákuye*
at	press against	come and look	come-stand	and	1SG.POR-relatives

oyásˀį”	*eyá*	*kéye.*	*“tókheškhe*	*ehą́ni-ȟci*
all	say	QT	somehow	for a long time-INT

luğą́-pi-šni,	*líla*	*o-kháta*	*škhá”*	*eyá*	*kéye.*
open.VT.2AG-PL-NEG	INT	L-hot	but	say	QT

“mi-tákuye	*oyásˀį.”*
1SG.POR-relatives	all

Two young Lakota men were living in a big city. They didn’t know anything about the Lakota culture. One of them got a very bad chest pain. His chest was hurting, and his stomach was also hurting. They were going downtown. He [the sick one] said: “Somehow I’m not feeling good at all. My stomach is hurting very much, and my chest is also hurting.” He [his friend] said: “There is an old Indian man, we’ll go to his house and ask him, maybe he has something that helps you." So they went up the hill and got to the old man's house. He said: "Hallo, what's the matter? What did you say brings you here?" He [the healthy one] said: "No [we didn't just come visiting], his stomach hurts and his chest also hurts. Maybe you can give him something that helps." He [the old man] replied: "Well, if you eat a turtle's heart you'll get well again." He [the young man] asked: "Where can we catch some?" He [the old man] gave them instructions. Then he said: "When you catch one, kill it, butcher it, and eat the heart uncooked. Swallow it. You'll be alright." When he had said that they left and went back on the road. Then, a turtle was passing by, crossing the road. They said: "There is one passing by! Let's catch it!" So they caught it and took it home. They took it home and then started wondering: "We were told to kill it somehow, but we don't have a big bucket and there is no place outside where we can build a fire, so what should we do?" Then one of them suggested: "Well, we have a microwave, when you put it in there it will die quickly." He [the other one] agreed: "Okay, we'll do that." The poor little turtle was still alive, but they put it in the microwave. They locked the door, and it started scratching a lot in there, but they sat down in another room and watched TV for a while. Then somebody was knocking, so they opened the door, but there was nobody. They said: "Maybe someone has come." They sat down again. Again somebody was knocking at the door in the back of the house. They looked there, but there was nobody. Then they were standing in the kitchen, listening, and the knocking sound was there again. They followed the knocking sound, and it came from the microwave. They said: "Maybe the turtle we put in there is scratching." They opened the door, and there was the turtle. It had taken off its shell, carrying it under its arm, and had crossed its legs and was looking out, leaning against the door. It was standing there, looking out, and said: "All my relatives. For some reason you didn't open for a very long time, it was very hot in here. All my relatives."

Note: Whenever people are entering or leaving the sweatlodge, they say *mithákuye oyás'į* 'all my relatives', which means, "We are all brothers and sisters."

6.3. The Wrong Answer

FLORINE RED EAR HORSE

Tape recorded September 1, 1995

ho lé į́š wichóˀoyake kihą wichášą wą akícita ópha kéye.
well this it story DEF man IDF.SG soldier join QT

nahą́ waníyetu yámni akícita kéye. ho na waná wikcémna
and then year three soldier QT well and now ten

šákpe są́m záptą hi-náží̜ kéye yųkhą́ wóˀokiye
six more five come-stand QT then pension

icˀí-la-kta cha waná yį́-kta cha héchel i-glú-wį̜yeya
3RFL-ask for-FUT so now go-FUT so so ST-POSS.INS-ready

kéye. yųkhą́ hé i-yá-ksapa-pi kéye. "ho lé ya-ˀí kihą
QT then that L-INS-wise-PL QT well this 2SG.AG-go to when

thokáheya wichóˀiye wąží i-ní-yųǧa-pi-kta cha 'ho hé
first word IDF.SG ST-2SG.PAT-ask-PL-FUT so well that

waníyetu tóna akícita o-yá-pha hé?' eyá-pi kihą
year how many soldier ST-2SG.AG-join QS say-PL when

'three" eyá yó' eyá kéye, 'hé waníyetu yámni yeló' eyá
three say IMP.SG.M say QT that year three ASS.M say

kéye. ho na hehą́l íyokhihe ki hé į́š 'waníyetu
QT well and then next DEF that it year

toná-ni-kheca hųwó?' eyá-pi-kta cha ho hé
ST-2SG.PAT-how many QS.M say-PL-FUT so well that

'sixty-five' eyá yó, 'waná waníyetu hená-ma-kheca'
sixty-five say IMP.SG.M now year ST-1SG.PAT-so many

eyá kéye. "thó" eyá kéye, "tókša hé ephį́-kte ló"
say QT alright say QT just wait that say.1SG.AG-FUT ASS.M

eyá kéye. waná yį́ na ektá í yųkhą́ wašícu wą hé waná
say QT now go and there go then white man LK that now

wóˀiyųğe wą k'ú ki hé thokáheya tuwá hé waná akícita
question IDF.SG give DEF that first who that now soldier

ópha ki hé waníyetu tónakheca ópha ki hé iyų́ğį-kte sˀe
join DEF that year how many join LK that ask-FUT like.AV

léchecha yųkhą́ thokáheya héchel "waníyetu toná-ni-kheca
like this then first so year ST-2SG.PAT-how many

hųwó?" eyá kéye. yųkhą́ "waná waníyetu yámni
QS.M say QT then now year three

hená-ma-kheca yeló" eyá kéye. "three" eyá kéye. ho
ST-1SG.PAT-so many ASS.M say QT three say QT well

hehą́l "waníyetu tóna akícita o-yá-pha hųwó?" eyá
then year how many soldier ST-2SG.AG-join QS.M say

yųkhą́ "sixty-five" eyá kéye. ho hé ųmáchetkiya eyá iyų́ğa
then sixty-five say QT well that the other way say ask

cha "sixty-five" eyá yųkhą́ líla-ȟci ayúta nahą́ke hé eyá kéye,
so sixty-five say then INT-INT look at and then that say QT

wašícu ki "who's crazy, you or me?" eyá kéye. "tuwá
white man DEF who's crazy, you or me? say QT who

witkó-tko-ka hųwó, niyé naˀįš tókha miyé hé?" eyá yųkhą́
crazy-RED-kind of QS.M you or maybe I QS say then

"both" eyá kéye. "ho hé nakų́ wóˀiyųǧe wą eyé ki hé
both say QT well that also question LK say DEF that

'tukté ųmá ya-chį́ hųwó, hayápi naˀį́š mázaska?' ehą́tąhąš
which one 2SG.AG-want QS.M clothes or money* when

'both' eyá yő" héyá kéye. ho tókhįš héyį́-kte
both say IMP.SG.M say that QT well FASS say that-FUT

sˀe léchecha yųkhą́ ipáyeȟ w-íyųǧa cha
like.AV like this then wrong NSP.PAT-ask so

"who's crazy, you or me?" eyá yųkhą́ "both" eyá kéye.
who's crazy, you or me say then both say QT

This story is about a man who had been in the military service. He had served for three years. Now he had reached the age of sixty-five, so he was going to ask for his pension. He was getting ready to leave. People instructed him [on what to say, since he didn't speak English]. One guy said: "When you go there they will first ask you a question. When they say: 'How many years have you been in the service?' say: 'Three. Three years.' The next thing they will say is: 'How old are you?' Say: 'Sixty-five. Now I am that old.'" "Alright," he replied. "I will say that." He went and arrived at his destination. He expected that the white man who asked him the questions would first ask those who had joined the service for how many years they had joined the service. But he [the white man] first said: "How old are you?" He replied: "Now I am three years old. Three." Then he [the white man] said: "How many years have you been in the service?" He replied: "Sixty-five." He asked him the other way around, so he said "Sixty-five." Then the white man looked at him with big eyes and said: "Who's crazy, you or me?" He replied: "Both." He had also been told: "When there is the question 'What do you want, clothes or money?' say 'Both.'" [In the old times people had that choice.] He had assumed that he [the white man] was going to say that, but he asked him the wrong question; he said: "Who's crazy, you or me?" That's why he said: "Both."

6.4. Red Holy Dog

FLORINE RED EAR HORSE

Tape recorded September 1, 1995

ho	*ehą́ni*	*oyáte*	*kihą*	*líla-ȟci*	*héchel*	*wašícu*	*iyá-pi-šni.*
well	old time	people	DEF	INT-INT	so	white man	speak-PL-NEG

yųkhą́	*átaye-la*	*wašícu*	*iyá*	*okíhi-pi-šni*	*cha*	*wicháša itháchą*
then	INT-DIM	white man	speak	can-PL-NEG	so	chief

wą	*wašícu*	*wą*	*kichí*	*w-óglakį-kta*	*cha*	*lé*
IDF.SG	white man	IDF.SG	with	NSP.PAT-POSS.tell-FUT	so	this

hąkéke	*slolyá*	*cha*	*iyé-kici-ska*	*chį́*	*nahą́ke*	*"ho*	*hiyú*
this and that	know	so	ST-BEN-interpret*	want	and then	well	come

wó,	*iyé-miye-ci-ska*	*yó,*	*wašícu*	*ki*	*lé*	*kichí*
IMP.SG.M	ST-1SG-BEN-interpret*	IMP.SG.M	white man	DEF	this	with

w-ó-wa-glakį-kta	*cha"*	*eyá*	*kéye.*	*ho*	*hé*
NSP.PAT-ST-1SG.AG-POSS.tell-FUT	QL	say	QT	well	that

šų́kawakhą́	*wą*	*gnúni*	*cha*	*hé*	*é*	*cha*	*ų́*	*w-íyųǧa*
horse*	IDF.SG	lose	so	that	IP	QL	because of	NSP.PAT-ask

chį́	*nahą́ke*	*héyá*	*kéye*	*"ho*	*o-mí-ci-yaka*	*yó,*
want	and then	say that	QT	well	ST-1SG-BEN-tell	IMP.SG.M

thakóža,	*'owákpamni*	*ki*	*lé*	*thoká*	*íyutaka*	*héhą*	*šų́kawakhą́*
grandchild	agency*	DEF	this	first	sit down	then	horse*

wą hį-ša cha wa-gnúni yelő' eyá kéye, "hé o-mí-ci-yaka
LK fur-red QL 1SG.AG-lose ASS.M say QT that ST-1SG-BEN-tell

yő" eyá kéye. yųkhą́ iyéska ki héyá kéye,
IMP.SG.M say QT then interpreter* DEF say that QT

"when the first agency sit down he lost a red holy dog." hé wašícu
when the first agency sit down he lost a red holy dog that white man

iyá iyé-kici-ska ki hé įšé hé wó'iȟaka hécha. eyá
speak ST-BEN-interpret* DEF that just that funny story COP say

ognáye-ȟci yu-'íyeska ki hé é cha lé obláke
according to-INT INS-interpret* DEF that IP QL this tell.1SG.AG

wó'iȟaka hécha. tuktógna ipáyeȟ eyį́-kte s'e
funny story COP somehow the wrong way say-FUT like.AV

léchecha yųkhą́ héchų s'e iwáyuphiya o-kíci-yaka cha lé
like this then that way* in a funny way* ST-BEN-tell QL this

obláke.
tell.1SG.AG

The old-time folks didn't have any knowledge of the white man's language. They couldn't speak it at all. One time a chief wanted to talk to a white man. He wanted another man who knew it [the language] in part to interpret for him. He said: "Come, interpret for me, I will talk to the white man." He had lost a horse. This was the reason why he wanted to ask around. He said: "Say for me, grandson, 'Where the agency was first located, there I lost a sorrel horse.' Say that for me." The interpreter said: "When the first agency sit down, he said he lost a red holy dog." [This is a possible translation of the original Lakota sentence.] The way he translated for him into English made a funny story. What he [the chief] had him [the interpreter] translate exactly as he had said, as I have reproduced it, makes a funny story. Somehow he must have said it the wrong way; I have imitated his funny way of saying it in this story.

Miscellaneous 7

7.1. Tanning Hides (Modern Version)

NEVA STANDING BEAR

Tape recorded September 9, 1994

ho lé thahá-kpąyą-pi ki lé é cha lehą́n lechála
well this hide-tan-IPS DEF this IP QL now recent

wichóˀichaǧe ki lená thahá ki hé yuzíl okátą-pi na
generation DEF these hide DEF that stretch pin down-IPS and

átaya lé iyéchįkyąke wígli sápa kapˀóžela hécha cha icú-pi
INT this car* oil black light weight such QL take-IPS

na átaya ų́ sla-yá-pi nahą́ kaȟlóg iyáye-šni
and INT with greasy-CAU-PL and then penetrate go-NEG

hą́tahąš akhé iyų́-pi na ho hé kaȟlóg iyáya hą́tahąš
if again apply-IPS and well that penetrate go when

lé haˀíyužaža hécha cha ektá haˀípažaža o-ˀíȟpeya-pi na
this washing machine* such QL in soap* L-throw-IPS and

icáhi yužáža-pi na yuškíca-pi nahą́ ho hená hehą́n
mix wash-IPS and wring out-IPS and then well those then

yuȟų́ta-pi chą́-šna líla yu-phí-ya-šna yuȟų́ta-pi. cha į́š hé
soften-IPS then-HAB INT INS-good-ADV-HAB soften-PL so it that

lechála wóˀechų. na hená lé phežíkakse ki lená
recent procedure and those this sickle* DEF these

hécha-šni-yą, hená lé haˀíyotke ki lécha cha yugmų́-pi na
such-NEG-ADV those this clothesline* DEF such QL twist-IPS and

máza ȟóta hécha cha yugmų́-pi na okáȟtag-ya lé
aluminum* such QL twist-IPS and sag-ADV this

otké-ya-pi chą́-šna héchel echų́ hená yuȟų́ta-pi chą́-šna
hang.VI-CAU-IPS then-HAB so do those soften-IPS then-HAB

phąphą́yela hiną́phe. na eháni hená táku ki waníca cha
soft come out and long ago those things DEF lack so

tuwéni hená héchų-he-šni. éyaš lehą́n hená táku ki
nobody those do that-PRG-NEG but now those things DEF

iyúha-ȟci yukhé cha. įšé lehą́n táku echų́-pi ki oȟˀą́kho-kho-ya
all-INT exist QL just now things do-IPS DEF fast-RED-ADV

waˀéchų-pi.
NSP.PAT-do-IPS

As for tanning hides, people of today's generation stake the hides down tight. They take motor oil, the black, light-weight type, and grease it [the hide] with it. If it doesn't get absorbed, it is applied again. When it is absorbed, people put some soap in the washing machine and wash it [the soap and the hide] together. Then they wring it [the hide] out. Then it is softened, softened thoroughly. That's the modern way of doing it. It [the softening] is not done with the sickle [blade], but rather, with a twisted clothesline, an aluminum [clothesline] which is twisted and made to hang loosely. When it is rubbed, it ends up soft. In the old times, people didn't have such things, so nobody did that [with these tools]. But today all those things are available. Everything people do today they do very quickly.

Note: An aluminum clothesline is twisted into a rope about three feet long. Each end is bent into a loop. Strings are attached to these loops, and then the rope fastened to a tree or pole. The wire is not pulled tight but rather sags a little bit. The moist hide is pulled back and forth over the wire construction until it is dry and soft. This procedure may take hours depending on the size and thickness of the hide.

7.2. Fry Bread

NEVA STANDING BEAR

Tape recorded October 31, 1994

įšé lená lechála Lakhóta kihą aǧúyapi blú nahą́
just these recently Indian DEF flour* and then

wínakapo na wígli ki lená wichá-k'u-pi k'ų
baking powder* and shortening DEF these 3PL.PAT-give-IPS when

héhą lená aǧúyapi ki kaȟ-wáyuphika-pi. cha héhą įšé
then these bread* DEF make-skillful*-PL so then maybe

wašícu eyá wašícu hį-šmá e-wícha-ki-ya-pi cha hená
white man LK white man hairy* ST-3PL-BEN-say-IPS QL those

aǧúyapi káǧa-pi cha hená ųspé-wicha-khiya-pi cha hé
bread* make-IPS QL those know-3PL.PAT-CAU-PL so that

ų́ hená héchel káǧa-pi éyaš isą́m iyé iyáya-pi nahą́
because of those so make-PL but more they go-PL and then

wígli ų́ káǧa-pi. cha hé thokéya aǧúyapi káǧa-pi ki hé
fry bread* make-PL so that first bread* make-IPS SYP that

wašícu hįšmá ki lená aǧúyapi paská-pi na maswíche'ųpe
white man hairy* DEF these dough* knead-PL and skillet*

šóka cha ektá mahél iyéya-pi na íyakaȟpe thų́-pi na
thick QL in inside send-PL and lid* apply-PL and

a-chéthi-pi hą́tąhąš lé ağúyapi ki napóğe. na
L-build a fire-PL when this bread* DEF swell and

ithánųg ği-yéla špą́ chą́-šna yuksá-ksa icú yúta-pi.
on both sides brown-ADV cooked then-HAB cut-RED take eat-IPS

ho éyaš lé Lakhóta ki iyáya-pi na lé wígli ų́ káğa-pi.
well but this Indian DEF go-PL and this fry bread* make-PL

ağúyapi blú tókhi napé-y-ožula šákpe akhígle o-yá-gnakį-kte
flour* about hand-EI-full six times L-2SG.AG-put-FUT

nahą́ akhé wínakapo kihą tókhi napé-y-ožula-šni-ya
and then again baking powder* DEF about hand-EI-full-NEG-ADV

iyókhiseyela i-yá-cu na él o-yá-kala-kte.
half ST-2SG.AG-take and there ST-2SG.AG-pour in-FUT

nahą́ asą́pi blú ki hé nape-y-ožula nahą́ napéphįkpa
and then milk powder DEF that hand-EI-full and then pinch

mniskúya o-yá-kala-kte. ho nahą́ chąhą́pi ki líla
salt ST-2SG.AG-pour in-FUT well and then sugar* DEF INT

cónala į́š i-cáhi-ya-yį-kte, napéphįkpa nų́m wa-hénakecha
few it L-ST-2SG.AG-mix-FUT pinch two NSP.PAT-enough

o-yá-kala-kte. héchena áta i-ˀícahi-ya-yį-kte nahą́
ST-2SG.AG-pour in-FUT thus all L-ST-2SG.AG-mix-FUT and then

mní sní-šni-ya-kel. mní ki kitą́la a-khál-ya-ke
water cold-NEG-CAU-kind of water DEF a little L-hot-CAU-kind of

sˀe, líla kháte-šni éyaš mní etą́ iwášˇtela
like.AV INT hot-NEG but water PART slowly

khal-yá-yį-kte na él o-yá-kašˇtą-kte. héchanų
hot-2SG.AG-CAU-FUT and there L-2SG.AG-pour-FUT do that.2SG.AG

na icáhi-ya-yį na tohą́n lé ağúyapi blú ki są́m šóka
and ST-2SG.AG-mix and then this flour* DEF more thick

áye hą́tąhąš ya-pá-tˀįzį-kte. napé ų́ ya-pá-tˀįzį na
PRC when 2SG.AG-INS-tight-FUT hand with 2SG.AG-INS-tight and

ho luksį na ağúyapi ipáblaye ų́ ya-pá-blayį
well cut.2SG.AG and rolling pin* with 2SG.AG-INS-flat

nahą́ míla ų́ wa-yá-ksa-ksa na lé wígli ki
and then knife with ST-2SG.AG-cut-RED and this shortening DEF

lé khal-ˀíluthį na kháte hą́tąhąš ektá o-ˀíȟpe-ya-yį
this hot-try.2SG.AG and hot when in L-ST-2SG.AG-throw

nahą́ ųmáchiyatą waná ğí hą́tąhąš ho luptą́yį
and then on one side now brown when well turn over.2SG.AG

nahą́ ğí áye hą́tąhąš ithánųgya ákhilehąyą
and then brown become when on both sides alike

yu-phí-ya napóğį na šˇpą́. cha hená héchų sˀe ağúyapi,
INS-good-ADV swell and cooked so those that way* bread*

wígli ų́ káğapi, káğa-pi. naˀį́š nakų́ wąží thąkál chethí-pi
fry bread* make-IPS or also one outside build a fire-IPS

héchel	*ya-káğį-kte.*	*nakų́*	*wąží*	*cha*	*hé*	*ağúyapi*	*chokˀį́*
so	2SG.AG-make-FUT	also	one	so	that	bread*	bake

káğa-pi	*eyá-pi.*	*cha*	*hé*	*į́š eyá*	*ağúyapi*	*ki*	*ya-páska*
make-IPS	say-IPS	so	that	also	dough*	DEF	2SG.AG-knead

nahą́	*lé*	*maswícheˀųpe*	*héchacha*	*ektá*	*iwáštegla*	*wígli*
and then	this	skillet*	like that	in	well	shortening

i-yá-kathąthą	*na*	*o-yá-gnakį*	*na*	*ya-pá-blaye*	*hą́tąhąš—*
ST-2SG.AG-rub on	and	L-2SG.AG-put	and	2SG.AG-INS-flat	when

napé	*ų́*	*ya-pá-blaye*	*hą́tąhąš—*	*na*	*íyakaȟpe*	*ya-thų́*
hand	with	2SG.AG-INS-flat	when	and	lid*	2SG.AG-apply

ki	*hé*	*napóğį*	*nahą́*	*ųmáchiyatąhą*	*ğí*	*ki*	*ho*
when	those	swell	and then	on one side	brown	when	well

akhé	*luptą́yį*	*na*	*íyakaȟpe*	*ya-thų́*	*ya-glé*	*na*
again	turn over.VT.2SG.AG	and	lid*	apply	2SG.AG-put	and

iwáštegla	*wígli*	*él*	*o-yá-gnakį-kte*	*hą́tąhąš*	*yu-phí-ya*
well	shortening	there	L-2SG.AG-put-FUT	when	INS-good-ADV

ithánųgya	*ği-yéla*	*špą́.*	*cha*	*hená*	*chokˀį́*	*ağúyapi*	*eyá*
on both sides	brown-ADV	cooked	so	those	bake	bread*	say

cažéyata-pi.	*hená*	*Lakhóta*	*ki*	*káğa-pi.*	*kštó.*
call-IPS	those	Indian	DEF	make-PL	ASS.F

When the Indians, in the recent past, received flour, baking powder, and shortening, they became expert at making bread. It is possible that some white men who go by the name of "hairy white men" [traders] taught them how to make bread. This may be why they make it at all, but they themselves went [one step further] and made fry bread. As the first step in making bread, the traders kneaded the dough, put it into a thick skillet, and covered [it] with a lid. When it was being baked this bread rose. And when it was baked brown on both sides it was cut into pieces and eaten. The Indians went and made fry bread. Put about six handfuls of flour [in a pan], one after the other, and then take, approximately, less than half a handful of baking powder and add it. Then add a handful of powdered milk and a pinch of salt. Then mix in very little sugar. If you add two pinches this will be enough. Mix all that together. Then heat water until it is lukewarm. If you heat the water slightly it will not be too hot. Heat some water slowly and pour it on. Do that and mix it [with the dry ingredients]. When the flour becomes thicker, knead it. Knead it with the hands and cut it. Roll it out with a rolling pin. Cut it into small pieces with a knife. Check the temperature of the shortening [that you have heated in a skillet], and when it is hot, put it in. When it is brown on one side, turn it over. When it becomes brown it rises pretty much on both sides. Then it is done. That way bread, fry bread, is made. Another type [of bread] you make by building a fire outside. Yet another type [of bread] is called "baked bread." You also knead the dough, then rub a skillet well with grease, put it in, and when you have rolled it out—when you have rolled it out with your hands—and when you have put a lid on, it rises. When it is brown on one side you turn it over again and put the lid on. When you cover it well with shortening, it cooks until it is well browned on both sides. This is called baked bread. It is made by the Indians. That's how it is.

7.3. Indian Christmas Tree

NEVA STANDING BEAR

Tape recorded November 16, 1994

yųkhą́ lé chą́ wazíȟąte thą́ka héchacha hená eyášna kaksá-pi
then this tree evergreen* big that kind those always cut-IPS

na tohą́n Waníkiya Thų́-pi Ąpétu chą́-šna hená owáchekiye él
and when Savior* Birthday* then-HAB those church in

é-gle-pi na wóšpi-pi. ho cha lé owáchekiye ki lé
L-put-IPS and pick.NSP.PAT-IPS well so this church DEF this

Lakhóta owáchekiye cha oyáte ki hél wachékhiye ya-pi na
Indian church so people DEF there pray go-PL and

tuwé kʔéyaš hél ya-pi nahą́ wachékhiya-pi. táku oyáte
whoever there go-PL and then pray-PL what people

kʔéyaš. cha hená hí-pi na tohą́n chą́ ki lé waná
ever so those come-PL and when tree DEF this now

kaksá-pi-kte hą́tąhąš ȟé ektá yá-pi nahą́ chąlí waphá́ȟta
cut-IPS-FUT when mountain to go-PL and then tobacco tie*

na chąlí héchiya é-gle-pi chą́-šna hé chą́ ki hé
and tobacco there L-put-PL then-HAB that tree DEF that

kaȟníǧa-pi na ohómni chąlí hená é-gnaka-pi na
choose-PL and around tobacco those L-place-PL and

wachékhiya-pi.	*na*	*chąnúpa*	*yuhá*	*wachékhiya-pi*	*nahą́*
pray-PL	and	pipe	have	pray-PL	and then

hokšíla	*wąží*	*naʔį́š*	*wichį́cala*	*wąží*	*kichí*	*iyáya-pi*	*na*
boy	IDF.SG	or	girl	IDF.SG	with	go-PL	and

kahų́-pi.	*hená*	*wakhą́*	*wichá-la-pi*	*cha*	*hená*
mark by striking-PL	those	sacred	3PL.PAT-consider-IPS	so	those

iyáya-pi	*nahą́*	*chą́*	*ki*	*hé*	*kahų́-pi*	*hą́tąhąš*	*ho*
go-PL	and then	tree	DEF	that	mark by striking-PL	when	well

hé	*íyohakab*	*chą́*	*ki*	*lé*	*kaʔų́ka-pi*	*na*	*makhá*	*ektá*
that	after	tree	DEF	this	fell-PL	and	ground	on

i-y-ápha-šni-yą	*iwą́kab*	*yúza-pi*	*na*	*akhíyuha*	*aglíyacu-pi*	*cha*
L-EI-hit-NEG-ADV	above	hold-PL	and	lift up	bring home-PL	so

hél	*íyohakab*	*lé*	*húte*	*ki*	*hé*	*é*	*cha*	*ohómni*	*chąlí wapháȟta*
there	after	this	base	DEF	that	IP	QL	around	tobacco tie*

iyápemni	*é-gnaka-pi*	*na*	*wachékhiya-pi*	*na*	*a-chą́nųpa-pi*
wrap around	L-place-PL	and	pray-PL	and	L-smoke tobacco-PL

na	*ho*	*hé*	*chą́*	*ki*	*hé*	*thi-yáta*	*aglí-pi.*	*owáchekiye*
and	well	that	tree	DEF	that	home-to	bring home-PL	church

ektá	*glí-pi*	*na*	*pa-wóslal*	*iyéya-pi*	*hą́tąhąš*	*hél*	*táku*
to	come home-PL	and	INS-upright	send-PL	when	there	things

ǧéǧe-ǧe-ya	*otké-ya-pi*	*cha*	*hená*	*ų́*	*aȟʔáyethų-pi*	*cha*
dangle-RED-ADV	hang.VI-CAU-IPS	so	those	with	decorate-PL	so

hená é cha oyáte ki hená iyóhi-la wicháša wą̨ží hiyú-pi

those IP QL people DEF those each-DIM man one come-PL

naʔį́š wį́yą na wakhą́yeža hená wą̨žígži glohí-pi na

or woman and child those one by one POSS.bring-PL and

hená wachékhiya-pi na chą́ ki hél iyákaška-pi. ho

those pray-PL and tree DEF there tie to-PL well

chą́-šna hé ómakha ki hé áta yį́ na echél

then-HAB that season DEF that entirely go and so

Ómakha Théca héchi isą́m yá héhą chą́ ki he-tą́ cha

New Year's Day* there more go then tree DEF that-from QL

hená wa-ȟʔáyethų-pi ki hená i-kí-k-cu-pi na

those NSP.PAT-decorate-IPS DEF those ST-PSS-EI-take-IPS and

tuwá tókhel waštélake héci yušpú-pi nahą́ ho akhé

someone how like.VT SUB pull off-IPS and then well again

thokáta ómakha héchiya akhé hená ikhóyag-ya-pi. ho chą́

future season there again those adhere-CAU-PL well then

hená į̌šé hų́ȟ wóphila eyá-pi na hų́ȟ wólakhota chį́-pi

those just some thanks say-IPS and some peace want-IPS

naʔį́š hų́ȟ hená khúža-pi cha akísni-pi chį́-pi naʔį́š

or some those sick-PL so recover-PL want-IPS and

táku i-kákiža-pi cha hená ų́ hená héchel į́š eyá

something L-suffer-PL so those because of those so also

chą́ ki hél táku iyákaška-pi. cha wašícu ki lé
tree DEF there things tie to-IPS so white man DEF this

Christmas eyá-pi ki lé Lakhóta ki waníce éyaš Waníkiya
Christmas say-PL DEF this Indian DEF lack but Savior*

Thų́pi Ąpétu eyá-pi. cha hél w-íyuškį-yą lená wóphila
Birthday* say-PL so there NSP.PAT-happy-ADV these thanks

éya-pi na'į́š eyá Lakhóta ki lé pte-są́ wą
say-PL and also Indian DEF this buffalo-white IDF.SG

thų́-pi cha w-íyuškį-pi ki héchų s'e. hená
give birth to-IPS QL NSP.PAT-happy-IPS DEF that way* those

wichóni-kta nahą́ wichózani-kta na wówa'ųšila-kta ų́
life-FUT and then health-FUT and love.N-FUT for

wochékhiye káǧa-pi. cha hé é Waníkiya Thų́pi Ąpétu eyá-pi
prayer make-PL so that IP Savior* Birthday* say-IPS

cha hé chą́ ki hé él é-gle-pi ki hél tuwá
so that tree DEF that at L-put-IPS DEF there someone

wachékhiyį na táku o-'ótke-yį na'į́š ųgnáš túwa
pray and something L-hang.VI-CAU or maybe someone

takún k'ú-pi-kte hą́tąhąš hená chąté i-y-á-gle-ya hená
something give-IPS-FUT when those heart L-EI-L-put-ADV those

hé echų́-pi. cha tuwéni hená otúyachį héchų-pi-šni. cha
that do-IPS so nobody those for nothing do that-PL-NEG so

lená	*wakhą́-yą*	*gluʔónihą-pi*	*į́š eyá*	*hená*	*wašícu*	*ki*
these	sacred-ADV	POSS.respect.VT-IPS	also	those	white man	DEF

étkiya	*šką́-pi.*	*hená*	*yu-wákhą*	*él*	*héchiya*	*chą́*	*ki*	*hé*
toward	act-IPS	those	INS-sacred	while	there	tree	DEF	that

é-gle-pi.	*ho*	*cha*	*chą́*	*ki*	*hé*	*tohą́n*	*yuʔų́ka-pi*	*hą́tahąš*
L-put-IPS	well	so	tree	DEF	that	when	take down-IPS	when

áya-pi	*nahą́*	*iníyothi*	*héchi*	*isákhib*	*aʔí-pi*	*cha*
take along-IPS	and then	sweatlodge	there	beside	take to-IPS	so

héchi	*iníkağa-pi*	*na*	*hé*	*chą́*	*ki*	*hé*
there	perform sweatlodge ceremony-IPS	and	that	tree	DEF	that

ų́	*į́yą*	*ki*	*hená*	*a-ʔíle-ya-pi*	*nahą́*
using	stone	DEF	those	L-burn.VI-CAU-IPS	and then

iníkağa-pi	*na*	*wachékhiya-pi*	*na*	*wóphila*
perform sweatlodge ceremony-IPS	and	pray-IPS	and	thanks

eyá-pi	*nahą́*	*ho*	*hé*	*hehą́yela*	*ihą́ke.*
say-IPS	and then	well	that	so far	end.N

The people [from the church community] always cut down a big evergreen tree, put it up in the church around Christmas time, and pick presents from it. This church is a Native American church. People go there to pray; anybody can go there to pray. Any kind of people. People come, and when the tree is to be cut, they go to the mountains. After putting up tobacco ties and tobacco, they choose the tree, place the tobacco around it, and pray. They pray with a pipe. Then they go, accompanied by either a boy or a girl, and nick it [the tree] with an ax. They [the children] are considered sacred. They go, and as soon as they [the children] have nicked it, the tree is cut down and secured so that it does not hit the ground. On the way back it is not supposed to touch the ground. After that, the tree stump is wrapped with tobacco ties and people pray and smoke over it. Then they take the tree home. They go back to the church, and when they put it up, they hang all kinds of dangling things onto it, decorating it with them. People come one by one, men, women and children, and bring their own contribution. They pray and tie the items onto the tree. The season proceeds, and through New Year's Day the decorations are taken off the tree. Everybody takes off what he likes, and the following year he or she puts it [the same thing] back on. On this occasion, some people just say thanks, others pray for peace on earth; some people who are sick want to recover, and those who are suffering from anything also put something on the tree for that reason. The Indians don't have what the white people call Christmas; however, they call it [Christmas] "The Savior's Birthday." On this occasion they [the white people] happily express their appreciation, pretty much the same way the Indians celebrate the birth of a white buffalo. They make prayers for life and health and for love among mankind. That is what they call "The Savior's Birthday." Whoever prays where the tree is put up and puts something on it, or maybe wants to give something away, does it wholeheartedly. Nobody does that thoughtlessly. The things that people honor in their religion they also practice toward the white people, and they put the tree up with blessing thoughts. When the tree is taken down [after the celebration] it is brought to a sweatlodge and put down next to it. People have a sweat there and use the tree as firewood for heating the stones. They have a sweat and pray and express their appreciation. This is the end [of the story].

Note: The treatment of the tree reflects many details of the sundance ceremony, which requires cutting down a tree which is used as the sundance pole, around which the ceremony evolves. The white buffalo is a central figure in Lakota spirituality. According to mythology, the Lakota received their religion, ceremonies, and beliefs from a woman called Ptesą Wį [White Buffalo Woman].

7.4. Twins

FLORINE RED EAR HORSE

Tape recorded September 27, 1995

Ho	*hehą́l*	*wichóʔoyake*	*wąží*	*obláką-kte*	*ki*	*hé*	*chekpá*
well	then	story	IDF.SG	tell.1SG.AG-FUT	DEF	that	twins

e-wícha-kiya-pi.	*lená*	*ehą́ni*	*wįyą*	*na*	*ehą́ni*	*wicháša*
ST-3PL.PAT-say to-IPS	these	old time	woman	and	old time	man

cha	*akhé*	*héktakiya*	*oyáte*	*wichó-ʔų*	*ki*	*él*	*wichá-hi-pi.*
QL	again	backwards	people	COLL-be	DEF	to	3PL.PAT-come-PL

thiwáhe	*wą*	*él*	*chekpá*	*ki*	*i-gláȟniǧa-pi*	*nachéce*	*hél*
family	IDF.SG	in	twins	DEF	L-POSS.choose-PL	perhaps	there

tąyą́	*ų́-pi-kta*	*cha*	*na*	*tąyą́*	*wichá-khuwa-pi-kta*	*cha*	*él*
well	exist-PL-FUT	QL	and	well	3PL.PAT-treat-IPS-FUT	so	to

wichá-hi-pi.	*hé*	*ų́*	*etą́hą*	*wakhą́yeža-pi*	*éyaš*
3PL.PAT-come-PL	that	be	from	child-PL	even though

wąžígži	*táku*	*héchel*	*ehą́ni*	*wichóʔiye*	*naʔį́š*	*ehą́ni*
certain ones	things	so	old time	language	or	old time

wichóȟʔą	*lená*	*slolyá-pi.*	*cha*	*ąpétu*	*wąží*	*iyá-pi*	*na*	*takún*
tradition	these	know-PL	so	day	one	speak-PL	and	something

héchel	*eyá-pi*	*naʔį́š*	*echų́-pi*	*chą́na-šna*	*hécheya*	*eyá*
so	say-PL	or	do-PL	then-HAB	really	LK

wichá-yuha-pi	*ki*	*lená*	*iníhą-pi.*	*éyaš*	*lená*	*ehą́ni*
3PL.PAT-have-PL	QL	these	surprised-PL	at any rate	these	old time

oyáte	*cha*	*wicháša*	*na*	*wį́yą*	*cha*	*thiwáhe*	*ki*	*él*
people	so	man	and	woman	QL	family	DEF	to

wichá-hi-pi.	*ho*	*į̌šé*	*hé*	*é*	*cha*	*obláke.*	*tákuni*	*él*
3PL.PAT-come-PL	well	just	that	IP	that	tell.1SG.AG	nothing	there

i-hą́ske-ya	*ephį́-kte-šni*	*éyaš*	*wa-héhąyela.*
L-long-ADV	say.1SG.AG-FUT-NEG	but	NSP.PAT-that is all

The story I will tell, then, is about what is called *chekpá* [twins]. These old-time women and old-time men came back to where their people lived [they were reincarnated]. In the family that twins [i.e., those who were reborn as twins] were likely to choose, they would live well and be treated well; to such a place they went [twins were considered special]. From then on, even though they were kids, they would know certain things about the old-time language and the old-time traditions [by themselves, from their former lives]. When they spoke some day and said or did something like that, the people who had them [the twins] were always really surprised. At any rate, these old-time people, these old-time men and women, came [back] to the families [after they had died]. I wanted to tell just that. I don't want to make a long story out of it. That is all.

Note: Florine adds that anyone who wanted to be reincarnated could come back to the world. Children who were very intelligent always came as twins. Twins always seemed to know things from a former life. Especially talented children who were born single were said to have left their twin brother or sister behind in the spirit world. Florine has given birth to twins.

7.5. Three Tongue Twisters

FLORINE RED EAR HORSE

Tape recorded October 25, 1995

#1

bloˀíyublu	*wą*	*blo-ˀáli-ya*	*blo-yúblu*	*ahíyaya.*
tractor*	IDF.SG	hill-climb-ADV	potato-plow	go by

#2

maštį́ska	*wą*	*ištá-ska-ska*	*na*	*sí-ska-ska*	*cha*	*psí-psil*
rabbit	LK	eye-white-RED	and	foot-white-RED	QL	RED-jump

iyáye.
go

#3 (INVENTED BY FLORINE)

šų́kawakhą́	*wą*	*glešká*	*cha*	*yeˀícˀiyį*	*na*	*glih-ˀícˀi-yį*
horse*	LK	spotted	QL	buck*	and	land on the feet-3RFL-CAU

na	*kaglá-pšų-yą*	*gliȟpáye.*
and	sideways-fall-ADV	fall

#1

A tractor is moving up a hill plowing potatoes.

#2

A rabbit with white eyes and white feet is jumping by.

#3 (INVENTED BY FLORINE)

A spotted horse is bucking and hitting the ground and falling sideways.

7.6. A Love Song or Lullaby

FLORINE RED EAR HORSE

Tape recorded October 25, 1995

į́kpa-ta	*na-wá-žį*	*na*	*šiná*	*chi-cóza-he*
end.N-on	ST-1SG.AG-stand	and	blanket	1SG.AG.2SG.PAT-wave at-PRG

na	*má éya,*	*má éya,*	*má éya,*	*léchi*	*kú*	*waná.*
and	oh my	oh my	oh my	here	come	IMP.F

I'm standing on a hilltop and I'm waving my shawl at you. Oh my, oh my, oh my, come here.

APPENDIX

Analysis of Neologisms and Idioms

The lexical items, compounds, and idioms contained in this section are marked with an asterisk in the interlinear gloss in the texts.

Entry	Translation	Analysis
akáb'iyaya	'leftovers'	*akáb-'iyaya* extra-go
akǫ́'iye'ic'iya	'to mount'	*akǫ́-'iye-'ic'i-ya* on-ST-3RFL-send
akǫ́yǫka	'to ride'	*akǫ́-yǫka* on-sit
anúkhasą	'bald eagle'	*anúkha-są* on both ends-white
aphíya	'to cure', 'to fix', 'to mend', 'to doctor'	*a-phí-ya* L-good-CAU
ağúyapi	'bread', wheat' 'dough'	*a-ğú-ya-pi* L-burned-CAU-IPS
ağúyapi blú	'flour'	*ağúyapi blú* wheat dust
ağúyapi ipáblaye	'rolling pin'	*ağúyapi i-pá-blaye* dough L-INS-flat
ąpétu wakhą́	'Sunday'	*ąpétu wakhą́* dawn sacred
ą́paó wicháȟpi	'morning star'	*ą́paó wicháȟpi* dawn star
blo'íyublu	'tractor'	*blo-'í-yublu* potato-L-plow.VT

chažé oˀígwa	'to sign papers'	*chažé oˀígwa* name POSS.write
Chasmú Okáȟmi	'Alliance NE'	*Chasmú Okáȟmi* sand bend
Chasmú Wakpá	'Sand Creek'	*Chasmú Wakpá* sand creek
chąˀíchipaweğa	'cross', 'crucifix'	*chą-ˀíchi-paweğa* wood-REC-cross.VT
chąˀógnaka	'casket'	*chą-ˀó-gnaka* wood-L-put
chąˀókaške	'prison'	*chą-ˀó-kaške* wood-L-tie
chą́ˀowįža	'wood floor', 'wood spread'	*chą́-ˀowįža* wood-cover.N
chąhá	'bark'	*chą-há* wood-skin
chąhą́pi	'sugar'	*chą-hą́pi* tree-juice (refers to the fact that the Native Americans made sugar by boiling the sap of certain trees, such as sugar maples)
chąhą́pi khúžapi	'diabetes'	*chąhą́pi khúža-pi* sugar sick-IPS (in this case, *-pi* functions as a nominalizer)
chąkáškapi	'fence'	*chą-káška-pi* post-tie.VT-IPS (in this case, *-pi* functions as a nominalizer)

chąlí wapháȟta	'tobacco tie'	*chąlí wa-pháȟta* tobacco NSP.PAT-fold (tiny pieces of cloth filled with tobacco which are lined up on a string; this is used as a gift to the spirits)
chąnákpa	'mushroom'	*chą-nákpa* tree-ear
chąpágmiyąpi	'wagon', 'covered wagon'	*chą-págmiyą-pi* wood-roll.VT-IPS
Chąphá Wakpá	'Cherry Creek'	*Chąphá Wakpá* cherry river
chąsákala	'twig', 'stick'	*chą-sáka-la* wood-stiff-DIM
chąšáša	'red willow' (*Cornus sanguinea*)	*chą-šá-ša* tree-red-RED
chąté iwášte	'happy'	*chąté i-wášte* heart L-good
chąté šíca	'sad'	*chąté šíca* heart bad
chąté wašté	'happy'	*chąté wašté* heart good
chą́wakˀį	'saddle'	*chą́-wa-kˀį* wood-NSP.PAT-carry
chuwígnaka	'dress'	*chuwí-gnaka* back.N-put
chų́kaške	'wire fence'	*chą́-ˀo-káške* post-L-tie.VT
chųwíyaphehe	'grapes'	*chą́ o-ˀíyaphehe* tree L-wrap around
haˀípažaža	'soap'	*ha-ˀí-pažaža* clothes-L-wash

ha'íyotke	'clothesline', 'hanger'	*ha-'í-y-otke* clothes-L-EI-hang.VI
ha'íyužaža	'washing machine', 'detergent'	*ha-'í-yužaža* clothes-L-wash
hąblécheya	'to seek a vision'	*hąblé-cheya* dream.VI-cry
héchų s'e	'that way'	*hé echų́ s'e* that do like.AV
hįgnáthų	'to get married' (for a woman)	*hįgná-thų* husband-acquire
hįgnáya	'to be married' (for a woman)	*hįgná-ya* husband-have as
hįšmá	'hairy', 'furry'	*hį-šmá* fur-deep
hógna	'that way'	*hé ogná* that according to
hokší o'ų́papi	'infant', 'baby'	*hokší o'ų́pa-pi* child wrap-IPS
hóyekhiya	'to call to'	*hó-ye-khiya* voice-go-CAU
hóyeya	'to call', 'to call out'	*hó-ye-ya* voice-go-CAU
huphéstola	'yucca'	*hu-phéstola* limb-pointed
ichą́tešica	'sad about'	*i-chą́te-šica* L-heart-bad
ichą́tewašte	'happy about'	*i-chą́te-wašte* L-heart-good
igláwa	'price'	*i-gláwa* L-POSS.count
ihą́kya	'to destroy'	*ihą́ke-ya* end.N-CAU

imásˀiyaphe	'hammer'	*i-máza-ˀi-y-aphe* L-iron-L-EI-hit
ipáblaye	'rolling pin'	*i-pá-blaye* L-INS-flat
išnáthi	'to have the menses or period'	*išná-thi* alone-live (women who had their period lived in separate tipis)
ištámaza	'glasses'	*ištá-maza* eye-iron
ištámniǧaǧa	'tear'	*ištá-mni-ǧaǧa* eye-water-flow
itípakįte	'towel'	*ité-ˀi-pakįte* face-L-wipe
itówapi naškąškayąpi	'movie'	*ité owá-pi* face draw-IPS *na-šką-šką-yą-pi* INS-move-RED-CAU-IPS
iwánaȟˀų	'radio'	*i-wá-naȟˀų* L-NSP.PAT-hear
iwáyuphiya	'nicely', 'in a funny way'	*i-wá-yu-phi-ya* L-NSP.PAT-INS-good-ADV
íyakaȟpe	'lid'	*í-y-akaȟpe* L-EI-cover.VT
iyéchįkyąke	'car'	*iyéchįkala įyąke* by itself run
iyéska	'interpreter', 'to interpret', 'half-breed'	*iyé-ska* speak-white
iyóškokpa	'ditch'	*i-y-óškokpa* L-EI-dip.N

į́yą okástakapi	'concrete', 'cement'	*į́yą o-kástaka-pi* stone L-pour in-IPS
kaslóhą hináži̧	'to park'	*kaslóhą hináži* slide stop
khąsúkhute	'to gamble'	from: *khą́ta sú khuté* plum seed shoot (plum seeds were used as dice)
khą́ta sú	'dice'	*khą́ta sú* plum seed
kįyékhiyapi	'airplane'	*kįyé-khiya-pi* fly-CAU-IPS
kįyékhiyapi oˀínažį	'airport'	*kįyékhiyapi o-ˀínažį* airplane L-stop
léchų sˀe	'this way'	from: *lé echų́ sˀe* this do like.AV
lochį́	'hungry'	*lo-chį́* food-want
makhíyuthapi	'mile', 'yard'	from: *makhá iyútha-pi* earth measure-IPS
makhóšica	'badlands'	from: *makhá o-šíca* earth L-bad
masˀápha	'to make a phone call'	*máza aphá* metal hit (originally refers to telegraphs)
masˀínaȟtake	'spurs'	*máza i-náȟtake* metal L-kick

maschą́ʔųpha	'bridle'	*máza chą́ o-yápha* metal wood L-bite
maštįca phuté	'buffalo berry'	*maštįca phuté* rabbit upper lip
maswíche'ųpe	'skillet'	*máza wa-í-che'ųpe* metal NSP.PAT-L-roast
máza ȟóta	'aluminum'	*máza ȟóta* metal gray
mázaska	'silver', 'money', 'coin'	*máza-ska* metal-white
mázawakhą́ often heard as: *mázakhą́*	'gun'	*máza-wakhą́* iron-mysterious
mní wakhą́	'liquor'	*mní wakhą́* water mysterious
mnináthakapi	'reservoir', 'dam'	*mni-náthaka-pi* water-lock up-IPS
mnipíǧa	'beer'	*mni-píǧa* water-boil.VI
mnišíca	'liquor'	*mni-šíca* water-bad
Mnišóše Othų́wahe	'Pierre SD'	*Mni-šóše Othų́wahe* water-muddy (= Missouri) town
mniwą́cha	'ocean'	*mni-ʔówąchą* water-all over
naʔíle	'traffic light'	*na-ʔíle* INS ('by itself')-light up
napíkceya	'by hand'	*napé ikcé-ya* hand natural-ADV
oʔíheye thípi	'outhouse'	*o-ʔíheye thípi* L-urinate house

ožą́(žą)glepi	'window', 'windshield'	*o-žą́-(žą)-gle-pi* L-transparent-RED-put-IPS
okhúže thípi	'hospital'	*okhúže thí-pi* sickness house
Ómakha Théca	'New Year's Day'	*Ómakha Théca* season new
Osní Makhóche	'Alaska'	*Osní Makhóche* cold land
othímahe(l) hiyú	'entrance'	*o-thí-mahe(l) hiyú* L-house-inside come
owákąyake	'chair', 'bench'	*o-w-ákąyake* L-EI-on-sit
owákpamni	'agency'	*o-wá-kpamni* L-NSP.PAT-distribute
owáphe	'hour'	*o-w-áphe* L-NSP.PAT-hit (refers to the beating of the clock)
owáyatke thípi	'bar'	*o-wá-yatke thípi* L-NSP.PAT-drink house
ową́yąg wašté	'good-looking', 'attractive'	*o-wą́yąg wašté* L-see good
owíyophe	'store'	from: *o-wa-íyophe* L-NSP.PAT-sell
ohpáye thípi	'motel', 'hotel'	*o-ȟpáye thípi* L-lie house
pa'ų́zi ektákiya yá	'to back up'	*pa-'ų́zi ektá-kiya yá* INS-back end to-to go
phahá	'scalp'	*pha-há* head-skin

phežíkakse	'sickle'	*phežíí-kakse* grass L-cut
phežíšaša	'buffalo grass'	*phežíí-ša-ša* grass-red-RED
phežíȟota	'sagebrush'	*pheží-ȟota* grass-gray
phežúta	'medicine'	*pheží húta* grass root
phežúta šíca	'drugs'	*phežúta šíca* medicine bad
phežúta wicháša	'herbalist', 'medicine man'	*phežúta wicháša* medicine man
phetížą̌žą ǧeǧéya	'lantern'	*phéta ížą̌žą ǧeǧéya* fire shine hang down
phetížąžąye	'lamp'	*phéta ížąžą-ya* fire shine-CAU
philámaya	'thanks'	*phi-lá-ma-ya* good-consider-1SG. PAT-CAU
philámayaya	'thank you'	*phi-lá-ma-ya-ya* good-consider-1SG. PAT-2SG.AG-CAU
po^ʔíphiye	'swelling weed'	*po-ʔí-phi-ye* swell-L-good-CAU
pteʔákąyąka	'to ride bulls'	*pte-ʔákąyąka* cattle-on-sit
ptebléška	'cattle', 'cow'	*pte-gléška* [*sic*] cow-spotted
Sápa Ų́	'Catholic'	*Sápa Ų́* black wear (refers to the black robes of Catholic priests)

Sichą́ğu	'Rosebud'	*Sichą́-ğu* thigh-burned (original name of the Brulé Sioux tribe who live on Rosebud reservation)
Ská Ų́	'Episcopal'	*Ská Ų́* white wear (refers to the white robes worn by the respective priests)
šųgwáthogla	'bronc'	*šųg-wáthogla* horse-wild
šųk'áką'iye'ic'iya	'to mount a horse'	*šųk-'áką-'iye-'ic'i-ya* horse-on-ST-3RFL-send
šųk'áką yąka often heard as: *šųk'áką ka*	'to ride', 'rider'	*šųk-'áką-yąka* horse-on-sit
šųká'ųspe	'to break or train horses'	*šų-ká-'ųspe* horse-INS-know
šų́kawakhą́ often heard as: *šų́kakhą́*	'horse'	*šų́ka-wakhą́* dog-magic
thakhą́	'sinew'	*tha-khą́* ruminant-string
thathą́ka	'buffalo bull'	*tha-thą́ka* ruminant-big
thawícuthų	'to marry' (for a man)	*tha-wícu-thų* ALP-wife-acquire
tháȟca	'deer'	*thá-ȟca* ruminant-proper
thąkáya	'to use the bathroom'	*thąkál yá* outside go

thąkáyąką	'to have the menses or period'	*thąkál yąká* outside sit (during their period women lived in separate tipis)
thąsák t'á	'struck with fear'	*thą-sák t'á* body-stiff faint
thíwichakte	'to commit murder'	*thí-wicha-kte* house-3PL.PAT-kill (in the old Plains culture, the killing of relatives was considered a crime, but not necessarily the killing of members of hostile tribes)
thiyóblecha	'tent'	*thi-y-óblecha* house-EI-square
thosą́	'light purple', 'lavender'	*tho-są́* blue-white
Thųkášila	'Christian God'	*Thųkášila* grandfather
thųkašilayapi	'government', 'president'	*thųkašila-ya-pi* grandfather-have as-IPS
tohą́n okíhilaka	'as much as can be'	*tohą́n okíhi-laka* whichever way can-kind of
tóktu nachéce	'who knows'	*tóktu nachéce* maybe maybe
Úta Wakpá	'Oak Creek'	*Úta Wakpá* acorn river
Ųcíyapi Thamákha	'England'	*Ųcí-ya-pi* grandmother-have as-IPS *Tha-mákha* ALP-land (refers to the Queen of England)

Ųžį́žįtka	'Rosebud SD'	*Ųžį́žįtka* rose
wachékiyapi	'altar'	*wachékiya-pi* pray-IPS
wachékiya wicháša	'pastor', 'priest'	*wachékiya wicháša* pray man
wágleyutapi often heard as: *wáglutapi*	'table'	from: *wa-'á-gle yúta-pi* NSP.PAT-L-put eat-IPS
wagmíza ikcéka	'squaw corn'	*wagmíza ikcéka* corn common
wahá'owį̨žapi	'comforter', 'bedspread', 'quilt'	*wa-há-'owį̨ža-pi* NSP.PAT-hide-spread.VT-IPS
wahútopa	'quadruped'	*wa-hú-topa* NSP.PAT-leg-four
wakhálapi	'coffee'	*wa-khál-ya-pi* NSP.PAT-hot-CAU-IPS
wakhą́ wicháša	'spiritual man'	*wakhą́ wicháša* spiritual man
wakhą́gli	'electricity', 'lightning'	*wakhą́-wígli* mysterious-substance
Wakhą́thąka	'Great Spirit'	*Wakhą́-thąka* mystery-great
wamákhašką	'animal'	*wa-mákha-šką* NSP.PAT-earth-move
wanáǧoyapi	'tape recorder', 'tape recording'	*wa-náǧoya-pi* NSP.PAT-scratch out-IPS
wanášlogyapi	'hominy'	*wa-nášlog-ya-pi* NSP.PAT-come off easily-CAU-IPS
Waníkiya	'Savior', 'Jesus'	*Wa-ní-ki-ya* NSP.PAT-live-BEN-CAU

Waníkiya Thų́pi Ąpétu	'Christmas'	*Waníkiya Thų́-pi* Savior give birth to-IPS *Ąpétu* day
waphíya	'doctor', 'healer', 'to doctor'	*wa-phí-ya* NSP.PAT-good-CAU
waphíya wicháša	'medicine man'	*waphíya wicháša* doctor man
wašícu wakhą́	'white doctor'	*wašícu wakhą́* white man holy
wašį́ ikcéka	'tallow grease'	*wašį́ ikcéka* grease true
wawíyopheya	'salesman'	*wa-w-íyopheya* NSP.PAT-EI-sell
wawóyuspa	'policeman'	*wa-w-óyuspa* NSP.PAT-EI-catch
wahpé okhíye	'arbor'	*wahpé okhíye* leaf row
wahtéšni inít'é ló	'doggone you'	*wahté-šni i-ní-t'e* worthless L-2SG.PAT-die *ló* ASS.M
wahúpakoza	'winged being'	*wa-húpa-koza* NSP.PAT-wing-flap
wayáwa	'to go to school'	*wa-yáwa* NSP.PAT-write
wayúphika	'skillful'	*wa-yú-phi-ka* NSP.PAT-INS-good-kind of
wazíhąte	'evergreen'	*wazí-hąte* pine-cedar
wątą́yeya	'sharp-shooter'	*wą-tą́-ye-ya* arrow-well-go-CAU

wicháša akątu	'human being'	*wicháša akątu* man on top
wicháša wašté	'handsome'	*wicháša wašté* man good
wíchoką	'noon'	*wí i-chóką* sun L-middle
wígli ikcéka	'tallow grease', 'suet', 'kidney fat'	*wígli ikcéka* oil common
wígli ų́ (káğapi)	'fry bread'	*wígli ų́ (káğa-pi)* oil with make-IPS
wínakapo	'baking powder'	*wa-ˀí-nakapo* NSP.PAT-L-swell
wípusye	'dryer'	*wa-ˀí-pus-ye* NSP.PAT-L-dry.A-CAU
wiwą́yąg wachí	'to dance the sundance'	*wi-wą́yąg wachí* sun-see dance
wiwąyąg wachipi	'sundance'	*wi-wąyąg wachi-pi* sun-see dance-IPS
wíȟpeyapi	'to practice give-away'	from: *wa-ˀíȟpeyapi* NSP.PAT-throw away (a Native American custom which was performed in connection with ceremonies; sometimes people gave away all they possessed on this occasion, but received material goods from other tribe members who also participated in the give-away in return)
wíyatke	'cup'	*wa-ˀí-yatke* NSP.PAT-L-drink

wiyáwapi	'month'	*wi-yáwa-pi* moon-count-IPS
wiyóhiyąpata	'east'	from: *wi-y-ó-hinąpa-ta* sun-EI-L-come out-at
wiyóȟpeyata	'west'	from: *wi-iyóȟpeya-ta* sun-go down-at
wíyukpą	'grinder'	from: *wa-ʔí-yukpą* NSP.PAT-L-grind
wį́yą wašté	'beautiful'	*wį́yą wašté* woman good
Ȟéská	'Rocky Mountains'	*Ȟé-ská* mountain-white
Ȟéská Oyą́ke	'Denver'	*Ȟéská Oyą́ke* Rocky Mountains city
yamnúmnuǧapi	'pepper'	*yamnúmnuǧa-pi* crush-IPS
yeʔícʔiya	'to buck'	*ye-ícʔi-ya* go-3RFL-CAU
yubláyapi	'page'	*yu-bláya-pi* INS-flat-IPS
yuȟlá	'to make a phone call'	*yu-ȟlá* INS-rattle
Zuzéca Pahá	'Snake Butte'	*Zuzéca Pahá* snake hill

REFERENCES

Boas, Franz. 1937. "Some Traits of the Dakota Language." *Language: The Journal of the Linguistic Society of America* 13(2): 137–41.

———, ed. 1911. *Handbook of American Indian Languages*. Washington DC: Government Printing Office.

Boas, Franz, and Ella C. Deloria. 1941. "Dakota Grammar." *Memoirs of the National Academy of Sciences* 23(2). Washington DC: Government Printing Office.

Brown, Joseph Epes. 1953. *The Sacred Pipe: Black Elk's Account to the Seven Sacred Rites of the Oglala Sioux*. New York: Penguin Books.

Buechel, Eugene, SJ. 1939. *A Grammar of Lakota: The Language of the Teton Sioux Indians*. Saint Louis: John S. Swift.

———. 1970. *A Dictionary of the Teton Sioux Language: Lakota-English, English-Lakota*, edited by Paul Manhart, SJ. Pine Ridge SD: Holy Rosary Mission, Red Cloud Indian School; Vermillion: University of South Dakota Press.

Campbell, Lyle, and Marianne Mithun, eds. 1979. *The Languages of Native America: Historical and Comparative Assessment*. Austin: University of Texas Press.

Chafe, Wallace L. 1976. *The Caddoan, Iroquoian, and Siouan Languages*. The Hague: Mouton.

Deloria, Ella. 1932. "Dakota Texts." *Publications of the American Ethnological Society* 14. New York: Stechert.

DeMallie, Raymond J., ed. 1984. *The Sixth Grandfather: Black Elk's Teaching Given to John G. Neihardt*. Lincoln: University of Nebraska Press.

Hassrick, Royal B. 1964. *The Sioux: Life and Customs of a Warrior Society*. Norman: University of Oklahoma Press.

Ingham, Bruce. 2003. "Lakota." *Languages of the World/Materials* 426. Munich: Lincom Europa.

Lakota Language Consortium. 2008. *New Lakota Dictionary: Lakȟótiyapi-English / English-Lakȟótiyapi, and Incorporating the Dakota Dialects of Yankton-Yanktonai and Santee-Sisseton*. Bloomington IN: Lakota Language Consortium.

Laubin, Reginald, and Gladys Laubin. 1957. *The Indian Tipi: Its History, Construction, and Use*. Norman: University of Oklahoma Press.

Mendoza, Patrick. 1993. *Song of Sorrow: Massacre at Sand Creek*. Denver: Willow Wind.

Neihardt, John C. (1932) 2014. *Black Elk Speaks: Being the Life Story of a Holy Man of the Oglala Sioux*. New York: W. Morrow and Co. Reprint, Lincoln: University of Nebraska Press.

Nurge, Ethel, ed. 1970. *The Modern Sioux: Social Systems and Reservation Culture*. Lincoln: University of Nebraska Press.

Parks, Douglas R., and Raymond J. DeMallie. 1992. "Sioux, Assiniboine, and Stoney Dialects: A Classification." *Anthropological Linguistics* 34(1–4):233–55.

Riggs, Stephen Return. 1852. "Grammar and Dictionary of the Dakota Language." *Smithsonian Contributions to Knowledge* 4. Washington DC: Smithsonian Institution.

———. 1890. "A Dakota-English Dictionary," edited by James Owen Dorsey. *Contributions to North American Ethnology* 7. Washington DC: Smithsonian Institution.

———. 1893. "Dakota Grammar, Texts, and Ethnology," edited by James Owen Dorsey. *Contributions to North American Ethnology* 9. Washington DC: U.S. Geographical and Geological Survey of the Rocky Mountain Region.

Rood, David S. and Allan R. Taylor. 1996. "Sketch of Lakhota, a Siouan Language." In *Handbook of North American Indians*, vol. 17, edited by Ives Goddard, 440–82. Washington DC: Smithsonian Institution.

Sebeok, Thomas A., ed. 1977. *Native Languages of the Americas*. 2 vols. New York: Plenum.

Shaw, Patricia A. 1980. *Theoretical Issues in Dakota Phonology and Morphology*. New York: Garland.

St. Pierre, Mark, and Tilda Long Soldier. 1995. *Walking in the Sacred Manner: Healers, Dreamers, and Pipe Carriers–Medicine Women of the Plains Indians*. New York: Simon and Schuster.

Standing Bear, Luther. (1931) 1988. *My Indian Boyhood*. Boston: Houghton Mifflin. Reprint, Lincoln: University of Nebraska Press.

———. (1934) 1988. *Stories of the Sioux*. Boston: Houghton Mifflin. Reprint, Lincoln: University of Nebraska Press.

———. 1978. *Land of the Spotted Eagle*. Lincoln: University of Nebraska Press.

University of Colorado Lakhota Project. 1976. *Beginning Lakhota*. 2 vols. Boulder CO: Department of Linguistics, University of Colorado.

Voegelin, C. F. 1941. "Internal Relationships of Siouan Languages." *American Anthropologist* 43:246–49.

Williamson, John P. 1902. *An English-Dakota Dictionary*. New York: American Tract Society.

Wolff, Hans. 1950. "Comparative Siouan." *International Journal of American Linguistics* 16:61–66, 113–21, 168–78; 17:197–204.

IN THE STUDIES IN THE ANTHROPOLOGY OF NORTH AMERICAN INDIANS SERIES

The Four Hills of Life: Northern Arapaho Knowledge and Life Movement
By Jeffrey D. Anderson

One Hundred Years of Old Man Sage: An Arapaho Life
By Jeffrey D. Anderson

The Semantics of Time: Aspectual Categorization in Koyukon Athabaskan
By Melissa Axelrod

Lushootseed Texts: An Introduction to Puget Salish Narrative Aesthetics
Edited by Crisca Bierwert

People of The Dalles: The Indians of Wascopam Mission
By Robert Boyd

A Choctaw Reference Grammar
By George Aaron Broadwell

War Paintings of the Tsuu T'ina Nation
By Arni Brownstone

The Lakota Ritual of the Sweat Lodge: History and Contemporary Practice
By Raymond A. Bucko

From the Sands to the Mountain: Change and Persistence in a Southern Paiute Community
By Pamela A. Bunte and Robert J. Franklin

A Grammar of Comanche
By Jean Ormsbee Charney

New Voices for Old Words: Algonquian Oral Literatures
Edited by David J. Costa

Reserve Memories: The Power of the Past in a Chilcotin Community
By David W. Dinwoodie

Haida Syntax (2 vols.)
By John Enrico

Northern Haida Songs
By John Enrico and Wendy Bross Stuart

Life among the Indians: First Fieldwork among the Sioux and Omahas
By Alice C. Fletcher
Edited and with an introduction by Joanna C. Scherer and Raymond J. DeMallie

Powhatan's World and Colonial Virginia: A Conflict of Cultures
By Frederic W. Gleach

Native Languages and Language Families of North America
(folded study map and wall display map)
Compiled by Ives Goddard

Native Languages of the Southeastern United States
Edited by Heather K. Hardy and Janine Scancarelli

The Heiltsuks: Dialogues of Culture and History on the Northwest Coast
By Michael E. Harkin

Prophecy and Power among the Dogrib Indians
By June Helm

A Totem Pole History: The Work of Lummi Carver Joe Hillaire
By Pauline Hillaire
Edited by Gregory P. Fields

Corbett Mack: The Life of a Northern Paiute
As told by Michael Hittman

The Spirit and the Sky: Lakota Visions of the Cosmos
By Mark Hollabaugh

The Canadian Sioux
By James H. Howard

The Canadian Sioux, Second Edition
By James H. Howard, with a new foreword by Raymond J. DeMallie and Douglas R. Parks

Clackamas Chinook Performance Art: Verse Form Interpretations
By Victoria Howard
Transcription by Melville Jacobs
Edited by Catharine Mason

Yuchi Ceremonial Life: Performance, Meaning, and Tradition in a Contemporary American Indian Community
By Jason Baird Jackson

Comanche Ethnography: Field Notes of E. Adamson Hoebel, Waldo R. Wedel, Gustav G. Carlson, and Robert H. Lowie
Compiled and edited by Thomas W. Kavanagh

The Comanches: A History, 1706–1875
By Thomas W. Kavanagh

Koasati Dictionary
By Geoffrey D. Kimball with the assistance of Bel Abbey, Martha John, and Ruth Poncho

Koasati Grammar
By Geoffrey D. Kimball with the assistance of Bel Abbey, Nora Abbey, Martha John, Ed John, and Ruth Poncho

Koasati Traditional Narratives
By Geoffrey D. Kimball

Kiowa Belief and Ritual
By Benjamin Kracht

The Salish Language Family: Reconstructing Syntax
By Paul D. Kroeber

Tales from Maliseet Country: The Maliseet Texts of Karl V. Teeter
Translated and edited by Philip S. LeSourd

The Medicine Men: Oglala Sioux Ceremony and Healing
By Thomas H. Lewis

A Grammar of Creek (Muskogee)
By Jack B. Martin

A Dictionary of Creek / Muskogee
By Jack B. Martin and Margaret McKane Mauldin

The Red Road and Other Narratives of the Dakota Sioux
Samuel Minyo and Robert Goodvoice
Edited by Daniel M. Beveridge

Wolverine Myths and Visions: Dene Traditions from Northern Alberta
Edited by Patrick Moore and Angela Wheelock

Ceremonies of the Pawnee
By James R. Murie
Edited by Douglas R. Parks

Households and Families of the Longhouse Iroquois at Six Nations Reserve
By Merlin G. Myers
Foreword by Fred Eggan
Afterword by M. Sam Cronk

Archaeology and Ethnohistory of the Omaha Indians: The Big Village Site
By John M. O'Shea and John Ludwickson

Traditional Narratives of the Arikara Indians (4 vols.)
By Douglas R. Parks

A Dictionary of Skiri Pawnee
By Douglas R. Parks and Lula Nora Pratt

Lakota Texts: Narratives of Lakota Life and Culture in the Twentieth Century
Translated and analyzed by Regina Pustet

Osage Grammar
By Carolyn Quintero

A Fur Trader on the Upper Missouri: The Journal and Description of Jean-Baptiste Truteau, 1794–1796
By Jean-Baptiste Truteau
Edited by Raymond J. DeMallie, Douglas R. Parks, and Robert Vézina
Translated by Mildred Mott Wedel, Raymond J. DeMallie, and Robert Vézina

They Treated Us Just Like Indians: The Worlds of Bennett County, South Dakota
By Paula L. Wagoner

A Grammar of Kiowa
By Laurel J. Watkins with the assistance of Parker McKenzie

www.ingramcontent.com/pod-product-compliance
Lightning Source LLC
LaVergne TN
LVHW050722220126
830376LV00001B/6
9780803237353